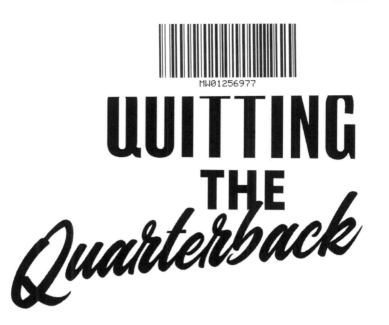

QUITTING
THE
Quarterback

LISA SUZANNE

QUITTING THE QUARTERBACK
© LISA SUZANNE 2025

Published in the United States of America by Books by LS, LLC.

ISBN: 978-1-963772-16-6

This book is a work of fiction. Any similarities to real people, living or dead, is purely coincidental. All characters and events in this work are figments of the author's imagination.

Books by Lisa Suzanne

THE NASH BROTHERS
Dating the Defensive Back
Wedding the Wide Receiver

VEGAS ACES
Home Game (Book One)
Long Game (Book Two)
Fair Game (Book Three)
Waiting Game (Book Four)
End Game (Book Five)

VEGAS ACES: THE QUARTERBACK
Traded (Book One)
Tackled (Book Two)
Timeout (Book Three)
Turnover (Book Four)
Touchdown (Book Five)

VEGAS ACES: THE TIGHT END
Tight Spot (Book One)
Tight Hold (Book Two)
Tight Fit (Book Three)
Tight Laced (Book Four)
Tight End (Book Five)

Visit Lisa on Amazon for more titles

Dedication

To the three people who make me smile every day.

Chapter 1: Tanner Banks

I Can't Believe It's Really Happening

"I'm not going anywhere without my brother."

The first time I remember speaking those words, our preschool teacher was trying to separate us into two different groups. One was going outside to the playground with the aide while the other was forced to stay inside and practice lettering with the teacher.

I wasn't about to let my best friend in the entire world have to deal with the nonsense of writing his letters, and eventually Miss Catherine relented.

He broke his arm that day jumping off the top of the slide, but that's irrelevant. Or an omen…I'm not really sure which one. But sometimes that happens. I do something that I think is protecting my brother, and in the end, it turns out I shouldn't have gotten involved in the first place.

I glance up, and my eyes meet the ones that have mirrored my own since the day we were born a mere twelve minutes and thirty-seven seconds apart. I wonder how many times I've spoken those words since I first learned how to say the words— or how many times he has.

I tighten my grip on the phone as I wait for a response to come through the speaker.

"They want Miller, too. They have an offer with a restructured contract, and they want to give you what you asked for. Both of you."

I grin at my brother, and his wide grin back mirrors mine. They want to give us what we asked for? We asked for guaranteed money for the next two years for both of us.

A *lot* of money.

Fuck yes.

"Then we're in," I say, forcing my voice to remain calm and businesslike despite the excitement coursing through my veins.

"Excellent. I'll get in touch with Mr. Hall, and I will have a contract for you to sign shortly."

"Thanks, Greg," I say to my agent, and I cut the call.

My brother holds his hand out like I should shake it, but I slap his hand with mine. We move back to slap hands backward, grab hands, shake once, let go, fist bump once, and hug. It's been our not-so-secret celebratory handshake since we were probably in that preschool classroom together twenty-five years ago.

Admittedly, a lot has changed since then. But one thing hasn't, and that's the fact that not only is my twin brother my best friend, but he's just about the only person left in this world who I can trust.

As we embrace for an extra second, I can't believe it's really happening.

We're trading the Arizona desert, where we've played football together for the last seven years, for the beaches of San Diego, where we'll continue playing on a team together.

We've never *not* been on the same team, and even though San Diego came knocking on my door for this blockbuster trade, they knew he was part of the package. He's the best running back in the league, so it would've been stupid of them not to take him.

We work in tandem. We read each other's signals on the field like nobody else can, which makes sense given our relationship. And together, we'll learn the signals of the rest of our teammates so we can have the sort of rhythm we've worked hard to build in Arizona.

But it's time. It's been time for a few years, and communication broke down enough that I was ready to move on. I was waiting for the right opportunity, and it fell onto my lap.

It's a blockbuster deal. Four trade picks and two players for my brother and me.

San Diego is rebuilding, and they acquired an excellent wide receiver last season who happens to be our half-brother, something we only learned recently.

And now they're getting the Banks brothers. Or...*technically* the Banks-Nash brothers, I guess.

We have a lot to work with in San Diego, and I've always wanted to move to the beach. I also don't hate the fact that we'll be moving a little further away from our mother, who is an Arizona native and, as we've recently learned, a pathological liar.

I love Arizona, but I could not be more ready for this new opportunity. It's coming at a time when my entire life has been thrown into chaos anyway, and the people of San Diego have been willing this to happen.

The trade deal was narrowed down to three teams, and I had my fingers crossed for San Diego. Perfect weather year-round and the chance to work with one of my new half-brothers along with the head coach and general manager over there? It's a dream come true, and even though I don't handle my own messages on social media, my PR firm and my assistant have communicated to me that I've gotten hundreds of messages from fans eager to hear whether I'll be joining their team.

They're welcoming me with open arms as they work to replace a quarterback who didn't give them what they were hoping for, and they get an all-star running back as well.

It's a huge deal. The Storm is considering me their new franchise quarterback, and they're going to build the offense around me and my strengths.

I can't wait to sign on the dotted line, get there, and start putting in the work.

Miller pulls back after slapping me on the back. "I've already looked up places, and I found a house not far from the practice facility. It's up in the hills." We agreed we'd live together as we get to know this new city even though we haven't lived together in years, and I'm excited at the chance to take on San Diego with my brother.

"Let's fucking go," I say, one of my mottos both on the field and off.

He pulls up the house on his phone and flips through a few pictures.

The panoramic views of downtown with the ocean in the backdrop are what sell me on the place.

"Vegas?" he asks.

We've already agreed that we're heading to Vegas as soon as we sign on the dotted line…not just to celebrate, but to be the first to tell our half-brothers who live there the big news.

"Fuck yeah," I say, and we do our secret handshake one more time to seal the deal.

Chapter 2: Cassie Fields

Fine, I'll Go to Vegas

"I'm not going anywhere without my kids." I purse my lips pointedly as I raise my eyebrows over FaceTime.

"Kids and Vegas don't mix, Cassie. *Come on.* You deserve this. They'll be fine with Alex for a couple days, and even if they're not, your parents are close." Jess, my best friend and cousin, is *very* convincing when she wants to be.

And she's right. Alex will have the kids this weekend, so why not take a quick trip to Vegas? It'll be both the getaway and the celebration I've been waiting for.

I sigh heavily. "Fine, I'll go to Vegas." I use my most dramatically annoyed voice to agree.

"You will?" she asks, total skepticism in her voice.

"Yes. Book it before I change my mind. And make sure to book us massages on you for forcing me to go."

"Eep! Wait until I tell Natasha and Katie!" Jess squeals, and then she cuts the call, presumably to go book some reservations.

I guess I'm going to Vegas this weekend with my girls.

Lily and Luca's bus from summer camp is set to arrive in ten minutes, and I use eight of those ten minutes to stare at the piece of paper that came in today's mail.

Judgment of Dissolution.

It took nearly seven months from when we filed for divorce to get this little piece of paper letting me know it's officially over—in the eyes of the state, anyway. It was officially over for *me* quite a bit longer ago than just today.

I think it was over the first time I caught Alex lying to me. But that lie snowballed, and when I found out he'd been cheating on me for two entire years, that was the end of the road for me. I refused to stay in a marriage with someone who could so easily betray me. The apologies meant nothing. The damage was done.

He slaughtered my self-esteem single-handedly as he really tried to make me feel like I wasn't good enough or pretty enough or *woman* enough for him, and now he can go fuck himself.

When the kids aren't over there, of course.

Even though he was an epic douchebag to me, at least he's good to our kids. I know how hard this has been on them—not the divorce, per se. They were sort of used to not seeing him much during the week when we thought he was putting all his effort into his work as a doctor but was secretly sleeping with his medical assistant—the oldest cliché in the book.

But now they have to be without *me* for nearly seventy-two hours every other weekend, and that's been rough on them, in particular Lily, my five-year-old. She's very attached to her mama, and I fear what long-term effects will hit her since she was so young while her parents went through a divorce.

I always worry about things like that. Even my son, Luca, who'll be starting second grade this year, seems affected by this whole thing, though we've done our very best to make it easy on the kids.

Still, it's hard to be fair and impartial knowing what I know about Alex, the fucker.

I should feel sad when I look at the paper in front of me. It's a physical representation of the end of the last two decades of my life.

Instead, all I feel is relief.

And a little bit of excitement for the road ahead. Maybe I'll find some excitement in Vegas to give me some little pieces of myself back again.

If nothing else, it'll be a break for four moms who desperately need a little time away.

I use the final two minutes before I need to head out to draft a text to Alex. My lawyer advised me to get everything in writing, and that includes text messages.

Me: *I'm going out of town this weekend. If you need anything for the kids, my parents can help.*

The last thing he ever wanted to do was to rely on them even when we were together, but I make the note that emergency help is available anyway.

His reply is immediate, which is more than I can say for the time we were married.

Alex: *Where are you going?*

It's none of his business, and I debate how to reply. It's such a game of politics now, to be honest.

So I don't reply at all. His question is out of line, and he doesn't deserve that information.

Instead, I head toward the bus stop and find Katie, who lives in my neighborhood, already standing there under the one tree that offers shade.

"Ahh!" she yells when she sees me, and she grabs me into a hug. "Congratulations!"

I giggle as I hug her back. "Thank you."

"Are you okay?" she asks, pulling back and holding me at arm's length to check for any signs of distress.

"I'm fine. Good, actually. Great, even. It's final, and it's like a huge weight off, you know?"

She presses her lips together and squeezes my shoulders. "I know. Any news on the job front?"

I nod. "I got called in for a second interview at the place that was my top choice, so fingers crossed." It's an office run by a physical therapist I used to work with, one who still works with my ex upon occasion, but he's willing to work around school hours so I can continue to be there for my kids. I'm both nervous and excited to talk to him again.

She nods and crosses her fingers for me. "When is that?"

"Next Tuesday, so all traces of hangovers need to be gone by then."

She giggles. "No promises, but you'll rock this. Cassie post-divorce is a force to be reckoned with."

I suck in a nervous breath. "Let's hope so. But first, girls' weekend in Vegas, baby!"

She squeals a little, and then some of the other parents from our neighborhood start to show up, so we keep our plans on the down low.

The bus arrives, and the kids bounce off. Lily's my mini me with her long, blonde hair and blue eyes, and Luca looks a lot like his dad with his darker eyes and hair. I stand in the middle and hold both their hands as we walk toward home, and they tell me about their days.

And then it's the usual chaos—snacks, more snacks, starting dinner, forcing everyone to eat when nobody's hungry because they ate too many snacks, baths, and bedtime.

I went from a stay-at-home mom to a divorcée today, and I've spent much of the last seven months trying to decide what exactly I wanted to do once the divorce was finalized.

Well, that day is here, and I have my answer.

I want to do whatever the hell I want.

And what I want is to be able to independently support my kids in all the ways that matter. I want them to see me stepping up and taking care of them, of sacrificing whatever I have to in order to ensure they're fulfilled and happy and have every opportunity to do whatever and be whoever they want to be.

Before I was *Mom*, I was Cassie. I was a Doctor of Physical Therapy. I was interested primarily in sports medicine, and I worked with a lot of gymnasts as I helped them through injuries with both therapy and training. Gymnastics was my thing when I was younger, but I knew it wasn't going to be a career for me, so I gave it up when I started high school. I didn't give up watching it on television, though, and I got Lily into it when she was two.

I kept up with continuing education courses even when I was at home with the kids just in case I ever wanted to practice again, and I started the process to renew my license the day I filed for divorce.

And now I'm ready to jump back in with both feet.

After my girls' weekend in Vegas, of course.

Chapter 3: Cassie Fields

A Fun Weekend with My Gal Pals

Excitement courses through my veins as the plane touches down. I look out the tiny airplane window as the famed hotels of the Strip rush by, and the plane starts to slow as we taxi toward our gate.

I glance over at Jess, who's in the middle seat beside me, and she's grinning at me. I can sense that she feels that same excitement, as do Katie and Natasha.

We're really here. We actually did this. My three best friends took time away from their kids and their families to celebrate *me*.

We each had a drink on the plane. We're on vacation, after all, and Natasha treated us to margaritas. After we grab our suitcases from baggage claim, we head to the Aria, where Natasha booked two connecting rooms for the four of us. I'll stay with Jess, and Natasha and Katie will share a room, and we're ready to get this party started.

We have reservations at one of the restaurants in our hotel tonight, and we'll head to some trendy nightclub afterward. I realized how very much my identity has become exclusively *mom* when I couldn't name a single nightclub in Vegas.

What happened to fun, party girl Cassie? She seemed to have died when I said *I do*, but I'm resurrecting her tonight. Or maybe she died before that. Maybe she never got the chance to live and thrive because she got tied up with Alex far too early in her college days.

I'm no longer tied to someone who gives me dirty looks when I laugh too loud or whose entire existence rides on the line of making everything appear a certain way.

I can laugh as loud as I want for the rest of my life, and the thought actually makes me feel sort of giddy.

In fact, I let out one of those giddy little giggles, and my friends all look at me like I've lost my mind. But the truth is, for maybe the first time since I was eighteen—half my life ago—I feel like I have my entire mind back again.

And it's a wonderful feeling.

We check into our hotel, and Jess and I are standing in the bathroom doing our makeup side by side when she says, "So what do you want out of this weekend? Like, just some girl time, or a hot hookup that stays in Vegas, or—"

"A hot hookup?" I wrinkle my nose. "Is that really me?"

She lifts a shoulder. "Doesn't everyone do it after a divorce? This is your time, Cassie. You can explore and have fun since you never really got to."

She's not wrong, and it marks the first time I've really thought about it.

"I figured I'd just have a fun weekend with my gal pals."

"Gal pals?" It's her turn to wrinkle her nose at me. "Let's start by not saying that again."

I laugh. "Fine. My besties."

"We need to work on your slang."

I roll my eyes. "Okay. Let's yeet our way into some fun."

"I don't think that's how you use that term."

I think over the words Luca came home from camp with this summer. "Let's have a bussin' weekend."

Her eyes meet mine in the mirror, and she looks downright horrified.

"Fine, maybe I'm not using those words correctly, but it's not like I'm going to start using Luca's new favorite word that he picked up at summer camp this year from the older boys."

"Which is…" She trails off and waits for me to fill in the blank.

"Nuts. As in *deez nuts*." I pick up my mascara as Jess bursts out laughing. "You think that's funny? Now Lily is walking around talking about her nuts since she wants to be like her brother." I purse my lips, and Jess can't stop laughing.

"I'd say second grade is around the age Dylan started with the *balls* talk. Just so you know, it gets worse."

"Great," I mutter. "Love that for me."

"Okay, anyway, hot hookup it is. Let's get you some hot hookup perfume." She rummages through her bag, and she hands me a bottle. "This is guaranteed sex perfume. Every time I wear it, I get lucky." She spritzes some on her wrists and down the front of her dress, and the soft, heady scent of vanilla and sandalwood fills the air.

I narrow my eyes at her but spritz some on anyway—for good luck, I guess.

We finish our makeup and check on our friends, and it's time to head down to eat. We've just ordered a round of margaritas when Jess announces, "We need to find a hot hookup for Ms. Fields."

My eyes widen as I give her one of those *shut your mouth* looks that best friends share, but she's not to be shushed.

"Listen, you haven't been with anybody except Alex. Tonight's your night, bitch."

"Oh my God," I mutter, and I set my hand over my eyes in total embarrassment—not that Katie and Natasha are witness to her words, but that she's not exactly being quiet, and anyone in the restaurant might hear her.

I glance over at the table next to us, and two older men are staring at me.

When I say *older*, I don't mean in their forties or fifties. We're talking closer to seventies or eighties.

And they're looking at me like they want to shoot their shots.

Great. Just lovely and wonderful.

Is that what I can bag these days? I think I can do better than that…especially in the black sparkly dress I borrowed from Jess that is nothing like my own personal style but perhaps should be.

I'm not demure Cassie Sinclair anymore.

I'm Cassie Fucking Fields, and I'm in Vegas. I'm here to have some fun, and maybe score a hot hookup.

That's all I want. One night with a stranger to knock boring old Alex Sinclair out of my muscle memory. Except I don't know how any of this works. I haven't had a one-night stand in my entire life.

Alex and I got together when I was a freshman in college. He was a junior, and he was my first. My only. I wasn't his first…nor was I his only, even after he vowed I would be.

I don't think this classy restaurant is where I'm going to find my hot hookup.

No…I think the club we're going to after the restaurant might be my spot.

Now if I can just find someone who isn't twice my age, I'll be all set.

Chapter 4: Tanner Banks

On the House for Grayson Nash

It's only been seven months since the Nash brothers tracked Miller and me down through our coach in Arizona.

That means it's been seven months that we've known the truth. Seven months that we've been angry with our mom and the man who raised us—not to mention the biological father we never even knew existed. Seven months of pent-up anger and frustration at the people who were supposed to be honest with us but chose to lie to us our entire lives.

Instead, it was our brothers who were honest, and we've been slowly working toward building bonds with them. Asher, the youngest, who happens to be our age, is the one who found out. He gathered up the rest of the Nash brothers, and they came immediately to tell us. The rest is history.

We're all busy. It's the offseason. We all have things to do, places to go, people to see.

Or…my half-brothers do, anyway. They all have women in their lives, and some of them have kids, but there's one thing we all share in common: football.

All six of us have played professional football, a gene we apparently inherited from the father we all share. The four Nash brothers are forces to be reckoned with. The eldest is the head coach of the Vegas Aces. The next in line, Grayson, played for the Aces when he retired to Vegas. Next is Spencer, who we'll get to play with in San Diego, and finally Asher, a tight end for the Aces and the one we're closest in age to but who has been very busy with a newborn.

It's a big deal stepping into a family like the Nashes, and I've admittedly struggled a bit with my identity.

I've been Tanner Banks my entire life. But Banks is my stepdad's surname.

I don't consider Eddie Nash my father. I don't really consider him much of anything other than an asshole, to be honest. I'm trying to see my mother's point of view in this whole mess. He paid her handsomely to keep her mouth shut about our true lineage, and she found herself stuck. She could give up the money and be honest, or she could give us the life she wanted us to have and keep the secret.

Obviously she chose the latter.

Still, it begs the question how many other women Eddie Nash was doing this to. It makes me wonder if there are more of us out there.

It's a weird way to fuck with someone's psyche when they're pushing thirty, but here we are, brand new *father-son conflicts* and all. I refuse to call them *daddy issues*, though Miller thinks it's a hilarious and apropos term.

But none of that shit matters tonight. Tonight is about going out with my brothers—all of them, at least that we know of—and fucking celebrating.

We get to play with Spencer. The three of us will be on offense together. We'll gain a new level of respect for each other in the locker room the way teammates always seem to do as they become family.

And the others, well, they're actual family now. Blood relatives, and I'm excited to celebrate with family.

It was always just Miller and me. We always wanted more siblings, and, well, this is definitely *more*.

"'Eyyy,'" Grayson says when Miller and I walk in. He holds up a hand, and I slap it first. He grabs on and bro-hugs me, and Lincoln's standing right behind him. He hugs me while Grayson greets Miller.

"Congrats on the new contract, man. What a hell of a blockbuster trade," Lincoln says to me.

"Thanks, bro. It's still sinking in." I smirk at him. "I bet you wish you'd have been in contention."

He raises his brows and nods. "We couldn't afford the two of you. Maybe one, but we knew better than to try to split you two up."

I laugh and slap him on the shoulder. "Thanks, Lincoln."

"You'll do incredible things for their offense, Tanner. I have every belief that we'll be in serious trouble when we face you this December."

I raise my brows. "You're goddamn right about that."

He laughs, and Asher slides over from the bar. He's holding a beer in one hand and wearing an obnoxious neon yellow shirt with a shark on the front. I swear, this guy's fashion choices are in a league of their own.

I greet him, and Spencer joins us next. Miller and I chat with him a little longer as he gives us some of the inside scoop on the locker room atmosphere, and he informs me not so subtly that the coach in San Diego is ready for me to come in with my strong sense of leadership.

I feel confident I can do this. I was given a leadership role on my previous team, and I ran with it…until a new head coach came in and had different ideas than I did.

I was stuck there for two years with him.

He didn't want me to be a leader, and it's part of why I wanted out. He didn't like having my brother and me play for the same team, and it's why Miller wanted out, too.

He had some sort of grudge against us, and I'm not sure why. But it's no longer my problem. I'm heading to a place where the vision not only meets with mine, but is the *same* as mine, and I can't wait to get started.

But first…we celebrate. I glance around for the waitress in our VIP area so I can order my signature drink—Casamigos tequila. I prefer it neat, no ice, and I like to sip it slowly to savor the oaky smoothness as it slides along my tongue.

I don't see a waitress anywhere nearby. I'm wearing a baseball cap, which should be enough to hide who I am. I'm also here with the four Nash brothers and my twin, but it's dark enough in here that I doubt I'll be recognized outside of the group.

I find a very crowded bar as I approach, and as one person walks away with a drink, I slide into the open spot. The woman beside me is ordering a margarita, and the female bartender looks at me next.

"Casamigos, neat," I yell across the bar.

"On the house for Grayson Nash," the bartender tells me as she glances up and down my frame.

I don't bother correcting her. I'm about the same height as my half-brother, and we share a lot of similarities since we have the same father. Beneath a baseball cap, it's an honest enough mistake. On the house is on the house.

"You're a football player?" the woman who was ordering the margarita says.

22

I glance down at her, and when our eyes meet, my breath hitches.

She's gorgeous.

She's a blue-eyed beauty with sandy hair pulled back into a ponytail, and she looks like one of those women who would go fucking wild if she let her hair down. She's maybe a few years older than me, and she's got this classy, real vibe going for her—so unlike the women who I've been going home with since my last relationship ended.

And frankly, I'm tired of my normal brand. Fake in every way you can imagine and the general opposite of classy.

I can't help but imagine pounding into her from behind as I yank on that ponytail. *Fuck*.

Before I get any crazy ideas, I glance down at her left hand out of habit.

No ring.

I wasn't *planning* on hooking up with the first woman I saw tonight, but I'm not opposed to it.

Not when it's with this woman, anyway.

Tonight's for celebrating, and what's better than celebrating with a woman who's already piqued my interest as she looks at me like she wants to see me naked?

I guess there's only one answer to that: celebrating with this woman and tequila.

Chapter 5: Cassie Fields

Don't Mention Your Ex

Oh my God, Cassie. Get it together.

Don't mention your ex. Don't mention your ex. Don't mention your ex.

I school my thoughts to remember this, but I *swear* Alex talked about the Nash brothers *all the time*. He was a huge football fanatic, and he particularly loved one of the Nash brothers. I can't remember which one, to be honest.

He loved football, and that sort of gave me an aversion to it. I know next to nothing about the game, but right now, I'm sort of wishing I'd paid a little more attention.

Meeting a Nash brother would be some incredible revenge on my asshole ex. I thought it on the trip here, but I never thought it would actually happen.

And now, as this man gazes into my eyes for a split second that feels like an eternity, I can't help but think that hooking up with one of them would be even more epic. I'd be *winning* this divorce.

I know it's finalized, and nobody *really* wins. But there's still someone who *wins* in a divorce after the fact. He's been fucking his assistant for a long time, but there will still be a time when one of us will go public with a new relationship first. One of us will have a better glow up. One of us will have a hotter partner than the one we left behind. One of us will upgrade first.

Can you imagine if it was *me*? With *him*? The guy next to me who's probably a decade younger than me and freaking *gorgeous* and who plays pro football?

That's the margaritas talking. I'm well aware of that. The chances of actually hooking up with this guy—Grayson? Was that what the bartender called him?—are slim to none, but I'm currently fueled by margarita confidence.

It's Vegas. What happens here stays here and all that jazz. It's the entire reason why I came here—to celebrate with new experiences.

My friends are on the dance floor. I excused myself to get another margarita, but then Grayson stepped in beside me, and maybe the rest is history. I'm pretty sure he plays for some Vegas team, but to be honest, I'm not entirely sure Vegas has a football team.

Yeah…I was *that* intent on avoiding anything my ex was interested in. Our problems started long before I discovered that he was cheating. He turned his nose up at anything related to gymnastics, so I turned my nose up at anything related to football.

"Yes, I am," he says, affirming my question from a moment ago when I asked if he's a football player.

I wrinkle my nose, and he chuckles.

"Are you not a fan?"

Don't mention your ex. Don't mention your ex. Don't mention your ex.

"It's just that my ex was a huge football fan, so I tended to avoid it." Goddammit. I mentioned my ex. Fucking margaritas.

He chuckles. "Recent ex?"

I narrow my eyes a little as I wonder why he's asking. "I'm here for the weekend celebrating the fact that my divorce is final, though we haven't been together in well over two years." I raise my eyebrows and enunciate *been together* to make it clear I mean in the physical sense.

Good Lord, Cassie.

Why are my lips flapping like this? I haven't even told Jess that Alex and I stopped sleeping together two years ago, but I'm telling a virtual stranger these intimate details about my personal life.

The bartender drops Grayson's tequila, and I'm still holding my empty glass with a bit of melted ice mixed with what was once a delicious concoction. He holds up his glass, and I hold mine up in response. "Congratulations," he says.

I press my glass to his, and he tips the glass to his lips. I watch as he takes a sip. The liquid seems to swirl around his mouth a little as he tilts his head back, and his eyes close as he swallows. His Adam's apple bobs up and down, and never before in my entire existence have I found Adam's apples sexy, but this guy? *Damn.* I could lick that apple all damn night.

He just *looks* like he smells good, like he tastes good. Like he fucks good.

I'm drunk.

And I want to have sex.

Two years is two years too long—not with the wrong person, I guess, but I'm suddenly totally ready for a wild weekend, and I'm not about to leave without getting exactly what I came for.

And this particular Nash looks like he can give me a really, *really* good time.

I'm a little out of practice. A little rusty. A sober Cassie would be absolutely *shocked* that a pro football player is even *looking* in my direction. But the why doesn't matter. The fact is that I'm interested, and I'm just drunk enough to believe this is a great idea.

"Thank you," I say stupidly after he opens his eyes.

"Are you here by yourself?" he asks.

I shake my head. "I'm here with three of my best friends."

"Where are they?"

I nod toward the dance floor.

"Do you want to get back to them? Or would you be interested in going somewhere a little quieter?" he asks.

My eyes are wide as they meet his.

He wants to go somewhere quieter? Is that code for sex? Because *yes, please.*

I'm finally in my era to sow some wild oats, and this attractive man standing beside me is the very definition of a wild oat. I know this won't go beyond this one night. The chances of me running into a pro football player ever again in my life are nil, so let the games begin.

"What would we do somewhere quieter?" I ask, not sure if it comes off as flirting or naivety.

He chuckles and takes another sip of his tequila, and if I didn't know better, I'd think he's almost…*flustered* by my question. He clears his throat. "Talk. Get to know each other. See where the tequila takes us."

I laugh, and then I nod. "Yeah. Sure. I'd like to see where tequila takes us."

He grins at me, and I swear, I melt a little just at that smile. I wonder how often he does this. Does he lean toward older women? Does he pick up a different woman every night? Because just that smile is enough to make me want to drop my panties for him.

You know…if I was wearing any.

This dress is tight as hell, and I didn't want any lines.

I worked my ass off to get fit over the last year. The day I filed for divorce, I also joined a gym. I wanted to get into the best shape of my life. I knew eventually I'd be getting back into the field of dating, and I wanted to go into that field looking my absolute best.

Two kids destroyed my body, but I'm slowly getting it back. And this football player hitting on me is the exact boost to my confidence that I've needed for a long time now.

The bartender pushes my margarita over and a receipt over toward me. I move to pick it up, knowing full well that it's going to be over twenty-two bucks for one drink, but the football player grabs it before I can. "She's with me," he says, and the bartender nods as he hands my bill back over the counter.

"Of course, Mr. Nash." He grabs some cash from his wallet, and he hands it over to the bartender.

It's a hundred-dollar bill.

He just tipped a hundred bucks on two free drinks, and honestly, I'm swooning. He's generous, he's gorgeous, and as he drapes his arm around my shoulder and starts to steer me through the club, he's definitely interested.

He drops his arm from around me and grabs my hand as we head toward the VIP area, and oh my God, am I going to meet more football players? I don't even get the chance to let my friends know I'm escaping with a football player.

He keeps his head ducked down, presumably to avoid being recognized. The music pumps loudly through the speakers—too loud for conversation as we walk.

Someone with a lot of similar features to him slaps him on the shoulder. I assume it's one of the other Nash brothers.

He's wearing a hat, too, and he says something close to Grayson's ear. They do one of those things men do where they sort of slap hands and turn it into a handshake that leads into a quick hug, and I can tell Grayson is close with his brothers.

He keeps walking through the room until we end up at a corner table, and he's right—it's quieter in here. The table doesn't have a speaker set right above it like there was out by the bar, and since this is the VIP area, we can sit with our drinks and have a private conversation.

Though my drink is nearing empty already. I should slow down.

Maybe I don't need to. Maybe it's better this way.

I guess I'll just go with it and see where the night takes us.

Chapter 6: Tanner Banks

The Splits

I feel out of my element, which is a strange feeling for me.

I don't usually have to work all that hard to pick up a woman who throws a line at me.

"You're a football player?" Those were her first words to me, and I thought it was because she recognized me. But then she said the whole bit about not being into football, and I don't know…it left me feeling intrigued.

That's a feeling I haven't felt in a long time.

I occasionally get the sense that the *only* reason women talk to me is because of my career. I guess objectively, I'm not a bad-looking dude. My twin is attractive to the female population, and my four half-brothers seem to do all right for themselves. As much as Eddie Nash is an asshole, he did pass down some decent genes.

Plus I have the whole pro quarterback thing going for me, which means intense workouts and eating right along with mental toughness, leadership skills, focus, discipline, competitiveness, charisma, and, of course, a healthy dose of arrogance.

That's me in a nutshell.

But this woman whose name I don't even know yet doesn't know any of that about me. All she knows is that I'm a football player along with whatever assumptions she carries with her based on that.

"You know who I am," I say once we're sitting in the quiet corner of the VIP area. "Tell me about you."

She licks her lips, and I can't help but study the little dart of her tongue as it sweeps across her bottom lip. It's just a peek, but it almost feels like a preview of something to come. I don't know why it gives me the strongest urge to kiss her…but it does.

"Well, I'm Cassandra, but everyone calls me Cassie." She snags that lip between her teeth for a second as if she's debating how much more to give me. "I love gymnastics, and I used to be able to do the splits."

I raise a brow, and she giggles a little.

Women don't tell men they can do the splits if they're going for innocence. Clearly she isn't.

"My favorite color is peach, I've never smoked a cigarette in my entire life, and I love, love, *love* avocados. Now you." She nods at me as if she just clued me in to the mysteries of Cassandra, but she isn't giving me much.

"My favorite color is green. I don't smoke, but I can't pretend I've never tried it. I don't drink coffee or anything with caffeine in it, and I wouldn't say I *love* avocados, but I don't hate them. I prefer the beach to the desert, though my favorite season is winter."

Her brows dip together. "Winter? Why?"

I shrug. "Football. You know, your favorite sport."

She laughs. "Right. I prefer fall, actually. I love sweater weather, jeans, boots, bonfires, and, of course, pumpkin spice lattes."

"Ah, you're one of *them*."

She narrows her eyes at me. "Exactly what is that supposed to mean?"

"A coffee drinker," I say innocently.

She grins, clearly proud of that fact. "Absolutely."

"I can get on board with fall. Except for the lattes. I'd gravitate toward cider, maybe."

"So you've *never* had coffee?" she asks.

I lift a shoulder. "I've tried it. It's fine. But caffeine throws off my sleep cycle, and except when I'm in Vegas celebrating, sleep is a top priority."

She leans in a little. "Are you saying you won't be sleeping tonight?"

"Depends." My eyes meet her gaze, and she's looking at me with something I've seen before—something that tells me exactly how the rest of this conversation is going to go.

"On what?" she asks—rather predictably—as she takes a sip of her margarita.

"On whether you're coming back to my hotel with me."

I half expect the margarita to come spraying at me, but instead, she swallows thickly, and her eyes heat on mine. "I think neither of us is going to get much sleep at all tonight, then." She raises her brows in a challenge, and goddamn, I really like this girl. Apparently my cock does, too, and he is *very* interested in getting to know her even more.

I'm curious to know more about her—things deeper than her favorite color and her preferred fall beverage.

But that's not what one-night stands are built for, and there's a clear undercurrent of understanding between us. There *has* to be when you pick someone up at a nightclub in Vegas. It's not like either of us is in this for the long haul. I'm not local, and I don't know whether she is. I just know she's here celebrating a divorce.

I'd offer to let her friends join us, but part of me wants to be selfish with her. I don't want to share her. I like having her full attention on me, and I like focusing on just her—which is what I told Grayson as I walked by him on the way back here. *Don't let anyone bother me.* I think I said it nicer than that, but he knew what I meant.

Clearly she's been hurt if she's just on the other side of a divorce, and I have the sudden urge to make her forget about that shitty ex of hers and be the only man on her mind—even if it's just for one night.

Every woman deserves that sort of attention, and I want to be the one to give it to her. She's here for a weekend she'll never forget. Isn't that why everyone goes to Vegas? So I'll give her that, and we'll part in the morning with a new memory.

I lean in a little closer. "Is it too soon to ask if you want to head back to my hotel with me?"

She twists her lips a little as she narrows her eyes. She chugs what's left in her margarita, and then she shakes her head. "To be honest, I thought you'd never ask."

I chuckle. "Do you need to tell your friends?"

She grabs her phone out of the little purse she's carrying. She taps a few words and tucks her phone back in. "Done."

Well, that's good enough for me. I grab her hand, and we head toward the exit together.

Chapter 7: Cassie Fields

Hot Hookup

What the hell am I doing?

I'm leaving my friends behind at a Vegas nightclub while I go to a hotel with a complete and total stranger.

But I remind myself that I'm a big girl, and I want this. I want this night where a hot football player can remind me that life doesn't always have to be so serious.

He pulls me into the back of an Uber, and the driver confirms his hotel. "Bellagio?"

"Yes," he says, and the driver sets off in the direction of the hotel.

I'm suddenly interested in what sort of room a pro football player rents out for the weekend in Vegas. I'm also wondering why he has a hotel room if he plays for Vegas. Doesn't he live here? Maybe not. I'm still not totally sure Vegas has a team at all.

"Bellagio?" I repeat.

"Where are you staying?"

"Aria. Though my cousin wanted to stay at the Luxor since that male dance show is there. She thinks if we're at the same

LISA SUZANNE

hotel, we have a better chance of running into one of the dancers outside of show times." I shrug with a laugh, but he doesn't laugh back.

Instead, his eyes burn with this new intensity into mine. "Are you interested in running into one of them?"

I shrug. "I was…until I met you."

His lips curl up at my words, and a warmth seems to hit me square in the chest. He likes that I only have eyes for him tonight. I like that he's taking me back somewhere private. I don't know how Vegas hookups work since I've never done this before, but it seems to me like a quickie in the bathroom or out back behind a bar would be a little less special than going back to a hotel.

The mere thought makes me suddenly nervous.

And then a text comes through from Jess.

I glance at my phone, trying to be discreet about it.

Jess: *Yes! I knew you were getting your hot hookup tonight! Be safe and have all the fun!*

"Hot hookup?" His voice is warm and low next to my ear.

I clear my throat, suddenly embarrassed that the driver might overhear what we're doing and judge me for it.

Not that I care. I shouldn't care. But for some reason…I do.

"I've just…never really done this before."

"Then let's get to know each other first," he suggests.

I wrinkle my nose. "Isn't that sort of defeating the purpose?"

He shrugs. "Depends what your purpose is." He says it in a way that gives me the green light to detail said purpose.

"Just some fun." I practically mouth the words to him as my eyes edge to our driver.

He turns his baseball hat around and leans in. He presses his lips just below my ear. "I can definitely give you that."

Holy shit.

My insides are quivering, and I shiver at the feel of his breath on my ear, at the feel of his lips on my skin. The scruff on his jawline. The soft, woodsy scent emanating from him at this close proximity.

Oh, yeah. He can *definitely* give me that.

"Jesus," he murmurs, drawing out the word. "You taste incredible." He kisses me again in that same spot, and I have to be sweating out tequila at this point, but if that's what he's into, then maybe we're a good pair.

I want to taste him, too, so I turn my head and catch his lips with mine.

Fireworks.

Freaking fireworks light up the entire sky through my closed eyes. Our lips are barely touching, and this is the first *new* man I've kissed since I was eighteen, and oh my God, thank you for margaritas and impaired judgment because this is the best damn night of my life.

It's just a kiss, a simple one that isn't even moving beyond the close-lipped stage yet, but it will. The promise is there as his lips mold to mine, and then his hand comes over to cup my jaw, and I'm freaking *done*.

My legs feel weak, and I'm thankful I'm sitting because I think they'd give out completely if I wasn't. I grip onto his bicep as a way to steady myself, and that's when his mouth opens to mine.

I'm roasted, toasted, whatever. I'm done. How do I move on from this? It's one kiss in the back of a rideshare, but it doesn't matter. Nobody has ever kissed me like this. Nobody else has ever made me feel sexy and wanted and like I could do anything I want the way he is right now.

I don't expect anything to happen after tonight, and that's fine. It's what I signed up for when I agreed to go back to his hotel with him.

But he's giving me something back that I thought I'd signed away forever in my marriage. He's restoring my self-worth and my confidence as he rebuilds my spirit. And when we part in the morning without each other, at least I'll be leaving here with all of that.

My heart feels full, and I push everything I'm feeling into this kiss.

His tongue swirls with mine as the kiss moves from slow to a little more urgent, and I'm about to let it get indecent back here as my hand starts to trail down from where it's gripping onto his arm.

But then the driver slams on the brakes, and I don't know if he slams on them because we were making out in his backseat like a couple of horny teenagers or because of traffic. Either way, it breaks up the intimate moment between us—not necessarily a bad thing since I was literally about to give him a hand job in the back of someone else's car.

It's not my first trip to Vegas, and I can see out the window that we're getting close to his hotel. His fingers slide between mine as we both turn in our seats so we're facing forward instead of each other, and we arrive at our destination a minute later.

We exit the car, and he grabs my hand again as we walk into the hotel. The casino is to our right, the reception desk is to our left, and straight ahead is the famed conservatory and botanical gardens. Without saying a word, we head that direction, hand-in-hand.

We wander around the conservatory filled with vibrant flowers, trees, and sculptures centered around a whimsical, romantic theme for summer. We stop and look at each display, and succulents the color of avocados will forever remind me of this moment as I take a beat to focus each time I spot my favorite color combined with my favorite types of plants.

It's cliché, maybe, but it's also romantic. And romance is something I thought I'd never get the chance to encounter again in my life. It's yet another thing this night with this man is giving back to me. Who knew a total stranger could be exactly what I needed?

I breathe in the scent of fresh flowers as we meander through the gardens, and the really strange thing is that neither of us is rushing through. It just feels natural to walk around here before whatever comes next.

I'm here in Vegas, holding hands with a pro football player I wouldn't have recognized if I hadn't heard the bartender say his name earlier, walking around the gardens at the Bellagio. If someone would've told me this is where I'd be a year ago, I never would've believed them.

And furthermore, I wouldn't have believed that the football player would pause in front of a display filled with peach flowers to give me a quick kiss on the lips.

"Peach flowers will always make me think of tonight," he says as he pulls back but doesn't let me go.

"Me too," I say, my lips tipping up into a smile.

I sigh contentedly as we continue our walk, and then I turn to him. "You said your favorite color is green, right?"

He nods, and I point to the green roses at the center of the display I'm studying.

"Green flowers will always remind me of you."

"Green and peach," he says. "Like a cantaloupe."

I'm about to open my mouth to say that Luca's favorite fruit is cantaloupe, but I stop myself.

I realize I haven't mentioned my children yet, and it's not that I don't want him to know about them, but I have this urge to protect them from whatever this is…to keep them out of it. Just like I'll keep *him* out of my conversations with my kids.

I'm not just *Mom* anymore. Meeting Grayson Nash tonight is giving me a chance to be someone else entirely, and I want to just be Cassie for a night.

We finish our stroll through the gardens and find ourselves heading into the casino.

"Are you a gambler?" he asks.

I lift a shoulder. "I have fun on slots upon occasion. You?"

"Yeah. I like cards, blackjack, roulette, dice. I don't get to take risky thrills with extreme sports and shit like that because of my profession, but high-stakes risks are still my jam."

"Really?" I ask, sort of surprised. He doesn't seem like a risk-taker.

"I need to feel that rush, you know? Especially in the offseason. If I go too long without taking a risk, it fucks with my balance. It's harder to react in the moment on the field." He stops in front of a slot machine with a hundred-dollar denomination, and he nods at it. "Want to try?"

My brows shoot up. "Not for a hundred bucks a spin. I'm more of a penny slot player."

"This one's on me." He pulls his wallet out of his pocket and grabs a few bills to slide into the machine. "What are the stakes?"

My brows crash together in confusion. "A hundred dollars a spin."

He shakes his head a little slyly. "No, I mean between us. If we double our money in the first ten spins, you set the prize. If we lose it all, I set the prize."

"How is it a prize if we lose?" I ask.

"It will be for me." He wiggles his eyebrows, and I laugh.

"Okay, hot shot. You go first."

He nods. "If we lose, you have to do a strip dance for me when I get you upstairs."

"I've probably had enough tequila that I'd do that for you win or lose, but okay. If we win, then *you* have to do a strip dance for *me* when *I* get *you* upstairs."

"Trust me, that's not something you want to see," he mutters.

I laugh. "Fine, then. If we lose, you have to give me oral sex first, and if we win, I have to give it to you first." I choose myself first for the one I think is most likely to happen.

"Jesus Christ," he moans. "You have yourself a deal. And for the record, it sounds like we're both going to win."

"Oh, we're *definitely* both going to win. I think we already did the moment you sauntered up to that bar and stood beside me."

"I think you might be right about that." He nods toward the slot machine. "You go ahead. Let's see who's going down first."

I hit the button, and on our first spin, three bars line up.

We win twenty times our line bet.

We win two thousand dollars with one spin.

Looks like I'll be going down first.

Chapter 8: Cassie Fields

A Deal's a Deal

We cash out our machine when it gets down to twelve hundred bucks—still a major win, but according to Grayson, that's the threshold where we won't have to be hand paid and report our winnings to the government.

He hands me six bills once we cash in our ticket.

"You don't have to do that," I say, trying to hand it back.

He raises a brow. "A deal's a deal."

I offer him a smile as I tuck the money into my purse. "Okay, then let's head upstairs."

He smirks. "Before all that, I need some fuel. You?"

"Fuel?"

"Food. Maybe another drink."

I narrow my eyes at him. "Are you asking me out on a date?"

"What if I am?"

What if he is, indeed. I'm finding myself incredibly surprised at every turn by this man. We both know why we're here, yet he isn't in a rush to get me upstairs. That fact alone makes me feel like he's a gentleman—one who it might be harder to say goodbye to than I first anticipated.

But I'm not naïve. I know where this is going, and I know the limit of where it *can* go considering the life I have back home paired with the life he leads.

It's not going to go beyond tonight.

But that doesn't mean we can't have a little fun while we're here in the moment.

"Then who am I to say no?" I ask.

He chuckles, and we head over toward the bar to order more drinks. Once those are in hand, we wander around until we find a place that serves snacks.

Once we put in our order for chicken tenders and sweet potato fries, we find a table and wait for our food.

"So…do you come to Vegas often?" he asks.

I shake my head. "I haven't been here in years." Since before I had kids. Instead of asking him why he's staying in a hotel, I ask an even dumber question. "Do you do this often?"

"Do what?"

"Pick up women at nightclubs and take them back to your hotel."

He chuckles. "I wouldn't say *often*, but I wouldn't say I've *never* done it before. I'll be honest, though. I never shared chicken tenders and sweet potato fries with any of them." He lifts a shoulder. "I've never walked through the gardens or stopped at the slots with them. Never made a bet like the one we made. And this part is going to make me sound like a total asshole, but I never found myself interested in any of them the way I'm interested in you."

I raise my brows in surprise. "In me?"

He nods and presses his lips together. "Yeah. You're…I don't know. You're real. You seem like a genuine person, and I don't come across that very often these days."

I reach over and squeeze his hand. I'm not sure why that's my reaction, but I guess his words sort of make me feel a little sorry for him. He deserves someone who's real, and part of me has this feeling like I wish it could be me. Like I wish this could go beyond tonight.

I mean…obviously it won't. It can't. We're from completely different worlds. I'm a mom trying to pick herself up and prove herself to the world as I try to figure out who the hell I even am as an individual, and he's a professional football player who lives in Vegas.

But just because we're only in it for one night doesn't mean we can't still be genuine with each other.

"What's your secret superpower?" he asks me completely out of the blue.

I twist my lips. "I don't think I have one. What's yours?"

"Throwing a perfect spiral. And probably staying calm under pressure."

"Oh, I can make it rain. And I can turn coffee into productivity." I shoot him a smug smile.

"You can make it rain?" he asks.

"Yes." I nod emphatically. "Every *single* time I wash my car, it rains the next day."

He laughs. "I know every word to every song by the Beatles."

"The Beatles? Why?"

"My mom is a huge fan." It's the first time he has mentioned anyone in his family, and I'm curious to know more. But I also don't *want* to know more. I don't want to leave in the morning with the image of him treating his mother well as he sings Beatles songs in the car with her, not when this is just supposed to be a hot hookup.

Those are the types of details that will make me wish this could have been more rather than one moment frozen in time.

"I have a lot of useless knowledge of early two-thousands Top Forty songs," I admit. "Lyrics, artists, song titles."

LISA SUZANNE

"What band is your favorite?"

I twist my lips as I think it over. "I always really loved Fall Out Boy, but I don't know if I've ever consciously called them my favorite."

He nods and squints a little as if he's trying to recall some songs by them.

"'Centuries' would be killer on a pregame playlist," I say nonchalantly. "Just saying."

He chuckles. "I'll be sure to add it."

I wonder if he really will. I wonder if I'll leave any sort of impression on him or if this is just another random night with another random woman to him. I like to think I'm special, but I'm also rooted in reality.

Our food is delivered, and we make small talk about our preferences between barbecue sauce, honey mustard, and ranch—both of us settling for honey mustard even though we both prefer ranch, but neither of us wants ranch breath given the next activity on our schedule.

We laugh as we eat, we finish our drinks, and he takes care of the check.

The *date* portion of the night is coming to an end, and I can't honestly remember a night where I've had this much fun with a man. I didn't know I could, to be honest.

But now I know because the man across the table from me is teaching me.

I wonder how old he is. I make a mental note to look that up later. It seems irrelevant to the conversation, and I certainly don't want to bring up the fact that I'm possibly five or more years older than him. But I'm still curious.

I've never been with someone younger than me. Even in high school, I gravitated toward older boys. I always liked the juniors and seniors when I was a freshman, and when I got to

46

college, the first guy I went for was Alex, who was two years older than me.

But none of that matters anymore, and it certainly doesn't matter tonight.

He stands from the booth and holds his hand out to me, and I slide my hand into his, surprised yet again at how natural it feels.

How *wonderful* it feels.

And I really can't wait for all the feels that are coming next.

It's a natural stroll from the casino toward the elevator, which is filled with others waiting to head upstairs in the main tower. My heart starts beating a little faster with anticipation as the elevator carries us up to the thirty-fourth floor, and we exit, still taking that same sort of leisurely walk. We both want to get to what's happening next, but we're both content just being together.

This is not what I was expecting from my first one-night stand. I was expecting clothes being torn off in different directions and that heady, lustful, heat of the moment sort of animal sex. I wasn't expecting to be treated like a lady on a date, but feeling all of his attention centered squarely on me has somehow been an even bigger rush than the alternative would've been.

He flashes his keycard at his door, and he holds the door open for me to enter first. It's a suite overlooking the fountains below, and I can't help when I head over to the window to check out the view. When again in my life will I ever get to see these fountains from this vantage point?

The answer is probably never again, so I take full advantage of it.

In fact, I take my phone out of my purse and snap a photo. The fountains are going off, and it's incredible from up here as I watch the water as it rises and falls to the beat of whatever song is playing outside that we can't hear in here.

I switch to video for a beat, and that's when I hear his voice behind me.

"What a view."

I end the video and turn at the sound of his voice, and I slide my phone into my purse and set it on the table in front of the windows. "It's gorgeous."

"Not to be cheesy, but I was talking about your ass."

"That was super cheesy, but I liked it anyway." I let out a nervous giggle, and he walks over toward me and pulls me into his arms.

His eyes are filled with something new and different when they fall onto mine.

I clear my throat nervously. The gaze we share is heated for a beat, and then his eyes flick down to my mouth.

His lips fall to mine, and I feel myself letting go.

It's very nearly like an out-of-body experience as I fall into this kiss. It's a kiss that's full of want and need and desire and all the things that have been sorely missing from my existence for far too long.

He opens his mouth to deepen the kiss, and my legs feel shaky like in the back of the car on the way here, but this time I'm standing. I grip onto his upper arms to steady myself, but I don't know if I *can* be steadied with this man.

He came in from out of nowhere and absolutely swept me off my feet, and I find that I sort of like being unsteady.

I sort of like that he doesn't know me. I like that I can be whoever I want.

And what I want to be right now is a woman intent on both giving and receiving the kind of pleasure I've never had before in my life.

Chapter 9: Tanner Banks

I'm Nothing if Not Disciplined

Who the fuck is this woman?

I never want to stop kissing her, and kissing has never really been my thing. It's fine, good even. It's a part of things, usually the part that kicks things off so we can get to the main event, but I don't want to just kiss her and move on.

I want to spend my time on her. I want this kiss to last since I already know it's one I'll think about again and again.

It's cliché—cheesy, even—to say that she's just different. But she likes my cheesiness, and maybe I'm fine with being a cliché if it means I get to kiss her a little longer.

I don't like the strange feeling in my chest as I kiss her. I don't like feeling things awakening that haven't been awakened before. But even though I don't like them…I'm addicted to them.

I know who her favorite band is. I know she likes pumpkin spice lattes. I can picture her in a bikini washing her car in her driveway only for it to rain the next day.

These are things that don't matter in the grand scheme of things, but they're things I don't typically take the time to get to know about the women I take to bed.

The last time I knew such details was with Heather, and the end of us was enough to make me stay far, far away from relationships. I learned from her that it's easier to just have a single night with someone instead of allowing feelings to get involved. It's easier to take pleasure and walk away.

Because let's be honest. Emotions aren't these things we need to be in touch with. They don't speak to who we are. They speak to how we react to situations, and in my experience, they're nothing more than distractions.

They stand in our way of doing the things we need to be doing.

And so I learned how to channel them into football. I took the pent-up rage over my last breakup and used it as fuel in my workouts. I stopped allowing myself to feel sadness and anguish over things I couldn't control, and instead I realized that love is only for fools.

That goes for family, too. My own mother taught me that love is a lie when she decided that loving her twin boys meant hiding their true paternity.

I've been lied to and disappointed enough when it comes to women, so I learned that getting close to them just isn't for me.

Yet in a single night, this woman is making me rethink all of that. I can't explain how or why, but she's opening things in me that I thought I'd killed off a long time ago. She's making me wonder if the door I closed on relationships long ago might be worth opening again. She's making me want to meet someone I can have a future with.

Maybe it's because she didn't immediately recognize me. She doesn't watch football. She doesn't care about who I am.

It's refreshing. It makes me feel like even if it's not her, there might be *someone* out there for me.

She pulls back from our kiss, and her eyes are hooded and lusty—a mirror reflection of mine, I'm sure.

Her fingertips come up to my jaw, and she stares at me in wonder for a beat, as if she can't really believe this is happening.

She moves out of my arms, and her hands trail down to my pants. She unbuckles my belt and works the button, and I grab her wrists in mine. I pull them up and twist us so her back is up against the window before she can get into my pants, and I hold her hands above her head.

I lick a trail from her neck down into her cleavage, burying my face there for a beat as I breathe her in. She smells like sweet vanilla, and my cock hardens painfully. I need release. I need sex. I need *her*.

I know we had that oral sex deal, but fuck, every instinct inside me is telling me to get inside her.

"I know we had a deal, but fuck, Cass. I need to fuck you like I need to breathe right now."

I move my mouth back to hers and press my body into hers against the window. I feel every inch of her body warm against me, and I gather both of her wrists into one of my hands as I trail my fingertips down to the bottom of her dress. I slowly gather the material in my hand and pull upward until I have it gathered at her hip, and that's when I realize…

She's not wearing any underwear.

Jesus Christ.

She's not wearing any fucking underwear.

"Holy fuck. Have you been naked under here all night?"

Her eyes meet mine, and hers are filled with need as she nods slowly.

My cock presses even more roughly against my zipper, and I thrust toward her, my clothes the only thing separating us. She moans as I yank her dress up even more, and I hold it there pinned between my stomach and hers as I let go of the material and reach between her legs. I slide a finger through her cunt, and a deep, throaty moan escapes from her lips.

I hiss out my own groan as I feel how wet she is, and I push a finger into her. "Jesus," I breathe close to her ear. "You're so wet for me. God, baby, you want this, don't you?"

"Yes," she cries. She shifts, her hands fighting against the binding I have on her wrists still held above her head as I push my finger in deeper. I slide my finger out and add a second finger as I push back in, and her hips start to sway with the rhythm of my hand as she rides it.

I move my mouth back to hers to kiss her while I finger her, and I swallow her moans with my kiss as I drive my fingers into her. I push them in as far as they can go and curl my fingers up, and I'm rewarded with the hottest, "Oh fuck," I've ever heard as she rips her mouth from mine.

Her body is tense as I keep going, and the need to taste her tits, the need to taste her entire body, slams into me.

I let go of her wrists and yank the top of her dress down so her tits spill out of it as my moves turn desperately rough. Her hands are immediately on me, one gripping onto my bicep as the other threads into my hair. The feel of her hands on me makes me feel completely out of control, like I could climax right here, right now, without her ever laying a single finger on my rock-hard cock.

But I'm nothing if not disciplined.

I focus on her—her sounds, her body, her pleasure—so that I'm not focused on my intense need to come. I'm still shoving two fingers into her as I grab onto one of her tits and move my attention to her nipples.

I squeeze her tit roughly as I suck the tight peak into my mouth, swirling my tongue around it as I suck. She's pure fucking heaven as I taste her body——a tiny preview of what's to come when I get my mouth on her cunt. My cock throbs with need as she tosses her head back with a thump against the glass of the window, and she cries out as I bare my teeth against her nipple, giving it a light bite that seems to drive her wild with need. My fingers are drenched with her juices as I continue to finger her, and *fuck* the need to taste her is out of control.

I let go of her tit and drop to my knees, tossing one of her legs over my shoulder and pulling my fingers out of her. I dive in face-first, licking a line through her folds as I find her sweet, swollen clit. I suck it between my lips and swirl my tongue around it the same way I did to her nipple, and she yanks on my hair as her legs start to tremble. I let go of the hold my mouth has on her clit to dip my tongue down inside her a few times before I move back up to focus on her clit, and I thrust my fingers back into her.

She grips onto the back of my head with both her hands, pulling my face closer into her so all I can see, all I can breathe, is her. It's an intoxicating, overwhelming scent that's somehow both sweeter and warmer than the vanilla of her perfume, and I find myself focusing on every detail, every sense, every pure, intense second I have with her.

I want to talk to her, to tell her how good she tastes, to say words that she'll think about tomorrow and the next day and the weeks after that, but I'm buried in her. I hum against her body instead, and that seems to be the thing that tips her over the edge.

"Oh yes, yes, mmm," she moans, and her knees seem to buckle as the trembles in her legs turn to full-on quivers. She yanks on my hair, and fuck, that's hot as hell. I don't dare stop what I'm doing, even though I want to watch her as she comes, but we have all night together. I'll make her come again and again and again.

She tightens up, pulling my hair even harder as her leg squeezes like a vise around me, and she cries out a string of *oh*s as she comes. It's intense as she battles against the pleasure, and I hang on for the ride as she fights her way through it. It's long, drawn out, and consuming as she alternates between moans and screams, and my God, it might be the hottest orgasm I've ever been witness to as my tongue is drenched with her sweet tang.

She loosens her grip on my hair as she tries to untangle her leg from around my neck. "Oh my God, I'm sorry," she says, and I sling an arm around her waist to hold her up as I easily lift to a stand from my knees.

"For what?" I ask, wiping my mouth with the back of my hand since my chin is currently glistening with her wetness.

She looks embarrassed for a beat, and I shake my head as my eyes meet hers.

"Don't ever apologize for getting exactly what you deserve." I lay a gentle kiss on her lips, surprised that she's so timid after that. I sweep her off her feet and carry her to the bed, and I lay her down.

She sighs softly as she lies there, and I excuse myself to the restroom. I return a few beats later to find that she has shimmied out of her dress, and she's a sight to behold as she lays naked on my bed with her eyes closed.

I stare at her for one unfiltered moment, and I allow myself the vulnerable hope that maybe I can see her again someday.

It's a foreign feeling for me to think that way when I haven't even gotten mine, but for the first time in my life, I feel like I could just be content to lay beside her. I don't need to *get mine* right now. She got hers, and I got to take her there. It feels like enough for tonight.

But tomorrow isn't promised. It never is, but even less so in this situation. It's just supposed to be one night. She's been clear that it's all she wants, and that's all I intended to give her.

Before I made her come. Before I kissed her. Before I felt a connection.

I run the washcloth I brought back from the bathroom along her pussy, and her eyes pop open at the first feel of me down there again. I gently take care of her, wiping her clean before I toss the washcloth on the floor, and she closes her eyes.

I grab the condom out of my back pocket and toss it on the nightstand, and I pull my shirt off and toss it on the floor. I yank off my pants, too. I'm wearing just my boxers as I slide into place beside her. I toss an arm across her stomach, ready to call it a night and just hold her close even though I want to kiss her more, want to suck on those gorgeous tits more, want to taste her more. Want to fuck her like I've never wanted to fuck anyone before.

What's meant to be will be, and even though I want all those other things, I also want to just lay here with her.

She shifts a little, and before I know it, she's on her knees as she pushes me onto my back. She moves in between my legs and bends over me, running her palm along the front of my boxers to find my cock primed and ready for her.

I watch her carefully, and her eyes flick up to meet mine as she grips onto me over my boxers. She moves her hand up and down a few times, giving me a hand job over my underwear, and fuck, it's hot as hell. She drops her mouth down to kiss me playfully through the material, and I groan.

"Fuck, Cass." I'm panting as she does it again, and then she slips her hand inside my boxers and pulls my cock out. She pumps her fist up and down my shaft a few times, and I groan at how good it feels.

She moves off me to pull my boxers off, and then she's right back where she was. She licks her lips as her eyes meet mine, hunger in hers as she takes me into her mouth. Her eyes don't leave mine as she starts sucking on me. I'm fucking mesmerized by her. She swirls her tongue around the head of my cock, moaning as if she's getting off on the very taste of me.

"You look so fucking gorgeous with my cock in your mouth," I tell her, and she moans as she closes her eyes and starts to really suck on me. She slides me all the way to the back of her throat, and *fuck* it feels good—too good. A little come leaks from the tip, and she swallows it down, the movement of her throat pure bliss on my cock. She bobs her head up and down, taking more of me with each thrust, and then she adds in her hand, sliding along my cock as her head moves up and down.

When she adds her other hand into the mix by lightly fondling my balls, that's it.

I'm fucking done.

"Your mouth is perfect," I grunt. "I'm about to come."

Instead of backing away like most women do at the signal, she seems to get even more enthusiastic, moving her mouth faster up and down my shaft as her hand follows along.

My abdomen tightens as my climax starts to tear through me, and she stops moving along my shaft to swirl her tongue over the tip as she cups my balls more tightly. I come *hard* with a loud growl as I let go.

It's been a while since the last time someone other than my own hand gave me a release, and I don't know that I've ever had one quite like this before.

Pulse after pulse of white hot come jets to the back of her throat, and she keeps sucking on me like she can't get enough, like she'll never get enough.

The pulses eventually slow, and she pulls back and swallows.

Fuck.

Just the mere sight of that makes me hard all over again.

I need a few minutes of recovery, but I wish I didn't. I wish I could keep going. I wish I could fuck her like she deserves.

She presses a few gentle kisses to my cock, and then she slides up my body, kissing my abdomen and taking the time to finger each of the ridges there before she moves to my chest, leaving wet kisses in her wake. She moves to my collarbone and then my neck, and she presses a soft kiss to my lips before she settles in beside me. My arm is under her, and she fits like a glove as she tosses one of her legs over mine, her pussy warm on my thigh as her head settles into the nook between my shoulder and my neck.

I reach around her with my arm that's beneath her, and I grip onto her arm as I lean down and press a kiss to the top of her head.

I'm rarely speechless, but *damn*.

What she just did is leaving me without words, and the sweet way she kissed me afterward is leaving me feeling a certain way that I can't quite categorize yet.

I think we both drift off to sleep, but I don't want that to be it. I don't want to wake in the morning only to have to say goodbye. I need a little bit of time, but I'm not done with her yet.

Certainly not without feeling her body as she writhes beneath me or over me or whatever myriad of ways we can invent.

She must feel the same way because I'm half-asleep when I sense movement beside me. I'm not sure how long we've been laying here, but I feel rested and recharged. She climbs over me, and my eyes open lazily as I watch what she's doing. She grabs the condom from the nightstand, and she moves back toward me. Her hand trails down to my cock, and her mouth is close to my ear when she says, "I need to feel you inside of me."

Her voice is low and throaty, and holy fuck.

As if her words are magic, I'm immediately hard.

It's time to give the lady what she asked for.

Chapter 10: Cassie Fields

Foreplay Was Really Never My Thing

I have to be honest here.

Foreplay was really never my thing.

I just simply don't have time for it——or maybe it's that my ex wasn't all that good at it.

We had a few minutes of moaning, and that was the end.

It wasn't always like that. When we were younger, we did all the things. I guess I figured it was the evolution of a relationship. At some point, you have kids and then you're just plain tired by the end of the day, so you forgo foreplay in exchange for an extra hour of sleep.

But *this* foreplay with *this* man?

I'll never sleep again if it means I can take and deliver pleasure like *this*.

I didn't know this sort of thing actually existed. I thought it was relegated to movies or books——or really good porn.

But he's good. *Really* good. Outstanding. So good, in fact, that where the events that led us here would've put me to sleep in the past, right now all I can think about is having sex with him, of feeling him moving inside of me while we each take and give more pleasure, of him kissing me and touching me again. It's addictive. *He* is addictive—and that's a pretty damn scary thought since this is only supposed to be for tonight.

And based on the way his skilled hands and mouth worked my body, I can only imagine how good he is with his dick.

I don't know who I am right now. I've never, not once in my life, told a man that I need to feel him inside of me, but something about Grayson Nash has me transfixed. I'm a new person, and maybe this is who I was always meant to be.

It's an incredibly freeing feeling. He doesn't know me, and I don't know him, and we can return to our lives with the memory of tonight.

I shift so I'm straddling him around his thighs, and I reach for his cock. I fist it and slide my hand up and down a few times to make sure he's ready for me, and his eyes heat up at the feel of my palm on his skin.

I tear open the condom wrapper and slide it down his cock, and he watches me carefully while I work. I'm about to shift upward so I can slide down onto him when he takes control. He sits up, reaching around my waist for me, and we're face-to-face. He leans up to catch my lips with his, and he kisses the hell out of me, which has the effect of unbearably intensifying the needy ache between my legs.

I feel like an animal as I try to move to get some friction between us, but he's in control now, holding me just out of reach. His mouth curls into a sly smile on mine, and I can tell he likes this. He likes seeing me desperate. He wants to make me beg.

And I will if I have to.

I claw at his back as I deepen the kiss, and he lets out a low groan as I try to move over him again. Instead, he shifts us completely so I'm suddenly pinned beneath him, and his mouth falls to my neck.

"Tell me how bad you want it," he demands, his deep voice low and hot near my ear.

I like that he tells me what to do. I'm tired of making every decision in my life for myself and my children. There's something thrilling about having someone like him take charge.

"So bad," I moan, and I arch my back as my hips seek out his.

He thrusts toward me, and I feel his cock as it settles near my entrance—near it, but not in it. Not where I need it.

He nibbles at my neck, and my skin feels like it's on fire as I wait for him to push in. I shift my hips again, arching toward him as I try to get him in.

"Mm, she's getting more and more desperate," he says calmly to himself, and I don't know how he can be so damn calm when I'm in a frenzy of need over here.

I'm writhing beneath him, and he's taking his time, slow and steady. It's how I'd picture him on the football field, I suppose, if I knew anything about football. It's as if he's choosing his moment, disciplined and practiced, and I'm a moaning, wet, needy mess as I wait for him.

I clutch the sheets with both hands as the ache between my legs throbs in time with my racing heart.

I wrap my legs around him as I try to pull his body into mine. "Do it," I demand. "Give it to me." I think about saying his name as I demand what I want from him, but something stops me. "Please," I beg, whimpering at the end, a stark portrayal of my mental turmoil as I go from insisting to pleading.

"Give what to you?" he teases.

"Your cock," I beg in a whisper, not used to this sort of dirty talk but finding that it's a total, extreme turn on as that ache grows still more violent. "Give it all to me."

LISA SUZANNE

"Where do you want it? I rather liked it in your mouth before…"

"Oh my God, please, please fuck me. Fuck me deep and hard until I can't see straight."

He growls before he rears back and grips himself in his fist, and his mouth crashes to mine at the same time his cock slams into me.

I moan into his mouth as he kisses me while he fucks me, and I find all I can really do is hold on for the ride. I cling on around his neck as I wrap my legs around his waist, our tongues battering together brutally as I think I start to see stars. The sexy scruff of his jawline rubs my mouth raw, and I've never experienced a more delicious, beautiful, sublime connection with another human before.

It's hot and carnal as he slams into me over and over, his athletic skills evident from both his rhythm and his stamina.

My God, it's incredible.

His eyes fall to mine, and a hot, intimate moment passes between us. It's downright erotic. It's totally unexpected as he moves inside of me, and I have a feeling this is the singular moment I'll think about when I think about this night. His eyes on mine.

He slows his strokes, and that's just as incredible as the fast ones. And then he pulls out, flips me over, and raises my hips into the air. "Palms on the headboard," he demands, and I do as I'm told because I'm afraid if I don't, the pleasure will stop, and I never want it to stop.

"Good girl," he says as he slides a finger into me from behind.

I've never been called that before, and something about it is hot as hell. It makes me want to do more things to hear more words of praise from him, and I give him a soft moan to let him know I liked it.

My hips sway in time with his hand for a few glorious seconds, and then he removes his hand and slides his cock back into me. It's a new angle, one that feels just as incredible as the last, and he reaches around me to grab one of my tits in one hand while the other moves down to stroke my clit.

I'm going to fall apart. I'm going to come for days if he keeps this up. I can't hold it together as I slam my hips back against him. He's tweaking a nipple and stroking my clit and driving into me over and over, and I feel it building as he drops his lips to my neck. He kisses me sweetly there, a heady contrast to what he's doing to my body, and then he starts in again with the dirty talk.

"Your cunt feels like it was made for my cock, Cass," he grunts. "Like you were waiting for tonight to give me all your come."

"I was," I cry. What the hell did I just say? I didn't even know who this guy was until a couple of hours ago, but maybe I was saving it all for him. I don't get in my head about it, though—instead, I just enjoy every second of this wild ride.

"That's right you were. I love how your sweet cunt is gripping my cock like you never want to let it go."

What the hell did *he* just say? Am I really doing that? Because I feel that way. I don't ever want this pleasure to stop. I don't ever want to leave this moment with him. I feel like my true, authentic, honest self for the first time in…

In eighteen years.

It's a thrilling realization to have as a total stranger drives into me in this Vegas hotel room.

"Oh God!" I cry, and that's when my body explodes over him.

I drop my hands from the headboard because I physically can no longer hold myself up as my body betrays me, and he continues pushing into me and touching me and kissing me as my body pulses all around him.

As I start to come down from that intense high, he slows his thrusts, and eventually he pulls out.

But he's not done yet, and even though I'm depleted and totally satisfied, I'm not stopping until he gets to come, too.

I roll over, and his eyes meet mine.

"You okay?" he asks.

"Mm," I say with a lazy smile. "I'm better than okay. Now get back inside and finish what you started."

He grins as he climbs off the bed, and he grabs my legs and pulls me to the edge. He rests my ankles near his shoulders as he slides into me, and he moves slowly, giving my body time to adjust to more pleasure than I've ever experienced in a single night.

"God, you're gorgeous," he says as he looks down at my body.

I try to believe his words. I try not to feel intimidated by them or like it's a lie. I'm not as firm as I was twenty years ago and two kids ago. I've worked my ass off to attempt to firm up again, but I still have the zones with imperfections—usually the only zones I see when I look in the mirror.

But when he's looking at me the way he is, I *feel* gorgeous. It doesn't feel like they're just words he's saying. It feels like he means them, and I want to believe him because he says them so convincingly, so honestly.

"Me?" I tease. "Have you looked in a mirror recently?"

He chuckles, and I'm not sure I've ever actually *teased* someone while they were inside me.

"What's the most you've ever come in a single night?" he asks.

"Counting tonight? Twice."

Surprise flashes in his eyes. "You've never come more than once in a night?"

I shake my head.

He splits my legs to the sides and leans forward, still filling me completely as he slows his moves. His face fills my vision, and I memorize it all for a beat.

Gorgeous blue eyes that are currently slate as they search mine. Full lips that know what I taste like. Dark hair that's messy from sex. Scruff on his jawline that scratched my thighs. The little scar on his chin, the straight nose despite probably taking hit after hit with the sport he plays for a living.

It feels like a dream.

"Let's see how high we can go."

He gives me another one before he can't hold on any longer, and we're both too exhausted for another round. I'm sure I'll regret having fallen asleep and wasting the time that could have been spent with him, but right now, we both need rest.

When morning dawns, I wake with a start. I'm disoriented for a second before it all comes rushing back to me, and I glance beside me as I stretch only to find the other side of the bed empty.

"Grayson?" I call out, and there's no answer.

I realize I'm naked, and I grab the blanket off the bed and wrap it around me as I pad through the suite looking for my date from last night.

The room is empty, and I guess that's how this works. The man ducks out so he doesn't have to face his regret the morning after.

It's a shame, but I guess that's what a hot Vegas hookup is all about.

I drop the blanket from around my waist and find my dress balled on the floor. *Sorry, Jess.* I slowly shimmy back into it, and it doesn't look wholly destroyed.

I should shower. I should change clothes. I should've worn panties.

Hindsight tells me a lot of things I probably should have done differently, but I refuse to leave this place with regrets. Last night was magical and amazing, and him not being here just makes leaving all the easier.

I still get to take all the things he gave me last night along with me. Him not being here this morning doesn't change the fact that for one night, I felt sexy and valued. I learned a lot about myself, and nobody can take that away.

Even if I feel a little cheap this morning.

I use the bathroom, and I think about leaving a note, but ultimately I decide against it. What would I say, anyway? Thanks for a fun time? Peach and green flowers will always remind me of you? And chicken tenders with honey mustard and blue eyes and multiple orgasms in one night?

No. That doesn't sound like something a thirty-six-year-old woman would ever say, let alone leave on a note for evidence.

I don't feel thirty-six this morning, though my muscles are deliciously achy. I feel refreshed and revived and *single*.

I finish up in the bathroom and head toward the door to leave this room, but it opens before I get to it.

And there stands my hot hookup…with a coffee cup in one hand and a bag in the other.

"PSL for the lady," he says, handing the cup over to me.

"PSL?" I repeat, and I glance at the side of the cup. *Cassie. Pumpkin Spice Latte.* "But it's July. They usually don't even carry the pumpkin stuff for another month, month and a half at the earliest."

He raises a brow and shoots me a cheesy wink. "I guess it pays to know people in the right places."

"Or it pays to be a professional athlete." I purse my lips.

"That too."

I lift a chin toward the bag. "What's in the bag?"

"I thought you might be hungry after all the, uh, working out we did last night, so I got some food." He walks over to the table set in front of the windows, and I follow him over. He pulls a couple of muffins and some of those little egg bite things out of the bag, and he nods toward the food. "Help yourself."

"Thanks for this," I say, holding up my coffee. "That was really sweet of you."

He ducks his head a little. "No problem." He seems almost embarrassed by my words as we both dig into the food. I wasn't expecting breakfast out of this deal, but I'm loving the extra time we're sharing.

"So you really never had more than one in a night?" he asks as if he's been thinking about it since I said it.

I laugh as I shake my head. "I really never did."

"Whoever you were with before me was a loser, then." He fixes his eyes down on the fountains below. It's quiet down there with little movement on the sidewalk, and the fountains haven't started yet. He seems almost wistful as he stares out there, and I can't help but wonder why.

"Tell me about it."

He chuckles, but he's quiet.

"I'd ask about your history, but I'm not sure I want to know." I wrinkle my nose.

His eyes have a touch of merriment in them when they meet mine. "Why not?"

"I don't want to picture you with other women. Last night felt so…" I trail off as I search for the right word.

"Intimate?" he guesses.

"Yeah." I nod. "Intimate. I feel like maybe you opened some things that had been locked up for a while."

"I think you might've done that for me, too."

I'm surprised by that. He seems so much more experienced than me even though he's younger than me.

I want to ask what those things were, but despite the intimacy we shared, it feels almost too private to ask. If I'm meant to know, I guess I'll find out someday.

But I don't want to push. I don't want to be the desperate lady who's never done the one-night stand thing. I don't know how to act in this situation at all, and as much as I want to leave my number, I don't think a hot young football player like him wants to get tangled up with a mom who's a recent divorcée reentering the workforce after a decade out of it.

There's too much going on at home right now for me to even consider something beyond the one night we shared, and he's about to start a new season anyway.

As if he can read my internal struggle, the next words he speaks take me by complete and utter surprise.

"I want to see you again."

"You mean like...tonight?"

He shakes his head. "I have plans tonight, but maybe next week."

I gasp the kind of gasp that's not very ladylike as I inhale a bit of my PSL, and I start coughing as I futilely try to get it down the right tube to no avail.

Next week?

He doesn't even know where I live. We haven't gotten into that sort of discussion with each other.

Is he just...going to fly out to San Diego and take me on a date? Meet my kids? Insert himself into my life?

It sounds lovely, but it also sounds completely and wholly unrealistic.

"You okay?" he asks, alarmed, and I nod.

I chug a few more sips as I try to calm the coughing. "Sorry," I croak. I clear my throat. "That just took me by surprise. I'd love to, really, but I don't think it's a good idea."

"Why not?" he asks, clearly affronted as his tone is almost cocky.

"I *just* got my final divorce papers a couple days ago. I've got a whole life I have to get back to on Monday, you know?" I try to let him down gently even though I'm positive he's just being nice.

"Yeah," he murmurs, and he seems melancholy about my answer. It has to be an act, right? We just met. He probably has a woman like me in every city, and he probably uses these exact same lines on all of them.

"You're amazing, and I had an incredible night with you," I say. "But we both know what it was."

"Right. Yeah, exactly." He presses his lips together and nods.

"I guess I should get going." I stand, and I grab my coffee since I've only had about half of it. I pick up my purse that's still sitting on this table. I realize for the first time I haven't checked my phone. I probably have a message from the kids, or maybe one from Jess.

I guess it's time to get back to reality.

"Of course." He lifts to a stand and walks me to the door, and I set my hand on the handle and turn around to face him.

He's close. Too close. He boxes me in against the door. "I had a great time with you, Cass."

"I had a great time, too, G—"

He cuts me off as he presses his lips to mine, and it's the sort of kiss I could stay in forever. I don't, though. I have to get back to my friends, and he has to get back to his life.

"I'll never forget last night," I whisper when he finally pulls back.

"Neither will I," he says, and then he backs up so I can open the door.

I clear my throat, which suddenly feels clogged with emotion. "Well, bye."

"Bye," he echoes, and I walk through the door.

"Wait," he says as I move to start the walk down the hall.

I turn back toward him, and he heads into the suite. I hold onto the door, and he comes back a few seconds later. He hands me a piece of paper, and it has a phone number written on it.

He clears his throat, and his eyes don't meet mine as he sheepishly says, "Just in case you change your mind."

I close my hand around the paper, and he leans in for one final kiss.

I breathe him in one final time, and then I head down the hall without looking back as I remind myself that a hot hookup is meant to be left behind.

Chapter 11: Cassie Fields

Turn Back the Clock

"Where have you been, Ms. Fields?" Jess demands as I let myself into the room we're sharing. She's sitting in bed scrolling her phone as she leans against the headboard, still in her pajamas.

I let out a sigh. "Only having the *greatest* night of my life."

"Then what are you doing back here?"

I laugh and keep my tone light even though it feels heavy in my chest. "It was a hot hookup. Aren't you supposed to leave when it's over?"

"I guess. You doing okay?"

"I'm fine," I say, and even I don't believe my own breezy tone as I walk over to the window. The view is different from this room despite the fact that only one other hotel stands between the Bellagio and the Aria. It was still a twenty-minute walk to find my way back to my own hotel room.

"Talk to me, Cassie," she says. "It's just us."

I turn to face her, and I collapse on my bed as I stare up at the ceiling. "Okay, truth. I didn't know men like him existed. He was just…God, he was everything. He was tender and gentle and, at the same time, wild and forceful. He made me feel things I've never felt before. And he made me feel...I don't know." My cheeks burn as heat travels along my spine at the admission. "Desirable again. You know?"

She swings her legs over the bed so she's facing me. "Of course I know. What your ex did...that was about him, not about you, babe. You know that, right?"

I nod. "I think I just needed last night as a reminder, though."

"Can I have all the details now? Like how you met, his name...all the things? Because your text just said you found a hot hookup, and then you totally left me hanging. I was worried about you *all night.*"

"I'm sorry." I sit up and face her. "And yes to the details. I was standing at the bar getting a margarita when he walked up beside me to order."

She claps her hands together and squeals a little. "Oh my God, the meet cute!"

I roll my eyes. "Can you have a meet cute when it's just a hookup?"

She lifts a shoulder. "Let me live vicariously through yours, okay?"

I chuckle. "Anyway, he ordered his drink, and the bartender said something like, 'On the house for Grayson Nash,' and I knew that name."

"Grayson Nash? The football player?" Her brows draw together.

I nod. "Doesn't he play for Vegas? So it makes sense why he was there."

"Yeah, sure, but..." She trails off as she pulls a face that clearly says she already said too much.

"But what? Why'd he have a hotel room if he's from Vegas?" I guess.

She shakes her head. "But…isn't he married?" She whispers the question, but it isn't any less of a slap in the face.

"What?" I gasp as a new realization hits me.

I was cheated on by my husband for over two years. I know how it feels to be the wife in that situation, and the fact that I might've been *the other woman* makes me feel sick to my stomach.

"And, yeah…like you said, why would he need a hotel room if he lives here?" she adds.

My stomach twists. "I don't know."

"Wait." She grabs her phone and taps around for a few seconds, and then she flashes her phone at me. "Is this him?"

I study the picture, and there are definite similarities there, but no…that's not *my* Grayson. I shake my head as something new slams into my chest.

He lied to me.

Oh my God.

If it wasn't Grayson…who the hell did I sleep with?

I feel cheap. Gross. Used.

I sort of wish I could turn back the clock ten seconds. I wish I'd never told Jess his name.

Or if I'm wishing things, maybe I should be wishing that last night had never happened.

Except I can't in good faith wish that. Maybe he wasn't who I thought he was, but he still gave me a pretty magical night.

"That's not him," I whisper. "But someone who looks a lot like him."

"Hm, there are a bunch of Nashes. Maybe you bagged a different one?" She's tapping around on her phone again, and I don't think I could take looking through photos of all the Nash brothers as I try to identify which one gave me an orgasm last night.

Multiple times.

You know…the one who brought me a pumpkin spice latte this morning. And muffins.

Heat pinches behind my eyes, and I don't want Jess to see. I lift a shoulder a little weakly as I collapse back on the bed.

"Didn't you just come from his hotel room? You should go back there and confront him. Ask him who the fuck he is!" Jess suggests, and I shake my head.

"I don't think I want to know. I need to go shower." I jump up and head to the bathroom, and I stand beneath the scalding water with a washcloth as I try to scrub away last night.

Is this always how people feel after a one-night stand? Because I feel dirty and disgusting even though I left his hotel feeling happy and hopeful less than a half hour ago.

It's a fresh cut that'll fade with time. I hope, anyway.

He gave me his number.

I could call him. I could ask him who he is.

Or I could just leave last night where it belongs.

I hear voices in the hotel room when I get out of the shower, and when I walk out in my towel, I find Jess talking with Katie and Natasha, who are both dressed and ready for the day. They all stop talking when they see me, and clearly Jess was giving them the lowdown on my night.

"There she is," Katie says brightly, and she flips her blonde hair back over her shoulder.

"Did you have fun last night?" Natasha asks, and she snags her lip between her teeth as if she's bracing herself for my answer.

"I had a great night," I say. "I mean, Alex sure as shit never gave me three orgasms in one night."

"Three?" Jess practically spits. "Is this dude some kind of magician or something?"

I laugh. "Must be. It was…enlightening. And now we have another day ahead of us." I'm trying to toss the attention away from me. I'm worried if I keep talking, I'll start crying, and nobody wants a crying Vegas Cass.

Cass.

Nobody calls me that. I'm Cassie to everyone, but I'm reminded of his voice rasping that nickname last night.

I know we had a deal, but fuck, Cass. I need to fuck you like I need to breathe right now.

An ache pulses between my legs as my stupid brain recalls the words.

I don't want to recall the words. I want to push last night out of my head so I can enjoy the rest of this trip with my friends. I'm here to celebrate, and last night was just part of that celebration.

"Do you want to talk about last night?" Natasha asks gently.

I shake my head. "No. It was great, and now I'm embarrassed, and I think it's safe to say I'm never sleeping with a random stranger again, so let's go take on Vegas. I'm thinking a new Hermès handbag will cure just about anything."

I realize my goal is to be financially independent, but considering the court is ordering Alex to pay me alimony, I have no qualms about spending that money on something nice for myself.

I force last night to the back of my mind as we shop, eat, and catch a show, and I'm spent when the show is over. I didn't get much sleep last night, and while Vegas isn't known as a place where you're supposed to get a lot of sleep, I'm too tired to have any more fun. The girls walk me back to the hotel, and I head upstairs while they head toward the bar in the casino.

And once I'm finally alone, I allow the memory of last night out of the little box I put it in. I let myself remember what an absolutely incredible night it was, and I let myself feel a little measure of hatred for—and a whole lot of anger toward—the man who lied to me.

As we board the plane for home the next day, I make the conscious decision that I will leave that night behind me.

It was always the plan anyway. I just wish I could leave it there fondly rather than bitterly.

Chapter 12: Tanner Banks

A Threesome Could Be Just the Thing

It's easy to pretend like that night never happened over the next couple weeks as I get to work with the Storm.

My brother and I officially move to San Diego, and we're thrust into the thick of things as training camp gets under way in another week. We're here with the rookies, training hard and getting to know people before the rest of the squad joins us.

It's our way of getting to know the team, the coaching styles, and the front office and how involved they get in the day-to-day field operations.

It's easy to push it all away as I'm immersed into a totally new life.

All I've ever known is Arizona, and when a new day dawns each morning, I find myself getting out of bed earlier than usual, pulling on some gear, and heading for the beach to run.

It's a hell of a workout on my legs, and there's something tranquil about being on the beach.

It also gives me time to think.

I'm so used to *not* thinking—to just reacting in the moment—that I've trained myself to shut down that part of my brain when I need to. It goes hand-in-hand with my theory that emotions are nothing more than distractions.

I can't let myself be distracted. I have an entire team looking at me to be their leader, an entire fanbase looking at me to lead them to victory. I can't let them down.

I *won't* let them down.

Miller knows this about me, and he understands this about me. We have the unspoken, intuitive understanding of each other in a way nobody else will ever be able to grasp, and that's a pretty damn powerful bond.

Like the fact that he picked out this house for us. He knew what we both wanted without me having to say a single word about it.

And normally that's a good thing.

But when I want to hide my feelings about something…well, I can't hide from him. Ever.

And that's why I'm out the door before he leaves for practice, and I meet him in the locker room instead of in the kitchen of the house we share.

We have different meetings and different practices since we play different positions, but I know I can't avoid him forever.

When Friday afternoon hits and the rookies are let out of practice early, I head up to chat with the coaches before I go home.

And I can't avoid my brother any longer.

"The fuck is going on with you?" he asks from his spot on the couch in the family room when I walk in.

I feign innocence for all of a few seconds before I slide onto the couch beside him. I stare at the television that's currently paused on one of the hosts of SportsCenter, and I sigh.

I can't hide it from him any longer. "I hooked up with someone that night in Vegas when I left the club early."

"I knew it." Of course he did. He always knows, just like I know when something's going on with him. "And that's what got you all twisted?"

"*She* got me all twisted," I admit. "I'm trying to distance myself from it, but I can't stop thinking about it."

"What about it?"

I shake my head. "I don't know," I murmur. I think back to that night. It wasn't just the way her lips parted when she moaned, or the way her body writhed as she came, or the way she looked at me.

I keep thinking about the part before I took her up to my room. Walking through the gardens with her at my hotel and seeing the joy on her face as she identified a flower. The way she licked her bottom lip when a drop of honey mustard fell on it and the way it felt like we were connected from the second our eyes met at the bar.

I can't tell Miller all that shit, though. It's emotions. I don't do emotions.

I blow out a breath. "She left an impression, that's all."

"The sex was that good?"

I chuckle. "Well, yeah. She had a magic pussy. But beyond all that, she wasn't into football."

"How'd she know you, then?"

I shrug. "She asked if I'm a football player, and we got to talking. I was a little buzzed from the tequila, but so was she. She just got divorced, and she was in Vegas celebrating. I was in Vegas celebrating. One thing led to another. By the time we got back to my hotel room, we were sober enough to know what we were doing, and we had a great night. But it sort of seems like that's all she wanted."

"You wanted more?" he asks, surprise evident in his tone.

"I don't know." I hear the frustration in my own tone. "It was a one-night stand. Her hot hookup. I gave her my number. She hasn't used it. I don't even know where she's from."

"You could call the club and maybe get a name from her receipt from that night," he suggests.

I give him a look like he's lost his mind. "And, what, call her out of the blue? To say what? 'Hey, it's Tanner from that night in Vegas. Remember how good the sex was? I'd love to do that again.'"

He shrugs. "Why not? Maybe she's thinking about you, too, but she's got the advantage since she knows who you are. Maybe she'd be thrilled to hear from you."

"And maybe our kicker will score a touchdown this season," I say, trying to think of something as ridiculous as what he's insinuating.

"Well, whatever you decide, I don't know how to say this kindly, so I'll be blunt. Get your shit together. It's affecting your performance, man."

"Thanks for the brutal honesty," I say dryly. "I know it is. I'm working on it, and I'll be good to go by Monday."

And then Monday comes, and "Centuries" by Fall Out Boy is blasting over the PA system while I'm out on the field practicing, and I'm not good to go as promised.

I don't know why I can't get her out of my head, but I'm running into reminders of her literally everywhere I go.

Sweet potato fries on the buffet table after practice.

Avocado with my morning eggs before practice.

Peach flowers in the flower beds in front of the practice facility.

Fall Out Boy on repeat.

She's literally everywhere, and I can't seem to escape her.

I guess having her as a distraction takes my mind off the fact that I don't even know who I am anymore. My jersey says

Banks, but I'm a Nash now. Am I supposed to take that last name? Eddie Nash didn't raise us, and I don't want to be associated with him.

But there's more to the name than just Eddie. There are my four half-brothers, for one thing. They're four great guys who I'm proud to call my brothers, and so is Miller.

And that's why, as practice comes to a close on our first day of training camp, neither Miller nor I decline when Spencer invites us out to dinner afterward.

We head to a restaurant near the training facility, and we're seated in a back corner booth for privacy.

"How are you liking San Diego so far?" Spencer asks after we order our food.

Miller and I glance at each other, and he nods for me to answer.

"Can't beat the weather. July in Arizona was basically hell on earth, so we're happy to be here."

"It's okay to go deeper than the weather with me," Spencer says gently.

"I like that Coach Dell trusts me," I say quietly. "I like that he wants to work in tandem with me rather than…well, rather than how it was before."

Spencer nods knowingly. "He's an incredible coach. One of the best." He turns to Miller. "You?"

He lifts a shoulder. "The food's just fair."

Spencer and I both laugh.

"He likes it spicy," I explain. "Arizona had decent choices when it came to his spicy food."

"Most restaurants here only offer Tabasco. I'm more of a Cholula guy," Miller says.

"I know some good places with spicy food," Spencer assures us, and we laugh. We make small talk about the offense while we dig into our dinners, and just as I've taken my last bite, Spencer narrows his eyes at me.

"So if you're enjoying it so much, what's going on with you?"

I swallow my food before I attempt to respond. "Excuse me?"

Miller rolls his eyes. "He's obsessing over some woman."

"I am not," I say both defensively and petulantly.

"Dude, yes, you are. You've had plenty of one-night stands before that haven't distracted you like this," he points out.

"I'm not distracted. I'm over it." More defensiveness. More petulance.

Spencer looks between us like he's watching some tennis match, and I nod toward him.

"How do you know something's going on with me?"

He shrugs. "I don't know. You just seem…a little distracted. And you know how bad distractions are for the field."

"Yeah, I'm aware, thanks." I'm also aware I don't need to be a dick about it, but I can't seem to stop that either. "Look, it's fine. It was a one-night thing, and I'll move on. Okay? Look, already moving on." My eyes follow two attractive women as they make their way into the restaurant, and I think a threesome could be just the thing that helps break me out of whatever this is.

The truth of it is that I'm going through a lot of life changes right now, and thinking about the night we shared gives me a warmth I'm not used to feeling…because I'm not used to allowing emotions in.

But I'm also not used to moving to a new city, or to finding out my mom lied to me my entire life, or to building my own plays with a new coach as we work to find our rhythm together. Or to finding out my biological father also fathered four other NFL players. Five if you count my twin.

QUITTING THE *Quarterback*

It's a lot for one person to take on, and while football was always my distraction, Spencer sitting across from us having a brotherly chat is just further evidence of how much has changed in the last few months.

It's also proof that I haven't dealt with any of it yet.

I didn't think I needed to.

But if someone who hardly knows me is calling me out on my shit, it's time to change *something*.

And that's why I make a vow. I'll push her out of my mind. She's in the past. I won't worry about the Nash thing for now. I'm a Banks, or a Banks-Nash, or a Nash. It doesn't matter what my jersey says as long as I get to play football.

I'll push it all away and focus on the game.

Because that's the healthy way to deal with things.

Right?

Chapter 13: Cassie Fields

Onward and Upward

"We're thrilled to offer you the position," Dr. Hayward says. "We'll start by having you shadow me for a few weeks before we give you your own patients, but I'm confident you'll pick things up quickly."

"Thank you so much. I won't let you down."

"I know you won't," he says, and he says goodbye before he ends the call.

I have a job. I can move forward and start taking my life back.

And maybe I can even stop dwelling on the one-night stand that I never should have taken part in.

Maybe it's silly to be stuck on it an entire week later, but given that it's my first—my *only*—I'm not sure exactly how I'm supposed to feel about it. I've given up talking to Jess about it. She doesn't get it because she's been with more guys than I have. She has a living, breathing manifestation of one of her one-night stands in Dylan, and I know for a fact that even though it's hard being a single mom, she wouldn't change that for the world.

So talking to her about the regrets I have about my night feels a little strange to me. Katie is a lot like I was, but back before the divorce, and I've never been as close with Natasha to discuss this sort of thing without the other women present.

So I'm kind of at a loss as to who I'd even talk to about this sort of thing. I tell myself it must not be that big of a deal. Maybe it's not. Maybe it's more common than I realized, and I'm building it up to this big thing in my head when it really isn't.

This job is my signal. It's my sign that I need to leave the past where it belongs and move onward and upward.

Easier said than done.

Today is the last day of camp for the kids, but school doesn't start for another week. Dr. Hayward was fine with me starting once the kids are back to school, and Luca comes running up to me excitedly after he gets off the bus.

"Mom, Mom, Mom," he says as he tugs on my arm.

"What, what, what?" I ask.

"Connor said his mom is taking them to the San Diego Storm's training camp next week. He said it's free. Can we go? Can we go? Please?"

"Oh, honey, I don't know anything about that," I say. And not that I would tell my child this, but I'm not exactly interested in watching football after my wild weekend in Vegas.

"Please please please," he begs, and I know he's serious when he's begging in threes like this.

I glance over at Lily for help. I'm hopeful she'll get me out of this one, but instead, the opposite happens.

"Claire's going too, and she said there will be a bounce house. Can we, Mama? Please?"

I blow out a breath. "I'll see if I can look into getting us tickets," I say. I'm hopeful they'll forget about it, but it comes up again a couple hours later at dinner.

"Did you look yet, Mom?" asks my seven-year-old in his sweet little voice.

The last thing in the world I want to do is let him down. "We'll get tickets together after you both eat a good dinner, okay?"

"Yes," he says, punching a fist into the air.

I keep my promise, and both kids are correct. It's free, and there are bounce houses and all sorts of kids' activities—including a chance for kids to meet some of the players, which I'm sure is the dream of many football fans.

Luca is thrilled to pieces, and he goes immediately to his iPad to look up a team roster. "How do you spell San Diego Storm roster?" he asks.

I tell him as he sits on the couch, and I clear the dinner dishes from the table. He punches in the letters as I say them. He's getting pretty good at reading, and he tries to sound out some of the names of players.

"Does QB mean quarterback?" he asks.

"I don't know. Probably."

"Did you know the Storm got a new quarterback this year?"

"Nope," I say absently. "I don't know who the old one was, either."

"He's supposed to be really, really good. That's what Connor said anyway, and Dad said that, too." He flips the television on and navigates to ESPN—clearly a habit instilled in him by his father—and they're talking about the NFL and training camps around the league. I'm only half-listening when I hear the name *Nash* mentioned.

I glance up and spot Asher Nash, who plays for the Vegas Aces. That's not my guy, either.

Maybe I'll never really know who he was other than some mystery. Maybe he's just a figment of my imagination created by one too many margaritas.

I finish the dishes and start the bathtime routine, which consists of me telling Lily for ten minutes to get in the tub, washing her, and then telling Luca for another ten minutes to go take his shower once she's out. Then it's another fifteen minutes each of our goodnight routine, and then I get the next hour to myself before I go to bed and start it all over in the morning.

And it's all going to be thrown into a tailspin in another week once school starts and I start my new job. It's been a lot of chaos over the last few months, first with me telling Alex I wanted a divorce and then him moving out. It's been upheaval and unpredictability, and I'm very much looking forward to the routine that school provides us.

But tonight, I pour myself a glass of wine and sit in front of the television to catch up on my favorite reality television—the show my mom calls trash but watches anyway because we both love a good love story.

Except in this episode, we discover that Chad still has feelings for his ex, and poor Fiona, who thought she'd found love with Chad, is shit out of luck.

I sigh. Are *all* men liars? It sure feels that way lately. First Alex, then Grayson—or whoever he was, and now reality star Chad.

I flip off the television and sit in silence with my wine. Honestly, men are simply exhausting, and the truth is that I'm just fine on my own. I don't want the complications that come from relationships, and I've never betrayed myself the way it feels like every man who's entered my life has.

I'm glad I have this new job to throw myself into, and I can't wait for one more week to get started. It's exactly the distraction I need since my personal life is at a complete standstill…just the way I plan to keep it for the foreseeable future.

Chapter 14: Tanner Banks

A Blonde Woman with Two Kids

Every Saturday, Monday, and Wednesday, the Storm opens up training camp to the public for a couple hours so they can come watch us practice. It's strange to me since a lot of what we do is supposed to be under wraps, but the stands are filled with people eager to get the first look at this year's team, and it's also a time for kids to have some fun while they're introduced to the game their parents love.

We run very basic drills during this time, and we run a little scrimmage where I swap places with the two backup quarterbacks so we all get a few turns at signal calling.

But every time I step onto the field, the crowd goes wild. It's a good feeling. It's a warm welcome. People are excited to have me here after the promising rookie quarterback the team drafted last year underperformed.

It's why they took me in the biggest trade deal San Diego has ever seen. I've proven my performance, and I have a lot of years left in me. I'm ready for this new challenge with the players who are here with me…and the rather healthy payday didn't hurt matters by any stretch of the imagination.

On Wednesday, I watch as the third-string quarterback, Jonathan Thomas, sets up a play. Even in scrimmage, he's a bit unsure of his footing. But that's the thing about quarterbacks. They *have* to be sure. They have to be confident and poised, and Jonathan doesn't have the pocket presence he needs to avoid sacks. It's almost like he's scared of the defensive line, which part of me doesn't blame him for since he was injured early in his career. Part of healing from an injury includes getting past the psychological effects from it, and I'm not sure he's fully recovered in that respect.

Ford Turner, our second-string quarterback, organizes the offensive line for the next play, and he's a good backup. Between the coaching staff and me mentoring him, I think we could see great things out of him in the future. He's a rookie this year drafted out of Michigan, and he was set to start before the big trade went through. Even so, he welcomed me in with open arms, and he seems like a good guy.

I run the next play, and I call the play. I toss a bomb down the field for Spencer to catch. It sails easily into his arms, and he runs it into the endzone. The crowd shouts their approval, and I grin at my teammates. I hope it's that easy when we're playing real opponents rather than our own defensive line.

And I hope our defensive line puts more pressure on our opposing quarterbacks, too.

Coach Q, also known as Quinten Walker, the quarterback's coach, approaches me after that play. He has some words of praise, and then he turns to Ford. "Can you head up to the kids' zone after practice for a meet and greet?"

Ford nods, and I knew some of the guys would be asked, but the coaches usually don't ask the starters.

Still, I say, "I'll go up with you." I don't have anywhere to be immediately after practice today, and it's not like we're going to have an offensive meeting without Ford there. Besides, I like meeting the next generation of football fans. I've always liked working with kids, and it's why I started a foundation benefiting kids. I can't wait to find ways to make an impact on the youth right here in San Diego, whether it's starting up a youth league like I did in Arizona, creating scholarships, running camps, or doing something else entirely.

Coach Q looks surprised that I volunteered. "Why don't you stay on the field and greet some of the fans in the stands?" He nods over toward where the fans are already lining up for the chance to get something signed by one of the players, and I nod.

We finish our scrimmage, and I glance at the crowd. A long line of people has formed in the stands as fans hope to meet one of their favorite players, and I can't help but feel a rush of excitement that all these people here are excited to meet us.

Us. We're just a group of dudes who like to play football, and somehow that has elevated every one of us on this field to a status we couldn't have been expecting when we first picked up a football.

And as a quarterback, the spotlight is even brighter on me. I'm looked upon as a leader, which has its benefits as well as its drawbacks. I like being a leader, but I don't love when I'm blamed for a loss. It's a team effort that can't be drilled down to one single person, but the truth is that if I'm having a shit game, it affects the field more than if anyone else is having a shit game.

I've had to grow a pretty damn thick skin over the years, and I'm at a point in my career where I've learned to allow the positive voices to be louder than the negative. Or that's what I tell myself anyway. I try not to be affected by the negativity.

From beneath my helmet, I eye the long line of people hoping some of us will come over, and I wonder if I'll hear any negativity when I walk over. And that's when my eyes fall upon a blonde woman with two kids. Her head is bent down as she tries to corral her two kids, but there's something incredibly familiar about her even though I can't see her face. She's talking to a crying little girl with hair a few shades lighter than her own, and then she turns to a boy who looks as if he's insisting upon something. She seems to be holding onto her patience tightly with the two of them from her body language, and I can't put my finger on why she seems familiar to me from the back.

I guess I've been to San Diego before. Maybe we've met.

I study her another beat, and that's when she turns forward and looks up from her kids toward the skies as if she's asking for divine intervention. She glances at the field, and even though I'm wearing a helmet, I swear her eyes fall onto me.

Holy shit.

It's *her*. Cassie. The woman from Vegas.

She's here in my new city. In my new stadium. A mere forty or so yards away from where I'm standing at this very moment.

I thought I'd never see her again, and as I watch her turn to the boy and say something, I piece together why she left that morning wanting nothing more than one night with me.

She has kids. She has an entire *life* that's clearly not in Vegas, and she's one of those people who subscribes to the *what happens in Vegas* theory.

I guess I am, too. I am *now*, anyway.

I'm rooted to my spot for a few beats as I try to figure out what to do. One half of me wants to run over to her. To talk to her. To ask her if she showed up here today to see me, if she wants to exchange numbers, maybe go out again.

The cocky part of me believes that of course she's here to see me. She knew who I was when she turned to me and asked if I'm a football player, and that's how our entire unforgettable night started.

The other half of me wants to run far, far away—to avoid them at all costs and leave the past in the past.

I don't know anything about her or her life. Clearly she hid a very big part of who she is from me since she's here with what are presumably her children since they look like little miniature versions of her. She hid it because we were only meant to share that one night.

And maybe seeing her here today with her kids is proof of that.

It feels like more lies, like I can't escape them. Like everyone in my life, including strangers, is lying to me.

Maybe she wasn't celebrating a divorce at all. Maybe she's married and went to Vegas for some conquest with her friends only to return home to her family and play the role of happy mother and wife again.

Maybe this was the thing I needed to fully get over that night. It's closure.

Except...

What if it isn't?

For a guy who preaches confidence on the field, I'm sure as fuck at an impasse in my own mind about what to do.

Miller sidles up beside me. "What are you doing?"

I clear my throat and glance over at him. "Debating whether I should go sign some shit or hit the locker room."

He nods. "Come on. I'll go with you." He takes off for the stands without another word, and when I glance up at Cassie again, she's not where she was standing a moment ago.

Instead, I watch her ass as she holds the little girl's hand and the boy walks in front of them as they make their way up the stairs and toward the concourse.

I guess that's my answer, then.

I follow Miller over, sign a few things, fake a smile, and head to the locker room as I try to piece together why the fuck I can't seem to get over that night.

Chapter 15: Cassie Fields

It's Him But Different

I've never been into football, but today has taught me that maybe I should rethink that.

All those men on the field in those little pants and jerseys? I had to fan myself because it was getting so hot.

Except, you know…kids.

We're heading to the kids' zone at the request of Lily, who started crying and throwing an epic fit that her brother wanted to wait to see which players would come over to sign things. He said there's some twins new to the team who are supposed to both be really good, and he was hoping to get his ball signed by them.

"We don't know who's going to run over," he whined, and Lily's crocodile tears turned into whale tears. That's the signal. As soon as the tears turn huge, the fit is coming, complete with screaming, and if I'm really lucky, she'll throw herself down onto the ground and her arms and feet will flail around dramatically.

I tried to maintain my composure. There is nothing I hate more than losing my shit in public, so I looked to the heavens as

I drew in a deep breath, and then I said as sweetly as I could to Luca, "If you agree to go to the kids' zone right now for your sister, you can have ice cream for dinner."

"You mean for dessert?" he asked.

I shook my head. "Nope. I mean for *your meal.*"

His eyes lit up, and he led the way up toward the kids' zone. Lily magically stopped crying, and it wasn't my finest parenting moment since I gave the screaming girl what she wanted, but I know the way to my boy's heart, and that way is paved with ice cream.

He's not exactly complaining now that he's in a bounce house, even if it is with his baby sister. In any event, both kids are happy, and as I glance around, I see lots of smiling, happy children and adults who look...well, as exhausted as I feel.

A day in public with the two of them is no joke.

I glance around at the huge photographs of players up on the walls, and the first one I see is Spencer Nash. My first thought is that it wasn't him, though the blue eyes match my mystery man. Was he a Nash? The bartender *called him* Grayson Nash. He didn't correct the mistaken identity. Was it because he was getting a free drink? Was it because he wanted to pretend he was someone else for the night? Was he even a football player *or* a Nash? Maybe he was some mystery guy related to the Nash family since he resembles them so much.

I'm still confused as to the answer to that, and that's when my eyes edge over to the next picture.

My chest tightens and my stomach twists.

Oh my God.

It's him. That's my guy. I feel someone tugging on my arm as I stare at the photo. *Miller Banks. RB #23.*

Miller Banks?

So...not a Nash? But yes...a football player?

"Mom, can we go play that game over there?" Luca's voice comes into focus, and I glance over at him.

"Who's that?" I ask, pointing to the picture I can't stop staring at. It's him, isn't it? It's him, but there's something different. The little slyness I remember from his eyes…it's not there. But who knows how much photo editing and retouching goes into these giant photos hanging on the wall? I can't tell if that little scar is on his chin, but it definitely looks like my guy.

"Miller Banks. Only the best running back in the entire NFL," Luca says. "Come on."

I can't stop staring at the photo. There's something off about him, but that's *him*. No doubt about it.

It's like he's staring back at me, but the light in his eyes, that innate charisma he has—it's not coming through in the photograph.

Maybe it was just my imagination, or the margaritas. Or maybe my memory is betraying me.

Still…Miller Banks. I have a name.

"Let's go," Luca whines, drawing out the *o* in *go*.

I blow out a breath as I pull myself together. I force my eyes from the image staring down at me, and I can't help but wonder how many women will look at that picture with the same sort of intimate knowledge I have of him.

I can't think about the specifics right now. I can't remember how he tasted, or what it was like as his cock bumped the back of my throat, or how it felt when he moved inside of me. I can't remember his lips on mine, or the way he was so tender and sweet with me before we ever even got back to his room. I can't remember chicken tenders with honey mustard and holding his hand as we walked around the conservatory.

I refuse to think about any of it, especially not here when I need to be present with my children.

Was he down on that field the whole time we were watching? I saw number twenty-three as he ran with the football, but he had a helmet on, and it's not like I'd recognize him from the stands—for one thing, my focus was on the kids, but for another thing, I thought he played for Vegas. I wouldn't have even thought to look for him here.

And yet…here he is.

I don't know what to think. He led me to believe a lot about him that wasn't true, furthering my theory that all men are liars.

I guess I know who he is now…but what the hell good does it do me knowing? Maybe I was better off in the dark.

I don't get a whole lot of time to dwell on it since Luca and Lily have all sorts of activities they want to do in the kids' zone. Face painting and crafts, churros and games.

We stay until the event ends, and I keep my eyes focused on my children, even though in my chest I can feel that he's in this building somewhere. He was the whole time we were here, and the thought leaves me feeling pretty dang hollow.

It doesn't matter that I know who he is now. I thought it would give me some sort of closure, but instead it just unlocked a whole host of other questions…along with the realization that there's absolutely nothing I can do about it.

Exactly how does one get in touch with a megastar like Miller Banks? Even if I had the answer to that, I wouldn't act on it. Because the truth is, he let me believe he was Grayson Nash. There was some reason he didn't want me to know who he was, and for me, that will always just be one of my life's great mysteries.

Chapter 16: Tanner Banks

Refreshed and Ready for Game Day

It's been a shitty training camp as I worked my ass off to get my head in the game, but our first game of the season is tomorrow, and I think I finally pieced together why that night affected me the way it did.

It was *her*.

She was genuine that night, and she seemed like the first person I'd met in a long time who didn't just tell me what they thought I wanted to hear.

Everybody *always* just tells me what I want to hear.

Except coaches. They almost never tell me what I want to hear.

She didn't acknowledge me at practice when I saw her that day, and the thought crossed my mind that maybe she didn't know who I was. Of course she did, though. She asked me if I was a football player. She had to know who I was. She must've just been distracted by the kids I didn't know she had.

Who the fuck knows?

All I know is that tomorrow is our first game, and I need my focus back.

We're at the hotel our team will stay at the night before every home game this season, and I'm shooting the shit with a few of the offensive linemen in a room a few down from my own when Miller walks in.

He tips his head at me in that silent way that says he wants to talk to me, and I finish up my conversation with these men before I excuse myself. We head a few doors down to his room, and I sit on the office chair.

I raise my brows and nod at him to say whatever it is he wants to say. He holds his hand out for our secret handshake.

I slap his hand, slap backward, grab his hand and shake, fist bump, and then I stand for a hug.

"We did it, man," he says as he pounds me on the back.

I pound him back, and I pull apart from him. "Season seven, dude. San Di-fucking-ego. Can you believe it?"

"San Di-fucking-ego?" he echoes, and he laughs as I slug him in the arm.

"Not bad having the beach out the window and salt in the air on the way to work, am I right?"

"No lie," he says. "You doing okay?"

I shrug. "Yeah, man. I'm fine."

"You know you can't hide it from me, right?"

I sit back on the chair, knowing full well he's not going to let me out of here without getting the truth out of me.

"Fine. A few weeks ago at one of the practices that was open to the public…I saw the woman I met that night in Vegas."

His jaw slackens. "The one that's got you all fucked up?"

I nod slowly and press my lips together. I haven't mentioned it because it felt like giving voice to it would only give it the attention it doesn't deserve.

"Yeah. And she had two kids with her. They looked just like her, and she left them out of the conversation the night we met. So…" I trail off. I'm not really sure where to go with that.

So it feels like she lied the way everyone else always lies to me. But did she? Is leaving her personal life out of it really that big of a deal?

"Anyway," I say, dodging the questions I know are coming, "I think I'm just stuck on it because she's the last girl I had sex with, you know? Rookie camp started, and then we were back on the field, and we're new to town, so I'm trying to build bonds with our teammates, and I just haven't had time."

"I get it. Neither have I," he admits.

"Yeah, but yours is a conscious decision," I point out.

He rolls his eyes. "Is it, though?"

"Dude, we all know you've been in love since you were fourteen."

He sighs, and he diverts the conversation back to me as he chooses to ignore the jab. "What are you going to do?"

I shake my head and blow out a long breath. "I'm going to let it go."

"Because that's worked so well for you over the last month and a half," he points out.

"Fuck off with that." I glare at him.

He holds up both hands in surrender. "Sorry, sorry," he says, not really sounding all that sorry. "Just show up tomorrow, okay? It's our chance to show this city what we're made of."

I nod. "I know. I'll be there. Guaranteed. We're in season now, and that's the only thing that matters."

I stick to that. I say goodnight and head to my own room. I take a shower, jerk off, and clear my mind. It's all part of my night-before-the-game ritual, a way to relax myself before bed.

It does the trick. I get a full nine hours of rest, and I wake refreshed and ready for game day.

I chug a BODYARMOR sports drink in my favorite tropical punch flavor as soon as I get out of bed, and I order breakfast to my room. While I wait, I do some light yoga to get my body warmed up and my mind centered. Once my eggs and Greek yogurt arrive, I spend the next hour eating and reviewing film Coach sent me to ensure I'm ready for what the defensive line is going to bring against us today.

I feel focused. I feel dialed in and ready.

I get on the team bus that will take us to the stadium, and I sit in silence next to my brother. We head our separate directions once we get to the stadium to talk to our position coaches about last-minute adjustments and to review game plans, and then we hit the field for warm-ups.

It's all going so well. Too well.

I'm listening to my pregame playlist, jamming the fuck out to Metallica as usual, this time to "Battery," and then the song switches and Fall Out Boy's "Centuries" blasts into my ears.

A chill runs down my spine as this sense of impending doom washes over me.

I immediately switch the song, and I make a mental note to take it off my playlist.

It's a great song, but there are too many emotions tied up in it, and right now I'm working hard to keep those emotions in check. The only emotions allowed on this field are game-related. The rest get put in a little box that I'll deal with later. Or never.

We head to the locker room, and we change into our uniforms. I pull my jersey on over my pads, and I stare quietly into my locker as I take a second to meditate, just like a lot of guys are quietly doing as we prepare for the game.

First, visualization.

I visualize my distractions, and then I force myself to let them go so that I can be present and grounded. I imagine myself throwing the ball down the field as it sails into the arms of a receiver. I imagine the perfect handoff to a running back— always my brother in these visualizations since he's one of the greats.

Next, affirmation and purpose.

You are ready. You are focused. You are a winner. San Diego is your home. The goal is to win and to make this new home proud.

Finally, gratitude.

I'm thankful I get to play for the San Diego Storm.

I'm ready. Coach Dell calls us to gather, and he gives us some motivating words.

"Every play counts. Get out there and do your job. You've worked hard over the last few weeks, and I know what you're capable of. Get out on that field and prove it." And then he asks, "Does anyone else have anything to say?"

As the new team leader and captain, I glance around the room and find myself speaking up. "We're a new team with a new mission, men. Let's believe in each other and execute. Let's make this town proud, and let's get the fuck out there and leave everything we have on the field." I stick my hand out toward the middle of the group, and my teammates gather around and do the same until we're huddled. "Let's fucking go."

I'm met with a resounding, "Let's fucking go!" from my teammates, and we all grab our helmets and head toward the tunnel where we'll head onto the field as we're announced.

Adrenaline courses through me as we hear the pre-introduction show start up on the public address system. I haven't actually seen it, but I remember posing for videos with my arms crossed over my chest as the cameraperson told me to give my fiercest, most intense glare to the camera as if it were for our opponent, so I assume I'll be up there at some point.

We hear, "Ladies and gentlemen, your San Diego Storm!"

The line starts to move—first the mascot, which is a big bear carrying a lightning bolt, then the flag runners, and then the players. I'm at the back of the line since I'll run out last, but this team doesn't do individual player announcements.

Still, the crowd is going wild as I make my way out onto the field, through the tunnel the cheerleaders are making with their pompoms, and toward the sidelines, where the coaches are already in game mode and making more adjustments to the plan.

I wave to the fans. My mom and my stepdad are here somewhere. She texted me to let me know they were coming, and I replied that I needed to focus on the game and wasn't ready to discuss our issues.

My biological father might be here, too, since three of his sons play for this team now.

I wonder if Cassie is here with her kids, and I immediately berate myself for allowing those thoughts to make their way in. I thought I locked those up and let them go this morning, and it would serve me better if I had.

I take my spot on the sidelines beside Coach Dell, and then we wait. I'm pumped as adrenaline floods me. I'm ready to take on the Cowboys.

We win the coin toss, and we choose to receive first. The Cowboys kickoff to us, and we take it to the thirty-yard line, which is where I'll go to work.

This is it.

Preseason games are over. This isn't just practice. This isn't me taking a few snaps and warming the bench to preserve my health and give the rest of the players a chance to show what they're made of.

I get to lead every offensive play for this game. I get to head out onto that field and do the thing I was born to do.

I get to prove to this city that I'm worth the money the Storm shelled out for me.

I'm one lucky guy, and I know that.

Not many people get to achieve their dreams, and my dream was to play professional football. Here I am, standing on the sideline with the rest of my teammates, all of us ready to take the field and play the game that we have a shared love and passion for.

It doesn't get much better than this.

I draw in a deep breath as I glance at my brother, and then together we jog out to our places on the field—just like we've done every single time we've taken the field together.

We head to the thirty-yard line where we'll start. Everyone on this field knows our first play, but I call it anyway as the offense gathers in a loose formation to give our opponents less time to prepare.

As it turns out, though, a tight formation might've prevented what comes next. Any different formation might've prevented it.

But we went with loose, and it fucked everything up. Everything.

Chapter 17: Tanner Banks

What a Way to Go Down

I get my hands on the ball, and I'm looking downfield to see if my receiver is open when I spot a defender who broke free of our offensive line. I dodge to avoid him, and I have a few more seconds for my receiver to get into place.

I plant my leg, and I see another defender coming at me, so I twist to get out of the way.

But when I twist, my planted leg doesn't move the way it's supposed to, and instead, my knee twists as a snapping sound echoes through my entire body, and my knee gives way to a crippling explosion of pain.

I toss the ball downfield as close to my receiver as I can as I go down, my eyes slamming shut as agony takes over. Tears pinch behind my eyes as panic starts to wash over me.

It's a noncontact injury. Nobody hit me or slammed into my knee, and recovery from noncontact injuries can be brutal.

I writhe around on the ground, grabbing onto my knee as if that'll make it any better, but I can already feel it swelling.

I've been around this game long enough to know what it is, but fuck that. This is literally the first play I've had with the San Diego Storm, and I'm not fucking going out.

Not like this.

My brother reaches me first. "What is it?"

"Knee," I grit out through a clenched jaw as I try to maintain my composure. It hurts like fuck, and the world is watching.

What a way to go down.

"Fuck," he yells, and one of the trainers, Nick, is running toward me with Coach Dell not far behind. Two more men are with them, names I can't recall as the pain threatens to consume me.

The medical staff reaches me, and they bend down to examine me, pushing my brother out of the way. But he's not to be deterred. He stands close by, shielding me from the cameras as best he can.

They start firing questions at me as they move my leg, and I'm trying to concentrate on answering them through the buzz of agony.

Nick takes one look at my knee and asks me, "Pain on a scale of one to ten?"

It's a fucking eleven on that scale, but I'm not about to admit that. If I tell the truth, they'll take me back to the locker room and force me to have an MRI. I'll be out for the season.

It's fine. I can brace up and play through this.

But my silence as I debate my answer is a dead giveaway.

This is bad. Really bad.

"Can you walk?" Coach asks.

I breathe through the pain.

"It's already swelling," Nick tells Coach.

"Don't say ACL," Coach says as if I'm not sitting right here.

"He needs an MRI."

"I'm fine. I can play." I grit out the protest, but it's weaker than it should be. If it were true, I wouldn't have all these men kneeling over me with concern in their eyes. I wouldn't hear the hush of an entire stadium whose hopes for the season are flushed down the drain on the very first play.

I wouldn't feel my chest cracking open and my heart fucking breaking for all I'm about to lose.

"Let's have Dr. Roberts determine that just to be on the safe side," Coach says, and Nick helps me up. He braces me around my waist with one arm while my brother takes the other side.

"You'll be back out here before halftime," Miller assures me, and I wish I had that same level of confidence.

I can walk, but every step is excruciating. I've managed pain before, though. I can put this in the same box I stuck all my distractions into before the game today.

Because that worked out so well.

Fuck. Fuck! I can't let this end my season. I was distracted, and I *knew* it would come back to haunt me.

I limp down the sideline toward the tunnel to take me back to the locker room still braced by Nick—but not my brother, who is returning to the field to play with Ford Turner instead of me. I hear voices on the sidelines.

Get your ass right back out here.

We're here for you.

We're playing for you.

The first emotion that hit was denial, but as I listen to their voices fading behind me as they get to play and I have to go get a fucking MRI in the locker room during the game, anger starts to step into its place.

"I'm fine," I roar at Nick.

"I know," he assures me even though we both know I'm lying. "We're just going to have Dr. Roberts take a quick look, and you'll be back on the field before halftime. Just like Miller said."

My clenched jaw works overtime as I try to create pain somewhere else in my body to take the attention away from my knee, but it's useless.

Nick takes me into an exam room, and Dr. Roberts is already waiting for us. Nick fills him in on his initial findings, and the doctor asks me to explain what happened.

"I twisted one way and my knee twisted the other," I say, and my voice sounds dead to my own ears. There's no emotion in it, and it scares me a little. "I'm fine. I just snapped it. It'll bounce back. Brace it up and let me go back out there."

Dr. Roberts shakes his head. "It's already swelling. Going back out now might be worse than season-ending, Tanner. We need to get some imaging done to see what's going on before it swells more. Excuse me." He walks out of the room and leaves me with Nick, who glances over at me.

"Let's get your jersey and pads off."

There's not much else to say.

He helps me out of my gear, and I glare down at my traitorous knee as I wish I could rewind the clock and do everything differently.

I take off my cleats and my pants, and Nick tosses me a gown to cover up with, not that I need one back here in a fucking locker room.

Dr. Roberts returns a moment later with a wheelchair. "Let's get you to imaging. The radiologist is here."

I blow out a frustrated breath. I don't want to go to imaging, least of all in a wheelchair. I don't want them to run an MRI to confirm what I already know. I'd rather live in the dark with a little bit of pain because that little bit of pain at least tells me I'm still alive.

Taking football away from me is taking that life away.

Maybe that's dramatic, but it's all I know. It's all I've done every goddamn year from July through February since I was eleven years old.

I don't even know what my life is if I can't step onto the grass every Sunday.

Fuck.

I do as I'm told.

I lay as still as possible on the table and slide into the tube that takes the images of the ligaments inside my knee. All I can think about is the doctor's words about how if I play through it, it could be worse than season-ending. What the fuck is worse than season-ending? What the fuck am I supposed to do if this is season-ending?

I can't even think about what would be worse than that.

It's a risk every time we step out onto that field. I've suffered broken fingers and cuts and scrapes, plenty of bruises, a couple of sprains. All shit I could play through. All shit that caused me to miss a game at most.

But this is different. The eerie quiet of this MRI machine *feels* different, and it leaves me feeling hollow.

Nobody will know what to say to me. Nobody will know how to react, how to make the quarterback feel better.

And the truth is that nobody will be able to. I'm a competitor. I'm a winner. I'm a hard worker. I'm an athlete.

That's my entire identity. Who am I if I don't have the game I love so goddamn much?

It shouldn't come as a surprise once I'm back in the exam room and Dr. Roberts walks in with my results. "It's a complete ACL tear, Tanner. I'm sorry. My recommendation is to wait a few days for the swelling and inflammation to go down and start some physical therapy. Reconstruction surgery in three to six weeks."

My heart drops at his words, and my chest tightens.

I knew it was coming, but it doesn't make the blow of the words feel any less harsh.

More words follow—words I can't focus on as a cloud of grief falls over me.

I already know all these things, but Dr. Roberts and Nick say the words anyway. They sound like those droning voices from the old *Charlie Brown* cartoons, or like I'm underwater as they talk. I hear the words, but they don't register.

"ACL tears are pretty much always season-ending. The surgery and recovery are tough, and the risk of reinjuring it is incredibly high if players return too soon."

"Things feel bleak right now, but you have the drive to return. You're mentally tough as hell, Tanner. You love this game. You can stand on the sidelines and call plays with the coaches. You can still study the game and our opponents. You can work your ass off to rehabilitate and get back to the game as soon as possible."

I just wish I believed the pep talk. I wish I had the mental toughness they think I do. I wish all those negative thoughts and distractions weren't slowly creeping out of the box I locked them in.

I wish I could get back onto the field, but I'm not medically cleared, and because of these stupid fucking images, I won't be for at least the next eight or nine months.

It's a noncontact injury. I don't even have someone else to blame, so I'll blame myself.

I'm out the next year because I was fucking distracted.

That's the last goddamn time I let some woman distract me from *anything* ever again.

Chapter 18: Cassie Fields

A VIP Patient

I'm sitting across from Dr. Hayward, my boss, as he goes over today's schedule with me. I've been sitting in on his patients as I've been trained on the system over the last month, and a couple weeks ago, we transitioned to me running the appointments and him dropping in to see how I'm doing. Last week, I had my own patients on Tuesday and Thursday, and it went really well. This week I expect to take on even more independent responsibility.

Dr. Hayward has a medical degree in sports medicine, and he opened Motion Orthopedics with his best friend, Dr. Barlow, one of San Diego's leading orthopedic surgeons. Between the two doctors and the staff of physical therapists, we work collaboratively to ensure our patients are receiving top-level care to accelerate recovery and restore mobility.

"We have a VIP patient coming in. Male, twenty-nine, a healthy professional athlete," Dr. Hayward says. "Because of your background in sports medicine, I'd like you to shadow me on this one."

Just telling me that he's a pro athlete tells me pretty much everything I need to know. He'll have the drive to return as quickly as he can to his sport, but his mental state is anyone's guess. Some athletes use injuries as the time when they can show the world what they're made of. Others fall apart and can't handle the mental aspects of being sidelined from the sport they love. Some of them hate being told what to do, and some *really* hate being told what to do by a woman.

"What's the injury?" I ask.

"ACL-MCL complex injury," he says, and I wrinkle my nose. That's a tough one for a pro athlete. It'll keep him out of his sport a while. "Happened yesterday afternoon, and he'll be in at nine this morning. We'll start prehab therapy next week after the swelling goes down. Dr. Barlow will examine him first and recommend a date for surgery, but we want to do some stabilizing and strengthening exercises with him ahead of that." He opens a file to show me the MRI report, and I scan through everything. It looks like a fairly complex but still standard ACL tear with a grade two MCL tear, and it'll require some physical therapy ahead of surgery with a lot more after.

"Once I consult with Dr. Barlow, we can put together a preoperative program for him, but I have some ideas in mind," he adds. "What about you?"

"Reducing swelling will be our first goal of prehab," I say, thinking through what challenges we might be facing based on the MRI report. "Then maximizing muscle strength and range of motion ahead of surgery. Depending on the patient's needs, I'm thinking a four-to-five-week program with balance training, knee extensions, quad work building up to squats. Swimming, biking, and elliptical work. A pro athlete is going to need to retain muscle strength, so we'll help with leg curls and press."

"Good, Cassandra," he praises. "We'll get that knee to look

and feel normal again before we go in and fix the root of the problem. Just so you know, this particular patient may be stubborn."

"That's why you hired me," I say smoothly with a grin. I'm a mom. I'm used to dealing with stubbornness all the time. I glance around for my water bottle, which I usually keep with me at all times, and I realize I left it in my car today.

He nods with a smile, and I glance at the clock. I have one patient to see before I sit in with this athlete, and she's currently in one of our exam rooms with a TENS unit getting some electrical currents to stimulate her calf before I head in to do a bit of muscle work with her on a strain that's been bothering her for weeks.

I double check her notes before I head in, and we've taken her pain down from a seven to a three over the last two weeks. I let her know we only need to see her once this week after I finish my muscle work, and I add a few notes to her chart before she heads out.

I have ten minutes to spare, even more probably since this VIP patient is meeting with Dr. Barlow first, so I take the opportunity to run down to the lobby and out to the parking lot so I can grab my water.

I rush back into the building and spot Gary, who works security, on my way by.

"Miss Cassie, always running," he says as he laughs and shakes his head.

I hold up my water bottle. "Left this in the car today. But, yes, running is good for you."

He laughs his hearty laugh. "We'll see about that."

I grin at him and head in the opposite direction from the elevators to take the stairs up to the sixth floor where our offices are in this medical building, and I'm still smiling as I head back into the office. I gulp down some water, leave my bottle in the break room, and head toward Dr. Hayward's office.

And then I wait for this VIP patient.

Chapter 19: Tanner Banks

Twin-Tuition

Was that her?

Or am I seeing things through the haze I woke under this morning?

I'm guessing it's the latter.

Everything feels pretty damn bleak at the moment, so my brain manifested an illusion of the one person I feel like I can blame for this even though somewhere deep down, I know it's not her fault. I'm angry at the world when there's really nobody to be angry with except myself.

I don't even know what to think this morning. The reality hasn't hit me yet. I slept like shit because how the fuck are you supposed to sleep when your mind is heavy with the truths that haven't hit you yet and your knee is throbbing and all you can do is focus on the pain?

And it's not just that.

I had about a million phone calls and texts from family and friends who saw me go down. I couldn't bear to reply to a single one of them, so I shut my phone off.

It didn't matter. They tried to get to me through my brother instead.

He fended off as many as he could, but he made sure I knew that Lincoln, Grayson, Spencer, and Asher all called to check on me, as did our mom and stepdad.

I made it clear to Miller that I don't want to talk to a single one of them.

He's been a shield for me, but to be honest, I don't really even want to talk to *him* about any of this. Talking about it feels like I'm acknowledging it's real, and I'm not ready to admit that yet.

My brother volunteered to accompany me to this appointment since the team won last night and we—*they*—don't have practice today, so he's here with me. Trainer Nick is also here.

The team sent him over to pick me up and drive me to this appointment—surely exactly what he wants to do with his Monday morning. He claims it is, but in reality, it's just part of his job. He can make sure I'm not moving the wrong way as I get in and out of the car, and he can make me sit in a wheelchair so I don't bear any weight before the doctors see me, despite the fact that I've been hobbling around on it all morning.

The team chose this orthopedic practice for me. I guess the surgeon is the best in the area. Fine. Great. Whatever.

All I can do this morning is second-guess my decision to move here to San Diego given that I was taken out on the very first play. Would I have had the same luck if I was still in Arizona?

It's a question I'll never have the answer to, but it's where my mind goes this morning.

"You look gray," Miller says. "Are you okay?"

"Fuck you," I hit back. Of course I look gray. I barely ate or slept at all since approximately nineteen minutes after one o'clock yesterday afternoon when my entire life changed in a split second. Hell, I've barely talked or acknowledged any of this.

Miller's quiet, but truth be told, he's a little gray, too. It's our twin-tuition, a term coined by my little brother. He feels what I'm feeling, and right now, complete and utter devastation is a pretty accurate portrayal.

Nick wheels me into the office, and a medical assistant is waiting for me to take me straight back to the doctor. I suppose it's one of the perks of my position—not having to wait in the reception area like everyone else does—but I'd rather not be here at all than be privy to that stupid perk.

The med assistant takes me directly to an examination room, and the doctor is already in there waiting for me when Nick wheels me in.

"Mr. Banks, I'm Dr. Barlow, and I'll be your surgeon. I'm so sorry to see you in here. How are you feeling today?" he asks.

"Pretty shitty, if I'm being honest."

He nods. "We'll do everything we can to ensure a safe and speedy recovery. I've reviewed the tape as well as the imaging. Let's get you up on the table so I can take a look."

Nick helps me up, and I lay on the table. The doctor starts to talk as he assesses the extent of the damage, moving my leg in various positions to check for stability. "Tell me how the pain is today."

I glance over at Nick and my brother, and I let out a frustrated breath. I thought patients and doctors were supposed to have confidentiality, but apparently not when you're a pro athlete. "Brutal. I can walk, but not without pain."

"That's to be expected. We want to prevent additional injury, so it's in your best interest to take it easy while we work to reduce swelling. We have a prehabilitation program to get your range of motion back ahead of surgery, and then we have extensive plans for after the surgery as well."

"If my range of motion is back, why can't I get back into the game and deal with surgery in the offseason?" I ask. I already know the answer, but I've also learned the answer is always no if you don't ask.

"You've torn your ACL, Tanner. You know that if you jump, cut, or try to run on it, you're risking more permanent damage that you won't be able to come back from. You're young. Quarterbacks play into their forties these days, and you're healthy enough and strong enough to do that. This isn't the end for you. It's a setback that we are here to guide you through so that you can return stronger than ever and lead this team to the championship since Lord knows we've been waiting for this for years."

I offer a wry smile at that. "And then I went and fucked it all up."

The doctor presses his lips together as he shakes his head. He holds a hand out to help me up to a sitting position. "It was an accident, and nobody thinks that of you. All I've heard is well wishes. This town is pulling for you and praying for you."

"Did you just say pull and pray?" I joke, and I'm not sure why I'm tossing out sex jokes at a time like this. The only thing I can come up with is that I've gone fucking delirious.

Or it's just what I do. I use humor as a defense mechanism. Or I try to…not always successfully, I guess.

Miller barks out a laugh at my joke, but Nick and the doctor remain stoic.

"We'll need our own imaging done ahead of the surgery, but based on what I'm seeing today and the MRI your team sent over, I'd like to schedule the surgery in four weeks," Dr. Barlow says. "We can reassess and move that date as needed. Any questions?"

I shake my head.

"Great. I'll have my partner, Dr. Hayward, come in next to go over the prehabilitation plan with you." He excuses himself and leaves me in the room with Nick and Miller, and a moment later, the door opens.

"I'm Dr. Hayward," the man says, sticking his hand out to me. "Are you comfortable having my new physical therapist sit in on our session?"

I shrug. "It's fine." I don't really care who's in here as long as they can fix this as quickly as possible.

He nods, and he opens the door for his PT to join us.

My eyes are on the ground as she walks in, and I hear a small gasp as the doctor starts to talk. "Cassandra, this is Tanner Banks," he says.

My head whips up at the name to find a blonde woman staring at my brother with a slackened jaw.

It takes a few seconds for it to register…but holy shit. It's *her*.

Same blonde hair. Same blue eyes. Same banging body.

She hasn't seen me yet, but my first thought is that I can't work with her. Are you kidding me?

My second thought is that even though I'm angry and frustrated and, obviously, *injured*, I'm stuck here for the next six to eight months. Having her here for the duration of that recovery might not be so bad after all.

She's staring at Miller in a way I've often seen people look at my twin after meeting me first, and it's yet another clue that maybe she has no idea who I really am. It's as if she knows him, but there's something a little off.

Because *there is* something a little off.

We look a lot alike—same hair, same eyes, same nose and mouth and facial structure. But there are obvious differences. He's two inches shorter than me and quite a bit bulkier, and he carries himself differently. He doesn't have the same air of cockiness I walk around with. He didn't fall off his bike and catch himself with his chin when he was eleven, so he doesn't have the same scar I have. And, of course, I'm better looking.

I'm staring at her as her eyes edge over to me, and I hear another little gasp as her eyes widen.

Holy shit.

It's really her.

And she's my physical therapist?

Or…she's shadowing my physical therapist, anyway.

And she's even more beautiful than my memory recalled.

Fuck.

If I say anything, they'll never let her work with me. But maybe I *shouldn't* let her work with me. Maybe it's an absolute mistake to work with her on my recovery when she'll only prove to be a distraction. That's all she's been since the night I met her, anyway.

She takes the reins.

"Nice to meet you," she says to me, clearly pretending we don't know each other, and she takes on an entirely different persona than the woman who was clutching the sheets in her fists as I drove into her in a hotel in Vegas. This woman is cold and clinical as she assesses my knee with the doctor.

I clear my throat but don't say anything. I don't want her to get in trouble, and to be frank, I'm still feeling quite a bit of anger about this whole thing. I'm still working through my own feelings as I try not to blame her for the entire reason I'm here, and now I'll have her to blame if my recovery goes south.

I know logically it's not her fault in any way, but I can't help thinking if my head had been in the game the way it should've been, the way it *was* before I ever met her, this never would've happened.

It was a freak accident. Could've happened to anyone. Hell, it *has* happened to tons of players in the league.

But not in the same moment it happened to me. Not under the same circumstances. And I bet none of them had to work with a physical therapist they'd already fucked but couldn't forget about.

"Once we get the swelling down, we'd like to start a comprehensive program ahead of your surgery," Dr. Hayward says to me, and he drones on and on about what that means.

I'm not listening.

I'm trying to have a silent conversation with Cassie, but she won't look at me.

What do I do?

Should I attempt to talk to her?

What the fuck would I even say? "You're the reason I'm here and oh yeah why didn't you use my number and whose kids were those and are you married or were you really in Vegas celebrating a divorce?"

My mouth often works before my brain does, and I'm about to ask everybody in the room to leave except her so I can have a word when Dr. Hayward says, "So we'll see you back here tomorrow."

"Huh?" I ask, and I glance at Nick, who's nodding as if to say he got all that and he'll take care of it.

"We'll see you then," Nick says, and the doctor leaves the room with Cassie trailing behind him.

She never even looked me in the eyes again…but it looks like I'll be back here tomorrow to try again.

Whether or not that's a good idea remains to be seen.

Chapter 20: Cassie Fields

I Still Thought His Name Was Miller

Of all the orthopedic clinics in San Diego, the Storm had to choose this one.

Of course they did. It's the best.

And now their star quarterback is in our care. It's up to us to help guide his pre-op work and post-op recovery.

What are my options? Tell Dr. Hayward I had a one-night stand with him, and he's a liar, so I can't work with him?

I just got this job. I can't afford to lose it. I can't afford anything messing it up, which is why I forced myself not to make eye contact with the liar and kept my head down when I saw him in that exam room.

I had *no idea* that he was the football player I slept with. None. Until I saw him in the exam room with his twin brother in the same room, I still thought his name was Miller.

Apparently, at least according to his records, it's Tanner. Tanner Banks, all-star quarterback for the San Diego Storm.

Dr. Hayward isn't going to give me this VIP patient. He'll take the lead on this, and even if he doesn't, he has other physical therapists at this practice who would give anything to be the ones to build their careers working with the famous football star.

But I suppose I can say the same. I can keep it professional. It may not be ethical to work with him since, well, I have intimate knowledge of his naked body.

But I know how to remain objective. I know how to treat him with respect—even if I wasn't treated the same way.

I shadow Dr. Hayward with his other patients, but I can't stop thinking about this guy. First I thought he was Grayson Nash, and then Miller Banks…and now I know the truth.

"Cassie?" one of the receptionists says to me as I pass behind the reception desk toward the end of the day.

I stop and raise my brows. "Yes?"

"There's a call for you on line four."

"Thanks." I rush to my cubicle and grab the call, nervous it's about one of my kids…though I'm not sure why the school would call me at work and not on my cell phone.

"Cassie Fields," I answer.

"So you're a physical therapist?" The rich, deep voice is familiar, though the last time I really heard it string together so many words, it was as he rasped it in my ear as he moved inside of me.

God, I have got to get a handle on this. That's not even true. It was at breakfast before I walked away without looking back…when he brought me a pumpkin spice latte and muffins.

I clear my throat. "Is there something you need?"

He barks out a laugh, and that is *not* what I meant.

I sigh.

"Can we talk?" he asks.

About what? I wonder, but I don't ask. I'm too scared to ask. "No."

"Excuse me?" he says. "I'm your patient."

"You're not under my care. I'd be happy to have Dr. Hayward give you a call."

"You know that's not what I mean," he says.

"I do," I say, and I glance around. I want to yell at him that using my work line to trap me isn't fair. Tammy, another physical therapist, is sitting two chairs down from me, and I know she can hear everything I'm saying. I need to be careful how I tackle this. "I can take down your number and get back to you."

The words slip out before I can stop them. I don't *want* to get back to him.

But I also want to draw a clear line in the sand, and maybe the only way to do that is to talk to him outside of the office and clarify the expectations up front.

"Fine." He rattles off his number even though I still have that little piece of paper with the same number written on it at home, and I jot it down. This is probably a huge mistake, but I'm not sure what else to do.

"I'll get back to you soon." I end the call before he can ask any other questions, and I stare down at the number I just scribbled down.

I'm angry that he lied to me. I'm angry that he's here. I'm angry that he's going to try to mess up this job for me.

I can't let that happen, and I intend to be very clear about that when we talk.

The only problem is…I don't know when to call him. I know I won't get to call him until after I get the kids down. There just isn't time.

I get off work at three, pray there's no traffic, and race over to bus pickup only to pull in right behind the bus. The kids get off and run to my car, and I drive through the neighborhood to get them home, that sense of dread building with every passing moment.

We do homework. Luca has baseball practice, during which I do my best to entertain Lily. We head home, and I whip up dinner. Then Luca needs to read to me for twenty minutes while Lily takes her bath. I read her a few books and get her to bed, and Luca and I watch this show he likes where an archeologist digs to uncover mysteries of the past together before I get him to bed.

I try my hardest not to rush things, but I'm nervous about this call.

And so, once both babies are down and the house is quiet, I pour myself a glass of wine and head into my bedroom.

I light a candle and stare at the flame flickering for a few minutes as I think through exactly what I want to say.

And then I pick up my phone and dial his number. My fingers tremble as I click the green button to place the call, and I listen to the ringing tone as I wait for him to answer.

"Hello?" It's the same voice, and I'm glad I'm sitting on my bed, leaning against the headboard, because my knees are a little weak as I hear it.

"It's Cassie."

"Cass," he says, his voice all deep and sexy when he says it, and I'm immediately transported back to the bed we shared as he moaned my name, sort of like when you hear a song that reminds you of a specific moment in your life. Only hotter, obviously.

I clear my throat and take a big sip of my wine to steel my nerves. It really doesn't work.

"Why did you lie to me?" I ask.

He's quiet a beat, and then he says, "What?"

"You lied about who you were. Why?"

"I never lied to you," he says. He does sound genuinely confused.

"Yes, you did. You let me think you were Grayson Nash."

"What? When?" he asks.

"The bartender said it's on the house for Grayson Nash, and then I asked if you were a football player, and you said yes."

"I *am* a football player. Well, I was...until I fucked up my knee. But where's the lie?"

"You let me think you were Grayson," I say.

"I let the *bartender* think I was Grayson. It was a free drink."

I can picture him shrugging as he says the words.

"You led me to believe you were someone you weren't."

"I had no idea you didn't know who I was," he protests. "I never lied to you. I thought you knew who I was when you asked if I played football. But if we're going to talk about liars, let's take a look at you, Ms. Fields."

"When did I lie?" I ask, my voice both defensive and loud. Much louder than I mean for it to be.

"Oh, I don't know...how about the fact that you're married with kids?"

"I'm not married!" I yell. "I just got divorced, and I can send you the proof if you don't believe me. But how the hell do you know about my kids?"

"I saw you. You were there at training camp with two kids."

I blow out a breath. "You saw me?"

"Yeah. I was about to head over to sign shit for fans when a little kid throwing a tantrum caught my attention. I glanced at the mom, and imagine my surprise when it was *you*. The woman who couldn't be bothered to use my number after the night we shared."

My stomach flips. "That aside...yeah. I have kids. That's *why* I didn't use your number. I'd never had a one-night stand before, but I'm not naïve enough to think the big football star ever wanted to see the mom from San Diego again. What happens in Vegas, and all that."

"I did," he insists. "You're all I've thought about since that night. It's why I was distracted on Sunday."

"Excuse me?" I squeal. "Are you blaming *me* for your injury?"

"No. That's not what I meant. I just mean…fuck." He lets out a heavy sigh. "I don't really know what I meant, but you fucked me up, Cass."

"Me? I'm just a mom trying to support my children post-divorce, and that's why I got a job with my old boss after eight years out of the field. I'm doing the best I can, and the only one who fucked anyone up was you. By lying to me."

"I never lied!" he yells.

"I don't know a goddamn thing about you. I don't even know your name other than what I saw on the records," I say.

"That's my name. Tanner Banks. I'm all fucked up because I learned the man I thought was my dad my entire life isn't. I'm a Nash biologically, so yes, Grayson Nash is my half-brother, and yes, I got mistaken for him when I was at a club in Vegas and I had a hat on. It is what it is. I'm sorry you were standing there. I'm sorry it was a case of mistaken identity. I'm sorry I didn't push harder to get your number that night, but something changed for me, Cass, and I don't know what, but I need to see you again."

"I can't, Tanner." It's the first time I've used his name, and to be honest…it's hot. Not that it matters. "That's why I called. I have professional obligations, and you're a patient now—and likely for the next year. I can't be with you as anything more than that."

"Then I'll switch practices and work with someone else."

"Dr. Hayward and Dr. Barlow are the best in the entire Southwest. It would be stupid for you to do that," I say.

He's silent on the other end, and I'm not sure what else to say.

"I guess I'll see you at your appointment tomorrow," I say.

"Don't hang up," he says softly, and I feel a twinge in my chest. Why doesn't he want me to hang up? What is it about me that he's hanging onto?

"Why not?" I ask quietly.

"Because you were different. Hell, you didn't even know who I was until I walked into the office. You were genuine. You were kind. Sweet, even. I just…it's rare to meet someone like that doing what I do. That's all. It feels like everyone's always lying to me, telling me what I want to hear, and you didn't do that. You were real with me."

"Yeah…but you weren't real with me. I didn't even know who you were," I point out.

"Then let me fix that."

"I can't. Not when I'm fixing your knee. Look, it's important for me to be financially independent from my ex-husband. It's important to me for my kids to see their mom working hard to achieve her goals. I can't let some football star mess that up for me."

No matter how much I want him.

My kids will always come first.

"I'll see you at your session tomorrow," I say, and I end the call.

Chapter 21: Tanner Banks

Focused and Clinical

So I'm just…out of luck?

I don't think so. Tanner Banks is a lot of things, but a quitter isn't one of them.

I'll be seeing her a few times a week at a minimum for the next few weeks, and possibly more than that after the surgery. I'm not sure how I feel about that yet, but my gut is telling me I shouldn't just walk away. I shouldn't just let her walk away, either.

Sometimes my gut says things I ignore, and rarely does that benefit me. But my gut told me not to say anything to Miller or Nick about Cassie. I tell my brother virtually everything, and I'm not sure why this secret bears protection.

Actually, that's not true. I need to keep this secret because I know what he'll tell me.

It's a conflict.

I mean…obviously. Of course it's a conflict. She could very easily get in the way of my full recovery, in particular if I'm distracted by her.

Again.

But I won't be. If anything, having her there might be exactly what I need to work even harder.

Miller isn't coming with me tomorrow morning since he's got workouts planned with the other running backs, though Nick will be there with me to listen to what the doctors say and report it back to Coach.

But he doesn't need to be in the room while I'm getting work done. It's not standard for a doctor to administer the physical therapy. It's why doctors hire physical therapists for their practices. I'm sure Dr. Hayward will want to oversee things, but I imagine I'll get at least *some* time with Cassie.

And if the doctor's office doesn't lead me straight to her, well, I'll demand that she's who I work with.

I need time. I need the ability to explore the connection I felt that night, and if this is my only option since she already said she can't be with me, then so be it.

I sleep like shit again, which is wholly unusual for me. My entire persona is the athlete who gets good rest, eats right, and kills every workout ever put in front of him. You don't get to the elite level I play at by slacking.

But I'm not currently playing at any level, and that's why I sleep like shit. I'm tossing one way as I replay the injury in my mind. I toss the other way and see her face. And every shift, every motion, every toss pulses a deep ache in my knee that leaves me feeling bitter and frustrated.

It's going to be a long, long road to recovery.

So long, in fact, that I briefly debate having a cup of coffee to start the day as I'm sitting with ice on my knee watching the highlights from the Monday Night Football game I watched in full with my brother last night—except for the part I missed to talk to Cassie.

He asked me who was on the phone, and I told him it was nobody.

She isn't nobody. I'm not sure exactly what she is, though.

I hobbled into the den for privacy while he continued watching the game, and I think the call left me with more questions than answers.

Will she tell her boss she knows me? Will she make it so we can't work together?

These questions plagued me during all that tossing and turning.

I'm tired and cranky, and I don't want to take that out on the people who are put in place to help me.

I also don't know if I can avoid it, though. Miller waits on me hand and foot, going so far as to bring me the ice pack before he leaves, and I hate that feeling. I can take care of myself. I *want* to take care of myself. I'm not used to asking for help, least of all from Miller. But I get it. He wants to make things more comfortable for me. Everyone does, which is nice, and I'm grateful…but I also want to figure out how the fuck to just make it stop.

It's annoying.

I can take care of myself. I can get my own goddamn ice, and having someone bring it to me is one of those little things that makes me feel like I'm not capable.

I *am* fucking capable.

Nick picks me up at eight forty, and he treats me like I can't fucking walk.

I can. It doesn't feel great, but I don't need the wheelchair he makes me use. I don't need his support with his arm around my waist. I just want to be left alone, and I start off on a cranky tone with him so it won't come as a surprise later when I ask him to leave the room so I can have some time with Cassie.

It's a stupid plan, obviously. I should get this out of my head and just let her do her job so we don't wind up fucking my knee up even more.

But I guess that's just not who I am.

The car ride to the doctor is quiet, and I still don't say much as we make our way through the lobby. Some security guard stops us. "Tanner Banks?" he says.

I nod and press my lips together into a tight smile.

"Sorry for the injury. The crew up at Motion are the best, so you're in good hands."

"Thanks," I say, and I give him a nod.

Great. I'm already recognized here, which doesn't bode well for me maintaining my privacy as we move forward. Word will get out that this is where I'm being treated, and because I'm a football player, people will show up wanting things from me. Photographs. My signature. Game tickets. My fucking shirt.

When I get up to the office, I am taken immediately back to the exam room again, where Dr. Hayward and Cassie are both already waiting for me. The doctor motions for me to sit on the table, and he starts to examine my knee with Cassie close by.

So close that I can smell her familiar vanilla sandalwood, and I'm transported back to the night we shared.

"The swelling looks about the same. Did you ice it yesterday?" he asks, pulling me out of my memories.

I nod. "Every other hour for fifteen minutes at a time."

"Great. Do that again today, and I'm going to have Cassandra get you started on some strengthening exercises today," Dr. Hayward says.

I glance at Cassie, but her eyes won't meet mine.

"I also need to mention that I was recognized in the lobby on the way up this morning, and I don't want any distractions. I think it might be better if we could shift the therapy sessions to at-home care." I say the words with zero ulterior motives, but then something happens that I wasn't expecting.

"That's understandable," Dr. Hayward says with a nod. "And we can certainly accommodate you, though home visits come with additional fees."

"I understand, and I want whichever therapist you send to be well compensated for the additional work."

"Of course," he nods. "I will clear Cassandra's schedule and have her come work with you if that's okay."

Is he kidding me? *If that's okay?* It's *absolutely* okay. *More than* okay. "That works for me."

"Cassandra, does that work for you?" the doctor asks her.

She looks uncomfortable but ultimately nods her agreement.

Of course she does. She's trying to build a name for herself in this field, and taking the reins of my recovery has the potential to make her a star. That's not me being cocky. That is just a fact.

"Great, then it's settled. You two can work out the schedule that suits you both, though Cassandra is only on the clock here from nine to three." He nods at Cassie as if he just did her a favor. He has no idea that he just did *me* a favor. "If you'll excuse me, I'm going to have Cassandra work on some strengthening exercises with you this morning."

"Mr. Banks, can you lie back on the table?" she asks as Dr. Hayward walks out of the room. We're not quite alone yet, so before I lay back, I glance at Nick.

"If you want to take five, there's not much for you to see in here," I say.

He nods and excuses himself from the room, leaving Cassie and me alone.

My first inclination is to pull her into my arms and make her remember why we were so good together that night, but I won't risk getting her in trouble at work.

"Do you really think this is a good idea?" she asks as soon as the door shuts behind Nick.

"What?" I ask innocently.

"The two of us alone together. Straighten your leg," she says, and she watches while I do what she says.

"I think the last time the two of us were alone together, we had a hell of a time," I say quietly.

She sighs then snags her lip between her teeth. "I'm less worried about flexion right now and more worried about strength. Let's do some quad sets, okay?" She takes me through some basic exercises where she has me tighten my thighs and hold for five seconds. "Make sure you aren't engaging any other muscles," she says, and she sets a hand on my thigh to feel the flex there.

Jesus Christ.

My dick swells at her touch, and this is probably a huge mistake, but I can't seem to stop myself.

She's nothing but professional, refusing to acknowledge the sudden bulge in my shorts as she's back to being focused and clinical. We do twelve reps before switching to another set of exercises, and she's not engaging in conversation, instead focusing on the task of rebuilding the strength in my knee.

"That's all for today. Be sure to ice as soon as you get home," she says. "What time would you like me to come tomorrow?"

I smirk at her question, but then I ask softly, "What time is easiest for you?"

"I'm on the clock nine to three, as Dr. Hayward said." Her tone is clipped.

I clear my throat. "Then nine to three." Miller won't be home since he'll be at practice, so it'll just be us. Unless Nick finds a way to insert himself into the equation, which he just might.

"Where do you live?" she asks.

"My brother and I are sharing a house near our practice facility up in the hills."

She presses her lips together. "The practice facility is about twenty minutes from my house."

"Then come over at nine twenty," I say. "I don't want this to be harder for you."

"Then why did you just make it so I have to come to your house every day to administer the same type of therapy I could do here in the office?" she demands. She's angry, but I can't puzzle out why.

"You're rehabbing a professional athlete. Don't you think that'll open doors for you?"

"How do you know what kind of doors I even *want* opened?" she asks.

It's a valid point, one I hadn't really considered, but a part of me thinks she's not really considering the full picture, either. "Well, what *do* you want?"

"I told you last night, Tanner." She sighs. "I'm just trying to rebuild my life. I don't need these kinds of complications."

"Neither do I," I say, my eyes averting to my knee as my meaning is entirely different from hers.

Her eyes meet mine, and hers soften for just a beat. She holds onto my gaze longer than I expect her to before she says, "Fine. I will see you tomorrow."

And then she walks out of the room, leaving me feeling hollow and empty despite the promise that I'll get to see her tomorrow.

Chapter 22: Cassie Fields

What I Want Doesn't Matter

"You want me over there *seven days a week*?" I say, and I know I sound baffled, but it's because *I am*.

"I know it's not typical, but he's a professional athlete, and we need to do everything we can to correctly rebuild his knee ahead of surgery," Dr. Hayward says.

"But I don't have childcare every weekend," I point out.

"We'll pay for someone to come watch them for a few hours. Make weekends lighter so it doesn't take as long."

I don't *want* to go over to his house on weekends. I don't want to go over to his house *at all*, but I'm stuck here. If I protest any more, I'll lose a patient, and I'll lose Dr. Hayward's respect.

"Aside from the weekends, I figured you would appreciate this since you can make your own hours. We'll clear your schedule, and he'll be your only patient. He wants you there overseeing his training."

"Isn't that what his team trainers are for?" I ask.

"You're the only physical therapist on staff with a degree in sports medicine. Given that I was your mentor out of college, I feel as though you are the only therapist we have that can properly manage this patient. If you'd rather let Rick have this patient, I'm sure he'd be eager to step in."

While it certainly serves as quite the compliment, it also makes me angry. I don't want to be the only one on staff who can handle this case. I don't want to give up the things I've just started building here in the office to tend to a grumpy football player I'm trying to avoid. I don't want to give up my weekends for him.

I don't want to give up the friendships I've started forming with the other therapists and the receptionists.

I also don't want to give this patient to Rick. I get weird vibes from him.

What I want doesn't matter. I'm new here, and now I'm going to be further isolated from my colleagues and coworkers as I'm forced to spend time with someone I'm trying to forget and leave in the past.

It's chaos when I get home from work until I get the kids to bed, and it all starts over again in the morning. I get them off to school and take a minute for myself.

I fix my makeup.

I spritz on some perfume—the same one I borrowed from Jess that night, not because it helped me get lucky, but because I like how it smells.

I double-check myself in the mirror.

I've never done this ahead of going into the office…that's for sure.

I drink an extra cup of coffee and brush my teeth before I head out the door at nine o'clock on the dot.

I navigate toward the address I got from Tanner's file, and I find myself up in the hills, standing at his front door fifteen minutes later. My heart is pounding loud and steady, but as I stare at the door, it feels like it's picking up the pace.

There's a Porsche in the driveway, and I wonder if it's his. It's green, and his favorite color is green. I can't imagine a Porsche is easy to get into with a torn ACL.

He's suddenly *real* to me. Yesterday and the day before, he was a patient. Before that, he was a memory.

But as I stand in this place that's his, I can't help but wonder what sorts of secrets I will unlock today.

"It's open," he says, his voice coming through the Ring doorbell.

I try the handle and push open the large front door, and I walk into a house that's surprisingly bright and cheerful. "Tanner?"

"In the family room," his voice calls. "Walk toward the patio doors."

I do as I'm told, my eyes fixed on the gorgeous view from here, and I find him exactly where he said he'd be—an even more gorgeous sight than the one out the windows.

Oh, hell.

I am so screwed.

How the hell am I going to stay away from him when we're smashed together every day like this? I don't know if I have the self-control to stay away.

He has a huge bag of ice on top of a towel balanced on his knee, and he's sitting on a sofa end seat that happens to be a recliner with his leg elevated up above his heart, just like he was told to do. There's something so...endearing about that.

No. I don't want to be endeared to him. Or enamored with him. Or excited by him. Or any other *E* word.

He's a patient. Nothing more.

A patient who you've seen naked.

Quiet, brain.

He's watching television, and he doesn't make a move when he spots me.

143

"Good morning," I say cheerfully. I glance at the television, and he's watching the same show I was watching with Luca last night.

"Is it?" he asks. He finally peels his eyes from the television to look at me, and I guess we're getting grumpy Tanner today. He looks rough, like he hasn't slept or shaved in a couple of days. He's wearing a T-shirt and basketball shorts, and the frown lines are deep with this one.

"Is that *Expedition Unknown?*" I ask.

He grunts out an affirmative response.

"I saw this one last night. No spoilers, promise, but it's a good one."

He looks surprised for a beat. "You watch this show?"

"My son loves it. And I figure it's educational, so why not?"

"I like it, too," he grunts. He's still grumpy, but it feels a bit like a breakthrough.

"Are you ready to get started?" I ask, setting my bag down on the little end table. I brought a few supplies for our session along with my tablet from work and, of course, my lunch.

He glances at his wrist. "You're early." He's still grunting.

"Sorry?" I say, and it comes out like a question.

"I have five more minutes with the ice."

"Okay." I pull my tablet out of my bag and tap around as I look through my notes for the types of exercises I want to run through with him today. Some are stretches he'll hold for twenty minutes or so, and others are a little more intense.

I decide to give him the rundown while we're just sitting here, so I sit beside him on the couch. He barely lifts his head to look at me.

"Let's go over what we want to accomplish today. We'll start with some different knee extensions, test out some heel slides and ankle pumps, and focus on some quad and hamstring exercises. Do you want me to show you the plan for your upper body workouts?" I ask.

He grunts out some reply that I can't really decode, so I start going through a comprehensive plan.

"What about running?" he asks.

I shake my head. "I'm sorry, but running is going to be off the table for a while."

"Great," he grunts.

"We can take some walks depending on how you're feeling. Eventually we can work light cardio in, but we have to get the swelling down first," I say.

His timer dings to signify that it's time to remove the ice, and I move to take it from him, but he stops me.

"I can do it," he hisses.

Okay. So clearly he doesn't want help today.

"Are you okay?" I ask tentatively.

He sighs heavily as he presses a button, and the recliner footrest moves slowly back down into place. "No, I'm not."

"Would you like to talk about it?" I'm about to launch into the fact that mindset plays a significant role in any recovery, but he just shakes his head and grunts again.

He limps over to the patio with his giant bag of ice, and he tosses the contents of the bag over the side of his deck. He hobbles back in with the empty bag and tosses it on the counter before he returns to me. "Let's get this going."

I take him through the first extension, and he's supposed to lay on his back with his leg extended in front of him for twenty minutes.

Rather than trying to strike up conversation, I examine his knee, take notes, and run through the rest of the day's plan while I wait for the timer to end.

It feels interminable. In fact, the entire day feels that way.

We ice his knee every other hour.

I try to make conversation, but it's impossible. I'm met with grunts.

And I get it. He doesn't want to be in this position, but he's letting himself get pulled under, and that's the worst thing he can do for his own recovery.

It's fresh, though. It's new, and it's a hard pill to swallow, so I'm being as patient as I can while giving him as much grace as I can.

Around noon, I pull my lunch out of my bag and eat it quickly while he's in the middle of another twenty-minute exercise. He limps out of the room without a word when the timer beeps and makes his own lunch in silence. I wait patiently for him to finish, but I really don't know how long I can make these house calls and sit here in silence waiting for him.

Maybe I'm more invested in him because of the fact that we have a one-night history. I want him to be okay. I don't want him suffering…even if a small part of me resents that entire night and the mistaken identity that followed.

"How late are you staying?" he demands at around two in the afternoon.

"I'm happy to give you a list of what you need to do for the rest of the day and go now, but that's up to you since you're the one who requested home care," I say.

These really are exercises he could do by himself, but he's certainly paying for it. In-home care doesn't come inexpensively, that's for sure.

I try to put it out of my head that he's doing it to indirectly pay *me*. I refuse to allow him to take away from my goal of financial independence. He had no idea that Dr. Hayward would offer me up on a silver platter when he said he preferred home care to going into the office every day.

And he doesn't *need* therapy every day. He could do this without my guidance. But since he's a VIP patient and he's a superstar, he gets what he wants. I wonder what else he gets because of that.

He clears his throat. "What time do you *need* to go?"

"The bus drops my kids at ten after three, so I need to be back by then. Usually I'm scrambling out of the office at three and praying there's no traffic." I offer a wry smile.

He glances over at me. "What if there is?"

I shrug. "I'll call a friend and beg her to watch them until I can get there."

"Nice to have friends," he murmurs.

"I have a great group of girlfriends. They were in Vegas with me that night," I say, and I realize my mistake a second too late.

I was trying to avoid talking about *that night*. I don't need to make the tension between us any worse, though the mention of that night seems to soften him just the tiniest bit despite the grunt of acknowledgement.

We watch more of the history show while we work, and I learn he's a bit of a history buff. History was never my favorite subject—science was—but I'm learning to appreciate it through Luca, who loves everything about it.

At two forty-five, he says, "You should go."

I nod. "Let me just go over what I want you to do toni—" I begin, but he holds up a hand to stop me.

"I've got it from here."

I press my lips together and nod. "Okay. I guess I'll see you tomorrow."

I head out the door without so much as a goodbye, and all I can do is hope he's in a better headspace tomorrow.

Chapter 23: Cassie Fields

The Pain Isn't So Bad With You Around

A dart of anxiety pings through my chest as I pull into the driveway for day two.

Is he going to be the grump I dealt with yesterday? Or did he magically change back to the Tanner I met in Vegas?

I ring the bell, and rather than being greeted by his voice through the Ring, the door opens, and his lookalike stands in front of me.

"Hi, I'm Cassie. I'm here to work with Tanner today."

"Right, we met in the orthopedic office that day. I'm Miller. Come on in." He's much friendlier than his grumpy brother, though hearing the same voice from someone else is a bit unnerving. "He's on ice in the family room, but he's just about done." I hear Miller's watch beep, indicating that the time is up.

"Good morning," I say cheerfully. "How's our quarterback doing today?"

I grab the ice from his leg before he can protest, and I dump it out over the railing on his patio like he did yesterday.

He sighs but doesn't answer with words, and he powers off the television today—a step in the right direction, anyway. Maybe it's because his brother is here.

I study him for a few seconds, and he looks about as grumpy as he was yesterday.

"How's it looking today, doc?" Miller asks.

"She's not a doctor," Tanner says.

"Dude, don't be a dick." It's funny hearing the same voice from two different men.

"I'm not. She's a physical therapist," Tanner clarifies for me as if I'm not standing right here.

"I'm technically a doctor of physical therapy, but nobody calls PTs *doctor*." I shrug. "My boss has an MD in sports medicine, so he's officially a doctor." I glance at Tanner's knee. "And it's looking a little better. Still some swelling, but not quite as inflamed as yesterday." I shift my gaze to his face. "Did you get any sleep last night?"

He shakes his head. "No," he grunts.

"That would explain the crankiness," Miller says in a loud whisper meant for Tanner to hear.

"I'm not cranky," Tanner protests petulantly. He's *definitely* cranky.

"Let's get started on the first knee extension, shall we?" I suggest, ignoring them both, and he stretches out his leg where he is on the couch.

"I have to get to practice, but can I have a word with you?" Miller asks me.

I wonder for the briefest second if he knows Tanner and I slept together.

"You can say whatever you have to say in front of me," Tanner says, contempt in his tone.

"Okay, I'll go ahead and do that. Doc, Tanner hasn't been sleeping at all. He's barely eating. Usually he's quick with a retort—too quick, if you know what I mean. I hear that complaint from his female visitors all the time, actually." Miller glances playfully at his brother as he insinuates his brother is a quick shot—which, by the way, I can confirm he is not, though it doesn't appear his brother knows about that—and I can easily see that they have a quick banter between them. He's trying to keep things light, and he's waiting for his brother to hit back.

"Fuck off," Tanner mutters instead.

Miller sighs, and I can see that he's worried. "Is there anything you can give him for his state of mind?"

"Are the sleep issues stemming from pain or from something else?" I ask, directing my question to Tanner.

"I'm fine," he hisses.

I drop it. For now.

"He's not fine," Miller says to me.

I reach into my purse and pull out a card, and I hand it to Miller. "If you need to get in touch with me for any reason at all regarding your brother, feel free to use the number on my card. It's my personal number."

I glance at Tanner, and I see him glaring at the two of us.

Miller holds my card between his first and second finger and presses his lips together. "Thanks. I need to head to practice, but I'll text you in a bit to check in on him, okay?"

"I'll be here. And Miller?" I say, and he turns toward me. "I'm happy to team up with you to get your brother back to one hundred percent."

He nods. "Thank you, Cassie. I appreciate that." He turns to his brother. "Want me to tell the team anything?"

Tanner just leans his head back and closes his eyes instead of replying.

Miller sighs. I can sense his frustration, and I wonder how much of it has to do with the fact that he's feeling some of his twin's emotions. I don't really know how all that works.

"I'll see you around," he says to me, and then he heads out.

I sit two cushions away from Tanner with my tablet while he works through his first knee extension.

"Let's go over the plan for today, okay?" I suggest, and he agrees. We run through today's goals, and I tell him a lot of what we're doing will be guided by me, but that I'd like him to do some of the same exercises tonight after I leave—just like yesterday. "I can write down a list for you to tackle each night after I go."

"If I pay extra, will you stay longer?" he asks.

I chuckle. "I can't. I have to pick up my kids. Besides, do you really want me here?" I ask bluntly.

He slides his head to the side so his eyes meet mine. "To be honest, Cass, the pain isn't so bad with you around."

My chest squeezes together at his words, and it feels like a tiny bit of progress.

He's quiet as I take him through his exercises, and around eleven, he asks, "What do you want for lunch?"

My brows dip together. "Oh, I brought my lunch."

"Yeah, I know. You did yesterday, too, and you deserve something better than a cheese sandwich and yogurt."

My brows rise. I had no idea he paid attention. It's all I had left when I made my lunch yesterday, and I didn't have time to hit the store yet, so it's all I had left again today. We're out of peanut butter, so no PBJ, and I saved the good Uncrustables for the kids.

He sighs as he taps on his phone. "I'm ordering from Fresh Market. What do you want?"

A text comes through, and it's the menu for the place he's ordering from.

"I'll take the Cobb salad with ranch," I say quietly.

He nods, and he adds that to his order. An hour later, our food arrives. We sit at the table together as I eat my salad and he attacks his chicken over brown rice, side salad, and fruit mix as he ices his knee.

I snap a photo of him with his food, and he glances up at me with a question in his eyes.

I shrug. "Miller said you weren't eating, so I'm just preparing to have the evidence ready when he texts me to check in on you."

He mutters something I don't quite catch under his breath, and I can't help a little smile. He doesn't love that his brother and I are going to team up, but I do. I have someone on the inside who's on my side, and that can only bode well for this man's full recovery.

Chapter 24: Tanner Banks

Fate Isn't Something I've Ever Believed in

"You want to sleep with her?" I demand from my brother the second he walks through the door.

"With who?" he asks, and he's clearly confused.

"Cassie. My physical therapist."

"Would it be a problem if I did?" Miller asks, and I shoot him one of those *if looks could kill* glares. "Come on, man. No. We're just teaming up to help *you*. I'm not going to be a distraction in that. Why, does she want to sleep with me? Oh! Or do *you* want to sleep with *her*?"

I can't tell him that I already have, and I certainly can't tell him I want to do it again. He'd never let me work with her if he knew the truth.

"Fuck you," I spit at him, and he rolls his eyes.

"Good one. Look, man, I texted her to check on you, and she responded with a photo telling me you were eating your lunch. Is she hot? Yeah, sure. Absolutely. Would I go near her with a ten-foot pole? Not a chance."

I clench my jaw as he admits he finds her attractive. I don't want him looking at her. I don't want *any* man looking at her except for me, and I don't quite understand the level of possessiveness I feel over someone I have no claim to.

It was one night, but now having her here in my home, caring for me, eating lunch with me...it's making me see a different side to her.

She's not just this hot woman who's an animal in bed. She's also caring and nurturing, kind and smart. I'm getting to know her beyond the one night we had together, and it feels like she's here not just for my recovery, but for *me*.

I realize she's getting paid to be here.

My feelings are likely misplaced. I'm falling for her because she's assisting in my recovery.

Except...it's not quite so simple as that. I think I started falling for her the night we met, and now that she's been put directly in my path, it feels like it's because of fate.

And fate isn't something I've ever believed in.

It only took two days' worth of home visits for me to feel this way. I'm not sure what the next eight or nine months will bring. For now, I don't plan to act on it. If anything, I'm only grumpier because of it. I'm dealing with a heavy load of grief as I look at a season where I won't get to play. The reality of that hits me square in the chest every time Miller leaves for practice and I'm left behind.

It's excruciating.

I want to go to the game Sunday, to stand on the sidelines and offer support and encouragement to my teammates, but I also don't want to be there at all. I don't want to see Ford Turner run out onto the field in my place. I don't want to watch as he makes plays I'd never dream of making because he's young and doesn't have the same years under his belt to develop his skillset.

But even though I *want* to go, I need clearance to go. I need Cassie to say it's fine for me to stand for three to four hours, and I already know that's going to be a no.

It's probably for the best. I'll watch from home, where I can sulk and be miserable rather than putting on the act on the sidelines. I need a little more time to allow myself to mourn the loss of this season.

Miller collapses next to me on the couch. "Are you okay, bro?"

I shake my head. "No. I'm not."

"Talk to me."

"This fucking sucks," I say.

"You're here to bitch about it. That's something positive, isn't it?"

I roll my eyes. It's something our dad—or our *stepdad*, I guess—would say to us all the time.

You know, back when we cared about his opinion.

"Have you talked to Mom?" he asks.

I shake my head. "You?"

He nods. "I called her on the way to practice the other day."

I clench my jaw, and it works back and forth. I don't ask him for more, but he says it anyway.

"You should call her, T. Holding onto anger is only going to impede your recovery."

"Yeah, yeah, yeah."

He means well. He's trying to help. But I don't really see how talking to her is going to help with anything except adding to my anger.

He clears his throat. "You need a hobby. A focus."

"My hobby is football. My offseason hobbies are running or golf. I can't do any of those things." I'm stating the obvious. He knows these things.

"I know. What about travel? Starting a business? Or a charity? You could do some good while you're sidelined," he suggests.

I shrug. "I'll think about it." The truth is that he's probably right. I have physical therapy, rest, and recovery. I'll have surgery, and I need to stay focused mentally as I work toward a full recovery. I can still be involved in other team activities, and I can study film and strategies while I'm away from the field.

But immersing myself in a game I can't even play right now feels unhealthy, and I know there's more to life than football. Maybe I should use my time away to explore some of that.

I just have no idea what I want to explore. It's *always* been football. I don't even know who Tanner Banks is without football.

But maybe it's time to get to know him.

"Are you watching tonight?" my brother asks as he nods toward the television.

"Don't know yet."

We're both quiet a few seconds, and then Miller sighs heavily. "What can I do?"

My brows dip together. "About what?"

"I feel antsy, and I know it's because you are. I need you to pull your shit together so I don't go out there and bust a knee."

"I just got hurt less than a week ago. Give me some space to grieve, man," I mutter.

"You can have that space, but I know you. I know you better than anybody in the world, and this isn't you. Sitting around feeling sorry for yourself…that's *never* been you. Grieve all you want, but you have to face reality at some point, and being a dick to everyone around you is only going to push people away."

I glance over at him in surprise. Miller has always been the quiet one—except when it comes to me. He's always told it to me straight, so I shouldn't be surprised that this isn't any different.

Maybe I just wanted a little sympathy, but Miller's too logical to offer it. You don't go to Miller for sympathy. You go to him for solutions.

Even when they're solutions you didn't ask for.

Is he right?

Am I being a dick to everyone around me? Am I pushing people away?

And if I am…how do I stop?

He heads upstairs for a while, and I realize that one potential answer to that is to call my mother.

"Tanner! How are you?" she answers.

She has tried to get in touch every day since my injury, and I've been ignoring her calls and texts.

A lump forms in the back of my throat as I try to figure out exactly how to answer that question. I'm not sure I've ever been worse. This feels like rock bottom. It's not, and the logical side of me knows that. But having to sit out an entire year feels a little bit like the end of the world.

"Oh, honey," she says softly, and even though I'm holding onto a lot of anger, hearing her voice causes something inside of me to give way. If Miller knows me best out of everyone in the world, my mom isn't terribly far behind him. "I can't imagine how hard this is for you."

I clear my throat, though it does nothing to make that lump go away. "It's been a hard few days…a hard few months."

"I know. I'm so, so sorry. I just want to be there for you, and I know you're angry with me."

"I don't want to talk about it," I say. I stare at the television that's muted as players run onto the field ahead of kickoff. I always watch Thursday Night Football with my brother, and he's upstairs giving me space and time. I'm not sure if I want to be alone or if I want to be surrounded by people. Both sound appealing, and both sound awful.

"Whenever you're ready, Tan. You know I'm right here. Always right here for my boys. No matter what."

"I know, Mom." No matter what.

If Charles Banks always said *at least you're here to bitch about it*, Mom always said, *no matter what*. It's their catchphrases.

I try to let go of a little bit of the anger I feel about the lies. They sacrificed a lot for us. I'm sure it was hard for a single mother to have to raise a set of very active twin boys. She did the best she knew how.

And now I can't stop thinking about a different single mother. It's a completely different situation given the fact that her ex-husband is still around and still a part of her kids' lives. But we had a father, too. Maybe I need to spend less time feeling anger and resentment toward them since they gave us the life we have now.

Still, just hearing my mother's voice tonight seems to have sparked something new in me. I'm just not sure what it is yet.

Chapter 25: Cassie Fields

Going Deep

Friday is much the same, and this is my weekend with the kids, but I'm going to have to miss time with them to tend to the cranky football star on both Saturday and Sunday.

This wasn't what I signed up for when I got a job that allowed me to work during school hours.

I'm not happy about it, but I'm thankful for my supportive and helpful parents who live close by. They agreed to come over in the morning so the kids can lay around the house in their pajamas, and my mom even said she'd make Mickey Mouse waffles for the kids.

Luca pretends like he's too old for them, but he secretly loves them.

I haven't told my parents anything specific about this patient. They both like football but prefer baseball, and that's how I was raised, too.

But they're proud of me for rebuilding my life post-divorce, and I know they want to do what they can to help me out when I need it. My mom also knows that I'm incredibly hesitant to call Alex for help. I'm hesitant to call *anybody* for help. I've always been that way. But my ex-husband falls somewhere near the bottom of my list when the time comes that I do need to ask.

Bedtime rolls around, and I tuck Lily in with our normal bedtime routine that includes four different versions of "Twinkle Twinkle Little Star." But as I stand to leave, she starts to cry.

"Mama, don't go!" she wails.

"Honey, I have to get Lukey down to sleep," I say, using his nickname as I stand by her door, ready to walk out.

"I don't ever want you to leave. I want to be with you all the time." She's sobbing, and I walk back over to her and sit on the side of the bed.

I get it. She's having attachment issues. Of course she is. I can't really blame her since first her parents got divorced, and then she was sent off to school full time. It's a lot of big changes for a little one, and I know I need to do my best to be understanding and patient as I help her the best way I know how.

But I'm coming up empty. I need to get her down, then I need to get Luca down, and finally, I need to get myself down. It's our routine.

I can't just leave when she's so upset, though. She probably already feels like I've abandoned her since she just started kindergarten, and I push her off to her dad's every other weekend.

I sing her another song. It's not enough.

"How about this," I say, moving straight into the bargaining phase. "Let me go get Luca down, and then I'll come back in and check on you. While I'm gone, you try your very hardest to fall asleep. Okay?"

She sniffles and nods, and I kiss her forehead and leave. I get Luca down, and then I head back into Lily's room.

She's still wide awake.

It's going to be a hell of a long night.

My parents arrive a little before nine on Saturday morning, and I head over to Tanner's place after a tearful goodbye with Lily. Miller's already out the door by the time I arrive, and Tanner opens the door to me as I fret over what sort of mood I'll find him in today. I'm not sure I have the patience for cranky Tanner after the shit night of sleep I had.

His beard is starting to grow in, and his hair is a mess. He still looks like he hasn't slept in a while, but I think I see a tiny bit of life back in those eyes.

"I iced a half hour earlier today," he grunts.

"Great. Let's go for a walk," I suggest. "Go get your shoes."

"A walk?" he asks. "Don't I need to rest it?"

"We can move slow, and I want you to use crutches, but I think a little fresh air would do you some good." I nod toward the hallway. "Shoes. Go."

He flattens his lips for a beat before he moves slowly to respond to my request, and I head into the family room to set down my bag while I wait. He returns a minute later, and I draw in a deep breath as I remind myself that this is a patient. I can't be thinking the thoughts I'm thinking.

I can't let the memories of that night plow into me unexpectedly.

I can't remember his strong hands as they moved along my body.

I can't think about how he made me feel more valued and cherished in one night than my ex did in eighteen years.

I can't think about how hot he is every time he walks into a room.

And I certainly can't stare into his blue eyes and hope for a repeat of that night.

"Let's go," I say.

He nods, and he grabs the set of crutches leaning up by the door as he flips on some sunglasses. We head out front, and he taps a button to lock the door.

We're quiet as we make our way along the sidewalk. I watch his gait as he moves, and I think he'd probably be okay without the crutches. One of his goals before surgery is to restore his normal walking, but we're only six days out, and I'm being cautious with him.

He's quiet for the first minute or two, and then he glances in my direction and says, "I hate silence. Tell me about your kids or something."

"My kids?" I repeat. And then I shrug. We're going to be spending a lot of time together, so I guess I can talk about my kids since it's one of those subjects I could talk about for hours. "Luca's seven. He *loves* baseball. Lily's five, and she just started kindergarten. She's really into gymnastics."

"Luca and Lily," he repeats, and hearing their names out of his mouth feels oddly personal. "We'll get him on the right path, don't worry."

My brows quirk at his words.

"Baseball? Pfft."

I laugh. "He's the one who convinced me to go to the training camp thing, so I don't think we're too far off. But the idea of him playing football scares me."

"It *scares* you? Why?"

I gesture toward his knee. "It's a contact sport. I'm nervous he'll get hurt."

"He could get hurt walking to the bus stop, Cass. Hell, this is a noncontact injury," he says, nodding down toward his knee. "Is that really a reason to keep him from playing?"

I sigh. "No, it's not. And I wouldn't stop him if it's what he wanted. But I'm a mom. It's my job to worry."

"Yeah. My mom is a worrier, too."

"Is she close?" I ask absently.

"No. She's in Arizona." He's clipped in his answer, and I vividly remember him mentioning some family issues he's been going through when we spoke the other night.

"Have you spoken to her much since you moved here?" I ask.

"She texts me almost daily. I reply almost weekly," he admits.

"Tanner," I admonish.

"She lied to my brother and me our entire lives. I need a little time to get past that."

I'm about to say something snide about how it runs in the family when I stop myself.

He's right. He really didn't lie to me. He didn't correct me, either, but he didn't realize I mistook him for someone else that night. Maybe it's time for me to bury that in the past.

"So how'd you find out about your mom's lies?" I ask instead.

He smirks at me, and it's hot as hell even though I can't see his eyes. "Going deep already, huh?" he asks, and then he twists his lips. "I suppose turnabout is only fair."

I choke on something in the back of my throat. Yeah, he went deep all right...

I clear out the blocked passage, and he chuckles.

"Do you know who Asher is?" he asks.

I nod. "Well, I mean...I do now. I looked up the Nash brothers when I found out you weren't Grayson, and I had no idea who you actually were."

He clears his throat. "I'm sorry about that, Cass. It must have felt like a huge betrayal to leave that night only to realize I wasn't who you thought I was."

"It did," I admit. "It hurt. It made me not want to do that one-night stand thing again."

"Good," he mutters, and I let that go.

"So…yes. I do know who Asher is. Now," I say.

"He found out his girlfriend was pregnant. He called his dad to tell him and, I don't know, ask for advice or whatever. His dad told him to do what he does with the twins, which was to say he sent our mom a check every month to keep her mouth shut about who our father truly was. And she did."

I gasp a little at that. "Oh my God. Then what?"

"Asher called his brothers and told them what he'd learned, and they all flew to Arizona to find us and tell us the truth."

"Are you close with the Nash brothers?" I ask.

"Yeah. I mean, sort of. We're getting there. Spencer is on the Storm, so Miller and I are closest to him just because we see him every day. Or I did, anyway, until this happened." He nods down to his knee. "And I guess if you have to go through something like this, it doesn't hurt to have a twin brother who can be there with you every step of the way." He stares straight ahead while he talks.

"What about your biological dad? Have you talked to him?"

"Not really. Sort of. We've been in the same room. We've met. That's about the extent of it. We didn't ask why. We haven't had the deep discussions, and I'm not sure we need to. He had an entire other family with four boys, and he didn't want to fuck up what he had with his indiscretions." He shrugs.

"But he's your father. Doesn't that mean something?" I ask.

"I don't know if it does, to be honest. He made it clear he didn't want the world to know about us. We went nearly thirty years not knowing, and I'm not sure what the hell good it does knowing now."

"I mean, from a health standpoint, since I'm in the medical field, it's important to know about your family history to be proactive in your own healthcare," I point out.

"I guess." He sighs. "Everything I know about the man is that he's a greedy, selfish son of a bitch. Just because we *know* now, it doesn't change anything."

"Does your brother feel the same way?"

He nods. "We've spoken at length about it. It was always just the two of us, and then out of the blue, we come to find out that there are four more. It's just…weird."

"But at least you don't have to go through it alone."

"How'd we end up talking about this shit when I started by asking about your kids?" he asks.

I laugh. "No idea. The progression of conversation, I guess. So you're thirty?"

"Twenty-nine."

"God, you're young," I murmur, the words slipping out without much thought going into them.

"How old are you?"

"You're not supposed to ask a lady her age," I scold, but then I laugh. "I'm thirty-six."

His brows rise. "So you're a cougar?"

"Tanner!" I say, smacking him in the shoulder, and he laughs.

"Hottest cougar I've ever been with," he mutters, pushing the joke a little further.

"I'm not a cougar. I've been with exactly two people in my life, and you were the second." I slap a hand over my mouth as soon as the words are out. What the hell is with my malfunctioning filter today?

He stops walking, therapy be damned, and he faces me. "I was your *second*?" he repeats. I wish I could see his eyes, but they're hidden behind those sunglasses.

My cheeks burn with embarrassment, and I avert my eyes to the ground. "I met my ex-husband when I was young, and he was my first—and only—for eighteen years. I was *not* his first—nor only—during that time."

"Jesus, Cass," he says, and he reaches over and grabs my hand—an interesting feat as he leans on his crutches. "I'm sorry. And then you ended up with me and didn't even know who I was. Fuck, I feel like such an asshole."

I know I need to push him back to walking, but I can't seem to force myself when I need to know the answer to one thing. "Why me?"

His brows quirk. "Huh?"

"What was it about me that made you take me back to your hotel when you could've had any woman you wanted in that bar that night? I'm just a mom. A former PTO board member who took back her career in physical therapy after a divorce."

"You're more than that. And I wish I knew the answer to that." He tugs on the ends of his hair with a bit of frustration. "It's not as simple as how gorgeous you are. I don't know. You're not a football fan. Hell, you had no clue who I was, which I know now. I've said it before, but you were genuine. You were easy to talk to. The last few women I've been with…" He trails off.

"The last few women?" I prompt, bracing myself to hear some hard words.

"They didn't have much going on. That's all."

"Let's keep walking," I say gently, and he listens. "Were any of them serious?"

"No. I don't really do serious. At least not anymore." He's staring straight ahead again, and somehow that's easier than having him looki at me. Even behind sunglasses, his gaze seems to pin me to my place.

"Why not?" I ask. We get to the end of the block, and we turn around and start heading back to his house.

"I was with someone I thought I was going to marry, and she broke my heart."

"Oh," I say softly, and I want to reach over and ruffle my fingers through his hair, but I refrain. "I'm so sorry. Can I ask what happened?"

"Eventually I caught onto the fact that she was only with me because of what I do, not because of who I was." He presses his lips together as if it's painful to talk about it.

"How long ago was that?"

"We ended things three years ago," he says. "It's dead and buried, but she broke my trust in women, so I decided I wasn't going to give another woman that sort of power again."

We're both quiet after those words, but the walk is coming to an end anyway. We head up the driveway and to the front door, and he taps in the keycode.

My phone starts to ring, and I glance at the screen to see Lily is FaceTiming me from her iPad.

"Sorry," I say, and I slip my phone back into my pocket with a heavy dose of guilt along with a bit of irritation that my mother let her call me on the iPad when she knows I'm working.

"Go ahead and answer," he says as he leans his crutches on the wall by the door. "I know I took you away from your family on a weekend, and I'm sorry about that."

My chest tightens a little at his words. "Are you sure?"

He nods, and I pick up the call as he heads toward the family room to give me privacy.

I see my baby girl's face fill the screen as I answer, and she's definitely crying…and wearing green eye shadow that I didn't approve before I left the house this morning.

"Hey, Lilypad. What's going on?" I ask, ignoring the makeup.

"Mama, I miss you." Her little voice shakes as she says the words through her tears.

"I'll be home in a few hours, baby girl. What did Grams make you and Lukey for breakfast?"

"Mickey waffles," she sniffles.

I give her my most serious look. "Were they the magical ones?"

Her little brows crash together. "I don't know. She made a bow on mine and said it was Minnie, but it still looked like Mickey to me."

I hear a bark of laughter coming from the next room.

"When are you coming home, Mama?"

"A couple hours, baby. Have fun with Grams and Gramps, 'kay? Ask Grams for a Fruit by the Foot." I suggest it because I know that'll keep her occupied for at least twenty minutes—and also because I know her grandmother can't say no to her.

"'Kay. Where are you?"

"I'm working with a patient to help make his knee better."

"You look like you're at a house," she says.

I nod. "He's a very important patient, and he's so hurt that I had to come to his house to help him get better."

"You're good at making boo-boos feel better. Make sure you give it a kiss because that *always* makes my boo-boos better." She pauses, and her eyes light up. "Oh! Can I come with you one time?"

"I don't think so, honey."

She frowns with disappointment, and then I hear my mom in the background. "Lily? Where are you?"

Of course. My mother doesn't even know where Lily is. That's comforting.

"You better go see what Grams wants," I say, and I make a silly face at her.

"Okay, Mama. Love you!" She ends the call before I can say it back. I slide my phone back into my pocket and head back to my patient in the family room.

Chapter 26: Tanner Banks

You're No Fun

"She's five?" I ask when she walks back into the family room. I don't know why listening to her conversation was so…light.

It's been darkness for days, but a little kid talking about trying to disguise a Mickey waffle with a bow is the first thing that has prompted a real, true laugh from me since the accident.

And listening to her be a mom was something else entirely. It was heartwarming. It's something that's been missing from my life for a long time, and even though I had a bit of a breakthrough last night with my own mother, there's something about Cassie's honesty with her kids that came through in just one simple conversation.

"Five going on seventeen," she says, and she rolls her eyes. "I'm so sorry about that."

"Don't be. You can bring them here." The words are out before I can stop them, but I heard the kid ask her mom if she could come with her, and she was sobbing when Cass answered the call. Clearly the kid misses her mom, and I feel bad that I'm taking her away from them.

She sits down next to me, and she checks my knee before she props it into the next stretch. "That's nice of you, but I can't do that. This is work, and trust me when I say they will only be a distraction."

Maybe it's the kind of distraction this place could use. "I'd say bring them tomorrow, but I'm not sure I'll be in the right headspace to entertain given it's the first Sunday since I got taken out. But maybe next Saturday?"

She clears her throat. "They'll be at their dad's house."

"Oh, right." I press my lips together. I'm sort of curious to know more about that dude. Mainly so I could kick his ass.

"Will you go to the game tomorrow?" she asks.

I shake my head. "I'm not ready, and I figured my PT would tell me to stay off it at least through the weekend."

"I can say whatever you want me to say," she confirms.

I offer a small smile. "How does your girl do when she's over at her dad's house?"

"Usually fine, but we'll see what next weekend brings. She's going through a bit of a mama phase."

"What's that?" I ask, and I know I should put a clamp down on all these questions, but I'm suddenly genuinely curious what life is like with kids.

She sighs as she leans back onto my couch while I do another one of those twenty-minute stretches. "Attachment. She just started kindergarten, and the divorce has been tough on her. I think she feels like everybody leaves her or is trying to get rid of her."

"And then I made you leave her to come here today."

I shake my head. "I could've sent someone else in my place."

"Why didn't you?" I glance over at her to try to catch her eye, but she avoids my gaze.

She folds her arms over her chest. "Because you're my patient."

172

I want it to be more than that. I want to tell her that, too, but I'm afraid she'll stop coming by every day if I do. And the one highlight in my day lately is getting to see her.

"Then tomorrow. Bring them with you. I'll come up with some shit for them to do."

She forces a thin smile. "That's nice of you, Tanner, really. But I don't think it's a good idea."

I don't want to push, so I don't. "Okay. That's fine. But the offer is on the table, and if you change your mind in the morning or she's having a hard time, bring her."

"Thanks." She shifts the topic to my next exercise, and we leave it at that.

I get a text the next morning a little after eight.

Cassie: *Lily is having a rough morning. I'm horrified to ask this, but are you sure it's okay if I just bring them?*

Me: *Positive. Pack their swimsuits.*

Miller hasn't left yet, and I yell his name. He appears in the family room a moment later.

"What?"

"I told my PT to bring her kids today. Can you make sure the game room is decent and set up for a seven-year-old?"

"Is that a good idea?" he asks. He relents with a sigh at my glare. "Anything else?"

"Are those lifejackets still in the deck box? I told her to bring their swimsuits."

"The ones the previous owners left?" he asks, and I nod. "Yeah. I didn't move them."

"Can you grab the towels and sunscreen too?"

He nods. "I'll grab the good snacks off the top shelf, too." He grins at me, and I laugh.

He takes care of everything, and he heads out to practice a little before the bell rings. I'm moving slowly, but I'm able to walk today, so I walk over to open the door.

I'm greeted by Cassie and her two kids, and they both look exactly like her. The boy is tall for seven and has spiky hair and blue eyes, and the girl is a mini version of Cass. Her blonde hair is pulled into two pigtails, and her blue eyes are bright as they look up at me. She tugs on her mom's hand, and I can't help but take in this whole scene in front of me.

Somehow it makes Cassie even hotter. I have no idea why, but my chest feels warm, and I feel lighter than I have in days with the three of them standing on my front porch.

Luca murmurs, "Whoa, it's really Tanner Banks."

I grin. "It's really Tanner Banks. And you must be Luca. Come on in."

"I can't believe I'm at Tanner Banks's house. Isaiah is going to be so jealous!" he says.

"Honey, I told you, this is confidential," Cassie warns.

"Mama, what's con-tent-shul?" Lily asks.

"It means you can't tell anybody you were here," she explains.

"You can tell whoever you want that your mom is friends with Tanner Banks, and I invited you to my house," I say, a gleam twinkling in my eye. I glance at Luca. "Remind me to grab a couple footballs to sign so you can have one, and you can give one to Isaiah."

My eyes move to Cassie's, and she mouths *thank you* to me. She looks truly embarrassed that she brought her kids, but on the one hand, it takes some of the pressure out of the day for me. It's shifting my focus just like my brother told me to do, though I'm positive this isn't what he meant by that.

Still, it gives me some ideas of where I want to put my focus—you know, if it's wrong for that focus to be on Cassie and her two kids.

I walk slowly through the house and back to my spot on the couch. "Make yourselves at home. There's a game room

174

upstairs, snacks in the pantry, soda in the fridge—if your mom says it's okay."

"Can we, Mama?" Lily begs at the same time Luca looks at Cass and says, "Please?"

She glares at me a little and purses her lips before she relents. "Fine." Both kids pump their fists into the air and head toward the kitchen as their mom calls after them, "But no sugar and no caffeine!"

"You're no fun," I tease quietly as they squeal over by the fridge, and she rolls her eyes. She follows them in to help with the sodas, and she gets them set up at the kitchen table with a snack, their tablets, and headphones.

"Okay, you two. Mama has work to do, so you sit here, okay?" They both nod solemnly, and they engross themselves in whatever it is kids watch on their iPads. She walks over toward me, and she says, "You didn't have to get them soda or snacks. I brought stuff to keep them occupied."

"I didn't. We had it around." I shrug. "But they might as well get something fun for having to spend the day with their mom while she works, right? Oh, did you bring their swimsuits?"

She nods. "Lily isn't quite independent in the water yet, though."

"Is swimming okay for me? I can get in with them."

"Swimming would be great for you, actually. Low impact, and we can add it into your rotation. Just no twisting. And absolutely no picking up my kids and throwing them into the water."

I roll my eyes this time. "You really are no fun."

She swats at my arm with a little chuckle, and despite my words, today *feels* a lot more fun.

But it's early, and the games haven't started yet. They will, and surely my mood will sour then…and that's why I decide

175

right then and there that I'm not going to turn on the television until Cassie and her kids leave.

I can watch football all night after that. And I will. I can review film, watch footage from our own game, look objectively at all the teams in the league in a way I usually can't on a weekly basis because I'm too busy studying our one opponent.

It's another new focus I hadn't really thought of before.

I clear my throat after Cassie outlines my first stretch, and I glance over at her. "My brother thinks I need a focus."

"What sort of focus?" she asks.

"I don't know. A hobby. Something other than football."

She stares thoughtfully at me before she says, "I agree. What are you into?"

"Football," I mutter petulantly. "Running. Golf."

"Okay, so activities. Exercise. You could do something low impact like swimming or cycling. Yoga would be great."

"Since we're already planning to swim today, maybe you could help me in the water," he suggests. "You said Lily isn't independent yet?"

"She's a little scared of the water," she says. "She's taken lessons, but she prefers a life jacket, and she won't jump in. Her brother, on the other hand, is fearless and will do flips and dives all day."

"I have a diving board."

"That you will stay off of, Mr. Banks." She purses her lips at me and raises her brows, and I have to admit, I like a woman who can set the rules.

Truth be told, I *need* a woman who can set the rules.

And the more time I spend with Cassandra Fields, the more I want it to be her.

We do a few more stretches, and then Lily comes over to watch her mom work on me. She seems curious at first, but then she loses interest since mostly it's twelve repetitive movements.

"Can we go swimming now?" she asks.

"Go get your swim stuff on, and we'll go in a few minutes. You can get changed in the bathroom down that hallway." She points, and Lily runs to the extra bag her mom brought, grabs her swimsuit, and darts down the hallway.

Our eyes connect, and I say, "You brought your swimsuit, right?"

Her lips tip up a little, but she's careful not to give too much away. "I did."

I lean in a little closer and whisper. "Please tell me it's a two piece."

She leans in, too. "It's not."

I don't hide my disappointment—or my erection at the thought of her in a swimsuit.

But the truth is that it's getting harder and harder to deny that I want Cassie.

Chapter 27: Cassie Fields

This Is All Sorts of Inappropriate

I walk over to Luca, who's still engrossed in whatever he's watching on his tablet.

"Do you want to swim?" I ask.

He nods, and I grab his swimsuit and tell him where to go change once Lily is out.

"Would you mind grabbing my swim trunks for me?" Tanner asks me, and he wrinkles his nose as if he feels bad asking. But the truth is, I don't really want him climbing stairs, and I assume his swim trunks are upstairs.

"Of course. Where are they?"

"Up in my bedroom," he says. "My room is the primary, so go up the stairs and all the way down the hall. The door's open. Top left drawer of my dresser. Feel free to change while you're up there. You know, and feel free to snoop. I don't have anything to hide."

I laugh, and I grab my one piece and head upstairs.

I find his room, and I glance around for a few seconds. His furniture is black, and his bedding is white. I spot his favorite color all around the room here, from the throw blanket over an armchair in the corner to the bits of color in photographs on the walls.

It's minimalist and regal, but it also screams of him. There are a few framed photographs on the walls, and they're all images of wild animals, landscapes, or football—no people. It's an interesting insight into the man I'm spending so much time with.

I shut the door and grab his swimsuit out of the top left drawer, and I realize I'm about to see Tanner Banks in just swim trunks.

My legs squeeze together as I remember his *abs*. God, he's gorgeous.

I pull off my clothes and realize I'm standing naked in Tanner Banks's bedroom, and I get a sense like I want this to happen again.

Pull it together, Fields. He's a patient. I can't get involved.

Except…

We *have* been involved. This is different.

I pull my swimsuit on, and I try to ignore the pulsing ache between my legs.

This is all sorts of inappropriate.

Not only is he my patient, but my kids are here—though, to be fair, back when I was married, we had sex when the kids were home…you know, after they were fast asleep for the night.

Still, I'm fully aware that I need to stay away. I know I can't get involved with him no matter how much I want to.

But knowing what's right and *doing* what's right are two completely different things.

I head downstairs with his swim trunks in hand and a T-shirt pulled over my swimsuit, and I toss him his trunks when I get downstairs.

His eyes drift along my legs and to my chest before they move to my face again, and I swear, I see lust in his eyes.

His tongue darts out to wet his bottom lip, and I feel all hot and achy with the way he's looking at me.

Damn. I need to get into that pool. Stat.

It can't possibly be true, can it? Does he want me the same way I'm fighting against wanting him?

"Towels?" I ask.

He stands, and he nods past the kitchen. "Miller left some in the laundry room."

I head that way and grab four towels from the stack, and both kids are waiting in the kitchen when I emerge. Tanner walks into the kitchen a moment later in his swim trunks, and my mouth waters.

Good Lord.

Tanner without a shirt on is even hotter than I remembered. Even though he hasn't been working out, the muscles in his abdomen haven't suffered because of it. Simply put, he's absolutely beautiful.

"Ready?" he asks, and his voice is low and sexy.

I clear my throat and nod. "Oh, wait. I brought Lily's wings. Let me just grab them from the car."

"Want me to get started spraying them with sunscreen?" he asks.

"That would be incredible," I say, and I grab the bottle out of my bag and hand it over to him. Our fingers brush, and it's the most clichéd cliché, but my God, does a spark of electricity pulse between us.

I head out to the car and grab Lily's puddle jumper. It's better to have her swim without it, but I want her to have fun in the water, not be nervous in it.

I find them outside. Luca is waiting by the edge of the pool.

And Lily is holding Tanner's hand.

She's standing there in her swimsuit, staring at the water as she *holds his hand.*

181

I melt. I freaking melt. They are adorable together, and I can't help but wish that *he* was their father instead of Alex.

I can't help but wish this was a regular Sunday afternoon as a family.

Tanner has known my kids all of a few hours, and somehow he just *fits*. It's in this strange way that I never expected, and it tugs at my heart.

"Can I get in now?" Luca begs, pulling my attention from the big football star holding my five-year-old's hand, and I chuckle.

"Go for it," I say, and he does a forward flip into the water.

"You ready to get in, Lily?" Tanner asks her.

"Will you hold my hand?" she asks him.

"Only if you hold mine," he says, and together, they walk down the steps into the water…without Lily's puddle jumper.

He's amazing with her. Patient and kind, even when Luca yells, "Tanner, watch this!" a hundred million times. He's encouraging my boy, and he's supporting my girl. He helps coach Luca with the proper way to dive off his diving board, and he helps Lily swim from one side of his pool to another…unassisted.

Normally, Lily only wants Mama in the water. Today, however, she only wants Tanner.

And so does Luca.

And you know what? So does Mama, just in a totally different and decidedly inappropriate way.

The more I watch him with my kids, the more attractive he becomes. He isn't just hot because of what he has on the outside, though believe me, it's nice to look at.

But it's this person who emerges when he's spending time with my kids that's making me feel these sudden, hot urges to have another night with him. It's the way he catches my eye and grins at me when Luca does a front flip off the diving board. It's the way he talks Lily through her fears. It's the way he's everything to both of my kids when I feel like I fail at that on a daily basis.

I can control myself, though. I have to. My entire career could be at stake here, and I refuse to lose it because of some guy.

But what if he's more than just *some guy*?

What if we started something that night in Vegas, and now we're a month out from it and we're getting to know each other on an entirely different level?

We're not dating, but we *are* seeing each other every day, and I *am* feeling feelings for him when I know I shouldn't.

It's okay. I can quit it. I can quit the quarterback.

Lily puts her head under the water and powers through across the pool.

It's the first time she's ever done that.

Tanner cheers for her when she comes up on the other side. She's grinning, Luca's celebrating her, and I'm practically crying.

When lunchtime rolls around, he says he'll grill hot dogs for the kids and chicken burgers for the two of us. I tell the kids to head inside and put their clothes back on for lunch, and that leaves the two of us out on the patio alone for a moment.

"Thank you for being so kind to my children," I say softly. I'm standing beside the patio doors before I head in, and he moves slowly over toward me.

He's close enough that I can reach out and touch those perfect, steel-cut abs, but I force myself not to.

"They're great kids," he says softly. He leans in a little closer to me, and he nuzzles my neck a little. I lean my head back to give him more space, and I force my hands down to my sides even though my instinct is to hold onto his upper arms to hold myself up. "And their mom is hot as fuck," he murmurs close to my ear, and then his lips move to brush mine.

It's just the softest whisper of a kiss, and I want more. I *need* more. My instincts kick in, and I can't force my arms down any longer. I grab hold of his upper arms, and I open my mouth to his. His tongue swirls around mine as we kiss passionately, urgently, out here on his patio. He boxes me in, his hips pinning me to my place as he moves his body closer to mine so we're chest to chest, and I feel his erection against my hip.

My God, I want this. I don't know if I've ever felt such a strong pulse of need for a man before. I thrust my hips toward him, and he groans.

We did this once before, and it's muscle memory at work as he kisses me. My body awakens to his touch, to his scent, to *him* as I feel myself coming alive in a way that I've only felt one other time, and that was in a hotel room with him.

And then we both hear a thump on the slider door beside me. We're out of view from whoever's on the other side, but someone is there, one of my kids, and he jumps back a little guiltily. He winces as he turns back toward the grill, and I'm not sure if he's wincing from pain in his knee or the pain of having to stop kissing me. Maybe both.

As it turns out, I'm not quite sure I'm going to be able to quit him after all.

Chapter 28: Tanner Banks

Princess and Buddy

Around three, her normal time to head out, Cassie starts getting the kids ready to leave.

Lily gives me a huge hug before she goes. "I hope to see you again soon, Mr. Tanner," she tells me. She's got ice cream on her chin, and I swipe at it with my thumb.

"You too, princess."

"Thanks for the footballs," Luca says to me, and I give him a hug, too.

"Any time, buddy."

I want to hug Cassie, but I'm not sure how she feels about affection in front of her kids, and besides, we're just supposed to be PT and patient.

I wave from my front door as she pulls out of my driveway, and I head back to the family room. It's quiet in here now—not that her kids were extra loud, but just having people around was nice. I'm not sure I like the quiet as much as I thought I would.

I'd planned to turn on the television the second they left to tune into today's games, but a part of me doesn't want to dampen the good mood I find myself in.

I do it anyway. I don't know if I've ever missed watching football on Sundays. Even before I learned how to play, Mom always had the television tuned to a game on Sundays.

I realize now it was because she was watching the man who fathered her children. I don't even know if Charles knew the truth about who our real dad was—he just knew it wasn't him even though he's on our birth certificates.

It's something I haven't really given my mom the chance to explain, but I'm suffering from a bit of an identity crisis. Not only was I struggling with who I am because I'd been lied to, but then football was taken away from me too, when I injured my knee.

But when I'm with Cassie, and even her kids, I feel like *myself* again.

It's only been a week since my injury, and I'm already making progress. I don't want to ruin that by getting too personal with Cassie, but it might be too late.

I shouldn't have kissed her, but I couldn't help it. It just felt natural after the sort of day we were having. She kept watching me with her kids, and I liked how it felt to have her eyes on me. She looked at me with approval and warmth, and it made *me* feel warm.

It made me realize that all it took was one night, and I fell.

Somehow, someway, I fell. It makes no sense, but it happened.

It's why I was distracted. We can't control who we develop feelings for, and to develop so quickly only to have her ripped away didn't do me any favors.

I'm thinking about her as I watch my brother run into the end zone.

I'm thinking about her as I watch Ford Turner get sacked. It would've been me, but I would've seen him coming from a mile away.

I'm thinking about her as I study the defensive line on the other side of the ball, and I watch their formations as I think through our own defensive line.

I'm not concentrating the way I should, but after today, I have a pretty strong sense that I've found something to focus on.

My physical therapist.

It's a terrible plan, and I know that. So I need to focus on something else, too. A hobby or a charity like Miller suggested.

Maybe video games with Luca. Maybe swimming with Lily. Maybe sex with Cassie.

It keeps coming back to that. To her.

Maybe it's because I'm horny as fuck. I haven't slept with a woman since the night I was with her, and my hand just isn't cutting it. It's no replacement for the warmth of her feminine body, for the feel of her hard tits pressed up against my chest, for the way her cunt wrapped around my cock so perfectly.

Jesus.

I mute the television as it goes to commercial, and I yank my dick over the top of my shorts. I stroke myself as I picture Cassie in her swimsuit, and then I picture her out of that same swimsuit as I call up the image that lives rent-free in my brain of her naked writhing beneath me. I think of driving into her sweet cunt as I pick up the pace on my own dick, and I grunt as I feel myself pulling closer to a climax.

And as I come all over my hand a few moments later, the relief is far too short-lived. I need more, and I need it with her.

I get up to clean up the mess I just made, and I have a text waiting for me when I sit back down on the couch, this time with a beer. I unmute the game so it's playing, but I'm more interested in reading the text on my phone.

Cassie: *The kids had a blast. Thanks for being so welcoming to them. I'm so sorry I had to bring them along with me.*

Me: *I had a great time today. The three of you are welcome any time, even outside of our sessions.*

Cassie: *By the way, princess and buddy? That was adorable.*

Me: *I aim to please.*

She sends me an LOL, and I can't help but think how much I want to continue this conversation with her.

We just spent the last eight hours together, and it's like I can't get enough.

I never felt that way with Heather. I liked having my own shit so we could have some time apart. Maybe that should've told me from the start something deeper about our relationship, but it didn't.

I decide to send her another text.

Me: *What are you up to tonight?*

Cassie: *Movie night with the kids. I just ordered pizza, and then we'll be getting ready for school.*

Me: *What movie?*

Cassie: *Some new SpongeBob one on Netflix. Luca got to pick tonight.*

Me: *What does getting ready for school entail?*

Cassie: *Packing snacks and lunches, making sure any forms are filled out. They don't get weekend homework, but we'll have that tomorrow when they get home from school.*

Me: *Homework? At that age?*

Cassie: *Yep. Lots of at-home practice. How's your knee feeling?*

Me: *The swimming felt good. It feels the best it's felt since the injury.*

Cassie: *I'll get you on the doctors' schedule for this week. I want them to take a look. You're doing so well that Dr. Barlow may want to move the surgery sooner.*

I like the idea of that. But I don't like the idea that she's shifting our personal conversation back to my knee.

Me: *Question for you since you have kids. Is there much need around here for an after-school football program for elementary school kids?*

The thought comes out fairly unfiltered.

Cassie: *I think Clayton Mack does one, but it's only in the summer.*

Me: *Okay, thanks.*

Cassie: *Why?*

Me: *I'm thinking about organizing something.*

Cassie: *Why?*

I chuckle at her repeated question.

Me: *I ran a program in Arizona. And I had a great time with you and your kids today. I want something I can focus on for the next few months and thought this could be it.*

Cassie: *I'm sure there's a lot of logistics to consider, but I think it's a great idea. Would you like the info of our activity director at my kids' school district?*

Me: *That would be great.*

She sends over the info, and I draft an email to the contact from my phone.

When I glance up after I hit *send*, I realize the Storm game is over.

We won, and I didn't even realize it.

I'm glad my team won, but it feels hollow that they won without me. I'm glad Ford is working out, but it should be me out there.

I didn't even watch to see how much harder they had to work without me there. I was too focused on Cassie, and not just her but her kids, along with the idea I had about starting up a program here.

I'm not quite sure what's happening to me, but it feels like something is changing.

And it feels like it all started the moment I stood next to Cassandra Fields at a bar in Vegas.

Chapter 29: Cassie Fields

We Have This Phone Call

I stare at my phone.

Why did you kiss me?

I can't make myself send the text even though I want to know. I need to know.

And when morning rolls around, I'm nervous.

I shouldn't be. I've been to his house every day, and it's been fine.

But he kissed me yesterday, and I don't know why. Even so...I want him to do it again.

In one day, my kids fell for him. Hard.

And seeing them fall for him made *me* fall for him a little bit, too. Then he follows it up with that text conversation telling me he wants to start up a football program for kids while he's injured so he has something to focus on...

Are you kidding me?

How am I supposed to act around him now that my heart is invested?

It was easy enough to play it off before. It was just a heated attraction, just the memory of our night. I convinced myself that he wasn't feeling the things I was.

But then he kissed me yesterday, and all hope I had of keeping things professional between us was completely obliterated.

It was a good run—for an entire five days.

God, what is wrong with me?

My first VIP patient and here I am, falling for him like some sort of idiot.

But it's not just that.

I could lose my job over this if I allow it to go any further than that kiss yesterday. I could get into serious trouble, and I absolutely will not stand in the way of his healing.

And that's why I'm nervous.

I decided I'm going to shoot my shot with him, and then if he takes me up on it, I'm going to resign as his physical therapist.

It's the only way we can move forward.

I can't risk my job for the unknown when I'm reaching the goals I set for myself and my kids.

My hands are trembling when I ring the bell, and Miller answers it.

"Come on in," he says. "Tanner is on the couch with ice, as usual. But for something different, he's doing a puzzle today. I gave him the challenge to finish the puzzle before the timer on the ice goes off."

I chuckle as I follow him through the house. Of course he likes puzzles. So do I. Still, disappointment lances through me that we're not going to be alone. "Great win yesterday. Congratulations."

"Thank you." He nods to Tanner, and I spot him on the couch with a laptop.

"Good morning," he says to me, and his voice is warm and friendly—a one eighty from the grumpy man I dealt with last week. "I finished the puzzle and got back to work."

"Good morning," I say, and my voice trembles a little.

If Miller notices, he doesn't say anything. "And thanks for whatever you're doing with him. He's in a good mood for the first time since the injury, and I think it has something to do with you."

I smile, though I'm surprised he told Miller about us. Maybe he didn't, so I play it cool. "Happy to help."

"He has his purpose back, you know? The kids' program, I mean. He was working on it when I got home last night, and he's working on it again this morning." He shrugs. "He's excited about something, and I'm relieved."

"How much do you feel what he's feeling?" I ask.

He shrugs. "It varies depending on the situation, but man, when he was depressed last week, I felt it."

"I've always been fascinated by twins," I say, and I hear a grunt from Tanner over on the couch that I choose to ignore since Miller doesn't catch it.

I'll ask him about it later once we're alone.

As it turns out, Miller has the day off since the Storm won, and he decided he's going to spend the day chilling at home.

With us.

I don't get to have the conversation with Tanner I need to have.

He watches our session, and we're forced to remain professional.

It isn't until after I get Luca down for bed that I spot a text from Tanner.

Tanner: *I'm sorry my brother was hanging around all day. I really wanted to talk to you, but I didn't mention anything to him about…well, any of it.*

Me: *I had some things I wanted to talk to you about, too.*

I click the send button before I change my mind, though I'm nervous about what his response might be.

Tanner: *Are the kids asleep?*

Me: *Yes.*

My phone starts to ring, and I answer it right away when I see his contact flash across my screen. "Hi."

"Hey."

I know I spent the majority of my day with him, but hearing his voice feels like a warm blanket wrapping around me.

He starts talking before I can say what I was planning to say. "I really wanted to kiss you again today, Cass. I can't stop thinking about our night in Vegas." His voice is low and raspy, and my God, it pulses a strong ache right between my legs.

"Tell me why you kissed me yesterday," I blurt.

He's quiet a beat as if I caught him off guard, and then he clears his throat. "I guess I just…couldn't let another moment go by without doing it. I did it because I wanted to do it. It felt right."

"I wanted you to kiss me, too," I say, and my voice is breathless. "And, you know…other things."

"My brother will be here tomorrow again, but we have tonight."

"I can't come over now. My kids are home. They're sleeping, and—"

"That's not what I meant," he interrupts softly. "We have this phone call."

"We can't kiss through the phone." I mean, maybe I'm stating the obvious, but I'm not sure what he's getting at.

"No, but we can talk. We can do other things."

"Such as?" I ask.

"You can touch your nipples and make them hard for me. You can reach into your panties and tell me how wet your cunt is with my voice in your ear."

Oh. Whoa. I wasn't expecting him to say *that*.

I clear my throat. "I, uh…" I stutter as I fail to come up with something to say, but I'm not exactly practiced in dirty talk these days.

"My cock is so hard for you, Cass," he murmurs. "All I can think about is getting inside you again. Tell me you want it, too."

"I do," I squeak.

"How bad do you want it?"

"So bad." Oh my God, I'm awful at this. I clear my throat and try again. "I haven't stopped thinking about our night together."

"When you think about it, what are you thinking?" He's gently urging me on, guiding me through this conversation as if he knows it's out of my comfort zone even though I want to do it.

"I think about when your mouth was on me. I think about when you were moving inside of me. I think about how your eyes connected with mine, and this moment passed between us that I wasn't expecting. It was more intimate and erotic than I thought I would have from something that was only ever supposed to be one night."

"Maybe it was never meant to be only one night," he suggests. "That's what I think about, too. And your gorgeous body. We were so close to being naked yesterday when we were swimming together. Can we swim again?"

"Of course. Tomorrow, if you want."

"Oh, no. Not tomorrow. Not until I can get you alone, and I can fuck you in my pool."

"Oh God," I moan.

"I want you to use my name when you moan," he demands, and he may be seven years younger than me, but I *love* how dominating he sounds in this moment.

"Oh Tanner," I moan.

"That's right. I didn't realize the night we were together that you didn't know my name, but now it's the only thing I want to hear when you're moaning."

Jeez. Where did this guy learn to talk like this? I always thought dirty talk sounded so…cheesy and corny, I guess. But coming out of his mouth with that dark little rasp to his deep voice?

It's everything.

"Mm, Tanner," I moan again as I practice it. Maybe it's because he isn't here looking at me that I can do this.

Maybe it's the glass of wine I had after I got Luca down.

I get up and lock my bedroom door just in case, and then I settle back into my bed.

"Touch your pussy. Tell me how wet you are," he demands.

I lift my shirt a little and reach down into my shorts, bypassing my panties, and I slide a finger into my pussy. "Mm, yes. It's so wet, Tanner. I'm so wet for you."

"Push your fingers in a few times and then slide them out and touch your clit for me."

I do it, and I let out a low groan. "What are you doing while I'm touching myself?" I whisper.

"I pulled my cock out of my shorts, and I'm stroking it. I did it last night while I thought about you, too. All I think about is you, Cass."

"Oh my God, Tanner," I moan as I start to rub my clit a little harder. "I'm going to come. I'm getting close."

"Come on your hand for me, baby. I want to be there with you. I want to be the one making you come."

"You are," I shriek as my body tightens. It's all him doing this to me, guiding my hand with his words. I start to come, and I tell him. "Oh God, I'm coming!" I squeeze the phone in one hand, and I squeeze my eyes shut as my legs thrash together, the orgasm plowing into me as I listen to his moans on the other side of the line.

"Yes, Cass. Jesus, you sound so hot right now. Fuck yes, oh fuck," he murmurs. "I'm going to come just from listening to you." He grunts a few times, and then I hear a louder moan as my own pulses start to slow.

We're both quiet a few beats, and then he says, "Oh fuck, that felt good."

"Just wait until we can do it in person," I say, and I have no idea where those words come from.

No part of this is okay. I still have things I need to say to him, and those words do not include me telling him to fuck me in his pool.

Even if that's exactly what I want.

I can't tell him the things I wanted to tell him now—not after he made me come just from his voice directing my hand over the phone.

"I can't wait."

"Neither can I," I admit.

He sighs, and we listen to each other breathe for a few quiet moments as we bask in the afterglow. It should feel weird that neither of us is talking, but instead, it feels comfortable—like neither of us wants to break the silence, and neither of us wants to let go of this conversation.

But then I hear my doorknob wiggle, and I hear a voice on the other side of the door. "Mama?"

"Shit," I whisper. "I have to go." I hang up, and I leap out of bed as I run to the bathroom and wash my hands before I head back to answer the door.

"Hey, Lilypad. What's the matter?"

"I had a bad dream," she wails, and she's distracted enough that she doesn't ask why my door was locked.

"Oh, honey, I'm sorry." I take her hand and walk her back to her room, and she climbs into bed. "Do you want to talk about it?"

"No. Just lay with me."

I do, and we both fall asleep.

It's Luca who wakes us up in the morning, and that's how our day begins…late. I'm discombobulated from a broken night's rest, and my neck is stiff from using a stuffed animal as a pillow.

Tanner texted me last night after I abruptly ended the call, and I feel bad I never replied.

I'll see him soon, but now I need to focus on getting the kids to the bus stop on time.

Then I can focus on figuring out how to deal with the Tanner situation.

Chapter 30: Tanner Banks

Rehab Before Romance

I can't hide it from Miller.

He's not just my brother. He's my *twin*, and I'm surprised he hasn't sensed it by this point.

Or maybe he has, and he's choosing to ignore it. Maybe he's chalking it up to me going through this injury. Maybe he's treading lightly around me. I'm not sure I like people treading lightly around me. I get it, but my patience for it is wearing thin. Just because my knee is all sorts of fucked doesn't mean the rest of me is.

But this morning, things *feel* a little different.

The swelling has gone down significantly. I think the swimming really helped, and it doesn't hurt quite like it did. But that's not what feels different today.

I didn't sleep well last night because I was worried about Cassie. She abruptly ended the call, and she didn't call me back. She didn't text me. I waited with my phone in my hand for a good twenty minutes before I finally gave up.

I'm sure it was nothing…but what if it wasn't? What if something's wrong with one of the kids?

A million scenarios ran through my mind. What does she do if one of them needs help in the middle of the night and she's the only one there? She'd have to drag one of them out of bed, or she'd have to wait on someone to get there to be with her.

Maybe she'd even have to call her ex-husband.

I don't know much about him. She hasn't detailed much about their relationship other than the fact that they were together for a long, long time, he was her first, and he cheated on her.

I can't begin to imagine how he could do that to her—to *them*. How he could destroy the sweet little family. How he could betray his wife and children that way.

She's such a catch—smart, funny, gorgeous—and she created these two little humans who are about as perfect as she is. I couldn't stop replaying Luca as he flipped into the pool or Lily as she grinned at me after she made her way across the pool, one of her bottom teeth missing from the smile since she just lost her first tooth a few weeks ago.

He gave that all up. And for what?

I'm not sure, but it doesn't make any sense to me.

I don't know why I find myself wanting to pick up what he gave away. Not just Cassie, though it definitely starts with her. But the whole thing, from grilling hot dogs for the kids to the fits over having to turn off the tablets because it's time to go. It was the messy moments of imperfection that stick out, and it was that feeling of loss when they left.

It was my first day meeting them.

I'm getting ahead of myself. Obviously. Very far ahead of myself. But it's a vision of the future I didn't allow myself to picture before, and now I can see it in vivid detail.

Maybe it won't be with them. It *probably* won't be. I have a feeling Cassie is going to fight her feelings when reality kicks in about her career.

But maybe it will be.

Maybe we'll fight our way to the end together after all.

And it's those thoughts that prompt me to mention it to my brother.

"You sleep okay?" he asks as he walks into the kitchen to make his breakfast.

I shake my head from where I sit at the kitchen table with a bowl of Greek yogurt filled with granola and berries.

"Thinking about how you should've been at the game or what?" he asks.

I shake my head again. "Or what."

"Care to elaborate?" His head is in the fridge, and I wait for him to turn around and face me. He sets the container of Greek yogurt down onto the counter.

I clear my throat. "I'm developing very strong feelings for my physical therapist."

His jaw slackens a little. "Cassie?"

I nod. I know I don't need to tell him to keep his mouth shut. He wouldn't tell anybody even if it wasn't about me. He doesn't gossip, and he doesn't spread rumors.

"Remember the one-night stand in Vegas in July?" I ask.

He nods. Of course he does. We talked about it at length.

"It was her," I mutter.

"It was *her*?"

I nod.

"What are the chances?" he asks in wonder.

"I don't know." I sigh as I debate how much to say, and then it all comes tumbling out of my mouth. "I've often wondered that myself, but I've also recently started subscribing to the theory that there are other dimensions at work in our lifetime, and people are meant to cross our paths more than once. For whatever reason, we met that night, and then I hurt myself, and here we are again."

"So you think it was fate that you'd get hurt and end up as her patient?" he asks, and when I nod, he makes a face and shakes his head. "Nah, man. I don't buy it. It's a coincidence." He spoons some yogurt into the bowl.

I feel like of the two of us, he's the more logical one. He's more rational. He's less likely to make decisions based on emotions. I always thought that described me better, but maybe my theories on emotions are starting to change a little.

Maybe they're not just there to get in the way. Maybe they do serve a purpose, and I've spent so much time ignoring them and pushing them away rather than dealing with them. I'm only starting to realize that now.

My anger and frustration over my injury are both fueling me to get to work on gaining my strength back in my knee, for one thing. Or maybe that's my resilience. My entire personality is being a confident achiever, and a large part of that is bouncing back from setbacks.

Whatever the case, I think Miller is wrong. I don't think it has anything to do with coincidence, and maybe that's my confidence speaking out, too.

"But either way, it doesn't matter," he says, his voice gentle. I know he's being mild to brace me for the next words that'll be harsh. "You can't work with her if you're banging her."

I sigh. I know he's right…in theory.

But I've enjoyed getting to know her over the last week. We've spent nearly six hours a day together every day, and instead of wanting her to leave, I find myself wanting her to stay a little longer.

That means something to me.

I've never felt that way about a woman before—not even Heather.

I'm becoming addicted to this woman, and I've only slept with her once. That's definitely new.

"Why not?" I ask. I mean...*technically* we're not banging. We did once, and then we had some phone sex last night. But that's it.

"It's an ethics issue for her, man." He grabs the granola and pours it into his bowl. "Do you want her to get in trouble?"

"Nobody has to ever find out."

"But what if someone does? It's a bad look for her. It could be her license on the line. Her entire career. Didn't you say she's recently divorced? Don't you think she's trying to build a reputation for herself? How would it look if she's fucking the first patient who came her way?"

"But we were together before my injury," I point out. I stir my yogurt without taking a bite, my appetite suddenly gone. It was as if the hope I felt hinged on Cassie, and with my brother trying to talk some sense into me, the hope is disappearing into thin air. "Feelings got stronger as we spent more time together."

"That doesn't help matters. You both should've been honest from the start. And what if something goes wrong with your recovery? Don't you think you'd blame her, and that would be the end for you two?" He's making solid points, but I don't particularly want to hear any of them. "Listen, I'm going to meet with a few of the running backs today for workouts, so I'll stay out of your hair. But talk to her, man. Tell her what you're thinking and how you're feeling, and maybe if you're honest, the two of you can navigate this together." He walks over, and he squeezes my shoulder. "You know how much I just want you to be happy."

"Then pipe down about all this," I mutter.

He presses his lips together. "I'm sorry, but you need to hear the truth, and you know I'm always going to give it to you straight."

203

"Yeah," I mutter, and I push my bowl of yogurt away. I prefer the Miller who's full of banter than the one doling out advice I don't want to hear.

"You gonna eat that?" he asks, and I nod toward it as if to tell him to have at it, and then I grab a bag of ice and head to the couch.

Miller's gone by the time the doorbell rings, and I walk over to let her in. She's standing there looking a little frazzled, and I'm *feeling* a little frazzled after my conversation with my brother.

I open the door a little wider, and the second I shut the door behind her, I pull her into my arms.

Jesus. She just *fits*. I'm not sure how or why, but she does.

I hold her close, and I kiss the top of her head as she sinks into me. It's quiet and intimate, warm and inviting.

"Why'd you hang up?" I ask.

"Lily had a bad dream. I felt…" She trails off and clears her throat before she finishes that sentence. "Caught. Speaking of which…is your brother here?" she asks into my chest.

"No."

We're both quiet a few seconds, and then she pulls back and tilts her head up toward me. I angle down to look at her, and a heated moment passes between us.

"I told him about us," I admit.

"About…us?" she echoes.

I nod. "About our night in Vegas. About, uh…"

"Last night?" she guesses.

I shake my head. "No. About the feelings I'm having for you." I duck my head a little at the admission.

She raises a brow. "Feelings of annoyance that I make you put in the work?"

I chuckle as I shake my head, and I lower my mouth to hers. It's a soft, tender moment of mouth to mouth, no tongue, no urgency. Just the two of us here in an intimate moment as we press our lips together.

I pull back to say, "Not at all. Strong, intense feelings. Feeling like I might be falling."

Her eyes widen a little as she stares at me. "Falling?" she squeaks.

"Yeah. Falling."

She pulls back from my grasp, and I'm worried I've overstepped. "My God, Tanner. I thought you just, you know…wanted me. Because our night together was so hot."

"I do," I protest.

"No, you said *falling*. That implies you want more than just sex."

"I do," I say, my voice less of a protest and much more resolute than the first time I said the same words.

She stares at me with some mix of confusion and horror, and I'm not really sure which is winning.

"Is this for real?" she asks. "Or is it like, you know, I'm helping you get better, and that whole transference thing?"

"It's not that," I say, and I grip my hair in a bit of frustration. "I know it's not that because I couldn't stop thinking about you after our night in Vegas. I've done the one-night thing before. Plenty of times."

"Rub it in a little harder," she mutters dryly.

"I'm sorry. I'm only saying it to add that I never left one of those and had another thought about the woman I was leaving behind. I know that makes me sound like a douchebag, but it's the truth. And then you walked into my life, and something changed."

She draws in a deep breath. "I, uh…" She shakes her head a little. "I *just* got out of a marriage. I have no idea what I'm looking for, no idea if I want to get married again someday or get into another relationship or…whatever. Any of it. I have kids. And we barely know each other."

It's a hit to my ego that she doesn't feel the same way, and a former version of me would clap back at that. But this new Tanner is someone I don't even recognize. "We've spent hours upon hours getting to know each other over the last week, Cass. You can't say we barely know each other. And you can't say you don't feel it too because I know you do."

She presses her lips together. "Of course I feel it. I felt it like crazy yesterday when you were with the kids. You were so natural with them, and it pulsed this feeling in the pit of my stomach I'm just not used to."

I glance out the window behind her as I think back to how much I enjoyed them. "I had a great time with them," I say. I don't want to scare her with the scary thoughts that are moving in my own mind about how I enjoyed feeling like a little family.

Maybe it's because it feels so goddamn much like my entire childhood was a lie. Her honesty with her kids is refreshing, and I feel like I want to be a part of it.

She sighs, and I need to touch her again. I pull her against me without words, and she speaks first.

"I was planning to say this to you yesterday, but then your brother was here, and…well, anyway. I want to see you. I want to *be* with you if you want it too, but I can't do that when I'm treating you." She pulls back and looks at me. "I need you to choose if you want me to be your physical therapist or if you want me to be something else."

I drop my forehead down to hers. "What if I want both?"

Before she can answer, my mouth collides with hers.

She resists for a beat, and then she melts into me for a moment. But ultimately, the resistance wins. She puts both hands on my chest and pushes herself back.

She's about to say something when she seems to think twice about it, and her mouth finds mine again only for her to pull back again. She's clearly wrestling with the right thing to do here, and I make it easier for her by letting her go.

"We need to set some ground rules," she says quietly.

I nod. I know she's right, and the last thing I want to do is jeopardize her career. "Let's get to work and talk it out while I stretch."

She nods, and we head into the family room where we always do our work. She checks my progress and guides me through a few new exercises before we get a chance to talk.

"What were you thinking for ground rules?" I ask.

"Work time is work time. If we're going to see each other, it has to be outside of our therapy sessions, and sessions remain professional."

I wince at her words even though I know she's right. I also know she's busy after our sessions, and it won't really be all that easy to date her. But I'll take what I can get. "Okay. What else you got?"

"If either of us feels like we can no longer be objective, we stop working together."

I clench my jaw. The last thing I want to do is to stop working with her. I'm not sure I'd let anyone else boss me around the way I've allowed her to. "Fine."

"Nobody can know," she says.

"Miller already knows."

"Fine. Then nobody *else* can know."

I nod. "Agreed. Anything else?"

"In the event of a situation that calls for it, I will prioritize your health over our relationship."

My brows dip together. "Like what?"

She shrugs. "I don't know. Anything. If I think you need additional therapies or emotional support I can't provide to you,

I will recommend you to other professionals. Rehab before romance, baby. That's going to be our motto."

I scrunch my nose up in distaste. "I don't like it, but if it's what it takes to give this a try with you, then I'll agree to all of it."

Her face lights up at my words, and I know we just said therapy first…but I have the strongest urge to kiss her.

As if she can read my mind, she says, "Save it for two forty-six."

And then we get to work.

Chapter 31: Cassie Fields

One Smitten Kitten

We share a steamy kiss before I need to head out to pick up the kids, and I feel like he's really making a lot of great progress. He seems to have moved onto the acceptance phase, and I'm sure he'll have his ups and downs—especially after surgery—but for now, I'm taking the win.

Tomorrow morning I'll meet him at the office instead of at his house, and Dr. Hayward and Dr. Barlow will both examine him as we chart the next stage of his prehab.

I get to the bus stop first, and Jess joins me a moment later. "How are things going with your patient?" she asks.

I clear my throat, and my cheeks turn pink.

"Cassandra Fields, do tell!" she goads me. "Please say you slept with him again."

I press my lips together. "No. But he did kiss me over the weekend, and we had this, uh…phone thing the other night."

"Ahh!" she squeals, and she holds up her hand for a high five. "He's *so* into you, Cassie. I knew he would be."

I giggle at her antics even through the little bit of guilt that pings in my chest. "He met the kids," I admit.

Her eyes widen. "Whoa. That's big."

"Not as my boyfriend or anything." My cheeks redden further at the word I just used. He's not. We're not there yet. I don't know if we'll ever actually *be* there. I try to backtrack. "Not that he is, you know. We're just…uh, messing around or whatever. But——"

"I know you, Cassie," she says, interrupting wherever I was going with that. "And I know this isn't just messing around for you. You wouldn't jeopardize your entire career for messing around."

Is that what I'm doing? Jeopardizing my career?

Yes, it absolutely is. If Dr. Hayward found out I was sleeping with this VIP patient, he'd fire me on the spot. And he'd have every right to. It's not just part of the code of conduct and ethics of a medical professional, but it's part of the contract I signed when I started working at Motion Orthopedics.

It feels like I haven't known him long enough to put all my goals on the line this way, yet I am. There's something there between us that I can't ignore. Something I don't *want* to ignore.

I blow out a breath. "Yeah. I don't really know what it is yet, I guess. Anyway, Lily has been having some separation issues, and she cried for my parents the entire time I was at his place on Saturday, so I brought them with me on Sunday. It was innocent, but good Lord, you should've seen him with them. They loved him, and he was so…" I trail off and shrug. "Just amazing with them. He watched Luca every time he did a flip into the water, and he helped Lily get her head down and swim and——"

"And you are one smitten kitten," she finishes for me.

I lift a shoulder. "Yeah. I am."

She smiles, and then another parent joins us, so that ends our conversation about that. But she put into words something I hadn't really allowed myself to consider, and now I'm not sure I'll be able to stop thinking about it.

Am I jeopardizing my future by being with him? How are we *really* going to keep this a secret?

I'm not sure, but the text I get from him later in the evening after I get Luca to bed pulls me right back in.

Tanner: *Since your kids will be at their dad's this weekend, spend the weekend with me.*

I have all the reasons in the world for why we shouldn't. Why it's a bad idea. Why I can't.

And yet, my fingers type out the response anyway.

Me: *I'd love to. Your place?*

Tanner: *Yes since Miller will be out of town and I plan to spend the weekend naked.*

Me: *Mr. Banks!*

Tanner: *Would you prefer I sugarcoat it? I don't need my bro cockblocking.*

I giggle as I read his text.

Me: *Not to worry. No cocks shall be blocked.*

Tanner: *When do the kids go to their dad's house?*

Me: *He picks them up on Friday from school, and they return home to me Monday after school.*

Tanner: *Does that mean seventy-two entire hours with you?*

Me: *Seventy-eight, if we're being technical.*

I stare at our text conversation as excitement fills me.

It's strange going into the office the next morning instead of starting my day at Tanner's house, but it'll be nice to see everyone.

The only problem is that my sentiment doesn't appear to be mutual.

I get in early so I can attend the weekly meeting with the other physical therapists in the conference room. Neither receptionist looks up to my cheerful, "Good morning!"

They both mumble some response, and I chalk it up to them being busy.

When I walk into the conference room, the meeting hasn't started quite yet, but everyone is already gathered. A hush falls over the room as I walk in and take a seat, and it feels like everyone is looking at me.

Do they know? Did they somehow find out that I'm planning to spend the weekend with my patient? Do they know I kissed a patient? Had phone sex with him? Crossed all the lines of what's appropriate?

It feels like they do.

Deep down, a thought claws at me that maybe they're just jealous that Dr. Hayward chose *me* to work with him instead of *them*. He had a good reason with my background in sports medicine, and these are professionals who should understand that.

But the truth is, having me go to his house every day and clearing my patient schedule only gave a bigger workload to some of the people in this room. Dr. Hayward didn't hire me thinking I'd only have one patient, and surely that's what this is about.

Still, I don't like feeling like I'm not a part of this team, and that's exactly how I feel as the rest of the PTs leave and Dr. Barlow joins just Dr. Hayward and myself to discuss Tanner's progress.

I give them the latest rundown of his progress and the different exercises we've been focusing on, and they agree that we can start to add in more strength training, which means we'll be spending more time in his home gym and less time in his family room. We detail a comprehensive plan, and I find that while I didn't love being in the meeting with the other physical therapists, I do enjoy this part of my job—creating a plan with the doctors and moving forward on Tanner's progress.

Melissa, one of the receptionists, interrupts our meeting to let us know that Tanner is in exam room four, and all three of us head that way.

I can't look him in the eyes as the doctors both take a look at his knee, and they're both happy with the way the swelling has gone down.

"We'll keep our initial date for surgery, but keep progressing like this, and your rehab afterward will be a breeze. I'd like to see you back in here again next Tuesday," Dr. Barlow tells him at the end of the exam, and I glance up to see him grin.

God, that smile. Those lips.

I sigh, and Dr. Hayward glances over at me after Dr. Barlow heads out.

"Coach texted me last night asking when I can return to the training facility," Tanner says.

Dr. Hayward glances at me. "It's fine for you to go to practices and team meetings, but under no circumstances should you participate."

Tanner nods. "What about strength training?"

"I'd need Cassandra there with you or in close contact with your trainer so we can ensure you're sticking to the plan. Just to be certain, is this arrangement still working out for the two of you?" he asks.

Tanner nods. "Obviously, given what you just said about my progress, I would prefer to keep working with Cassie."

Dr. Hayward glances over at me, and I swear, sometimes men are so freaking clueless. If I was having an issue with this patient, does he really think I'd bring it up in front of said patient?

"I agree," I say, and I offer a tight smile as I do my very best not to raise any eyebrows in here. I clear my throat. "It's been conducive to my schedule with my kids, and I've enjoyed helping Mr. Banks on the road to recovery."

As it turns out, nothing I possibly could've said would have raised the eyebrows any higher than they already were.

Tanner heads out, and Dr. Hayward stops me before I walk out of the room.

"A word, Cassandra."

I stop and turn back toward him as I pray that the guilt isn't in my eyes.

He sighs. "Alex said you brought the kids over to meet Mr. Banks. Is that true?"

I clear my throat. I don't even know how Alex would know that…except the kids talk to him a few times a week, and I wouldn't put it past Luca to brag about it.

The fact that my boss is also friends with my ex-husband shouldn't matter. This is my career, and I won't be intimidated by my ex.

"Mr. Banks invited them," I say quietly. "He felt bad taking me from my family on a weekend when they're with me rather than my ex-husband, so he asked me to bring them along."

"Be careful there, Cassandra. Be mindful of your professional obligations."

"Always, Dr. Hayward." I smile sweetly even though I'm positively *seething* on the inside that he would have the nerve to say that to me.

Only…he's right. I'm *not* minding my professional obligations. Instead, I'm planning an entire weekend naked with this man.

And I can't wait.

Chapter 32: Tanner Banks

When Have I Ever Not Been Careful

Clearly I need to get laid, and obviously Cassie Fields is the only woman I want to bang.

I don't get nervous about sex…usually. It sort of feels like we're building up to something here, and I'm not sure how to manage the expectations we'll both layer onto this weekend.

What if everything goes south? What if it's not like it was the first time we were together since that was two strangers and now it's two people who know each other? What if we decide we're better off not pursuing this at all?

The thought tugs at my chest, but the truth is, there's always that possibility. Only…a lot hinges on the two of us continuing to work together. Like, for example, all of my hope for a full recovery.

I can't imagine going through this with anybody else by my side…which my brother calls out after I get home from my appointment.

"Where's Cassie?" he asks from his spot at the kitchen table where he's digging into his yogurt.

"The office. She's reviewing my plan with the doctors, and she'll be by in a bit." I head into the kitchen to grab a banana.

"How are things going for you two?"

"We set some ground rules, and we're going to quietly give this a try. But, in her words, rehab before romance."

He chuckles at that. "Like you'll be able to keep it in your pants."

I narrow my eyes at him, and he holds up both hands.

"Okay, okay. I'll stop. I'm happy for you, bro. Seriously. But just be careful."

"When have I ever not been careful?" I ask.

He glances at my knee and tilts his head as if he's speaking to a child. "Do you really want me to answer that?"

I clench my jaw. "Too soon."

"I know. And it was an accident. I'm sorry. What did the doctor say?" he asks as his spoon clanks on the side of the bowl as he scoops up whatever's left in there.

"He's happy with the progress. Keep doing what I'm doing, but add in strength training. The surgeon wants to keep our date the same but says post-op should be easy."

"That's great news," he says, and he walks his empty bowl over to the sink. He rinses it out and places it in the dishwasher. We're both fairly clean people, but of the two of us, I'd peg him as the neat freak, while I'm more normal about it. "So you'll be coming back to the training facility?"

"I asked about that, and they said it's fine but not to do any drills or anything. Cass would need to either work closely with Nick or come with me if I plan to do any workouts."

"Would it be weird having her there?" he asks.

I shrug. "No. But it doesn't matter since you're all leaving for Pittsburgh soon. I'll swing by for this afternoon's meetings and a welfare check, and then two weeks from Monday is the surgery."

"You ready for it?" he asks.

"I'm ready to be back on the fucking field, that's for sure."

He walks over and claps me on the shoulder. "I'm sorry, bro. But look at the bright side. You're getting all this time with this woman you couldn't stop thinking about."

"I thought you didn't buy that it was fate stepping in." I narrow my eyes at him.

The doorbell rings, and he moves to get it as he tosses his answer over his shoulder. "I don't. But if she's helping you fight your way back, then what I believe doesn't really matter."

He's got a point.

And speak of the devil, I hear Cassie's voice after my brother greets her.

"How are you?" she asks him.

"Doing well. Keep doing whatever you're doing for Tanner. It's working."

She's blushing as she appears in the room just behind my brother. "I'm heading out to practice. See you this afternoon," he says to both of us, and we say our goodbyes as he leaves.

"It's working?" she asks as she pulls out a chair and sits across from me while I finish my banana.

"You heard the doctors. They're impressed with my progress."

She presses her lips together with a nod. "As they should be."

"I'm going to the team meetings this afternoon," I admit.

"How does that make you feel?"

I twist my lips as I avert my gaze out the window. I told Coach I'd come, but I didn't really think about how it might affect me emotionally.

"Honestly? It makes me feel like I want you there with me," I admit as I sneak a peek over at her.

Her eyes soften. "What time?"

217

"It won't work. The meetings start at three."

She twists her lips and scrunches her nose in apology. "I'm sorry. I'm happy to swing by earlier with you, provided we get our work done. Or if you'd like to use the training room there, like Dr. Hayward had mentioned."

I stand from my chair at the table and walk around to her side, and I drop a kiss down to her neck. "I rather like our private sessions here."

She leans back into me. "Mm. As do I."

The welfare check goes well, and even though it's nice to see my coaches and teammates, I hate answering the same questions over and over, so I say a few words about how my prehab is going, when the surgery is scheduled, and how I'm rooting for the team. I get emotional as I tell them I wish I was out there with them, and I stay for most of the meeting. But I duck out early so I don't have to answer questions, and I head home and crack open a beer as I sit on the couch and brood.

I wish she was here with me.

I'm not sure why that would make me feel better, but I just know it would. She brings light where it's dark, and right now, things feel pretty damn bleak.

It was a mistake going there. It was another reminder that I don't get to play this season. I thought I had come to terms with it…but it doesn't appear that I have.

The doorbell rings about the time I'm expecting Miller to arrive home, but he's not here yet. I get up, and I'm surprised to find Spencer standing on the other side of the door.

"Come on in," I say, opening the door a little wider so we're both standing in the foyer.

He glances at the beer in my hand, and then his eyes move to mine. "Are you doing okay, man?"

I nod and hold up my beer. "This is my first."

"You don't have to explain it to me." His tone is gentle, and while I appreciate him stopping by, I'm not really in the mood for sympathy. "I just didn't get a chance to talk to you at the facility, so I thought I'd stop by. Miller said you're fine, but I wanted to see for myself, I guess."

"I'm about as good as can be expected."

"You'd be better if you had a bottle of Newlywed's finest instead of that piss water you're drinking," he jokes, mentioning his wife's family vineyard.

I chuckle. "Thanks. You want to come in and stay awhile?"

He shakes his head. "I should get home. Grace is making dinner tonight, and I need to pack. Listen, if you want to come over for dinner, she's a pretty good cook."

"I appreciate the offer," I say, but honestly, dinner with newlyweds sounds taxing. "I've got dinner plans." He doesn't need to know that my plans consist of ordering something local and having it delivered, which is my plan pretty much every night.

It's gotten worse since I've been injured. It's easy to play it off like I shouldn't be navigating my kitchen, though in truth, it's probably fine for me to move around enough to make a meal.

Ordering in is easier than cooking and cleaning, though Miller scolds me for my habits all the time. If he's home, he'll cook for the two of us, but he's been spending a lot of time with the running backs as he works to build his place with the team.

I should be going out to dinner with the other quarterbacks or the wide receivers or the offensive line. Instead, I'm stuck here at home as I pine for a season that was never meant to be mine.

And truth? It sucks.

The only thing getting me through it is knowing I'll get to see Cassie…and that's why I can't wait for Friday, when we'll have seventy-eight uninterrupted hours together.

.

Chapter 33: Tanner Banks

Sex O'Clock

When she arrives at my house on Friday morning, she's carrying an overnight bag likely filled with clothes she's not going to need.

I grin at her and grab her by the waist to haul her into my house, and she laughs as she drops her bag to the floor and gives into a quick embrace.

Much too quick.

It's short-lived as she presses gently on my chest, and it has the effect of pushing me away. "Rehab before romance, remember?"

I sigh as I force myself to let go of her. "How's that going to work for you tomorrow morning when you wake up in my arms?"

She purses her lips. "We can do whatever we want until nine fifteen. Once I'm on the clock, so are you. We work until two forty-five, and then we're free to, you know…"

"Get naked?" I supply, and she laughs.

"If that's what we agree to, then sure."

"I agree." I wiggle my eyebrows, and honestly, if she wasn't here and I was missing my team's first away game, I'd likely be in a much worse emotional state than I am. So I guess I have her to thank for that. She's not just good for my physical recovery. She's good for the mental and emotional sides of it as well.

She works me hard all morning, and it feels like some odd sort of foreplay. We move into strength training my quads. Leg day was never my favorite, but she makes it fun.

My brother and I chose this house in part because of the home gym, and Miller and I set it up with equipment that we'll use even though we'd both planned to spend the majority of our time training with our teammates at the team facility.

Neither of us anticipated that one of us would be using it for rehabilitation when we bought this place.

I guess I'm glad it's here even though I wish the injury never happened in the first place.

When lunchtime comes around, she pokes around in my pantry and my fridge for something to pull together, but she comes up short.

"I'll order something," I offer.

"Let's cook dinner together tonight," she says.

I nod. "Okay. We can order groceries instead."

She chuckles, but it's exactly what we do.

We're sitting at the table with grilled chicken and fresh veggies for lunch a short while later, and the groceries come while we're eating. She gets the door and unpacks everything for our meal tonight, and when she sits back down, I study her for a few seconds.

"You know, Miller didn't believe me when I told him it was fate that brought you and me together," I say.

She looks surprised as she glances up at me. "You think it was fate?"

222

"I have this theory that people cross into our life multiple times. Sometimes we know it, other times we don't. Like, for example, what if you and I had never spoken at the bar in Vegas? What if we hadn't spent the night together? Would that have changed the course of whether or not I'd gotten hurt?"

Her brows dip as she narrows her eyes at me. "Are you saying fate caused your injury so it would bring the two of us back together?"

I shake my head. "No. I'm saying fate introduced you to me before my injury because it somehow knew that you were the only one who was going to be able to handle nursing me back to health."

Her eyes seem to get a little misty at that, but she still gives me her standard Cassie answer. "You don't think Rick could've handled you?"

"Sassy Cassie." I chuckle with an eyeroll in jest. "But really…I don't know who Rick is."

"One of the other PTs at the practice who was not so thrilled when Dr. Hayward gave the newest VIP patient to the newest therapist on staff."

"Why did he give you my case?" I ask.

"I think for a couple reasons. For one, I'm the only PT on staff with a degree and background in sports medicine. For another, I have a lot of patience, and working with a stubborn athlete is not always easy. And—"

"Excuse me? *Stubborn athlete?*" I interrupt.

She widens her eyes pointedly. "Prove me wrong."

I laugh and hold up both hands. "Touché. Did you have another reason?"

She lifts a shoulder. "I worked under him years ago, and he trusts my instincts. He saw it all come right back to me the first month I was at Motion, and that trust came right back."

"Bet he never thought you'd end up banging your patient."

She laughs. "No, likely not. Though the only time we've banged, it was prior to you being my patient."

"You won't be able to say that after approximately two forty-six this afternoon." I widen my eyes pointedly at her this time.

We finish our lunch, and it feels like the clock is barely moving as we continue my exercises.

My phone dings at two forty-five.

"Oh my God, did you set a sex alarm?" she asks with a laugh.

Instead of answering her, I stop the exercise I'm doing, turn off the sex alarm, and grab her around the waist.

"It's sex o'clock," I say, my voice low and raspy, and she laughs.

"I cannot believe you just said that."

My lips move to her neck, and she grips onto my shoulders as she tilts her neck back to give me more space. "Tell me you're ready for this," I say, and I thrust my hips to hers to make sure she knows exactly what I'm referring to.

"I'm ready," she says, her voice breathless.

"What's the best position for an ACL tear?" I ask, my lips moving along her neck to her collarbone.

"Nothing with weight or pressure on the knee," she says. "You standing behind me. You could sit in a chair and I could get on top of you. Spooning with your leg supported. Me on top." She lifts a modest shoulder as if every new suggestion doesn't pulse a painful, achy need right through me.

"I pick all of the above," I say. I shift my hips again so she can feel how hard my cock is, and my lips drop to hers as my hand moves beneath her shirt and moves up to finally, *finally* get one of those perfect tits back in my hand.

I press my lips to hers as my other hand climbs into her hair. Her mouth opens to mine as we deepen the kiss, and her hand trails down toward my thigh as she touches me over the front of my shorts. I shove my cock into her palm as she rewards me with a moan right into my mouth when she feels how fucking hard I am for her.

Of course I'm hard. I've been hard since she walked out of my hotel room in Vegas months ago, and the only one who can alleviate the need I've felt for months is her.

My tongue batters against hers, our mouths both fully open as we make out in the weight room. I massage her tit as she massages my cock over my shorts, and it feels like this weekend won't be enough.

I don't know if I'll ever get enough of this woman.

She moans as I squeeze her tit, and she responds by fisting my cock. Desperation lances through me, and as much as I want to spend the rest of the day kissing her, my body can't take another minute here on the outside.

"Fuck, Cass, I've missed you so goddamn much."

"I'm right here," she moans against me, the desperation evident in her voice, too. "Fuck me, Tanner. Fuck me now."

Instead of giving her what she asks for, I lower my hand from her tit down into her pants. I slip my finger right into her pussy, and she grinds down on my hand. She's so hot and wet for me, and my mind has only one laser focus as animal instincts take over. I need to fuck her. I need to feel that wet pussy gripping onto my cock as I slide in and out of her.

I trail my lips from her mouth to her neck. "Are you on the pill?"

She nods her answer.

"Is it okay if I don't use a condom?" I ask as I move my hand out of her pants.

"Yes," she whispers, her voice a plea for me to do exactly what I'm saying.

"Take off your pants," I demand, and she strips right out of them as I pull my cock out. It's hard and heavy against my palm as I slowly stroke myself, a little come leaking out the top in anticipation of what's about to happen.

I pull her shirt over her head and toss her bra to the floor, and she's standing naked in my workout room. I glance around for the best place to do this, and I spot the back of a chair. "Bend over the chair," I say, and she nods as she walks over to it. "Jesus, you're gorgeous," I say, admiring the view of this naked woman as she bends over and waits patiently for me.

I decide to play a little first. I run my hand along the curve of her hip and down her ass. I reach forward and slide my fingers back into her, and as much as I want to kneel down to the floor and suck her cunt until she screams, I know I can't. She'd stop me from getting down on my knee anyway. This stupid fucking injury might stop me from playing football, but it's not going to stop me from having sex.

She moans as her hips sway to the motion of my fingers, and I'm transported back to the last time I had sex.

I push two fingers in all the way to my knuckles, and her moans turn louder. I twist my wrist as I pull back only to thrust in again, priming her for my cock that's so hard and ready for her. I reach around her with my other hand, her hard nipples brushing my fingertips before I take one in between my forefinger and my thumb, and she yells out.

"Oh, God, Tanner!"

"What do you want, Cass?" I murmur close to her ear.

"Mm," she moans. "You. I just want you." Her voice is nearly a cry, and I can't wait a second longer.

I move my hands from her body as I position myself behind her, and I line my cock up with her slit. I swipe through her once, the heat and her scent nearly overwhelming, and then I slide into her.

We both grunt at my entrance, and it's like I'm fucking home again.

"Fuck, I missed you," I mutter as her cunt sucks me in and grips onto me so warmly, so tightly.

"I missed you too," she cries, the end turning into a moan as she bucks backward into me as if she wants me deeper inside of her.

I grip onto her hips so I can control the speed and depth as I start to move. I bear as much of my weight as I can on my right leg so as not to anger the left, and I rock into her over and over again. She meets me in the middle, pushing back against me as the need to come starts to tear through me.

I push in as deeply as I can, and I reach around her to grasp one of those perfect tits in my hand. She bucks against me as I hold onto her tit, her sweet moans fucking music to my ears, urging me to keep stroking into her as deeply as I can.

I reach around with my other hand to touch her clit. "Tell me how it feels," I murmur close to her ear.

"It's good, Tanner. So good."

"Do you like when I fuck this tight pussy?" I grunt.

"I fucking love it," she curses, and Jesus, the words push me to fuck her even harder. I'm pummeling into her when she yells, "Oh God, Tanner! Don't stop! I'm about to come!"

I don't dare slow my pace even though I'm about to come, too. My abdomen tightens as fire rips up my spine, and I can't stop the freight train as pleasure takes over and my body gives into it.

"Fuck!" I roar, and she screams out at the same time as come streams out of me and into her, jet after hot jet. We're in complete unison as her pussy grips more tightly onto me, milking every last drop out of me as I give all of my pleasure over to her, and she gives me hers in return.

It's both beautiful and sexy, and it bonds us even more closely as that feeling of falling turns into something else entirely…something it's too soon for, something inexplicable. Something completely outside of my character and my history.

Something that could only be the other half I didn't know I was searching for.

It's her. She does this to me, and it doesn't matter if it was two weeks or two years. I'm in a place I never thought I'd find myself with a person I didn't think I was ever supposed to know beyond one intimate night.

Warmth hums through my entire body, and I'm not sure I've ever felt closer to another human being before. We shared that one night in Vegas, and it was incredible, but we both knew what the expectation was. It was just supposed to be one night. It was what it was.

This is different, though.

She'll still be here in the morning when we wake. And the next morning, too. And then she'll have to leave, but she'll be back, and we're just at the precipice of whatever this could turn into.

And as we sit in the quiet eroticism of a brutal orgasm before either of us moves, it feels like it could turn into forever.

When both of our shudders start to slow, I reluctantly pull out. I reach down to feel the heat of my come as it spills out of her, and I massage her pussy gently for a few hot seconds before I grab her clothes from the floor and set them on the chair she was just leaning over.

She lets out a long, low sigh as she straightens, and I glance over at her as I pull my shorts back into place.

"Don't get dressed on my account. I'm all for naked Fridays," I say.

She laughs as she rolls her eyes, and I have a feeling we're just at the start of the kind of weekend that I'll keep on repeat in my mind until we get to have another one.

Chapter 34: Cassie Fields

Morning Swim

I laugh at something in the movie he put on for us after the sex before we start dinner, and I feel him gazing at me, so I glance over at him.

"What?" I ask.

He shrugs. "Nothing. Just…I like the sound of your laugh. We've spent so much time being serious, and…I don't know. It's been a rough year between finding out about my family, then the blockbuster trade followed by the ACL tear. I don't even know who I am half the time anymore, but you make it easier. I guess I'm just used to everything in life being so serious all the time. You make me want to lighten up a little."

My chest warms at that. It was a sticking point between Alex and me, I think. I lost count of how many times I told him to lighten up, and it was always as if even love wasn't enough for him to listen.

But maybe he never really loved me. How could he when he was cheating on me?

I still have no idea how long that was going on for, but I imagine it was longer than I ever would've thought.

My phone starts to ring, and I pull it out of my pocket to see Lily is FaceTiming me.

"Give me a sec, okay?" I tell Tanner, and he nods as if he gets it—he shouldn't be in this video. I pick up the call, and I say, "Hi, Lilypad!"

"Mama! We got ice cream!" She holds up her cone, and I laugh for her even though my chest tightens inside.

The cone is both large and candy-coated, which means Alex is trying to do things that please the kids. I hope that's what it is even though it feels very much like he's trying to be the fun dad he didn't bother being when he had me as a safety net.

"Wait, are you at Tanner's?" she asks.

My eyes widen as I stare at my child. I can't lie to her, but I also don't want her dad to know where I am since presumably he's within earshot. I clear my throat.

"That's Tanner's couch. I remember." She says it so resolutely that I know I'll never be able to tell her it's not.

"Yeah, he needed a little extra work today, so we're just finishing up. I better get back to him, but you enjoy that ice cream!" I tell her. We exchange I love yous before we end the call.

"Extra work, huh?" Tanner teases as he elbows me a little.

"Their dad *never* let them get ice cream when we were married. The only time we got it was when he was working late and I decided to treat them," I say, clenching my jaw.

"I'm sorry. That's shitty. But on the bright side, the kids get ice cream, and he'll have to deal with the sugar high."

I giggle as I try to imagine the very impatient Alex dealing with one of Lily's epic tantrums, and I guess karma will come for him if he had any sort of ill intentions when it comes to giving treats to the kids.

We make dinner together, we eat out on the deck overlooking the city with the ocean in the distance, and we make love—this time with me on top as he drives me to yet another orgasm that feels like it was even stronger than the last one.

It's really the perfect evening, and it feels like our weekend is just getting started.

He wakes up before six and has breakfast ready for me when I saunter down from his bedroom shortly after he does, and we enjoy yogurt and granola before we'll have to get started on today's therapy sessions.

"Morning swim?" he asks me, and the gleam in his eye tells me exactly what sort of swim this is going to be.

"I'd love to," I say since I haven't showered yet, and he heads outside, strips naked, and lowers himself into the pool.

I laugh as I watch him, and then I decide to step out of my comfort zone and do the exact same thing.

After all, my swimsuit is all the way upstairs in my overnight bag, and I'm pretty sure his plan is just to get me out of it anyway.

His patio might be up on a hill, but it's definitely private. I dive into the water and send up a big splash, and when I come up from the water, he's grinning at me. As I come up out of the water, I hope I look like some sort of mythical sea creature. I'm sure I at least got the *creature* part right.

Regardless, this is *definitely* the way to wake up on a Saturday morning. It's just easier this way since we're both going to end up naked anyway.

It only gets better from there.

Tanner swims over to me and grabs me into his arms. He hugs me to his chest, and I wrap my arms around his neck and my legs around his waist as I angle my head down to catch his lips with mine. He hugs me close, and it's perfect here in his arms.

He grabs onto the back of my head and deepens our kiss. This connection we've formed is freaking addictive.

He reaches beneath us and shifts me down a little at the same time as he slides his cock into me. I hold on tight for the ride as he bounces me up and down, the water only helping our movements as it rushes around us.

He continues to kiss me, our mouths pure magic together as our bodies find a quick rhythm. He breaks from our kiss to lean his head into the crook of my neck as he groans.

"Goddamn, you feel so fucking good." His lips are against my neck as he continues to angle into me in his pool, and all I can do is simply hold on and enjoy the ride. "Oh fuck, fuck, fuck," he groans, and I feel him starting to tighten beneath me, which sends my own body into a frenzy.

"Oh God, Tanner, yes," I moan into his ear as I squeeze my arms around his neck, and my body starts to convulse all around him.

He groans as he shoves into me, and I'm not sure I'll be able to look at this pool again without thinking of the way he is giving me so much pleasure in this beautiful moment.

He continues to pump into me well after both of us have climaxed. In the past with Alex, he'd pull out, roll over, and go to sleep regardless of whether I got mine. But with Tanner, I feel like I never want him to let go. I'm ready to go again.

It's like I'm insatiable. That's never happened to me before because I've never been with someone who knew my body so well.

He is still inside me as his lips move back to mine, and he kisses me slowly, sensually, his tongue firm and confident against mine as he gives no indication that he's trying to rush through this moment.

He drops his lips from mine and moves them toward my ear to whisper, "I'm still so fucking hard for you, Cass."

He continues to pump into me with those words. I lean my head back, the sun warm on my skin as he fucks me slowly right here in his pool.

"Oh God," I moan. "Don't ever stop." He leans forward to suck one of my tits into his mouth, and I arch my back to give him easier access as I keep bouncing up and down his inexplicably still hard cock.

I don't know if it's the water or what's going on, but as he continues to move inside of me, my body starts to unravel again for him.

I claw at his back as I fight my way through the second climax of the morning, this one more brutal than the first.

"Goddamn, you're so fucking gorgeous when you come," he murmurs as his eyes study me. "I want to make you come over and over just so I can watch it."

My heavily lidded eyes fall onto him. "I'm not going to fight you on that one."

His lips lift into a small smile before he shifts me up and pulls out of me.

I groan with obvious dissatisfaction that he left, but I know we have to get moving since time is running short this morning.

"We have half an hour until we need to get started," he tells me.

He gets out of the water first and grabs a couple towels. He hands me one to dry off before we head inside, and I take a quick shower. I meet him in the family room before our work session begins, and he kisses me one last time before nine fifteen hits.

And then we both get down to business, as if a switch flips for both of us at the time we typically get started together. We work hard on exercises and stretches until lunch. We take a quick lunch break, and then we head back in until two forty-five, and as soon as our session ends, it's a repeat of last night.

Snuggling on the couch to a movie. Laughing together as we munch on popcorn. Making dinner together. A glass of wine for me, a glass of tequila for him.

Sex.

So much sex.

Moaning and climaxing, coming and kissing.

Laughing and talking.

I've never felt closer to a man in my life. It's as if he anticipates everything I need without me needing to say a single thing, whether it's something to eat or the way he touches me or asking about the kids just when I'm missing them.

It's pretty much the perfect weekend. The only downside is that it has to end. We have to snap back to reality, and reality sort of begins as we wind down our session on Sunday afternoon.

The San Diego Storm is playing the Sunday night game, and I can sense the shift in his mood as we get closer to game time.

"Do you want to talk about it?" I ask quietly, and he twists his lips.

"I should be out there, you know?" he says.

I nod and press my lips together. "You should be. But you're here with me instead, and we're going to get you healthy. You'll go back stronger than before, Tanner."

His eyes shift to the ground as he nods sullenly, and we watch the game together snuggled under his covers in bed.

He talks me through the plays and teaches me about the game, and I listen with rapt attention to the passion in his voice as he shares pieces of himself with me—the same way I've been sharing pieces of my own passion as I help him heal.

If we need to look for something good in all this, it's that it's giving us a chance to blossom and grow.

We just have to be careful about making sure nobody finds out about us.

Chapter 35: Cassie Fields

That Continues to be Unethical

We've just finished homework on Monday after school, and I'm about to get dinner started when my phone starts to ring.

I glance at the screen to see it's my ex-husband calling.

As much as I hate dropping the kids at school on a Friday and not getting to see them again until Monday after school, the major benefit—and the entire reason we set that up as our custody plan—is that I don't have to see or speak to Alex.

At first it was because it was honestly harder on the kids to have to leave one of us and go to the other one. Getting picked up from school is a different feeling than being separated. But now I see the additional benefits.

"Hello," I answer curtly. I assume he's calling about something regarding the kids since they are really the only reason I need to ever communicate with him at all, but my assumption is wrong.

"Luca couldn't stop talking about how you took them to some football player's house," he says.

I sigh. I was never really trying to keep it a secret, but I also wasn't expecting to be confronted about it by Alex. "So?"

"Why are you introducing the kids to a patient?"

"It wasn't like that. It was my weekend with the kids, and I'm doing house calls for a VIP, and not that it's any of your business, but the patient felt bad he was taking me away from the kids, so he invited them. That's all."

"I don't want them around your patients."

I bite my tongue at the thought that runs through my head. *Well, I didn't want you fucking some other woman when you were married to me.*

"Okay," I say instead. "I just brought them to my new friend's house, then."

"You're making friends with your patients now? I know you've been out of the field a while now, but that continues to be unethical," he says dryly.

Oh, if he only knew how unethical we were in his pool yesterday morning.

"Thank you for the opinion I didn't request. Is there anything else?"

"Lily left her stuffed avocado here."

"Shit," I mutter. "Can you drop it by?"

"I'm at the hospital until seven, and then I have dinner plans," he says. "But I could swing it by in between." The way he says it sounds like he's doing me a huge favor, and I roll my eyes.

"I would appreciate that," I say, and I just get the feeling that I'm going to pay for this.

I really need to talk to Lily about being more careful not to leave anything over there.

The doorbell rings at seven fifteen, and Lily is already out of the tub and in her pajamas. I'm thankful Alex actually remembered, but one thing I know about him is that even though he was willing to destroy his family, he loves his kids.

"Lil?" I call since she's in her bedroom playing. "Door's for you!" I make my way to answer it, and there stands Alex.

He's leaning on the door, perhaps in some attempt to come off as a bad boy, but he just looks like a cliché. "I miss you, Cassie," he says quietly, as if he knows the kids are going to appear any second.

This time, I have zero qualms about whether or not to hold my tongue. I hear Lily's footsteps coming down the hall, but she's still far enough away that she's out of earshot to my hissing voice. "Is that what you were thinking when you were with Sydney?"

He flinches at my words, but he can't defend himself because his daughter appears at my side.

"Daddy!" she says as her eyes light up.

"You left Guac at my house," he says, holding up the stuffed avocado.

She snatches it out of his hands. "Guacky!" she squeals, and she hugs it tightly to her chest. "Thank you, Daddy!" she says before she runs back down the hall presumably to add Guacky to her play rotation.

"Thanks for dropping it by," I say.

"For what it's worth, I'm sorry." He looks into the house a bit forlornly, as if he misses living here with the three of us. And I get that. We had a sweet little family dynamic, and he chose himself over it time and time again.

Was it nice having his extra hands around? Yes, sure. You know, when I wasn't doing all the same things but also taking care of a grown man who was out late at work most nights. Or out late screwing other women. Po-ta-to, po-tah-to.

But that's sort of the whole thing. He misses me…but I don't miss him.

Especially not after this weekend. Especially not after having the smallest taste of what else is out there. I know now that I always deserved more than Alex ever gave me, and even if things don't pan out with Tanner, at least I have that knowledge to hold onto.

The next morning, I head to the office to meet with Dr. Hayward and Dr. Barlow as they examine Tanner's progress over the last week. I arrive as early as I can after getting the kids off to school so I can sit in on the team meeting again, and once again, I'm met with a bunch of cold shoulders.

I'm starting not to like it here very much, but does it really matter when I'm hardly ever here? I can deal with the dirty looks once a week.

Except…my patient's surgery is in thirteen days. He'll have a lot of recovery and months of rehabilitation afterward, but once he's healthy again, he won't need me making house calls anymore.

And then what?

I'll be back here in this office getting dirty looks from Rick, Melissa, Jordan, and Brett. I'll always be looked at as Hayward's favorite physical therapist, the one he'll give the VIP patients to. I'll stand little to no chance of actually fitting in here—just when I was starting to.

And now I'm spending the weekends I do have free with Tanner, which means I'm isolating myself from my friends, too. I only see the girls at bus pickup, and I'm usually screeching my tires up to the curb to get there on time, which decidedly inhibits our former gossip time.

I'm still adjusting to my life post-divorce. It's a lot to be literally *everything* to the kids for eleven days out of every fourteen, and just like Tanner said he's struggling with his identity lately, I'm realizing that I'm having the same sort of crisis.

I'm a mom when I'm with my kids.

I'm a physical therapist when I'm with Tanner, but in the hours we're not working…I'm becoming someone I've never known before.

And now I need to know…exactly who is Cassie Fields?

I left Cassie Sinclair behind in the divorce, and I only have myself to rely on now. But Tanner makes me feel like I don't have to bear all the weight alone. Rather than stressing about all the changes or feeling guilt or shame in them, I feel like I have someone who is starting to know the sides of myself that even I don't know.

And I love that feeling. I want to feel more of it. I want more of Tanner.

"Cassandra?" Dr. Hayward says, and I snap back to attention.

"I'm sorry. What?"

"Can you talk to us about the different quad exercises you've been working on with Tanner?"

"Right. Uh…sorry." I clear my throat as I try to make myself present here in the meeting. It is, after all, the entire reason I'm here. "We have a whole program we run through every day that starts with hamstring curls, leg raises, and mini squats. We've added in additional training at this point to keep his core and upper body strong."

"Rick, you also have an ACL patient, is that right?" Dr. Hayward asks.

Rick nods. "We've been doing a lot of the same, which begs the question how the newest member of the therapy team is the one most qualified to work with an NFL quarterback."

Dr. Hayward turns to him with surprise. "I'll thank you not to question my decisions, Rick. Not that I need to defend myself, but I was planning to handle this patient myself until he requested in-home care, which wouldn't have worked with the additional patients in my care. Cassandra has a background in sports medicine and performed her clinicals in that industry, so she was the next natural choice. Given the fact that she was so new and was just starting to establish her patient care, choosing her was both the best for the patient and the least intrusive to the rest of the staff. Did you have any other questions?" He's incredibly sarcastic as he asks that final question, and Rick remains silent for the rest of the meeting.

But one thing is clear.

He's not happy I got the patient he wanted, and I don't know him very well, but I wouldn't put it past him to figure out a way to sneak in and blow everything up for me.

Chapter 36: Tanner Banks

Because of You

In a million years, I never thought I'd be excited for a physical therapist to arrive at my house to guide me through ACL surgery, yet here we are.

The doctors examined me and determined Cassie and I should keep doing what we're doing. Now that we're less than two weeks until the surgery, I plan to spend my daytime hours with her and my evening hours going to the training facility to be with my teammates.

It was a fairly rough road to get here mentally over the weeks that have passed since the injury, but what I told Cassie was true. She makes things lighter, and everywhere I go, I'll arrive equipped with that light.

I'm concerned I'm banking all my hopes of recovery on her, but the only reason I have that hope is because of her. I want to work harder when she's around. I want to get better faster.

Miller is here with us on Tuesday, though he's mostly staying in his own room, probably playing video games or jerking off.

I pull her into me for a quick hug when she arrives, and she stiffens a little. Concern immediately darts through me.

"What's wrong?" I ask cautiously.

She clears her throat as her eyes move away from me, and that concern flips to something a little darker.

"Cass, what's going on?"

"First Alex told me he didn't like the kids coming over to a patient's house with me, and then he told me he misses me. But that's not even the worst thing." She sticks her tongue over her top teeth as if she's warding off tears before she sucks in a breath. "One of the other PTs called me out in the middle of a meeting before you got in today. He asked Dr. Hayward why I got to be your therapist when I'm the newest member of the staff. And it hurt to be called out like that in front of everyone. He made it seem like I'm not good enough."

"Oh, Cass," I say softly, and I pull her back into my arms and press a kiss to the top of her head. "If it makes you feel any better, just before you got here, I was thinking about my recovery and how I'm working so goddamn hard because of you. I want to be better because of you, and I don't just mean my knee."

She pulls back to look up at me, and her eyes are misty.

"I have hope because of you. I'm lighter because of you. Theoretically, this should be the absolute worst time in my life between all the shit that I keep getting clobbered with, but it's not. Because of you."

She moves up to her tiptoes and presses her lips to mine.

I give in for a few beats before I rest my forehead to hers and draw in a fortifying breath. "So if anyone makes you feel not good enough, I just want you to know that you are *more* than good enough. You are everything, and the only reason I'm progressing the way I am is because you're here to guide me through it."

More words almost slip out. *I love you.*

But my fear stops me.

There's only one other woman I've ever said that to, and she broke my heart. I don't know if this is love or something else, but I've never felt so close to a woman before, and certainly not in such a short amount of time.

And it's not just that. She's a package deal. She has kids, a history, and an ex-husband. She's been married before. She's seven years older than me and just starting over.

Speaking of her kids…I don't know if I'm in a place where I'm ready for that sort of life. I enjoyed one Sunday afternoon with them, but that doesn't mean I'm ready to commit to a woman with two kids. I don't even know if I *want* kids. I haven't known the truth about Eddie Nash and Charles Banks long enough to know if I want a family of my own.

But I have time to figure it out.

Does Cassie? She's thirty-six. Does she want more kids? And if I want them with her—a question that *should* be really, really far into the future—how much time does she have left to have them?

On top of all that, this is her entire career we're talking about. She's just getting back into the swing of things, and she's already running into trouble at her office. Because of me. Because I demanded home care and never thought in a million years that Dr. Hayward would assign *her* to me. But he did, and now we're in this precarious position where I'm beyond the falling phase but too goddamn scared to admit that to her.

And besides all that, I don't even know what this is for her. Is she just recklessly enjoying her freedom? Is she doing everything she can to help a patient? Is she living it up after being tied to her ex for half her life?

She presses her lips together, and then she backs away from me as she swipes at a tear that splashed down onto her cheek. "Great, now you made me cry," she says with a laugh.

I thumb away her tears. "Sorry, but it's the truth."

She presses her lips together. "Thank you, Tanner," she says softly.

I lean in and press a gentle kiss to her cheek, and while I'm there, I murmur, "And for the record, that slimy ex-husband of yours can fuck all the way off."

"And take a left and keep fucking off some more," she agrees.

I laugh, and then I pull her in, shut the door behind her, and head to the training room so we can get to work on today's exercises.

Chapter 37: Cassie Fields

Banks Ten

Things are relatively quiet over the next week, and I have the kids over the weekend again. Out of respect for Alex's wishes—and to avoid further complications—I have my parents watch them on Saturday and Sunday, though I'm debating telling Tanner I can't work the weekends when I have the kids.

Not because I don't want to.

But because I've been working every day nonstop, and even though it doesn't *feel* like work because I get to spend time with Tanner, it is. And I can't give up every weekend with my kids and also not bring them along with me. It just isn't sustainable for the next eight months or so.

Each day that carries us closer to his surgery, he falls a little quieter. He's starting to turn inward, though I do my very best to pull him out of it.

His surgery is on a Monday, and the weekend before it, Alex has the kids. I'm glad I'll get to spend the time ahead of the surgery with Tanner both for the final moments of prehabilitation and the moments where I can be there for his mental state.

And, you know…the sex.

He throws me for a loop on Saturday evening, though.

Miller is at the team hotel since it's a home game, and we're lying together in bed after another incredible climax when he says, "I think I want to go to the game tomorrow."

My brows shoot up. "You do?"

He nods. "It's the last game before the surgery, and I want to be on the sidelines. I have no idea what state I'll be in after the surgery or how long it'll take me to feel ready to be out there, and I don't want to miss out."

I nod. "Then you should do it. I'm sure the team would love to have you there."

"Yeah," he murmurs. "Coach invited me to wear a headset and help with play calling, and I think it's important for me to engage with the team when I can."

"Why haven't you?" I ask.

He lifts a shoulder. "The thought of stepping back onto the field was a little intimidating, but I think I'm ready."

I lean over and kiss his shoulder. "I think you are, too."

He presses his lips into a tight smile, and he angles his head down to kiss me.

He holds me in his arms as we sleep, and I wish we had more than just every other weekend to do this—to fall asleep beside one another and wake up in the same bed, to share breakfast together, and to steal sweet kisses.

In the morning, I start packing my bag to head home for the day when he stops me. "What are you doing?"

"I figured I'd head home for the day while you go to the game."

His brows dip together. "Oh, no." He shakes his head. "Sorry. Did I not make this clear? I'm going to need you on the sidelines with me. I need you to ensure I'm not moving around too much or doing anything overly strenuous."

I hold a hand to my chest. "Me? You want *me* on the sidelines with you?"

He nods as if it's a silly question.

"What about Nick? What about…am I even allowed on the field?" I stutter.

"If I say I need my personal medical staff, the team will have to deal with it." He pulls me against his body. "Stop packing and change into a Storm shirt."

"Tanner, this is crazy!" I protest.

"What is?"

"Well, for one, I don't have a Storm shirt."

He chuckles. "Good thing I've got you covered then." He heads to his closet and returns with a soft T-shirt that features his last name and his number.

"Banks Ten?" I read from the back of the shirt.

"Banks Ten," he confirms. He leans in a little closer. "Better be the only Storm number I ever see you wear."

I laugh. "That's pretty much a given."

He drives since he doesn't need his left knee for that activity, and he has all the correct credentials to get us onto the field on game day. I find myself walking down the sideline where the coaches are already gathered together, the natural grass on the field crunching beneath my feet as I look around from this vantage point.

It's incredible.

It feels like I'm a part of the team as I trail behind Tanner and look up into the grandstands. People are trickling in already to watch warm-ups before the game, and I feel like over the last few weeks, I've learned a lot about the game.

Surely I'll learn even more at this up-close-and-personal lesson, and still more once Tanner is back on the field because I will not miss an opportunity to watch him play now that I have intimate knowledge of him…and now that I know who he is.

247

He walks up to the coaches, who all embrace him. They ask him questions about his knee, and he introduces me. They ask *me* questions about his knee, too, and he tells them he's ready for his surgery tomorrow.

The stands continue to fill, and the team heads back into the locker room to prepare for the game. Tanner goes with them, but I stay here on the sidelines as I check in with the medical staff. Nick, the trainer who was with Tanner at his first appointment at the office, remembers me, and we chat for a bit about Tanner's progress.

Tanner comes back out with the coaching staff, and I'm still standing toward the back of the group as he slips an earpiece in on one side. He glances at me as if to make sure I'm okay, and when he sees I'm fine, he turns his attention to the offensive coordinator.

I observe the other players and the game, and I glance over at Tanner every few moments to ensure he's not doing anything that could possibly jeopardize tomorrow's surgery.

I take a moment to really study him when the third quarter starts.

He's in his element there on the sidelines. Black training pants, a gray Storm sweatshirt, a hat with the Storm logo on it…damn. That man is *fine* as hell.

And there's this connection between us that's absolutely insane.

Sometimes a little thought nags at the back of my mind. Is he only into me because I'm helping him get better? Will he drop me the moment he's cleared to return to the game?

I remind myself that he slept with me long before he was injured—long before he knew I was a physical therapist. He had an interest in me way back then, and I believe in us. I believe what we have has legs, that we can make it the distance.

There's just something special about our chemistry and our connection. So special, in fact, that I get a call about it after the game.

We're just finishing dinner when my phone starts to ring, and when I see it's Alex, I answer it as fear pulses in my chest that something is wrong with one of my children.

"Hey, everything okay?" I answer.

"You went to the game today?" he demands.

"Excuse me?" It's all I can think to say.

"What were you doing on the sidelines of the San Diego Storm game?"

"How is that any of your business?" I ask.

"Well, when the kids start asking, I guess it sort of becomes my business," he says.

"They know I'm working with Tanner." I refuse to feed more into it, and at the same time, I really don't want to lie because there *is* more going on than I'm admitting to.

"The way you two were looking at each other, it looked like a hell of a lot more than that. The announcers saw it, too."

"The announcers?" I echo. Silence pulses between us. "What did the announcers say?"

"They wanted to know who the woman on the sidelines wearing number ten was. They talked about how they saw you walk out with Tanner."

I blow out a breath. "That sounds innocent enough."

"It was the way they said it, Cassandra," he says, and I hear the accusation very clearly in his tone.

"Well, they're announcers. Did you need something?" I ask. "I'm eating dinner."

"Where? With *him*?"

"I'm not dignifying that with a response. Tell the kids to call me before bed." It's a mistake since they'll call me with video chat and see I'm at Tanner's house, but I want to see the kids. I feel like I have a pretty damn good excuse for being here considering Tanner's surgery is in the morning, and I'm allowed to be with my patient before he goes in.

I hang up and blow out a breath of frustration.

"You okay?" Tanner asks carefully.

"Yeah. My ex said he saw me on the sidelines, and the announcers made some comment about you and me walking out together."

"Oh. I hadn't really considered that," he says.

Truthfully, I hadn't, either. It's only a silly rumor that has no weight to it anyway.

But it's one more spark to add fuel to Rick's fire. One more reason for Alex to look deeper. One more justification for Dr. Hayward to remove me from working with this particular patient.

And it's the last thing we need to be worrying about the night before Tanner goes in for his surgery.

Chapter 38: Cassie Fields

Nervous Cleaning

I glance at my watch. He should be coming out of surgery any minute, and he'll be in recovery a while as he comes out of general anesthesia.

And then the real work begins. I expect he'll be in a good bit of pain the first few days following the surgery, but knowing him how I do, I have a pretty good feeling he'll fight his way back. There doesn't seem to be anything he wants more than to return to the field, and he's come a long way since the injury a mere four weeks ago.

Since it's not standard practice for a physical therapist to be at the hospital during a patient's surgical procedure, I'm at home today. Dr. Hayward gave me the day off since he knows I haven't had one since Tanner was injured.

I almost wish I didn't have the day off. It's too quiet here with the kids at school, and I can't seem to focus.

And so I'm cleaning.

I already vacuumed and mopped the whole house, and now I'm going through Lily's bedroom for clothes that no longer fit and toys that no longer get played with. I'll do Luca's room next.

I think about checking in with Miller for an update, but I know he'll text me when he knows anything.

Tanner asked him to.

I gave Tanner a kiss before his brother loaded him into the car at six this morning, and then I headed home. At least his brother is there, and that's what I keep reminding myself.

I wish I could be there.

The last few weeks have been mostly incredible as we've transitioned into this place where we now find ourselves, and he very much feels like my boyfriend. But if he actually was, then I'd be there next to Miller.

I'm not.

I'm at home.

And by the time he's out of surgery, the kids will be home.

I asked my parents if they could swing by to watch the kids for a few hours this evening so I could pop over to visit my patient, and they were happy to help. But Luca has baseball tonight, and that means my parents will have to run the kids around, and my kids can be a lot to take on.

I'm letting it go, though. I'm learning that sometimes I need to lean on the people closest to me because, as much as I pretend like I'm a one-woman show who can do it all…I know I can't.

My doorbell rings just after lunch, and Jess is standing there holding a box.

"What's in the box?" I demand, and she laughs as she flips open the lid to reveal a half dozen cookies.

I yank one with lots of chocolate chips out and take a huge bite. "Mm, these are delicious. Come on in."

"I saw your car in the driveway and knew Tanner had his surgery today. I figured you could use some cookies."

"Always. Thank you."

She looks around, and her brows dip together. "Why does it smell so...so..."

"Clean?" I supply.

"Yeah. That."

"Because I've been nervous cleaning all morning." I shrug.

"Oh, that reminds me, I have a stack of Dylan's old clothes for Luca." She walks in and sets the cookies on the counter, and she pulls one out for herself as she sits on one of the stools at the counter.

I sit beside her. "I can come get them." I say the words around the mouthful of cookie, and now that I've taken a break from my nervous cleaning, I'm nervous eating.

I shove the whole damn cookie in my mouth.

"Let's get down to the real reason I'm here. How are you holding up?" she asks.

"I'm okay." I lift a shoulder, and she knows me well enough to know I'm lying.

"How are things going with you and the QB?"

"We spent the weekend together since the kids were with Alex, and it was..."

"Full of sex?" she guesses.

"Well, I mean, *yeah*, but that's not what I was going to say."

She laughs as she closes her eyes for a second. "I could just imagine how that body—"

"Grasshoppers!" I yell, and she jolts back to reality.

She hates grasshoppers.

"Get the image of my man's naked body out of your mind," I hiss.

She laughs. "Sorry. I was picturing his twin brother."

"Right," I say dryly. "Anyway, it felt like we were really *together* this weekend. But then I'm snapped back to reality today when I don't even get to be in the waiting room as he goes through this surgery."

"Oh, Cassie," she says, and she sets her hand over mine. "I'm sure that's tough."

"His brother is going to text me updates, and I'm sure Dr. Barlow and Dr. Hayward will keep me in the loop. And I know ACL is a really common surgery, so I'm not worried...but I'm still worried. You know? And I can't *be* worried because I have to be Mom in a few hours."

"But you can collapse right now here with me, and I'll pick you up and dust you off," she offers.

I shake my head. "I wish I could, but I haven't seen the kids since Friday morning. I need to be at bus pickup."

"Can I watch them later so you can go see him?" she offers.

"I called in my parents."

"Good ol' Aunt Kim and Uncle Stu."

I nod. "My mom is bringing dinner, and my dad is bringing corny jokes and a Hawaiian shirt, most likely."

"Sounds like them." She giggles. Our moms are sisters, and we grew up the best of friends because of it. She's two years younger than me and has been my best friend since the day she was born.

"Tell me about what's been going on with you," I say, hoping for a distraction.

"My boss is throwing around the idea of making us come in a few times a month," she says. She's worked remotely for years, and every few months, her boss tosses around the idea, and there's such pushback from his employees that eventually the idea dies. "I think this time he's actually got a point, though. Our new hires have no idea what they're doing because nobody is in the office to train them." She launches into some description about her work that I'm doing my best to listen to since she's the kind of person who will pepper in questions to make sure I'm listening, and I think I do a pretty good job.

But I'm distracted.

I'm worried.

I want another cookie.

And eventually, my phone dings with a text.

Miller: *Surgery was a total success. They're waking him up now. He'll be discharged and home by six.*

Relief filters through me, and I show the phone to Jess before I type out my reply.

Me: *Thank you so much for the update. I'll be by around six if he's up for a visitor.*

Miller: *If it's you, he will be.*

My chest tightens at his words, and feeling this way all day about him is telling me something important.

This isn't just messing around to either of us. Feelings are involved. Deep feelings. The kind of feelings I wasn't sure I'd ever feel again—especially not so soon after the divorce.

But he's going to be my patient for the foreseeable future.

At some point, we're going to have to give up one or the other. Either we're together as a couple, or I'm his physical therapist. I don't see a way forward for us to have both…but I don't know if I can give up either.

Chapter 39: Tanner Banks

Not Ready to Introduce You to My Mom

When I open my eyes, she's standing in front of me.

At first I think it might just be an illusion, something left over from the grogginess of anesthesia, but she gasps when her eyes connect with mine.

The anesthesia has long worn off. Everything hurts. I just took the hydrocodone pill my brother offered me, and it hasn't kicked in yet.

But having her here is helping in a way nothing else today has. It's helping my *spirit*, which felt pretty damn smashed as they put me under earlier.

I'm reclined on the couch after my brother helped me into place, and I don't think I'll be leaving here anytime soon.

I know I'll have to. They can bring me food, but they can't use the restroom for me, and I'll need to start rehab in a few days.

But for right now, I'm not moving. "Come here," I say softly, and Cassie moves around the couch, taking a good, long look at the wrap around my knee before she sits beside me. I move my arm around her, and she leans into my chest as she tosses one arm over my stomach. I lean down and press my lips to the top of her head.

"I was thinking about you all day," she says.

"I was dreaming about you while they had me under," I joke, and she laughs as she lightly hits my chest.

"You were not."

I crane my neck to see my brother standing nearby, so I lower my voice. "I was thinking about the first time in the pool."

"I totally heard that," Miller says.

I smirk, and Cassie's cheeks flush. Honest to God, that's what I dreamt about when I was under.

It was vivid, and I can only imagine talking in my sleep while I was under anesthesia. Is that a thing? I might've made it one today.

The next few days are somehow both never-ending and a complete whirlwind at the same time.

Everyone I know calls to check on me, but much like how I felt immediately after the injury, I don't feel like talking to anyone. The pain pills make me sleepy, but if I don't take them, my knee screams in pain.

It sucks. Plain and simple. I'm back to the grumpy asshole I was when it first happened, and every single day, I have to admit that Cassie is a goddamn saint for dealing with my cranky ass.

I have Miller field my calls when he's home. I mute my phone when he's not.

Cassie reviews all my post-op reports, and Dr. Hayward continues to send her to see me even though I can't get started on rehab right away. We'll start slow and work our way up, and according to their plan, I'll be ready to go by next season.

Still, it's only mid-October right now. Organized team activities start in May, and they don't think it'll be safe for me to participate. Training camp isn't until the end of July.

That means it'll be nine entire months before I get to play football again.

Since I started, I have never gone nine months without playing.

My mom always had us in one camp or another. She was damn near obsessive about feeding our passions, and she saw from an early age that football was it for both of us.

She put us in soccer. She had us try T-ball. We even did bowling one weird summer, as if she could somehow avoid what was in our very DNA.

Not that we knew it was part of our DNA until more recently.

The fact is *she* knew.

And that's why, when the doorbell rings the Friday morning after my surgery and I check my Ring cam…I tell Cassie not to answer it.

"Who is it?" she asks.

"My mother and stepfather."

Her eyes widen. "Tanner." She purses her lips at me. "You can't make them stand there and pretend you aren't home."

"I don't want to see them," I say.

"Which is probably why they decided to drop by uninvited. She's your mom. You might be angry, but she just wants to see for herself that her boy is okay."

"I'm not ready to introduce you to my mom," I say, going for a light, joking tone, but she's already on her way to get the door, and I can't pretend like I'm not totally pissed off about that.

I listen to their introductions. "I'm Cassie, Tanner's physical therapist."

I hear my mom's voice next. "Nice to meet you, Cassie. Sandra Banks, Tanner's mother, and this is Charles, his dad."

"Stepdad!" I yell from the couch.

"Come on in," Cassie says after an awkward beat of quiet. "Tanner is due for another pain pill soon, so he may be a little grouchy."

I hear the door close behind them, and my mother appears in front of me.

Curly dark hair. Brown eyes. And Charles with his brown eyes, too—neither my brother nor I paid enough attention during biology to question whether that was usual or not.

We were more interested in PE. And, you know…girls.

"How are you feeling?" my mother asks tentatively.

"Like shit." I curse because I know she hates it.

She purses her lips, and Charles comes to sit beside me. I wish Miller was here to buffer me from this shit. I'm not in the position to deal with any of it, but I'm also not exactly in the position to run away from it. Probably why they chose this moment of all moments to show up.

"We're so sorry to see you down, but we know you, Tan-man, and we know you'll power through this obstacle and come out stronger than ever," he says.

"Is that another lie?" I ask through a clenched jaw.

"Tanner!" That's Cassie, berating me for not being positive all the time about this surgery. "You *will* come back from this stronger than ever." She hands me the hydrocodone, and I set it on the table beside me.

I don't want pain pills right now. I want to *feel* the pain because it gives me a clear target to focus on instead of this conversation with my parents.

"Look, I don't want to do this now," I say.

"We don't have to do anything, Tanner," my mom says. "We just want to be here for you. Regardless of what you're feeling about us, we are the two people who raised you and love you more than anyone in the world, and I'm not going to take a back seat while you're suffering."

I blow out a breath, and she moves in behind me and plants a kiss on the top of my head.

"I know you're a big, tough NFL star now. But no matter what, you will always, *always* be my little boy. The one who got into mischief with his brother from the day he was born. The one who snuggled in my lap before bed. The one I made peanut butter and jelly sandwiches for every day. The one who fell off his bike when he was eleven."

"The one who turned into a man with forgiveness in his heart?" I ask through a clenched jaw.

She sighs as her eyes avert to the ground. "The one who turned into a good man who's struggling with a lot right now but can always lean on his mom and dad."

"I don't even know who you are anymore," I spit. "My entire childhood feels like one big goddamn lie."

She glances over at Cassie, and I'm sure she's wondering what my physical therapist knows. I wonder what Cassie's thinking. She knows all this dirty laundry, so it's not like we're airing anything new in front of a stranger, but my mom doesn't know that.

"Watch your tone with your mother," Charles says sharply beside me.

I flinch, frankly a little surprised that he decided to pipe in. "And you…" I press my lips together and shake my head. "You pretended to be something you weren't our entire lives. What the fuck brought you two to the conclusion that we were better off not knowing? What made you think we'd never find out the truth? Would you *ever* have told us?"

"No," my mom says simply, shaking her head. "I never planned on telling you." She presses her lips together as they start to tremble, and she looks up at the ceiling as if she's warding off tears. When she speaks again, her voice trembles. "We were good parents to you and your brother, Tanner.

261

Whatever you think about us now, we did what we did to protect the two of you. We did it from a place of love."

"You did it from a place of greed," I hiss. "You accepted those checks every month to buy your silence."

"So I could provide a better life for the two of you. Charles and I didn't meet until you were two. We didn't get married until you were four. We didn't have it easy, and we agreed early on that we would use anything we got from Eddie for you. So if you ever wanted to know how we afforded the exorbitant fees of high school football and camps and college and gear...that's how."

I'm silent as I seethe. I want to believe the worst. I want to believe that they were rolling in dough because of the extra cash he sent every month, but the truth of it is that I know what she's saying is true. We never saw them struggling to make ends meet, but my mom was a schoolteacher. Charles worked in insurance. It makes sense that they didn't have a lot of extra cash each month, yet we never felt that strain. We were never told we couldn't do something because it cost too much.

They're silent, too, and I think it's because they're waiting on my reaction to that. But what is there to say? We're at an impasse. It's been just under a year since I learned the truth, and this is really the first time we've had it out like this.

I'd like to say that someday I'll understand. But I'm not sure I will.

Cassie's the one that breaks the silence. "I'm so sorry, but Tanner has some stretches he needs to do."

"Of course," my mom says, nodding. She turns to me. "Is there a good time we can come back? Maybe have dinner with you and Miller while we're in town?"

"You'd need to ask Miller that." My voice is flat.

"Tanner is free most evenings after three o'clock," Cassie says, and I shoot her a look that very plainly tells her to zip her lips. She ignores me. "You're welcome to stay now with these stretches, but he's also quite tired and could use some rest."

"Thank you," my mom says to her. She glances at me. "We'll let him do what he needs to do. I'll give Miller a call and see if we can work out a time for dinner in the next couple of days." She squeezes my foot on my good leg as Charles stands.

"Take care, son," he says, and I lean back on the couch and close my eyes in response.

"I know he's so angry," my mom says to Cassie in the hallway, as if I can't hear her from the family room. "We shouldn't have dropped by, but he's been ignoring my calls, and I didn't know what else to do."

"I understand. I'll talk to him and see if we can work out a good time for you to talk." I hear a bit of rustling, and then Cassie says, "Why don't you give me your number so I can get in touch with you?"

My mom says her number, and Cassie presumably types it into her phone. They say their goodbyes, and they leave.

Cassie walks back into the room, her arms folded across her chest.

"What?" I spit.

"Did you have to be *such* a dick to them?"

"Excuse me?" I ask, royally offended by her insinuation.

"You can't talk to your mother like that."

My brows dip together. "What business is it of yours?"

"I'm something to you, something more than your physical therapist, and I love you, so I'm going to give it to you straight."

I freeze at the words, and I'm not even totally sure she realizes what she just said.

"What?" I whisper.

It's as if she reviews the words she just spoke in her head, and then she freezes. Her eyes widen as she slaps a hand over her mouth.

"You love me?" I ask, and suddenly it's as if all the pain evaporates from my knee. It's as if I've taken ten of those pain pills, but instead of the groggy side effects, everything feels about a million times better.

She lifts her chin a little defiantly as she squares her shoulders and looks me dead in the eye, her arms still folded across her chest. "Yes. I love you, Tanner Banks."

Silence spans between us for a few long seconds before I say, "Come here."

She obeys, and she sits beside me on the couch, taking the space my dad just vacated.

I take her hand in mine, and I yank her so she falls against my chest. She turns and looks up at me. "I love you, too, Cassandra Fields." I guide her head up toward mine and press my lips to hers, and for as scary as I thought it would be to say those words, it's not actually scary at all.

It feels *right*.

It feels perfect.

She pulls back, and she stares up into my eyes before she pulls back and sits up. "I didn't mean to say it like that, but I'm glad it slipped out anyway."

"So am I," I admit.

"But we're in the middle of another important conversation, and one I want you to hear."

My brows dip.

"And it's not like I'm going to mount you and bang you to celebrate our three not-so-little words a few days after you had surgery."

I narrow my eyes at her. "Why the hell not?"

She laughs. "Because I have things to say."

"And then sex?" I ask hopefully.

"No. First of all, it's work time. Second of all..." She draws in a deep breath. "I just want to say that having kids changes you. That's all. Priorities change, and life changes, and as a mom…I get where your mom might've been coming from all those years ago, and I think about the future sometimes as a boy mom and get scared that Luca won't want anything to do with me someday. I can't imagine that world. It makes me want to cry. And your mom, she was alone, raising twin boys, and I think of my own kids and what lengths I would go to protect them. I stayed with Alex for *months* after I found out he was cheating on me because I thought I had done something wrong or somehow deserved to be in the position I was in. I thought it would be better for the kids for their parents to stay together. I thought a lot of things, I guess, but my point is that she did what she thought she had to do to protect her two boys. You had a great childhood, didn't you? You had everything you could've asked for. You had a loving home and two parents who were there for you. Isn't that all that matters?"

I'm about to say that the *truth* is all that matters, but she plows forward.

"She was all alone, and she made a decision because, at the time, she thought it was best for her children. And now she wants to be here for you when you're suffering, and you aren't letting her. But the truth is maybe you'd heal even faster if you could find it in your heart to forgive them for the lie so you can focus fully on your recovery and your future rather than on your grudge."

As much as I'm not ready to admit it…I think she might be right.

And truly, I think only the words from someone I love as deeply as I've grown to love her could be enough to make me see that.

Chapter 40: Cassie Fields

I'll Tell Them You're My Girlfriend

My heart breaks for him, and as a mother myself, it breaks for his mom.

At the same time, my heart is so completely full after the words slipped out in an unfiltered moment. I *do* love him, and I'm not sure when I would've gotten up the nerve to say it to him if it didn't come out during an impassioned speech the way it did.

I get that he's on pain meds and he's just coming off surgery, but he didn't hold back his anger with his mom or his stepdad. I just hope I got through to him.

I hope I made him see what I—someone on the outside—can so easily see.

But it's always easy to see those things when you're on the outside. It's harder when you're in the thick of it on the inside. And I have my own life experiences to add to the mix. Mother to mother, I see why she did it. I don't blame her for doing what she thought was best for her kids.

Especially since she admitted that she'd never planned to reveal the truth.

Which begs the question…why did Eddie admit to it?

I don't know much about the man, to be honest, and most of what I've heard isn't great. He seems greedy and selfish, and if those two traits accurately portray him…then it makes sense that eventually he'd want to cut off his spending. The twins are nearly thirty at this point, and I'm surprised he paid her off as long as he did.

These are the thoughts swirling around my mind when my phone rings just after I finish the dinner dishes. I'm surprised to see it's Tanner calling.

"Hey," I answer, and I finish drying a couple dishes while I cradle the phone between my ear and my shoulder.

"Are you busy?"

I glance up and see both kids occupied on their iPads, so I say, "I can spare a minute or two."

"That's all I need. I have a few things I need to fill out for the school district to get my football program up and running, and my publicist thought it would be a good idea to get an in-district parent to write me up a recommendation. Know anyone who might be able to do that for me?"

"Hm, maybe one of your coaches?" I tease.

He laughs.

"I'd be happy to do it, though I don't know why you'd need one since everyone knows who you are," I say. "We can work on it tomorrow in between stretches if you'd like. That way you can tell me about the program, and I can include whatever you need in the letter."

"Would it be okay if I talked to Luca about some of the ideas I have for the program? Just to see if it's stuff he'd be interested in."

"I think that's a great idea. Now? Or do you want us to come by tomorrow or something?"

"Well, there's sort of one other thing…" He trails off, and I wait patiently for it. "I agreed to dinner tomorrow with my parents, and I'd like you there. And I know you have the kids, so I was thinking you could just bring them, and I could talk with Luca there."

"The kids?" I repeat. "*My* kids?"

"Well…yeah. I assume you don't want to bring someone else's kids."

"I mean, that's very sweet of you, but have you ever been to a restaurant with children?"

"No. Why?"

I chuckle. "Do you want to see for yourself? Or do you want me to tell you?"

"Oh stop. It can't be that bad."

"No, you're right," I agree. "It's probably worse than whatever you're thinking."

"Is it any worse than dumping a bowl of spaghetti on my brother's head at Olive Garden when we were in first grade?" he asks.

"Probably right along those lines," I say dryly.

"Bring them. It'll be a nice distraction."

"How do you plan to explain to your mom and dad why I'm accompanying you to dinner with my children?" I ask.

"Easy. I'll tell them you're my girlfriend." His voice is so flippant, so casual, and I freeze.

"Your…your *what*?"

"What? You think you can just profess your love to me out of the blue and I'm not going to think of you as my girlfriend? Cass, there's no one else. Okay? Only you. Hell, I don't even have time for somebody else since you're here all day, and you're all I think about after you leave. So deal with it. You're my girlfriend."

Tears heat behind my eyes.

It's way too soon for me to have a boyfriend. I *just* got out of a marriage, and I should probably take a little time on my own.

Except I'm starting to learn that society's expectations of timelines are a load of trash, and I can do whatever the hell I want. I only get one life, and the more time I spend with him, the more confident I am in the fact that our lives were meant to intersect.

"Well, I guess I can't argue with that." I glance over at my kids. Luca is wearing headphones as he plays his game, and Lily is singing, so she isn't about to hear a thing I say right now. "Boyfriend."

He chuckles. "Hearing that word feels better than I was expecting."

"Deal with it," I tease, throwing his own words back at him.

A sense of joy climbs through me…even though reality sort of hits me at the same time.

"Would you really tell your parents that, though?" I ask. "Don't you think it's safer to keep it between us for now?"

"Us meaning you, me, my brother, and your cousin?" he asks.

I laugh. "Yes. That's exactly what I mean."

He chuckles. "Yes. I was mostly teasing when I said I'd tell them that. I don't have to say anything at all, or I can say that I need you there since it's my first venture out after surgery."

"Whatever you're comfortable with."

"Well, I'd be most comfortable not going to dinner at all and instead getting you naked," he says.

"That's sort of off the table until next weekend. Unless I get a babysitter."

"Do that." His voice is low and needy, and it pulses an ache down low.

"Okay," I agree. I don't need any more convincing than that. It's been a week, and I miss that intimacy with him. "Do you want to talk to Luca now, then?"

"Sure."

"Hang on." I pull the phone from my ear, and I walk over and tap Luca on the shoulder. He pulls his headphones off and looks up at me expectantly. "Hey, Tanner Banks is on the phone and wants to talk to you."

His eyes light up as I hand the phone over. I listen to Luca's end of the conversation, and I let them chat while I finish what I'm doing in the kitchen. They only talk for a few minutes before Luca calls me over to hand the phone back to me.

"Get everything you needed?" I ask.

"Not from his mother," he mutters.

I giggle. "Let me get that babysitter lined up."

"Listen, spend the morning with your kids tomorrow since I'm taking you from them tomorrow night," he says.

My heart warms. "Thanks, Tanner." I run through the list of stretches I want him to do, and I remind him to listen to his body and take it easy if anything feels off before we say our goodbyes.

My parents, who are the best, by the way, agree to watch the kids tomorrow night instead of tomorrow morning, so everything is lined up.

I decide to take the kids to one of our local waterparks in the morning complete with waterslides and a lazy river, and we spend the day laughing and splashing. I'm sun-kissed as I slip into a casual black dress for dinner, and my parents show up right on time.

I draw in a deep breath as I realize…I'm about to go to dinner with my boyfriend and his parents.

Chapter 41: Tanner Banks

A Distraction While We Wait

Cassie is coming at seven, and we're meeting my parents at seven thirty. I'm ready to go at six and debating whether we'll have enough time for sex when my phone rings.

It's a number I don't recognize, and I can count the times I've answered a number I don't know on one hand…but something compels me to pick up.

I wish I hadn't.

"Hello?"

"Tanner?" the voice on the other end asks.

"Yeah?"

"It's Eddie Nash. Uh, your father," he says.

I can't think of a single word to say in response to that.

"I just wanted to see how you're doing. Spencer says he's checked in with you and you're doing well, but I wanted to know for myself." He's rambling a bit, and since I found out about him, I've sort of put him into an unlabeled box in my mind. I've spent so much time feeling anger at my mom for lying to me about him that I haven't really allowed myself to feel emotions toward him.

He didn't want us. He chose his other family. We weren't anything to him other than a monthly expense. Allowing myself to think about that sort of fucks with my head, so I push it back into that box.

"I'm fine," I grunt. It's a lie. I'm not fine. My knee is all fucked, I'm meeting my lying parents for dinner, and I'm angry that I'm not prepping for a game tomorrow.

I wonder how much of that this man would understand. I know of him, but it's not like I looked up his career. I know he was a cornerback for the Giants for a number of years, and I know he had four boys before our mom had Miller and me. I know he was married a long time, and now he's divorced. I wonder if we had anything to do with that. I wonder what his ex-wife knew and what he hid from her. I wonder if there are more of us out there. I wonder if his monthly expenses got too high to handle when he was blacklisted from the league for being an asshole.

I really don't have much to say to him. I don't care if he understands me or not.

"All right. Well, if you need anything—"

"What?" I interrupt him with a hiss. "You'll be there for me? To be honest, this feels like nothing more than a desperate attempt to try to get something out of me, and I have nothing for you."

I surprise even myself with those words.

Potentially he has things for me. Like Cassie once said, for example, knowing his medical history could be important someday, or maybe he has tricks of the trade when it comes to the sport we both love.

Or maybe he even has answers to the questions that have swirled through my mind since we found out the truth. Maybe I should ask rather than make assumptions.

But I don't currently find myself in a place where I want those answers.

"Thanks for calling," I say, and I end the call. I realize my hands are shaking as I set the phone down, and I draw in a few deep breaths as I try to push him to the back of my mind.

But I can't.

Maybe his call came at the perfect time. Maybe I can head into this dinner tonight and get the answers I clearly so desperately seek.

And that's why I invited Cassie to come with me.

It has nothing to do with my knee and everything to do with the fact that when she's in the room, somehow I find myself calm. Centered.

Maybe it's her age. Her experience. The way being a mother has rubbed off onto her in other ways—patience, and a firm hand, and this tender way she responds to me and my needs.

I'm starting to rely on her for more than just my physical therapy. I'm starting to need her in other aspects of my life, too. It's a scary thought since we haven't really talked about what lies beyond my rehabilitation, though I've thrown around some ideas in my own mind.

Could she work with me as my full-time trainer? Could I hire her privately beyond the rehab part of my PT to work with me and ensure my knee stays strong?

Could I ask her to move in with me?

We're not there, obviously. She has more than just herself to consider.

Am I destined to fuck up my future kids and stepkids because of the way I was fucked up well after the statute of limitations should've run out on mommy issues?

Is that all this is for me? I'm having issues with my own mother, and so I'm clinging to the first person I find who is the very definition of a *good* mother?

275

Somehow I doubt it. There's something very real and very pure between Cassie and me, and it has nothing to do with any of that.

But she's also seven years older than me. I'm turning thirty soon, and she's turning forty in a few years. Is there too much of a gap between us to sustain something long-term? And how will my career affect any of that?

It's too early to tell. For now, she's my physical therapist, and that's all the outside world needs to know.

I push thoughts of Eddie Nash back into that unlabeled box, but when Cassie walks in and finds me sitting on the couch, she immediately knows something is up.

"What's wrong?" she asks.

I blow out a heavy breath. "Eddie Nash called."

"Oh, Tanner," she says softly. She sits beside me and touches my good leg. "Are you okay?"

I press my lips together as emotion seems to clog the back of my throat. I'm surprised by the emotion I feel over it. It shouldn't affect me, and part of me wants to talk to my brother about it, but he's out of town for a game, which just feels like one more thing to add to the list of offenses against me.

I'm doing my best not to take it personally. I know in my heart that it *isn't* personal, but it doesn't make it hurt any less.

Football is where I always channeled everything I was feeling, and maybe that's why I never acknowledged that I actually do have emotions. I didn't have to bottle them up when I could leave them out on the field.

I can't do that now, and it's all starting to catch up with me.

"No," I admit. "I don't want to go to this goddamn dinner. I don't want to get caught off guard by Eddie Nash. I don't want to be stuck on this couch when I should be with my teammates preparing for tomorrow's game."

"I know," she says softly.

276

I glance over at her. "The only good thing out of all of this shit is that it means I get time with you."

"There's the positivity I'm looking for," she says, and she offers a small smile. "If you don't want to do dinner, then we don't. We decline, and we stay here. It's probably better for you *not* to go out to dinner anyway. The logistics are tough with a wheelchair, and you're only five days out from surgery. You need to stay home resting, and you can blame me for that if you decide to cancel."

She's right. I don't know why I didn't consider that before. I pick up my phone, and I text my mom.

Me: *My physical therapist said I need rest. She doesn't think a restaurant is a good idea.*

I show her the text before I click send.

"Do you think you should call her instead?" she asks.

I shake my head. "I don't want to."

"You're so stubborn."

My phone vibrates with a reply, and I roll my eyes when I read it. "Guess who I get it from."

Mom: *That's fine. We'll come to your house instead.*

Cassie presses her lips together. "Do you need me to say no dinner at all?"

I shake my head. "No. Let's get this over with."

"Want me to distract you while we wait?" She raises her brows, and a rush of blood travels straight to my cock.

"Oh yeah. Most definitely," I say, and I'm about to reach down and pull my cock out when she starts to talk.

"Okay. Luca was *so* excited about the camp. We had a playdate with some other kids from school, and—"

I clear my throat.

"What?" she asks.

I shake my head with a wry laugh. "Nothing. I just…misinterpreted what you meant by a distraction, I guess."

277

Her brows crinkle together, and I look down at my cock, which is still getting harder at the promise of the sort of distraction I was thinking of, and she glances down there, too.

Her eyes are wide when they meet mine. "Ohhhh," she says. "Yeah. Oh."

She laughs. "Well, I can do that, too." And then she proceeds to reach into my shorts, pull my cock out, stroke it a few times, and slide her lips down over it.

"Oh, fuck," I murmur. I shift my hips up into her mouth as she takes me to the back of her throat right here on the couch. She sucks on me, and I groan at how good her mouth feels. "Yes, baby, suck on me just like that," I say, and I set my hand on the back of her head.

Now *this* is exactly the sort of distraction I needed. This woman's mouth on my cock? Perfection.

She bobs her head up and down as she takes me deep, and I hold her in place for a few beats as she swallows around my cock. My mind clears and my body relaxes for the first time in days.

"Fuck, yes, Cass. That feels so goddamn good. Take my cock like the good girl you are," I mutter as she lets go to take in a breath of air, and then she licks around the tip before she slides her tongue up and down my shaft.

Fuck, she's good at this. She sucks one of my balls into her mouth while she jerks off my shaft, and that's it. My complete undoing.

I come hard all over her hand, grunting her name through the entire release as she strokes my cock through the whole thing. She licks her way back up my shaft when I finish coming, and my legs start to tremble as relief filters through my system.

She gets up and rinses off her hands at the kitchen sink, and she returns a minute later to the seat she just vacated. "Was that more along the lines of what you were thinking?"

I laugh as I pull her against my chest. "Absolutely. And, you know, I can't get on my knees to return the favor, but you're always welcome to sit on my face."

She laughs. "I will take you up on that…but after dinner when you're ready to go again."

Hell. With her? I'm ready to go again right now.

Chapter 42: Cassie Fields

Playing House with a Football Player

The absolute one eighty of his personality from when I arrived to now is nearly comical.

He was a tightly wound ball of stress, but he's not anymore.

I pat myself on the back for that genius idea even though it was sort of his idea, and I pull up his favorite restaurant to place our dinner order. He texts his mom to see what she and his dad want to eat, and they arrive shortly after we place the order.

"Oh," she says in surprise when I open the door. "What a lovely surprise. Is Tanner doing okay?"

I nod. "He's doing well." I gesture for them to head into the family room, and I hear the greetings ahead of me as I lock the front door. I wonder if she's wondering why I'm here, but if she is, she doesn't say anything. At least not with me in the same room.

I join them and find his mom sitting beside him in the place where I was sitting before they arrived, and I take a spot on the opposite end of the L-shaped couch so I can keep an eye on Tanner.

"Dinner should be here soon," Tanner says a little awkwardly.

"Honey, I know you have questions, and—" His mom cuts herself off as she glances at me. "And, well, I thought tonight I could answer whatever you need to know."

"I really don't. You made a choice, and you're sticking by it, and you're the one who wants to keep talking about it," he says.

"Because you keep pushing me away. We used to be so close, and now I feel like we're worlds apart."

"We weren't really all that close if you felt like it was okay to lie to me for my entire life," he snaps.

"Don't talk to your mother like that," Charles warns.

Tanner turns to him next. "Or what? You don't get to tell me what I can or can't do. Not when you were her accomplice."

"It's not like that," Charles says, raising his voice. "We made a choice when you boys were very, very young. We decided together that I would be your father in all the ways that mattered. Don't act like I wasn't there for you every step of the way, Tanner. For you and your brother. We didn't make that decision lightly, and it wasn't always easy. But I wouldn't trade it for the world."

I hear the emotion in his voice, and for just a second, I try to put myself in his shoes.

I really don't think they acted out of malice. The opposite, in fact. They acted from a place of love, and I felt that the last time they were here, too.

But Tanner can't see it. Of course he can't. He isn't a parent…but if he was, I think he'd be more apt to see it, too.

Silence fills the room for a few awkward moments, and then I say, "Why don't you tell them about your youth football program?"

He launches into some details about the program. I learn quite a lot about the program as he talks, and I hear the passion in his voice about it. He's excited about this, and it's a project that will feed his soul as he spends the next several months without the game he loves so much.

He's still talking about it when dinner arrives, and I grab plates and set the food out for everyone before I help him over to the table.

His parents ask him questions about it, and it feels like they're closer than Tanner would like to admit.

I get that he feels betrayed. I get that he's hurt by the lie. But maybe I can help him see how much these two care about both him and his brother, and maybe someday he can find it in his heart to forgive them.

"I have several former players already on board, and as soon as the school district approves the plan, we'll be able to pilot the program at Cassie's son's school," Tanner says.

"Oh, you have a son?" Sandra asks.

I nod. "Luca. He's seven, and I also have a little girl, Lily, who is five."

"They're both great kids," Tanner says, and I sense a bit of pride in his voice.

"You've met them?" Sandra asks.

"Cass brought them here a few weekends ago. Lily is really attached to her mom, and I've been eating up her weekends," Tanner says.

Sandra and Charles exchange a glance.

"Is their father in the picture?" Sandra asks.

"We're recently divorced," I say quietly. "They go to his house every other weekend, but they live full time with me."

"That must be hard," Sandra says quietly, and the understanding in her voice makes me think once again about how, as mothers, sometimes we're forced to make decisions for our kids, and all we can do is hope we're doing right by them.

Sometimes we don't find out the answer to that until they're nearing thirty, and other times the answer is obvious right away. I wish there was a guidebook to all of this because when I'm apart from them, I feel like I'm failing them. At the same time, I know it's important for them to see their mom working hard and reaching her own goals.

Except I'm not sure that's what this is.

I'm not even going into an office. Instead, I'm playing house with a football player seven days a week for six hours a day, and now I'm sitting at dinner with his parents when I should be at home playing Chutes and Ladders with my kids.

He doesn't need me here as his physical therapist, yet I'm here. I know it's more than a doctor-patient relationship at this point, but the more time we spend together outside of our work times, the higher the chances become that we'll be caught.

Especially when an ex-husband swings by on a Saturday night in some ridiculous attempt to try to win his family back only to find his ex-wife out with another man.

Chapter 43: Tanner Banks

Cone Commander

Cassie seemed like she pulled back in the middle of dinner, and I'm not sure what happened or how I lost her. It was like she faded away when she mentioned her ex, and rage pumps through me that a single person could have that strong of an effect on her.

I suspect it's more than that, and I'm surprised when she opts to head out when my parents do.

Maybe she's just doing it for show for them since there really was no need for her to be here at dinner from the perspective of her being my physical therapist.

Or maybe I should take her at her word—that she doesn't want to miss getting her kids down to bed tonight.

But she doesn't call me on her way home, and she doesn't call me once I assume the kids are down, either. It feels like something is off between us, so I text her even though it's late.

Me: *Thanks for joining me at dinner. Are you okay? I was hoping you'd stay for…dessert.*

It's nearly an hour before she replies.

Cassie: *I'm okay. I'm sorry I left. Like I said, I wanted to be home to get the kids to bed.*

I'm not sure what else to say to that. I feel a distance starting to span between us, and I don't like it.

Me: *Hope they went down easy.*

Cassie: *They did. My mom said Alex stopped by and was surprised I was out.*

Me: *Did they tell him where you were?*

Cassie: *No. I haven't mentioned anything to them about us, but I'm worried he's going to figure us out. This sneaking around…it's a lot.*

Me: *I know it is. Maybe we don't have to.*

Cassie: *If you want to continue working together, we do.*

Me: *Not if you quit and I hire you as my full-time personal trainer.*

It's not the first time I've mentioned it, and I can't see any reason she has to say no.

Except the one she gives next.

Cassie: *You know I can't. I have lofty goals with this job, and I can't put myself in a position where I'm relying on someone else to financially support me. I did it for the last eight years, and I can't go back.*

Me: *I understand. But it's not the same. I'd be paying you to perform a job.*

Cassie: *And what happens once you're well and back on the field and running off to Vegas for your next one-night stand? What happens when someone a decade younger than me catches your eye?*

My chest tightens at her words. She's never expressed that sentiment to me before, but considering the fact that her slimy ex cheated on her combined with the way we met, I get it. She's usually so confident, so sure of herself…but this is obviously her insecurities coming out.

Me: *The only one my eyes are focused on is you, Cass.*

She doesn't reply, and I fear it's because she doesn't believe me.

My finger hovers over the call button. I want to say the words to her. I want her to know this isn't just me clinging to our one night or to her because she's taking care of me.

I've fallen for her hard, and I'm not going anywhere.

I'm not entirely sure the same can be said for her, though.

Is she just giving me what I want while I'm her patient? Is she the one who's going to run off to Vegas for her next one-night stand? Is she projecting that onto me so she feels justified in doing it later?

I shouldn't let her insecurities become mine, and yet that's exactly what I find myself doing.

She's pushing me away because she's scared, and I need to figure out how to man up and not let her do that.

She seems okay on Sunday, but my head is in a bad space since it's game day. I watch my brother and my teammates on the field and pine for the day when I get to be there with them.

I feel like I'm on a roller coaster ride over the next few weeks. Some days I'm up, some days I'm down. Some days I'm thrown for a loop, and some days feel like an uphill climb.

Things seem to settle between the two of us, but we're focused on new stretches and exercises. With her training in sports medicine, she gives me massages, and I fight every single urge I have to request a happy ending.

It's not easy.

November hits, and the weather starts to cool.

November is also the start of my after-school program.

The first Wednesday of the month is our first session, and I'm finally done with the crutches, but I still have to be careful. I've been deep in planning mode with former San Diego Storm wide receivers Bryce Morris and Thomas Scott, who signed on to run this entire season with occasional appearances by yours truly. I can't wait to show up today and get this party started.

We end our therapy session a little early so I can head to the school and meet with the principal, and both Bryce and Thomas are waiting in the parking lot for me when I arrive. The three of us head in, and we're given a warm reception from everyone in the front office. The principal takes us out to the field where we'll meet every Wednesday, and Bryce starts setting up cones for the different drills we plan to run.

We had room for twenty-six kids, and the program sold out in minutes. The three of us wait for the kids to start to show up once the final bell rings, and they come barreling out to the field after school.

We get started right away on attendance, and I say a few words about working hard and grinding, and then we get moving on our first drill.

Bryce and Thomas explain what to do while I stand back and observe. Parents start to show up, too, some with younger siblings to watch our program. I spot Cassie, and I catch her eye and flash her a grin. She smiles back, and I immediately feel at ease.

I explain the drills as Bryce and Thomas demonstrate how to do them, and I find myself having a lot of fun.

After some fundamentals with cone drills, we move into some backpedaling and shuffling drills, and then we start a game of flag tag.

The kids are running around, laughing, and having a great time, and I wish I could run around some more with them. Instead, I walk along the field and talk one-on-one with kids while Bryce plays on one side and Thomas plays on the other.

I can't wait to chat with Luca later about what he thinks about this whole thing, but I can see it on his face. He's having a blast, and he's learning about football at the same time. My chest feels warm at the thought that we could be making an impact on the next generation of football stars. This could be where they get their start, right here on this field. This could be one of their core memories as they look back on when it all began.

I glance over at Cassie, and I see her holding Lily in her arms almost like a baby, as Lily seems to be throwing some sort of fit, legs kicking as Cassie tries to talk to her rationally.

I walk slowly over toward them, and I can't quite kneel down to be eye level with Lily, but I bend over at the waist.

"What's the matter, Lilypad?" I ask, using the name I heard Cassie use once.

"She's upset that her brother gets to play with you but she doesn't."

"Oh, man. I'm sorry, Lily. This program is for ages seven through ten. But you know what we need?"

Her eyes grow wide as she looks at me, and I scramble to come up with something she can do. "I need a cone commander. Do you know anyone who can handle that?"

"What's a cone commander?"

"It's someone who makes sure all the cones stay lined up where they need to be, and when we switch drills, it's the person with the *very* important job of picking up the cones and bringing them to Mr. Morris. Wait a minute...do you think *you* could do it?" I ask as if the idea just occurred to me.

She stands from her mom's lap and wipes her cheek before she nods solemnly. "I can do it."

"Come on," I say, and I hold out my hand for her. She slides her little hand into mine, and I glance at Cassie, who mouths *thank you* to me.

I shoot her a small smile. She doesn't need to thank me. I gently squeeze Lily's little hand, and I glance down at her to see her looking up at me. I grin as I lead her over toward a row of cones. "Ready, cone commander?"

"Ready," she says with a resolute nod of her head.

"Okay, now just so you know, cone and commander both begin with the letter C, so if you hear me shout CC, that means you. Got it?"

She nods with those sweet little wide eyes again. "Got it."

And that's how I started calling Cassie's daughter CC.

Chapter 44: Cassie Fields

A Small Victory. Or a Huge One.

Okay.

Fine.

I give up.

I can't fight this anymore.

I've tried. I've been back and forth. I've tried to pull back, but every time, it's like I'm swept right back into it. And now he's calling Lily *CC*? It's too cute. I can't with this.

It's like watching Tanner work with kids has changed everything for me. And when it's *my* kids, it's even more special. I'm sure the other parents are watching Lily walk over there with jealousy in their eyes. They got to watch as Tanner walked over to me to take my kid out onto the field.

It feels like a small victory. Or a huge one. It feels like the only friends I have left after the divorce are my three girls, and everyone else sits around in judgment. Well, let them judge this, then.

It's just making me want to go public with this relationship. Not to rub it in their faces, though that would certainly be an added bonus, but because I want to take the kids to dinner after

Luca's football practice, and I want Tanner to join us. I want him to spend the night at my house once in a while. I want date nights and all the things you get to do in a normal relationship.

Instead, we're sneaking around hoping we don't get caught because if we do, the repercussions would be catastrophic.

And so I take the kids out to IHOP for dinner. Thursday night, I cook for them. Another week comes and goes, and then another. I watch Tanner interact with my kids on Wednesdays, and I fall a little harder each time. They love him, and I can literally see him falling in love with them, too.

It feels like we have our entire future laid out in front of us, and I can't wait to grab on with both hands and get started on it.

I find myself daydreaming about that a lot. It might be further off than I realize. It's not like I'll just move into the house he shares with his brother with my kids. It's also not like he'll move into the house I used to share with my ex-husband to help me raise my kids.

But finding a place we can call our own is potentially in the future, and every time I sit at the after-school program and watch him call CC over to help him with cones, every time I watch him interact with Luca on the field, every time I see him giving my babies extra attention and glancing my direction to see if I caught it all…my heart latches on a little more.

I'm all the way in with him, and the more time he spends with my kids, the more I see that he's all the way in with me, too. We haven't talked much about it, but he knows we're a package deal. I don't come solo. I have kids, and I have them with me eighty percent of the time. It's a lot to ask of someone, but we're not at the point where we have to decide anything yet since we still have another six months or so to keep what we're doing under wraps.

After the next set of away games, he'll be cleared to stand on the sidelines at the home games. We won't have our Sundays anymore, but I can tell how excited he is to get back on the field with his teammates, even if it isn't in the capacity he wants it to be quite yet.

And this Friday, the kids will be heading to their dad's house, and Tanner has invited me to spend the weekend with him again.

His gaze lingers on mine as we work through quad sets and hamstring curls, through calf raises and the leg press. We do some balance drills, and he's getting stronger with every session.

He moves in to kiss me as we take a quick break, and I hold up a hand. "Rehab before romance," I remind him, and he sighs.

"Can we just…not do that this weekend?" He sounds annoyed.

"Not do what?" I ask.

"Look, we spend a lot of time together, right? Six hours a day, give or take. I know I'm not always all that pleasant to be around, especially not for that many hours. But Cass, I love you, and I just want to spend the weekend with *you*. Not with my physical therapist, but with my girlfriend. The whole weekend."

"So…no PT tomorrow and Sunday?"

He nods. "That's right. I'll still do my stretches, but I want to take you somewhere this weekend where we can just be together."

My brows pinch together. "Where?"

"You'll see."

I narrow my eyes at him, but he's not giving anything away.

"I can't go too far in case the kids need me."

"I know." He reaches for me and pulls me against his body, and I don't fight it. "But the Storm is in town which means Miller will be home tonight, and I want you and this gorgeous body of yours all to myself."

I nod. "Okay." I'm already packed to spend the weekend with him anyway, so I see little reason not to agree to this plan of his.

When our time is up for the day, he says, "Are you ready?"

"For what? Sex o'clock?"

He chuckles. "For our weekend plans."

I narrow my eyes at him. I'm not entirely sure what I'm supposed to be ready for, but if it's the two of us alone for the weekend, I think I'll be just fine with whatever it is. "Yep."

"Then get in the Porsche because I'm taking you somewhere."

I laugh, and I grab my little suitcase. He grabs his duffel, too, and then we head out to his car. Fifteen minutes later, we're pulling up to a house that's situated right on the beach. "Your weekend accommodations, ma'am," he says after he puts the car into park.

"Cut out that ma'am nonsense. It makes me feel even more ancient than I am."

He shakes his head, his eyes twinkling when he turns to look at me. "You're perfect."

I offer a very unladylike snort in return.

He taps a code into the keypad, and he opens the door to allow me to walk in first. And it's perfection. It's a huge beach house that he obviously rented for the two of us, and I walk through it toward the patio doors on the first floor. The large patio is steps away from the beach, and even though I've never lived directly on the beach, I've been within twenty minutes of it for most of my life.

It's pure, tranquil perfection.

"Come with me," he says, and he walks toward the corner where there's an elevator I didn't even see. We head up to the top level, and then we take a small staircase that leads us up to the rooftop deck.

I breathe in the salty ocean air, and a sense of peace washes over me.

He wraps his arms around me from behind as we both look out over the water that's really just steps away. This deck offers tons of privacy, and yet it's out in the open. It's the first time he's held me in his arms in a place other than the privacy of his own home, and it feels nothing short of totally spectacular.

I turn in his arms, and I tilt my chin up to look into his eyes.

"Something about the natural light in your eyes makes you even more beautiful than usual," he murmurs, and my lips tip up at that.

"I was just thinking the same thing about you," I admit, and he angles his head down as he drops his lips to mine.

We stand there on the rooftop deck kissing slowly, sensually, tenderly, under the warmth of the afternoon sun with the salty ocean air surrounding us, and I'm not sure if there's a single scenario more perfect than this.

Until he leads me over toward one of the lounge chairs on this deck after a while. He sits, and he pulls me down on top of him. We continue to kiss there, and his hands move under my shirt to caress the skin of my back as he thrusts his hips up toward me. He's ready to go, and feeling how hard he is beneath me is making me ready to go, too.

I move off him and slide my panties and my jeans off, and I unbutton his shorts and reach into them. His cock is hard for me, and I take him into my fist and pump up and down it a few times before I climb over him and slide him right into me.

"Yes, baby," he murmurs, and I start to move over him as I brace myself with my hands on his chest. He reaches up under my shirt to touch my breasts as I move, and I moan when he bypasses my bra and takes my nipples between his fingers.

We find a quick rhythm and move together, pushing each other toward bliss as our bodies communicate in the language they've so quickly and easily learned.

I moan, and he asks, "Do you like when I touch your tits?"

"Mm," is my moaned reply, and he rubs my nipples, which only pushes me closer to bliss.

"Your cunt is so hot for me, so greedy," he pants. "I want to taste it, but I don't want to stop fucking it."

"Good thing we have all weekend," I manage before my body starts to give way to the intense pleasure.

The sound of seagulls on the beach and the rush of water on the shore fills the air around us, but all I can focus on is this connection we share. It's intimate and deep, and the chemistry between us is pure fire——so unlike anything I've experienced before. So addictive.

So explosive.

But that's sort of the whole problem with fire.

It's not meant to burn forever.

Chapter 45: Tanner Banks

Eternal Flame

We order dinner, and we eat on the rooftop.

In fact, we spend the majority of our weekend up there, and it's Saturday evening when I call out something that's been on my mind.

"Are you worried about something?" I ask.

She snags her bottom lip between her teeth. She nods a little as she ducks her head and glances out toward the water. "Yes. I've been trying to figure out how to say this all weekend."

My brows pinch together as alarm pounds in my chest. "It's me," I say gently as I reach over to squeeze her hand. "Just say it, babe."

She draws in a steadying breath. "I've never felt anything this powerful before, and I'm scared it's burning too brightly. Too hot. You know what I mean?"

I shake my head because…no. I don't have a clue what she's getting at.

"I keep thinking how hot it is between us. We're on fire together. But fires…" She trails off with a shrug.

"They burn out eventually?" I guess.

She nods, but she doesn't make eye contact with me.

I shake my head, and I look out over the water where her gaze is focused. "When I was in tenth grade, I wrote a research paper on eternal flames. They're rare, and only certain conditions can cause them to exist."

She glances over at me, and our eyes connect for a beat before I continue.

"There's one in New York. Eternal Flame Falls. There's a natural gas spring at the base that supports the flame. Every once in a while, when conditions are too windy, the flame goes out. But someone always comes by to light it up again." I shrug as I pause. "I think since I wrote that paper, I had it in the back of my mind that it was all I wanted out of life. Those things that burn so brightly inside of us, and when the flame dims, we have someone there to help light the fire again."

Her brows dip as she stares at me, and then she swipes a tear off her cheek. "Tanner. That's beautiful."

I reach out to thumb away a tear on the other side. "My flame burned out when I fucked up my knee, but there's one person who has been here with me working hard to relight it every time we're together." Her eyes meet mine as I say the words I've been too scared to say. "I think you just might be my eternal flame, Cassandra Fields."

She stares at me a few seconds before she leans forward and brushes my lips with hers.

I really didn't think love was in the cards for me. I thought when I ended things with Heather, that was it. I was done doing the relationship thing, and I was destined to have night after meaningless night with women.

But then I met Cassie Fields at a bar, and the entire course of my future switched tracks.

We've seen each other every day for more than two months now, and I'm not sure I've ever shown more of myself to another person. She's the one person who will call me out on my shit, who will help nurse me back to health, and who will listen when I just need to bitch.

She's become my best friend over the last couple of months. For everyone else, life kept moving when mine came to a standstill.

Miller is playing ball, and I only get to see him when he isn't at practice or at games. I moved to this new town where I knew of some people but didn't really have any friends. I expected to bond with my teammates, and I started to during training camp as I found my footing.

I bonded with Spencer. I found a whole family of brothers I never knew existed.

But they all have lives. They have things to do, a game to play, a bakery to run. They're good about checking in with me, about talking to me, about making sure I'm not falling down into the darkness.

But the only reason I'm not falling is because I have Cassie to lift me up.

We spend the night showing each other how we feel, and when morning dawns and she's in my arms, the fact that today is Sunday and time to watch another round of games doesn't hit me with as much brute force as it has on the days when we don't get to wake like this.

I want with everything to be able to progress this relationship forward, but right now, it feels like this is all we can do. Secret weekends where we don't leave our rental. A stolen dinner here, a quiet kiss there.

I'm not sure we can sustain the secret nature of what we're doing and still be able to grow. I'll be asked to attend various events, and I can only get away with bringing my physical therapist along for so long.

I want to protect her, to protect her job and her goals and her ambitions, but I don't know how it's possible to do that and level up our relationship at the same time.

We need to be content where we are. It's only until my rehab is over. It's only until next season starts.

But then what?

What happens to *us* when we're not forced together for six hours a day? I wish I had the answer to that because for once in my life, it feels like I found someone who I can trust when everyone else except for my brother has let me down.

Maybe I lost my identity over the last year, but Cassie makes me confident in who I am, and when I'm around her and even her kids, I know exactly who I strive to be.

But none of that will matter if we can't figure out some way to be together that isn't a huge risk to both of us.

Chapter 46: Cassie Fields

Car Trouble

When the doorbell rings just as the kids are settling into homework after school on Monday, Luca is all too happy to abandon his math problems and rush to the door to answer it.

"Dad!" he says, and I suck in a breath as I force myself to come to terms with the fact that I'm going to have to deal with my ex.

I walk up behind Luca. "Did Lily leave Guac again?" I ask.

He holds it up, and part of me feels like he purposely pulled it out of her bag to have an excuse to come by.

I take it from him. "Thanks." I'm about to turn into the house with it when he stops me with a hand on my arm.

"Can we talk for a second?" His eyes shift to Luca, and then back to me. "Alone?"

I press my lips together. "Lukey, can you bring this to Lilypad for me?"

He nods, grabs the stuffed avocado from my hand, and rushes back into the house. I step outside and close the door behind me to seal us into privacy. "What?"

"Luca couldn't stop talking about your patient this weekend," he grunts.

"So? He instituted a football program at Luca's school. I wasn't going to prevent my child the opportunity to work with current and former football players because you're jealous of one of my patients."

He raises a brow. "Jealous? I never said that. Is there something to be jealous of?"

"Oh, come off it, Alex. You don't want the kids over at his house, and you hate that I have a connection to something you love."

Don't say it, Cassie. Do not *say that you slept with him.*

God, I want to say it *so badly.*

He raises a brow. "We came by last night to see if you wanted to go to dinner with us. You weren't home."

"Are you insinuating I was with my patient?" I ask.

"Were you? Because we stopped by Saturday, too. Lily wanted her iPad. You weren't home then, either."

"It feels an awful lot like you're keeping tabs on me, but you lost that right when you slept with Corinne. And Jamie. And Carrie." I mean, not that he *ever* had the right to keep tabs on me, but I'm making a point here.

He clenches his jaw, and I watch as it works back and forth. I brace myself because I know his tells, and the clenched jaw is the signal that he's about to say something hurtful.

To my shock, he doesn't. "Fine. Just watch it with the football player. I know you, Cassie, and I know you have this romanticized view of what life should look like. If you knew football players the way I do, you'd know he ain't it."

I nearly laugh in his face. He's *way* more it than Alex ever was.

He deserves to hear those words, and someday he will. But right now, I need to keep a tight leash on both my emotions and my big mouth.

But as it turns out, it's too late. Mostly because Alex does *not* keep a tight leash on his own emotions…nor his big mouth.

I head into the office for the Tuesday morning meeting ahead of Tanner's exam, and just like the last time I was here, everyone in the office essentially ignores me.

What a warm reception.

I'm not sure what's going to happen once I'm done with Tanner's rehab and I'm forced to work with these people on a daily basis again. I'm sure everything will be fine by then, but the thought makes me a little nervous.

"Cassandra, a word?" Dr. Hayward says to me as the meeting draws to a close, and I hang back, presumably to give him the latest update on Tanner before we head into the exam room.

Once the rest of the physical therapists leave, though, he shuts the door. He draws in a breath before he turns to me, and an ominous vibe fills the air between us.

"Ms. Fields, it's been brought to my attention that there might be something inappropriate going on between you and your patient. Can you please clarify?" He seems a bit off as he asks the question, as if he's almost nervous to have this conversation with me.

My hand moves to my chest. "Excuse me?"

He clears his throat. "The relationship between a patient and a medical professional can be complicated. I just need to ensure that—"

I hold up a hand. "What are you asking me?"

"Are you engaging in something other than a professional relationship with Tanner Banks?" The question comes out rushed.

I take a step back as if I've been dealt a physical blow.

I don't know how to answer that. I don't want to lie to my boss, but I also can't admit the truth to him.

"Why are you even asking me this?"

He pulls out his phone, and he shows me a photo. It's from Luca's after-school football practice—the one that first week when Tanner asked Lily to be his cone commander. He's holding Lily's hand as they walk toward the field. He flips to the next photo, and it shows Tanner's head bent down low talking to Luca. And the final photo is Tanner looking at me while I'm trying to calm Lily down.

The look in his eyes is unmistakable even from a distance.

But none of these are incriminating. It's not like he flips to a naked one of the two of us up on the rooftop deck this past weekend…but he does flip to a photo of my car in Tanner's driveway, and it's dark outside.

"Where did you get these?" I ask quietly.

"It doesn't matter."

"It's a total invasion of my privacy, and it does, in fact, matter," I hiss.

"Your car was parked in your patient's driveway for the entire weekend, Ms. Fields. Would you care to explain why?" he asks, sliding his phone back into his pocket.

He flattens his lips as he studies me, and I know I'm caught. I don't have a defense, and lies aren't exactly a solid way to go about it.

"Car trouble," I finally lie weakly.

He doesn't buy it. I don't expect him to.

"I also received photographs of you and Mr. Banks arriving at a house near the beach together this past weekend." His voice is flat, and maybe there actually is a naked one of us on the rooftop deck.

I'm mortified. I have no idea what to say, no idea how he found any of this out. We were being so careful, and it still didn't matter. I open my mouth to apologize so we can move on and not keep Tanner waiting, but he cuts in first.

"Cassandra, I decided to give you a chance by giving you a job here even though you'd been out of practice for quite some time. I gave you our VIP patient despite the protests from others on staff because I thought out of everyone here, you would maintain professionalism. I cannot begin to tell you how disappointed I am in your ethics. I'm going to have to let you go effective immediately for violating our practice's code of conduct."

All the blood drains from my face, and I feel like I might pass out for a second. "Let me go?" I echo. "But what about Tanner? What about—" What about the fact that I'm the only PT who can handle him? What about the fact that I need this job to support my kids? How will I become financially independent from Alex when I can't even hold onto a job for more than a few months?

"I'll put Rick on Tanner's rehabilitation. You can pack your things and go."

"But I need this job," I beg. I know it's useless, but I say it anyway.

"I'm so sorry," he says firmly, as if he found his footing. "Best of luck to you." He opens the door and walks out, and I close my eyes as I try to wake up from this nightmare.

But when I open my eyes, I'm still in the same room. Same place. Same feelings rushing through my chest. Same pit in my stomach.

Maybe I had it coming all along. I mean…he's right, in the technical sense. I didn't give my weak defense that we'd met before he was ever even injured. I didn't mention the fact that there are actual feelings involved on both sides of the equation. I couldn't find my voice when he fired me so quickly. So out of left field.

If only we hadn't gone to that beach house. If only we would've thought to park my car in his garage.

If only we hadn't slept together. If only I hadn't thought a one-night stand with a football player my ex admired was a great idea.

That thought pulses a new realization in me, and suddenly I have an incredibly sneaking suspicion I know exactly who is behind Dr. Hayward finding out.

It doesn't matter how he found out, though.

In one two-minute conversation, all my personal dreams and aspirations just came crashing down all around me, and I'm not quite sure how to pick through the rubble to find my way out of it.

Chapter 47: Tanner Banks

Where the Fuck Is Cassie

I've been waiting a full ten minutes when Dr. Hayward walks into the exam room, and it's fine. Most people wait longer than that at a doctor's office, I guess, but I've never had to wait here before.

But Cassie isn't behind him. Some other dude is.

"Tanner, good to see you again. How's the knee?" Dr. Hayward asks. He starts his exam, poking and prodding at various places on my leg and checking my knee.

"Fine," I say carefully. *Where the fuck is Cassie?*

I want to ask, but I don't.

"This is Rick," Dr. Hayward says. "He'll be taking over your rehabilitation starting today. If you'd like to continue with your in-home care, he's more than happy to accommodate you."

"Hey, man," Rick says, sticking out a hand to shake mine. He gives me a smile, and he reminds me a bit of a slick salesman. "It's great to me—"

"Where the fuck is Cassie?" I demand, interrupting him in the middle of his sentence.

Rick clears his throat as he drops his hand, and Dr. Hayward looks surprised by my question.

"We've reassigned Rick to your case," Dr. Hayward says, still poking at my leg.

"I heard you, but I've made excellent progress with Cassie, and I'd like to continue working with her," I say thickly.

"Unfortunately, that's no longer a possibility. Rick is an incredible healthcare provider, and we're excited to work together to get you ready for the field." He finishes his exam and takes a step back.

That's no longer a possibility? What the fuck happened from yesterday afternoon when Cassie left my place to this morning? Will she still come over today?

How many questions can this asshole sidestep?

I clear my throat. "What do you mean it's no longer a possibility?"

"She's no longer with Motion Orthopedics," Dr. Hayward says.

"As of when?" I demand.

"Employee information is confidential. Rick is ready to get started with you, so why don't you two work out that schedule? If you'll excuse me, I have other patients to attend to." He bolts from the room, and I'm just supposed to sit back and work with some other dude now? What the fuck is going on?

"If you'd like to continue in-home care, I'm happy to accommodate that. The office here will clear my schedule as needed to ensure we give you the highest level of care, and…" He goes on and on, but I started tuning him out somewhere in the middle of his words.

"Yeah," I murmur, and I get up and walk out of the room while he's in the middle of whatever he's saying. I start wandering the halls. "Cassie?" I call. "Cass?"

Rick appears behind me. "She's not here, Mr. Banks. Now if we could get our schedule worked out—"

"I'll be in touch," I mutter, and I bolt from the building.

Her car isn't in the parking lot where I spotted it when I came in less than a half hour ago.

She's gone.

What the hell happened?

I slip into my car and pull out my phone, and I check to see if I missed a call or a text from her.

I didn't.

I dial her number as I sit in the driver's seat, the car not even on yet.

After six rings, I hit her voicemail box.

I leave a message. "Cass, it's me. What's going on? Hayward said they're reassigning me to Rick. What the fuck? I don't want some weasel named Rick. I want you."

I blow out a breath as I end the call, and I sit in the car for a few beats as I try to figure out what to do. I don't want to head home to my quiet house where there is no Cassie, and anxiety pulses through me as I try to imagine what the hell happened.

I'm only coming to one possible conclusion.

She's not at the office. She's not picking up my call. Someone else is going to take over my rehab.

Somehow the doctor at her office found us out. Somehow we were discovered. And somehow…she's no longer working there, which means she's also no longer working with me.

I don't know what the fuck that means for my rehab, but I sure as fuck know what it means for my heart…and it's not good.

Instead of heading toward my house, I head toward hers. I push the gas pedal to the floor of my Porsche as I take the highway to get to her place, and my tires screech as I pull into the driveway. I might not be able to run to the front door, but at least I can still drive fast.

I ring the bell and bang on her door at the same time, and I start to yell her name. "Cassie? Cass! Open the door!" I bang on the door some more, and magically, it opens.

She's standing in front of me, tears streaking her cheeks and eyes rimmed in red. I rush in and pull her into my arms, but she stiffens.

She doesn't reach around me to hold me back.

She doesn't make a move to get closer to me. She doesn't tip her chin up so I can lean down and meet her lips with mine.

Instead, she *stiffens*.

"What's going on?" I demand as I pull back, recoiling like I've been physically struck.

"Dr. Hayward fired me," she says. She sniffles, and the tears streaming down her face don't slow.

"For what?" I roar.

"Unethical relationship with a patient."

"Jesus, Cass," I mutter, and I move to pull her into me again. But she stops me.

She holds up a hand, and she shakes her head as she closes her eyes and presses her lips together in some attempt to stop more tears. "Us—this relationship—it just cost me my job. *You* cost me my job. You cost me my entire identity, everything I've been trying so hard to build. I fell out of a marriage and jumped into bed with you, and I haven't had the time or space to figure out who the hell I am on my own."

I open my mouth to say something—anything that will stop her or comfort her or keep this freight train from going completely off the rails where I already feel it going—but she keeps talking.

"I never even got the chance to figure out if I can support my kids on my own, and now I don't know if I'll *ever* get a job anywhere else. I was fired for violating the code of conduct. Rumors will hit the media because you're famous, and I won't be able to show my face anywhere." Her tears start to fall harder. "I can't do this anymore. It's over. I never should've introduced you to my kids, never should have gotten involved with you. I never should've taken you on as a patient." She's shaking her head, her eyes refusing to meet mine, and all of it feels like a giant punch to the gut.

It feels far, far worse than twisting my knee and snapping some ligaments. Hell, it hurts worse than finding out Charles isn't my real father.

This hurts my chest. It's clawing at me, sending me into a dark place I'm not sure I'll know how to climb out of.

She's cutting this off just when it was getting good. She's pulling out everything from beneath us, and she's leaving exactly zero hope on the table that there's any chance we'll be able to come back from it.

"Don't do this, Cass," I whisper.

"I need you to go," she says. Her voice rings out loud and clear, echoing down the hallway where we stand. "I wish you all the best with your recovery."

"I can't do this without you," I say, and I hear the begging in my own voice. It doesn't sound like me, but I guess that's what the weight of falling in love with someone will do.

"You can," she assures me, but her tone is less than convincing. "Please see yourself out." She turns and runs out of the room, and I stand there for a few seconds staring after her, my stomach churning and my chest feeling as if someone just set a thousand heavy bricks on it, before I give her what she asked for.

Chapter 48: Tanner Banks

Man Up, Douchebag

I stare out over the view, and I tip my glass of tequila to my lips only to find it's already empty.

It's done nothing to dull the ache in my chest.

It's done nothing to stop the churning in my stomach.

My phone rang, and it wasn't her. I didn't answer. It rang again. Still wasn't her.

I left her house a few hours ago, and I don't know what to do. I don't know where to turn.

Miller's not home. I don't know where he is. It's a Tuesday—his day off.

Every day is a day off for me.

It shouldn't be, I guess. I should be doing my stretches and exercises, maintaining strength in other areas, and getting excited that I'll finally be cleared to get back into the Storm's training facility so I can work out with my teammates as I continue to make progress toward getting back in the game.

But all of it feels so goddamn pointless right now.

I had a light in this tunnel, a light that I thought was an eternal flame…but all it took was one conversation for the light to burn out.

And with the flame went my hope.

Hope for gaining strength. Hope for returning to the game. Hope for a future filled with laughter and family and kids.

Kids.

I wasn't sure I even wanted them, and then this single mom brought not just a breath of fresh air into my life, but a whole new perspective.

But her words from earlier are on repeat in my head, crushing the perspective and the hope.

You cost me my job.

I never should've introduced you to my kids.

I get that she's hurting. I get that this is fresh. I get that she was shocked by this turn of events.

But those words were a fucking knife to my soul.

I thought we were building something.

I thought that when I walked away from her with Lily's little hand in mine on Wednesdays and called her *CC* that it meant something more than me just letting a kid participate.

I thought that when I gave Luca some extra pointers on the drills and worked with him after our practice was over that she'd see it was because I care so much about her, that I know that her kids are an extension of her.

Seeing her be a mom and watching her respond to situations with *honesty* only made me fall harder for her, and I was led to believe that feeling was mutual.

But it was all some illusion. If she could so easily bow out at the first sign of trouble, it's hard to believe I ever meant anything to her at all.

I was always just a patient to her, and maybe she's right. The second we saw each other in that room, we should've spoken up.

But I needed more time with her.

Well, I got it. And now I'm worse off because of it.

I hear the scrape of the patio slider opening, and my brother's voice interrupts my brooding.

"What are you doing out here?" He sits in the chair next to me and leans over to sniff my drink. "Is that tequila?"

"It was."

"Where's Cassie?"

"Not here." I tighten my grip on the empty glass as I keep my gaze focused out over the view.

Would things be different if I'd somehow ended up in another city? Maybe I'll never know the answer to that.

"Dude, what the fuck is going on with you?" he asks, and I glance over at him to find his gaze fixed on me, worry creasing his brow.

I blow out a breath. "Cassie's boss found out about us. I don't know how. He fired her, she blames me, and now I'm out the best PT in San Diego and apparently one girlfriend."

"What?" he breathes.

"You heard me."

"Fuck, man. Let me get you some more tequila."

I hand him my glass, and he returns with a glass of water. "The fuck is this?" I demand.

"Man up, douchebag."

"Excuse me?" I say, offended by the name calling.

"You heard me. I don't know how the fuck long you've been sitting like this, but it ends now. Get your ass up and do whatever exercises you've been assigned. You're getting back on that field in July if I have to fucking carry you there. I didn't move to San Di-fucking-ego with you to do this shit by myself, you hear me?"

"You don't have a choice," I roar at him. "I'm fucked until then."

"So you spend every second from now until then getting better so you can make your big triumphant return. You don't sit on the patio and drink away your sorrows. Goddammit, Tanner!" He's angry, and truthfully, I get it. He's feeling a certain way because I'm feeling a certain way, and it makes everything that much harder when you're a twin who feels not just your own shit, but also someone else's.

It's both a blessing and a curse.

"You've been dealt a shit hand. But the Banks brothers don't just fucking fold when we have a bad hand. We discard the shitty ones and try again."

"Yeah, well, maybe I'm more Nash than Banks," I say.

"You think the Nash brothers give up? Have you fucking *met* them?"

"Yeah, I have met them," I hiss. "And I've met Eddie Nash, who we can all agree is a selfish piece of trash. And maybe I have more of his blood running through my veins than any of us realized before."

He rolls his eyes. "Fuck off with that load of shit, Tanner. Pull yourself together. I'm not going to sit here and let you talk shit about my best friend."

I know he means me, and I know he's trying the tough love route to try to make me feel better.

But this is different. This isn't some *pull me up by my bootstraps* moment.

It's not me sulking because of a bad day.

This is heartbreak. Pure and simple.

I *thought* I knew heartbreak. I thought we were old friends. When the end of my relationship with Heather came along, I thought I learned what it was. When I learned that Charles wasn't my father but that our biological father had been paying off our mother to keep silent for my entire life, I thought I knew what heartbreak was again. When I tore my ACL and was told I'd need a year away from the game I was born to play, I thought that was the worst thing I'd ever endure.

But take those three things and add them together, and it's still not as intense as the pain I feel at this moment knowing that Cassie blames me for losing not just her job, but her goals and dreams.

"Fuck you. I'm not going to sit here and take this." I stand and head inside, moving a bit more quickly than I should given my condition. I grab the tequila bottle on my way through the kitchen and head up to my bedroom to be alone with my liquor.

And then I do exactly what my brother just told me not to do.

Chapter 49: Cassie Fields

He Shouldn't Have that Problem with Rick

We're walking to the bus stop in the morning when Lily's little voice asks, "What's the matter, Mama?"

It's not like I can tell her, but it's not like I can put on the façade the way I did when her father and I got divorced. And I'm not quite sure why.

"Nothing, sweetheart," I lie, brushing away a tear from behind my sunglasses. I told myself I wouldn't cry in front of the kids, but, well…I can't exactly help it.

I keep thinking about what after school is going to look like today. Luca has his football practice, and Lily and I usually sit on the side until Tanner comes over and calls for his CC. He flashes that beautiful grin at me, and an ache pulses in me that we share this secret.

Only…that's not how today's going to go.

"But Mommy, you're crying," she says as I sniffle.

"I think it's just allergies, honey." Deep down, I hate the lie. I know it's healthy for children to see their parents expressing their emotions, but I'm not going to tell a five-year-old that I ended a secret love affair with a patient yesterday and my heart feels like it'll never be whole again.

It's the right move. I know it is.

But if it's the right move, why does it *feel* so wrong?

I don't have the answer to that, and as we approach the area where parents gather for our bus pickup, I spot Jess and Katie already chatting with their heads bent closely together.

I haven't mentioned anything to Jess, and truthfully, I haven't been the greatest friend to them lately. Usually I drop the kids and bolt to get to Tanner's house—not because he's my boyfriend, or *was*—but because I had a job to do there.

And, yes, it was nice getting there a minute or two early since it elongated our day.

But I don't have to worry about that this morning since *I no longer have a job.*

I suck in a shaky breath.

"Morning!" Jess says cheerfully when she sees us approaching.

"Morning," I say, mustering up everything I have to pretend like I'm okay for the next few minutes. Then the kids will get on the bus, and I can head home where I can have a proper breakdown.

Except Jess doesn't allow that. I kiss my babies before they leave for school. Katie heads home, and Jess walks with me down the sidewalk back to my place as the grilling begins.

"What's up, Fields?" she asks.

"Nothing," I mutter. "You?"

"Lies." She's calling me out, and I don't like it.

I play innocent. "What do you mean?"

"Why are you hanging around here and not darting off to the football star's house?" she asks.

I can't help it. I burst into tears.

She stops on the sidewalk to give me a hug. "Oh my God, Cassie. What's going on?"

I fight my way out of the hug and continue the journey toward home. She's right beside me the whole way.

I snag my lip between my teeth and bite down as I try to draw the pain away from my chest to focus on something else so I stop crying. It's not fully successful, but it allows me to blurt out what happened. "Dr. Hayward found out about Tanner and me, and he fired me. Then I broke up with Tanner."

She gasps. "How'd he find out?"

I press my lips together. "I don't know for sure. He wouldn't tell me. But I'd put my money on Alex."

"That ass!" she yells. "Fuck him! I'll go find him and kick him in the nuts. God, I hate him."

"So do I," I commiserate, and I sort of hope she *does* go find him to kick him in the nuts. The guy has it coming.

"Are you sure it was him?"

I lift a shoulder. "Who else would it be? He's been stopping by the house when he has the kids, and he hasn't found me there."

"You mentioned in passing that the others at the practice were jealous that you got the VIP patient. Could it have been someone there?" she asks.

I hold a hand to my forehead as I consider the possibility. "Hayward said my car was spotted in Tanner's driveway for the entire weekend, but Alex doesn't know where he lives. I mean, I suppose he could've checked the hospital records and figured it out…"

"But so could someone at your office," she points out.

"My *former* office," I correct. Everyone was standoffish toward me once I scored Tanner, and the truth is that I don't know any of them well enough to say whether one of them might've been behind this. But I know Alex, and I know he's capable of something like this.

"Right. Former."

I blow out a breath. "I don't know. But either way, it doesn't really matter. It feels like I lost my job because of Tanner. I've lost my identity as someone who's more than just *Mom*, and I can't be with someone when the cost of a relationship is that high."

Even as the words spill from my tongue, I get a sense of what Tanner's been through over the last year. He lost his own identity when he found out about his father, and again when football was taken away from him.

The hurt in his eyes when I told him to leave flashes through my mind. I've seen it no less than twenty times an hour since I walked away from him.

But like I told him when I tried to convince him that his mom was acting in his best interest, sometimes parents have to do things to protect their kids.

And this is me doing that for them.

They love him. They've fallen for him, too. And the more I study it, the more I see that there's just no scenario based in reality that would see us past his rehab and into the future together.

He's seven years younger than me, and he's a famous quarterback. He shouldn't feel obligated to take on a woman a few years away from forty whose weeknights are filled with baseball and homework and gymnastics and dancing, who has an ex-husband trying to figure out a way to ruin her relationships, who can't hold onto a job for more than a few months without finding a way to ruin that, too.

It was a simple case of developing falsified feelings for his healthcare provider. Well, he shouldn't have that problem with Rick.

Jess follows me up to my front door, and I turn to face her.

"I think I'd really like to just be alone right now," I say.

She rolls her eyes. "Too bad for you then that I have the day off."

"For what?" I ask, my brows dipping together.

"For taking care of my cousin. Now get inside, and let's put together an action plan."

I shake my head. "I appreciate it, Jess, really. But it's too fresh. I need a minute to figure out where the hell I even go from here."

She squeezes my shoulder. "I don't want you to be alone."

"I'll be fine." It's a lie, and not even a good one.

I don't know if I'll be fine. I don't know how to go to the after-school program and watch him running around with my kids, knowing there's a divide between us.

I don't know what comes next for me. Can I even get a job as a physical therapist when I was fired from my previous job for breaking the code of conduct? Would Hayward give me a recommendation, or is my career in healthcare done forever?

I want to show my kids that women can do anything. I want to prove to Alex that I never needed him or his money.

I guess I had a lot of plans, and then I went and screwed everything up by falling for the first guy I slept with after the divorce.

God, I'm such an idiot.

I don't have a job. I don't have the man.

But I have two kids who are relying on their mom to show up at the football practice after school, where I have to face the man I'm heartbroken over.

I guess that gives me a solid six hours to prepare.

But when I get there…he's not there.

The other two former players run practice. They pick some other girl to be the cone commander, and Lily throws an absolutely epic fit.

I end up walking over to the swing set with her and pushing her until she stops crying.

Luca's in a mood when we get in the car. Lily's still upset she wasn't the commander.

I'm exhausted from crying half the day away, and now I'm worried about Tanner since he didn't show up to practice.

And our night is just getting started.

Chapter 50: Tanner Banks

The Coward's Way Out

I didn't want to cause her any more pain, so I told Bryce and Thomas that I had a conflict. They knew what to do. They don't really even need me there. It's my program, yes, but when I'm back on the field, I won't be there anyway.

It's not a lie. I do have a conflict, a major one, and it's with one of the parents. Miller says I took the coward's way out, but the reality is that I did it from a place of trying to protect her and her kids.

She said she wished she'd never introduced me to them, and that seems to be the thing that's heaviest on my heart.

I want to know *why* she said it.

I want to know what it is about *me* that made her say it.

Miller said it had nothing to do with me and everything to do with her kids, that she was lashing out from a place of anger, but I don't buy it. I guess she was right when she said that sometimes parents do things to protect their kids…but I don't understand it.

I was starting to, I think. I was starting to feel that sense of protectiveness over all three of them. But now, I guess it's not my place.

Thursday happens to be Thanksgiving, and practice is earlier in the day than usual so everyone can head home to be with their families.

Mom and Dad—Charles, whatever I'm supposed to call him now—arranged to visit us for the holiday, and they'll be at the house cooking all day while I head into the practice facility with Miller. I can't practice, but I can stand on the sidelines and analyze.

It's partly me needing to get out of the place that reminds me so much of her, but it's also partly me not wanting to spend the extra hours with my parents.

Though truth be told, the anger I was holding onto seems to have dissipated a little. Or maybe I'm just learning how to numb the shit I don't want to feel. The tequila helps, though that's really more of a late afternoon into evening activity.

Once we arrive at the practice facility, I ask Nick if I can talk to him privately. He immediately pulls me into his office.

"How's the knee?" he asks.

"I need a new PT. Can you do it?" My tone is flat, but hell if I'm going to work with any other person at that practice than Cassie Fields.

"What happened to Motion?" he asks.

I blow out a breath. "Long story, but the woman I was working with is no longer there."

"And you can't see anyone else at the practice?"

I shake my head.

He gives me a strange look but doesn't press the issue. "Okay. I'll need to take a look at their post-op reports, and I may need you to take me through what they were having you do. Of course I can help you, but I don't do home visits. It'll have to be here."

I don't tell him that I don't want to do this at home anyway. Everywhere I turn, I see her, and that doesn't seem conducive to being ready to return to the game in a few months.

Getting out of the house feels like it'll help.

"Thanks, Nick," I say, and he nods.

I start out on the sidelines with the coaches during practice, and it feels good getting back on the field with the grass beneath my shoes. Coach Q calls me over, and together we work with Ford and Jonathan as they run drills together with the wide receivers first and the running backs second.

It's a good way to get back into the game, anyway, and I find I like encouraging the younger players as I guide them with my own experience. It sort of reminds me how much I enjoyed working with the kids at Luca's school, and it makes me think for the first time how maybe someday I'll follow in my oldest half-brother's footsteps and look toward coaching once my playing days are over.

I'm not sure whether it's what I want, though. Part of me always figured once I decided I'm done playing, I'd just be *done*.

Like Grayson, who retired to run a bakery with his wife. He's still very connected to the football world considering all his siblings are still involved in the game, but he gets the luxury of sitting out practice as he throws his time and energy into something that *isn't* football.

It's hard to imagine a life like that, but in all honesty, when I was allowed a glimpse of what life could be like when I wasn't constantly on the go…I didn't hate it as much as I thought I would.

I tend to think it's because Cassie was there for it.

327

I push her out of my mind. Or, I try to, anyway. She never strays very far—even when I'm focused on watching Ford hand a ball off to my brother.

Nick pulls me aside after practice and runs through a few stretches with me, and he tells me he sent additional stretches to my iPad. It's some interactive thing where I can watch on the screen and it'll guide me through what to do.

It's not a replacement for Cassie, but I guess it'll have to do.

But when I get home, I can't seem to find the motivation to do any of it. It doesn't help that my parents are here. I need a few days, maybe. I need some time to process what happened with Cass. I need to figure out where the fuck I go from here.

Part of me wants to fight for her, but the other part of me can't find the fight in me as her words dig into my chest and leave permanent scars there.

Maybe Miller's right and it has nothing to do with me and everything to do with protecting her children, but I was in this thing with her. I was willing to fight to protect them, too, because they're an extension of her.

It's been seventy-four days since I was injured. Seventy-one of those days—not the day it happened, and not the last two days—were spent at least in part with Cassie. To just have that cut off makes me feel as if there's something missing.

Because *there is*. Cassie is missing. She became a huge part of my life over the last seventy-four days. I guess I just need a minute to adjust to that.

But nobody wants to give me a minute.

Mom is stirring something by the stove, and Dad is checking the blade on the electric knife when we walk into the kitchen. It smells like heaven in here, and I know I have a lot to be thankful for, but I can't seem to banish the negativity from my thoughts.

I'm thankful for my career…that I don't get to participate in.

328

I'm thankful for my family…who lied to me my entire life.

I'm thankful for my home…that reminds me too much of Cassie.

The only person I can think of to be grateful for that doesn't come with strings attached to it is my brother.

He's the only person who has been there for me my entire life. The only one who doesn't lie to me because I can see right through him. The only one who understands me like nobody else.

The only one who will call me out on my shit…just like I do for him.

But he's got his own shit to deal with. Maybe the best thing I can do is skip town for a while.

Chapter 51: Cassie Fields

A Load of Horseshit

We spend Thanksgiving Day at my parents' house with extended family, including Jess, her mom, and Dylan. I try to focus on all the things I'm thankful for.

My kids. My parents. Jess and my friends. My health. A roof over my head. There's always a lot to be grateful for. And even though I try my hardest to focus on those things, Jess still calls me out when Dylan is keeping Luca and Lily occupied with a loud and boisterous game of Mario Party.

"You doing okay, Cassie?" she asks, bumping my shoulder with hers near the back of the kitchen. My mom and aunt are by the stove, our dads are outside checking the turkey they're smoking, and our kids are busy. It's just the two of us.

"Honestly? No."

She rolls her eyes. "Then call him," she says.

"I can't. You know that." I take a sip of wine as if it'll help me feel any better, but nothing has over the last couple days.

"Why not?" she asks.

"Because it's not just him. It's losing him on top of losing my job. It's feeling like an idiot for giving in when I knew it was wrong."

"What if it wasn't wrong?"

I flatten my lips. I don't have a response to that. It had to be wrong if I was fired because of it.

Something was wrong, anyway. I shouldn't have taken him on as a patient, and I knew that all along. But I couldn't resist the temptation, and now I'm paying the price.

Jess sighs. "I know it sucks, mama. I love you."

"I love you, too," I say, and I clink my glass to hers. We each take a sip, and she tosses an arm around me as she rests her head on my shoulder.

"I'm here for whatever you need." She straightens.

"I know, and I appreciate you. It's just new. I need a second to land and figure out where I go from here."

She nods. "Have you thought about what you want to do?"

"About what?"

"About work."

I shake my head. "It was always PT, and there's no way anyone will hire me with that mark on my file."

"You never know. Have you thought about training? What about at Lily's gym?"

I lift a shoulder. It's not a bad idea, and I know the owners of her gymnastics place are always looking for staff. But they're looking for coaches, not for physical therapists. I don't want to coach.

Still, it wouldn't hurt to talk to them next time I'm there.

"I'll think about it."

"That's the spirit. Now about this Tanner situation," she says, and my mother chooses that moment to perk her ears. She saunters over toward us as my aunt moves to watch the kids play their game.

"There's a Tanner situation?" she asks, a gleam in her eyes.

I give Jess one of those *thanks a lot* kind of glares, and I glance over at the kids, who are still occupied. "We were sort of seeing each other, but we're not anymore."

"Oh, come on, Cassandra. You were more than '*seeing* each other,'" Jess says, putting air quotes around my words.

"And now we're not," I say pointedly.

"Have you told your mom any of this?" she asks.

I was really hoping not to get into this today, but here we are. I clench my jaw for a second, and then I tell my mom the truth. I keep my voice low so my kids won't overhear, though with the cheering over by the television, I'm sure they won't. "I was fired because my boss found out most likely via Alex that I was in a relationship with my patient."

"Oh, Cassie," my mom says, and she gives me the kind of warm, tight hug that pulses tears behind my eyes. "I'm so sorry. So you ended things with him?"

"I did," I confirm. "It shouldn't be this hard. If it's right to be with someone, we shouldn't have to sneak around and risk getting caught. Besides, I didn't take the time I should have for myself after the divorce. All I wanted to do was succeed in my career and find a way to prove I didn't need Alex or his money, and I'm back to square one. Only sadder this time around."

A timer dings at the same time the game ends, and Lily loses to her brother, effectively ending the adult conversation. We eat, we give thanks, and my kids are in turkey comas, so we head home before I have to spend more time defending my life choices when I don't even want to be talking about them at all. It's earlier than we usually bolt after the holiday feast, but I'm exhausted and don't have the energy to pretend I'm not.

Lily's in the bath when the doorbell rings, and I blow out a breath as I head up to answer it. I glance through the peephole to see Alex standing there.

"What?" I hiss at him when I open the door.

"Happy Thanksgiving," he says, and he holds up a small bouquet of flowers he brought with him.

He gave me flowers a lot when we were married. I didn't know they were guilt flowers at the time, but I do now, and I narrow my eyes into a deep glare.

"What are these for?" I ask as he holds them out. I don't accept them because I have a sneaking suspicion I already know.

"For Thanksgiving. I'm thankful we can coparent and remain a part of each other's lives."

"What a load of horseshit," I mutter.

"Excuse me?"

"You heard me." And then something dawns on me.

Something I never even considered before.

"How'd you know we were back from my parents' house?" I demand.

We usually stay another hour or two at a minimum on a holiday.

How did he know I wasn't home all those weekends I spent with Tanner?

I can't help it. My eyes move to the doorbell beside me, and they're wide when I move to look at him. "Have you been spying on me on the Ring cam?"

"*Spying* is a bit misleading, don't you think? I'm just watching out for my family."

What the hell?

"It was you, wasn't it?" I demand. "You told Hayward about Tanner and me."

"Tanner and you?" he asks innocently. "What are you talking about?"

"Oh, come off it, Alex. I know it was you. You've been jealous of my relationship with him since the second I started treating him. Hell, since the second he was traded here and your son started idolizing him."

His jaw locks for a beat, and he looks menacingly at me. "Your relationship? I thought you didn't have one."

I roll my eyes. The damage is already done. "You know damn well what happened, so stop acting like you don't." I reach over and rip that goddamn doorbell off the wall. I let it drop to the ground as I realize I'm not even safe anymore in my own home. What if he has other cameras here? "Get off my property."

"I came to wish my children a happy holiday," he says.

"You can speak with them when it's your weekend." I move to slam the door in his face, but he catches it before it closes.

"Fine," he says. He holds up both hands. "Fine. You're right, okay? I was jealous, and yes, upon occasion I checked the cam to see if you were coming or going. I'll delete the app."

"And running to Hayward?" I ask, folding my arms across my chest.

"It wasn't just me. I had help."

He had *help*? Oh, that's fresh.

"From?"

"Rick," he admits.

I shake my head. "Fuck you," I hiss, and then I really do close the door in his face. I bolt the lock, too, and I make a mental note to get a locksmith here next week to change the locks. Better yet, I'll just put the godforsaken place up for sale. The whole idea of me staying here with the kids was so they could ride the same bus, go to the same school, and not have their lives completely upended because of the divorce. Or Luca, anyway, since Lily is new to kindergarten.

But fuck that.

I'm not staying in a place where I'm not safe from someone whose only goal is to sabotage me.

I realize as I lean back against the front door that I just closed in my ex's face that I never had a chance. He *never* would've let me succeed in the medical field—*his* field—without him. He always would've figured out some way to make me depend on him, whether it was for a recommendation or a job or a house.

I refuse to depend on him.

I wonder if spying on your ex-wife and kids is grounds for suing for full custody because I sure as hell would love to never have to have anything to do with him ever again.

I can't do that to my kids. As much as I hate him, I know he loves them. As bad a person as he is, he's still a good dad.

After I get Lily to bed, watch some *Expedition Unknown* with Luca, and get him down to bed, I pour myself another glass of wine and wonder how the hell I'm going to get my life back in order.

Chapter 52: Tanner Banks

A Bottle of Casamigos with Your Name on It

My flight is after the Sunday night game. The Storm wins at home, and next week we play the Thursday night game in Seattle, a game I won't travel to anyway. I'll miss practice this week, but I'm out anyway, and I need this time for my mental health.

Nick sent me with a whole regimen of stretches and exercises for my knee, and it's not like my athlete brothers are going to let me get away with flaking on any of it.

I text Asher as I'm waiting at the airport.

Me: *Heading your way for the next few days. Let me know if you can get away for dinner. Killer catch in the fourth today, by the way.*

His response is quick, and it makes me laugh.

Asher: *Thanks. The throw could've used some work, but he's no Tanner Banks. You're welcome to stay here if you like teething babies and an old man about to turn thirty.*

Me: *Thanks for the incredible offer, but I booked a hotel. Miller and I aren't too far behind you, you know.*

In fact, we're only three months younger than him.

Asher: *I have a bottle of Casamigos with your name on it if you want to stop by tonight.*

Me: *I will take you up on that.*

Once I land, I grab an Uber over to Asher's place, and I text him to let him know when I've arrived so as not to wake the baby. His wife is in the family room rocking the baby, who looks like he just fell asleep, and she gives me a big smile and leans in for a friendly hug before she heads upstairs to get him down.

Asher gives me a hug, and then he slaps me on the back. "How's the knee?"

I glance at his shirt, not sure if I can take him seriously with enlarged characters from the *Toy Story* franchise staring back at me, but I give him the latest. "I just switched PTs, but overall it's doing well." I follow him into the kitchen, and he grabs the familiar bottle and slides it across the counter. "How'd you know I'd need a drink?"

"You flew to Vegas immediately after tonight's game. Guys who are doing well don't tend to do that. So why are you here?" he asks. He grabs a glass out of the cabinet and slides it toward me, and he gets a second for himself. I pour us each a few fingers from the bottle.

I hold up my glass, and he clinks his to mine. We each take a sip before I answer.

"Aside from the obvious family shit on top of the injury?" I ask.

He nods. "Was Thanksgiving with your folks too much to take?"

I shake my head as I let out a sigh. "It was fine." I clear my throat, and then I blurt out the truth. "I was sleeping with my physical therapist. Her boss found out about us and fired her, and she ended things with me." I shrug. "I guess I just needed to skip town for a few days." I realize it's not as simple as all that, but those are pretty much the basics.

"Hm," he grunts.

I bare my soul to this dude and he gives me a *hm?* I stare at him as I wait for something more. "What?"

"Well, the way you said all that makes it sound like no big deal, yet you're here, so it must be." He raises his brows pointedly.

"Yeah. It got serious." I take a sip of my tequila.

"So let me get this straight. You found out about Eddie. You tore your ACL, sidelining you for an entire season. And then you lost the girl?"

I press my lips together as I raise my brows and nod. "Yeah. That pretty much sums it up."

He tips the tequila over my glass generously, and I chuckle as I hold it up in his direction. "It's not helping the way it should," I admit.

"You just haven't had enough." He laughs, but he turns serious. "What can I do?"

I lift a shoulder. "Nothing. I just needed some time away from all of it."

"Let's start at square one. I know the family thing was a big shock, but we've had a year to get used to the idea. Have you talked to Dad at all?"

I shake my head. "He called after the surgery, but I blew him off."

He takes a sip of his tequila. "Look, out of all of us, I guess I've always been the closest to him. It wasn't by my choice, but it is what it is. He does shitty things, but deep down, there's a good side to him. We just need to give him the chance to let it out."

"I've made progress toward forgiving my mom," I admit. "Cass—that's the PT I was seeing—she's a single mom, and she made me see that sometimes mothers do what they have to do to protect their kids."

He glances up at the ceiling, presumably thinking of his wife and kid. "Yeah, they do. And fathers do, too. Eddie knew he couldn't give you and Miller the life you deserved when he already had the four of us to deal with, and he panicked."

"I guess what gets me about all of it is the fact that he panicked when he found out she was pregnant, but he doubled down by paying her until we were twenty-eight. Why? Why did he stop paying her to keep quiet?" I ask.

"He had nothing left to lose," Asher says quietly. "He already lost it all, and he couldn't afford to keep paying her. He made it seem like he accidentally let it slip to me, but it was calculated. He knew I wouldn't keep it quiet."

I reach over and slug his arm. "I'm glad you didn't."

His mouth tips up in a faint smile. "I'm glad, too. It's nice having little brothers for a change."

I laugh. I'm taller than him, and Miller's bigger than him, but I guess technically we're his little brothers—by three months.

"The knee is progressing, so what are you going to do about the girl?" he asks as if he's solving my problems one at a time.

"She ended it. I'm not sure what else there is to do."

"Uh…you fight?" he suggests.

"She's got two kids, man. She lost her job, and she blames me. I can fight all I want, but it's a losing battle." I tip the tequila to my lips.

"If you say so."

I guess I was expecting him to try to push a little harder to convince me, to tell me about his personal experience where he fought for the girl…but one thing I've learned about Asher is that I should expect the unexpected.

The way he says it tells me he doesn't believe me, and I let those words play in my mind as he tells me he's going to call it a night, and I head back toward my hotel.

I'm not ready for sleep yet, so I find myself in the high stakes room as I blow through a little cash and drink more tequila. Cass is on my mind as always, and I think back to the words she said to me the last time we parted. It hasn't even been a full week yet. The words are still fresh, and they still hurt.

Maybe he's right. Maybe I need to fight. But I have no fight left in me. I've taken too many hits. I'm down for the count.

And I'm not sure how to climb back up out of it.

Chapter 53: Cassie Fields

Motivation to Start Putting My Life Back Together

The kids asked about Tanner all weekend.

"Why aren't you at his house today?"

"Can we come with and swim again?"

"Is he all better?"

When I told them I'm no longer working with him, they were devastated. Luca cried. Lily went to her room and slammed her door.

When I told him it was a mistake introducing him to my kids, this is what I meant. It's not just him and me ending things. It's all of it. It isn't just my heartbreak to suffer alone. It's theirs, too, and knowing they're sad about it only hurts me all over again.

They fell for him. Admittedly, it was in a different way than how I fell for him, but they still did, and now their feelings are hurt. The last thing I ever want to do is hurt my kids, and that's why I find myself standing at the bus stop chatting with Jess long after the bus is out of sight.

"Did I make a mistake?" I ask softly when it's just the two of us.

"You want my brutal honesty?"

I purse my lips. "No. I want you to lie and tell me I did the right thing."

"You know I won't lie to you."

I sigh.

"Yes, you made a mistake," she says flatly. "You're putting blame in the wrong spot because you're hurt you were fired, and you're sad over losing your job. But just for a moment, I want you to visualize your future. Think beyond high school. Lily's graduating college, Luca's finding success in his chosen field, and you're officially an empty nester…is it your job that you're turning to, or is it your partner?"

"It's not that simple," I whine.

"Yeah, it actually is, Cassie. And I'm not going to protect your feelings by sugarcoating it. You have to do what's right for you and your kids, but at this point, you're the only one who can fix it." She shrugs at the end, and maybe she's right.

It doesn't *feel* that simple, though.

Maybe I should call him.

I flip on the television as I start breakfast, and the channel lands on some celebrity gossip show—one I never watch, to be honest, but I just cracked an egg and I can't grab the remote to change it. Just as I'm drying my hands on a towel, my ears perk up as my head whips to the screen at the mention of his name.

"In celebrity sightings, Tanner Banks, injured quarterback of the San Diego Storm, was spotted last night at a club in Vegas." The screen shifts from the host to a video clearly recorded on someone's phone. It's definitely Tanner, and he's chugging from a glass while someone sprays a champagne bottle nearby. He slams the glass down with a laugh, and it feels like divine intervention.

344

It's a sign.

I'm sad and sulking, and he's...

Well, he's in Vegas. At a club. Like the one we met at.

And he's chugging liquid from a glass and laughing with people I don't know.

I flip off the television—both with my finger and with the remote—and I decide that I need to use it as motivation.

Motivation to start putting my life back together.

And with that in mind, I finish my eggs and head over to the gym where Lily takes her gymnastics lessons.

I spot the owner at the front desk, and I march over toward her. She's shuffling some papers around as she spot-checks something from the paper on the computer.

"Good morning, Janet," I say brightly.

"Cassie, it's good to see you in here. What can I do for you?" she asks. She sets the papers down and focuses her attention on me.

"I'm sure this is a longshot, but I'm a practicing physical therapist, and I was wondering if you have any staff openings. I've loved gymnastics my whole life, and I'm really interested in working with athletes." I stand confidently even though I'm no longer feeling that confidence inside.

"Oh, I had no idea you were a physical therapist. Unfortunately, we're not hiring, but I'll keep you in mind," she says, and her voice is apologetic.

"Do you have a PT on staff?" I press. "Because I'd even consider part-time work where I could do some additional training with the athletes before or after their sessions."

"We don't. But you bring up an interesting idea, and it's something I'll discuss with Nate," she says, naming her husband.

"I appreciate that," I say with a smile. "I'm transitioning from stay-at-home mom back to the work force, and it's not as easy as you might think."

"I'm sure it's not," she says. "Best of luck to you, and I'll certainly be in touch if something opens."

"I appreciate that." I don't want to get too pushy, so I walk out toward my car after that. I went in with such hope, and I'm leaving it all there in the lobby.

I don't know what to do with myself. I realize this is just one of what will likely be many rejections, and it was a soft one at that since she's going to consider a new position—if she really meant that. But getting the job at Motion Orthopedics felt so easy.

And it was all taken away pretty easily, too.

I head toward home because I'm not sure what else to do. I put on *Expedition Unknown*, grab the bracelet supplies, and give in to both my kids' favorite hobbies even as I realize how much this episode makes me think of Tanner.

I find myself stringing a bracelet with his name on it, tears in my eyes, and I realize that even this task, doing my kids' hobbies, somehow connects back to him.

Maybe it's time to find some hobbies of my own.

Chapter 54: Tanner Banks

Doubt Equals Hope

I slept in.

It's not my usual style. On a typical day, I'm up and at 'em bright and early to get in a workout before workouts.

But on a typical day, I'm not mourning the loss of whatever it was that Cassie and I had along with not being able to play football. I guess this is my new normal, and I hate the fuck out of it.

I drank too much last night. Stayed up too late. Spent too much money. Ran into an old buddy I played with in college, and somehow we ended up at a club together. It was innocent enough, and it was nice to get out and blow off some steam with an old friend.

But I'm paying for it this morning. I'm not the same guy I was the last time I drank with the buddy from last night, that's for damn sure.

Grayson told me to come to the bakery for lunch today, so I head that way after a long shower that mostly helps with the headache. I park behind the back door and knock, and Grayson opens the door a minute later.

For just a second, something washes over me. Cassie didn't know who I was—or who Grayson was—but she'd heard his name, and that's who she thought she was sleeping with the night we were together here in Vegas.

It feels like a lifetime ago. So much has happened over the last four months.

"Hey, man. You look rough," Grayson says candidly. He gives me a quick hug with a pound on the back, and I dish it back.

"So do you."

He laughs. "Asher said to make you a box of Nash's Nibbles, so it must be serious. What's going on?"

"Something cookies can't solve," I say dryly.

"Oh, shit. Must be really bad."

"He told you, didn't he?" I ask.

He nods and slings an arm around my shoulders. "Yeah, man, and I'm sorry. Bring her a box of Ava's cookies. It'll fix everything."

I laugh. "If only it were that simple. I will take a box of cookies on my way out, though."

We head through the bakery and toward the break room, where I spot Missy, Grayson's mom.

I've met her a couple of times, though we really haven't had the sort of conversation that meant much to either of us. It's awkward. I'm the product of a relationship my father had with my mother while he was married to this woman, and frankly, she deserved better than the hand she was dealt. By all accounts, Missy Nash is a force to be reckoned with. She'd have to be. She raised the four Nash boys, and they all turned out pretty damn great.

"Tanner, so good to see you," she says as she lifts to a stand. She gives me a quick hug, and she sits back down to her sandwich. "You have to get one of these. They're amazing."

"One of what she's having," I say to Grayson, and he chuckles.

"Be right back."

It's just Missy and me for the moment, and I sit across from her. "How have you been?"

"Me? Oh, I'm fine. Never better. But tell me about you, honey. How's your knee?"

The way she addresses me with a term of endearment and so much genuine care tells me whatever awkwardness I feel between us is of my own making.

I slide into the chair across from her. "The knee is progressing. Surgery was seven weeks ago, and the swelling is gone at this point. Things are going well."

"And how are you doing? I've seen firsthand how hard it is to sit and watch the game when you want to be out there in the thick of it." She gives me the kind of sympathetic look I wish my own mom would give me, and I find myself opening up to her.

"I can't honestly think of a time I've felt worse."

"Oh, honey," she says, and she reaches across to squeeze my hand. "Things will get better. Just get through the season, and you'll be back out there in a few months."

"It's not just that," I admit.

Her brows rise as she waits for it.

"It's a woman."

Her lips tip up in a smile. "Always is. I watched all four of my boys go through it, and trust me when I say a mother can always tell. What happened?"

"Are you sure you want to talk about this? Isn't it weird, you and me connecting like this?"

She shrugs as she shakes her head. "It's not weird for me. Is it weird for you?"

"A little. I just mean…knowing what I know. About where I came from."

She twists her lips. "Look, Tanner. Some football players were built differently back then, and so were some football wives. I swept more under the rug than I should have. It's not like I didn't know what he was doing, but for a long time, I thought it was what I'd signed up for. I wasn't exactly innocent in all of it. He did his thing, and I did mine, and we stayed together for the kids until it no longer made sense. For what it's worth, I told him to be honest from the start. But he had this vision of what he wanted out of his life, and I took a step back to let him have it. And your mom…she and I had a conversation once, and I learned that she didn't know he was married. She's not to blame in any of this, and I really hope you're not holding any of it against her."

"I have been," I admit.

"Imagine being a woman, twenty-one years old, still in college with twin boys relying on you for their every need. She did what she had to do to survive, and it's as simple as that."

I never thought of it like that, but she's doling out quite the truth bomb. And it doesn't end there.

"Now about this woman who has your heart," she says once she's satisfied that she's getting through to me. "What's going on with her?"

"She was my PT, and her boss found out about us. Fired her, she ended it with me, and here we are."

"Can you get her back?" she asks.

I shrug. "Doubt it."

"Doubt is uncertainty, and uncertainty means there's hope left. So to me, doubt equals hope."

Doubt equals hope. I feel like that should go on a T-shirt or something. But more, I feel like I should take that advice to heart.

QUITTING THE *Quarterback*

Is there hope left where Cassie and I are concerned?

Everyone around me is telling me to fight for her, and I thought I was doing the right thing by backing away and giving her space. But maybe they're all right.

Maybe I was meant to skip town and get far away from everything to try to look at things from a different perspective. Well, this is certainly perspective, and I think after lunch, I need to head to the airport, get back to San Diego, and start fighting to get Cassie back.

The door opens, and I'm expecting Grayson to walk in with my chicken salad sandwich. It's Grayson, but his hands are empty.

And his face is blanched.

"Grayson?" Missy says tentatively. "Are you okay?"

He shakes his head a little, and his eyes seem to come into focus on his mom. "Asher just called."

She seems to stiffen, and I glance over at Grayson.

"It's Dad," Grayson says. "He's dead."

351

Chapter 55: Cassie Fields

My Own Hobbies

I pile the clothes that no longer fit Lily on top of the dresser, and I reorganize the drawer with what's left. I put the clothes into a tote, and then I'm done.

The house is organized. Completely. Top to bottom. All of Luca's clothes are organized, and so are Lily's. I even went through my own. The kitchen is spotless. The playroom is organized.

It's all done.

Every task on my list is done, and I don't know how we got here. I don't know if I've ever actually *been* here. It's always running from one thing to the next, but right now...I have nothing else to do. Not until the kids get home from school, anyway.

And I still don't want to live here, but I'm not sure where else to go. I'm not sure what to do with myself. I don't even really have my own hobbies anymore.

I used to love running. Maybe a run would do me some good.

I used to love doing puzzles. Maybe a puzzle would do me some good.

I used to enjoy scrapbooking. Maybe working on the baby books that have gone far too long without any attention at all would do me some good.

I have no hobbies that are just for me anymore. I gave them up when I had kids so that I could focus on them and their needs, their likes, their desires.

But they're both at school, and I'm here. I feel restless. I'm tired but don't want to sleep, antsy but don't want to do anything. I can't help but wonder if these feelings are because of the divorce, because both kids are at school full-time now, or because I got fired.

Maybe some combination of all three.

I can't stop thinking about Tanner being in Vegas having fun and moving on while I'm stuck here in neutral. I feel lost, and I think it's because I was starting to let Tanner be my compass. Or we were each other's compass, anyway. Something along those lines.

I sigh heavily as I realize I've been kneeling in front of Lily's dresser for the last ten minutes. I push to a stand, using the dresser to help lift up, and I hear each of my knees crack as I straighten.

I'm stiff, and I think a run—or a light jog, at least—might do me some good. I change into my running gear, and I head out the front door and take a lap around my neighborhood. I jog by my neighbor's house, and three down from that is Katie's place. I run around the corner toward Jess's house, and a little further down by Natasha's.

They're my three closest friends in this neighborhood, my three only friends in the neighborhood now. When a divorce happens, it's not just the husband and wife separating. It's years of friendships, too. I run by Gemma and Michael Collins's house. Alex got them in the divorce. I run by the Xaviers' house and the Gladstones. Alex got both of them, too.

I hate how divisive it all feels. He doesn't deserve any of them since he cheated on me, and yet friendships seemed to split based on who was closer. I was always closer to Natasha, Katie, and Jess, so I got them.

But really…nobody wins in any of it, and least of all when one of us is deceitful by nature. I thought the cheating was the worst of it, but that was before he conspired to make sure I lost my job. To make sure I'd always be dependent on him.

So maybe I'm not meant for a path in physical therapy. Maybe I'm not meant for anything medical at all.

Does anyone pay to put puzzles together? Or to scrapbook?

I make my first loop, and I pause by the driveway to pant for a few seconds before I take off for a second lap around the neighborhood. My lungs are burning and my legs are wobbly, but at least I feel it. And that's definitely something.

I run a third lap, and I walk the fourth to cool down. I head inside and take a shower, and then I put together a puzzle. Before I know it, it's time to pick up the kids.

The whirlwind of the evening begins, and it's snacks and homework, baseball practice and making dinner. Through it all, Tanner is never very far from my mind.

I thought after a week things would start to get easier. I thought giving it a little time would help me pick up the pieces.

Apparently a week isn't enough time.

I do another puzzle once I get the kids to bed, this time in complete silence. I don't have a show on in the background. No music. Just me and my thoughts, the direction of which I do my very best to force on fitting one puzzle piece into another.

But even now, he sneaks his way in.

Is he still in Vegas?

Is he thinking about me?

How's his knee?

Is he okay?

One little phone call would answer all of those questions, but he's busy moving on.

I guess maybe a week just isn't enough time to move on.

But what will be? Another week? A month? A year?

The way things feel right now, I'm not sure any amount of time will ever be enough for me to move on from Tanner Banks.

Which is funny considering how easy it was to get over Alex in the grand scheme of things.

But the more I think about it, the more I wonder whether I really *have* to get over him. Maybe he's moving on, and maybe that's okay.

And maybe it's equally okay if I *don't* move on. Maybe I can't because I'm hopelessly, madly, desperately in love with him. And I wish he was with me, too. But even if he isn't, at least I got to experience a few months where it sure as hell felt like he was, and maybe that just has to be enough for this middle-aged single mom.

It was sure one hell of a few months with the quarterback, and the more life takes me on a pattern of rinse and repeat, the more I wonder whether we'll ever be able to find our way back to each other.

Chapter 56: Tanner Banks

What the Fuck Was I Holding Onto

Strange how you can hold a grudge against someone, but the moment they're gone…so is the grudge.

What the fuck was I holding onto? I missed my window, and I haven't had enough time to process how to feel about that yet.

I need to call Miller. Grayson is making calls now, and Missy, too. Grayson's wife, Ava, is in and out of here as she brings her husband and mother-in-law what they need.

Family is pulling together in this tragic moment, and I find myself a part of it. The moment. The family. All of it.

I wait until I know Miller will be home before I head out back to my rental car and slip into the driver's seat for a moment. I stare at my phone as I try to make sense of any of it, and eventually I realize I can't.

I dial my brother, and he answers right away.

"Saw the TMZ report about you at the club last night. Score any pussy?" he answers, his voice full of merriment.

"I, uh…I'm calling with some news."

He clears his throat. "What's going on?" His voice loses the merriment as a bit of fear steps in, something only I would be able to detect because I know him so well.

"Eddie Nash is dead."

He's silent for a beat before he mutters, "Jesus Christ. What happened?"

"Assault."

"Give it to me straight, bro."

I clear my throat. "He was stabbed." It was sudden, and it was intentional—according to the secondhand account I got from Asher, anyway.

I don't know all the details. All I know is that Asher found out first. Asher called Lincoln first, Grayson second, and presumably Spencer third.

"Stabbed? What the fuck?" he asks.

"That was my first thought, too." I tell him what I know. "I guess he'd gotten tied up with some local bookies. He had his kids bail him out in the past, but he wasn't quick enough this time."

"Jesus," he curses again.

"I just found out about an hour ago, so I don't know about plans or anything yet. I'll keep you updated."

"We play Thursday night this week," he reminds me.

"I know. Missy is working out the details, and I know she's working to make sure all six of us can be there. It's a short flight from San Diego, so Thursday morning might work out so you can be back by game time."

"How is Missy?" he asks.

"Wiser than me. We had a good chat, but we were interrupted with…well, this."

"Makes you think, doesn't it?" he muses.

"I can't seem to grab onto exactly what I think. You?"

"I don't know," he mutters. "How life is short. We're not guaranteed anything. All the tired clichés."

"Yeah," I murmur back. He's right, though. If I hadn't spent so much time in my anger, maybe I could've had the chance to get to know the man who was biologically my father. Asher said there was some good in him deep down, and now I have to live with the regret that I never got to see it because I never gave him the chance.

Maybe forming a relationship with him would've just messed me up even more. But now I'll never know the answer to that.

"You want me to call Mom to tell her?" he asks.

"Let's do it together," I suggest.

"I think that's a good idea."

I blow out a breath as I connect her to our call. "Tanner?" she answers.

"Miller too," my brother chimes in.

"What's going on, boys?" She sounds guarded, and she has every right to since this isn't a typical call. I don't know if we've ever three-way called her before. Usually we're just in the same room and grab the phone out of the other's hand.

"I have some news," I begin quietly. She's silent as she braces for it. "Eddie Nash passed away late last night."

"Oh," she squeaks. "What happened?"

"He, uh...he was assaulted," I say. I'm not sure why I censor it.

"Oh, how awful," she breathes.

A beat of silence fills the line as we all sit with that.

"I don't know anything about arrangements yet, but I'll let you know," I finally say.

"I'd like to be there," she says. "So, yes...if you could keep me in the loop, I'd appreciate it."

"Mom?" Miller says.

"Yeah, honey?"

"I just wanted to say…" He pauses as he gathers his thoughts. "I know it's been a strange year, but I would love to put all this behind us. Tanner and I, we didn't give him a chance, and I would hate to turn around and feel like I didn't get to say the things I needed to say to anyone else, you know what I mean?"

"I know exactly what you mean," she says quietly.

"Same for me," I grunt. "I'm sorry, Mom. And I want you to know that I understand why you did what you did."

"You do?" she asks, surprise evident in her tone.

"It was Missy Nash who made me see it," I admit.

"I just want peace in our family again," Miller says.

I nod even though they can't see me. "So do I."

"Then that's what we'll have. I love you boys," she says.

"Love you, Mom," the two of us say at the same time.

"Tell Dad we love him, too," I say, and a lump seems to clog the back of my throat after the words are out.

"I will," she says, and I hear the emotion in her voice, too.

Missy makes things happen, and when I head back inside, I learn she has planned a small, private service for Thursday morning.

I head to my hotel after I help with the arrangements and make sure my half-brothers all have what they need, and I sit at the bar with a glass of tequila for a while as I contemplate my next move.

I could go home until then, but I'm not sure I want to. My brothers here in Vegas all have someone to lean on—significant others as they deal with their loss. And their loss is much wider and deeper than mine. It's their father—the man who raised them.

That's not what he'd ever be to me because that's not what he chose for us.

I've lost out on the chance to get to know someone I'd easily written off, and I think the *what-ifs* are fueling my grief. To be honest, I don't know if I can grieve someone I never knew.

I think about calling Cassie. I think about Asher's words to fight.

I think about a lot of things, and ultimately, I drink until I don't want to drink anymore, and then I head up to bed.

Things aren't any different come morning. I'm still indecisive about what I want to do. I want to talk to Cassie. I want to hear her voice as I go through this strange gamut of emotions. But I don't want to call her with news like this. I want to call her to tell her I want her back, that I don't know how to do this life without her…

But she regrets me. She regrets introducing me to her kids. She regrets losing her job because of me. And I don't know how to put a bandage over that to heal it. I don't know that calling her with a personal need outweighs her needs.

I'm not sure I've ever put someone else's needs before my own.

When I call her, I want it to be because I figured out how to reconcile with her. I don't want it to be because of the pulsing desire to talk this out with someone outside of the equation.

But as soon as this all blows over, as soon as I get back to San Diego, I'll start fighting to win her back.

Chapter 57: Tanner Banks

The Man Who I Never Got to Call *Dad*

My parents arrive Wednesday afternoon, and I head over to Lincoln's place for dinner.

With them.

Spencer and Miller are in San Diego since they play tomorrow night, but the rest of us—Lincoln, Grayson, Asher, and me—are meeting up at Linc's place along with Missy, my parents, and some of the Nash in-laws for dinner.

It's a huge family affair, the kind reserved for weddings and funerals, I suppose. I arrive at the same time as my parents, and Missy greets us at the door.

I brace myself for…something. Fireworks. Awkwardness. I don't know what.

But to my utter shock, Missy pulls my mom into a hug. *A hug.*

"I'm so sorry for your loss," my mother says to Missy. "And for, well, everything."

"Water under the bridge, Sandra," Missy says. "Our families are merging, and whatever brought us here is in the past. But we can make a better future. For our boys."

Mom hugs Missy again, and it really does feel like it's in the past. It's quite the model of forgiveness, and I take it as the kind of example I want to model myself. Charles gets in on the hug, too, though he's more reserved than usual.

The Nash boys share memories of Eddie as we sit around a huge dinner table, and it's allowing me to see a completely different side of the man who I never got to call *Dad*.

From the sounds of things, his entire life was football. It's not surprising that Miller and I found our way there, too. Maybe he pulled strings behind the scenes for us, but I think that's something I never really want to know the answer to.

I glance over at Charles and think about how utterly weird this must be for him. He's quietly listening to the memories of the man who biologically fathered the children he would go on to raise as his own, and I can't imagine the sort of feelings he has rushing through him.

I think about Luca and Lily and how I formed an attachment to them over a short period of time. I could only dream about how that could grow and thrive if given the chance, but maybe I'll never know. And there's a distinct difference there. They have a dad. He may have treated his wife like garbage as he broke up his family, but he's still very much a part of his kids' lives—as he should be. It's his place to be.

But that doesn't mean I couldn't have found my place in there, too.

And that's a place I intend to fight for.

We stay far too late drinking and laughing at Lincoln's house, and I ride with my parents back to the hotel we're all staying at.

"How are you doing with all of this?" my mom asks me from the backseat while Charles drives. She made me sit up front since my legs are longer.

"I don't know," I admit. "The whole thing is just…" I trail off.

"Strange?" Charles supplies, and I nod.

"Yeah. I sort of just want to get through the funeral and move forward, you know? I love having four new half-brothers, but over the last year, I guess I realized that it never really mattered who biologically fathered me. What matters is the family that raised me, and I'm sorry it took me so long to see that," I say.

I hear my mom sniffle in the backseat, and that damn lump is back in my throat.

Charles reaches over and pats my leg. "It doesn't matter how long it took. I'm just happy that's where you landed."

My mom reaches over the seat to squeeze my shoulder. "Whatever got you there, I'm just glad to have my boy back."

I set my hand over hers on my shoulder. "I never went anywhere, Mom."

I hang out with my parents in Vegas, which makes for a much different trip than the last time I was here. Miller and Spencer catch the first flight on Thursday to Vegas. Miller texts me when they land bright and early a little after eight, and less than a half hour later, I'm meeting him for breakfast at a restaurant in the hotel.

He invited our parents, too, and they're meeting us. But we gave ourselves a fifteen-minute buffer to check in on each other first.

We hug at the entrance to the restaurant for a long time, neither of us wanting to let go as we cling to what's familiar in this very strange situation.

"I thought we had time," he admits quietly once we finally part.

"So did I," I say.

We head into the restaurant, and we're taken to a table, and before I even glance at the menu to figure out what I want to eat, Miller says, "Really makes you think about how life's short, doesn't it? How we're not guaranteed anything."

"Yeah," I murmur. I glance up at him and find him studying me, and I have a feeling I know what's coming. I jump in before he can. "So are you going to shoot your shot or what?"

He chuckles. "Take your own advice, man."

"It's easier to give it than to take it."

"Exactly. I was about to tell you to call Cassie," he admits.

"I'm going to. I'm going back home on Saturday. Asher's birthday is tomorrow, so I said I'd stay and hang out. But when I get home, I'm going straight to her place."

"What's the plan?" he asks.

I reach into my pocket and finger the box in there. I wasn't about to leave it in my hotel room, but I don't really want to carry it around with me, either.

And then I decide to keep it to myself. I tell Miller everything, but there's a reason why I felt compelled to bring this to Vegas with me. I didn't want it at the house I share with my brother. I didn't want him asking questions when I wasn't ready to answer them.

So maybe this one thing deserves to be kept under the vest a little while longer.

"I don't know yet," I say instead. "What about you?"

He sighs a long, deep sigh. "I can't exactly tell Sophie how I've felt about her all this time."

"Why not? It's only been…" I glance at my watch as I calculate in my brain. "What, fifteen years?"

His jaw tightens. "Aside from you, she's my best friend, and she has been for half my life. I can't blow that. And besides, she's seeing some guy."

"Doesn't it kill you to hear her talk about whoever she's seeing? How do you do it?" I ask.

"I'm a masochist." He shrugs, and I chuckle. "The truth is that I just want her to be happy."

"With you though. Right?"

"Shut up," he says petulantly. "I keep trying to find someone who compares, but nobody does."

I shake my head and clench my jaw. "All for some chick you've never even fucked."

He glares at me, and I wait for him to lecture me on how it would be *making love* when it came to her, but he glances over my shoulder, and we both see our parents are here. He stands and greets them with a hug for each of them, and that's the end of that conversation.

I tease him, but the truth is…I feel bad for him. I know he's been in love with Sophie since we were freshmen in high school, but how do you tell your best friend that? They grew close, but she had a boyfriend. When she split with him, Miller had a girlfriend. He split with *her* to shoot his shot with Sophie only to find her making out with another dude.

Their timing has always been off, and that's how it's been for the last fifteen years.

Maybe someday they'll get it right. I hope for his sake they do…but if they don't, I hope Miller can fall for someone who makes him happy.

Because that feeling of falling for Cassie is one of the single greatest events of my life even though it happened during one of the darkest.

After breakfast, the four of us will head together toward the funeral home where we'll pay our last respects to the man we never knew, the man who duped everyone who will be in attendance, the man who hurt so many of us yet still has people who loved him and showed up for him at the end.

We walk through the hotel lobby on our way out, and my parents head to the valet with Miller while I hit the restroom before we go. I'm walking through the lobby toward the valet station when I hear a voice.

"Tanner?"

I freeze, and then I slowly turn around and glance up only to find myself face to face with Cassandra Fields.

Chapter 58: Cassie Fields

I Can't Believe You're Really Here

"Cass?" he whispers softly. "Wh—what are you doing here?"

I wring my hands together nervously as I clear my throat. What *am* I doing here? I suck in a breath. "Miller texted me about your—uh, about Eddie. I had to come. I had to see you…to make sure you're okay."

He's frozen in place as he stares at me as if he's seeing some sort of illusion, as if he's hallucinating and can't quite piece together whether this is real or not.

And then he moves slowly across the lobby and stops short of me. He's clearly holding himself back, doing what he can to restrain himself. "Why?" There's a hesitance in his voice, and I hate that I put it there.

"Because I love you," I blurt. "Because I'm sorry for what I said, sorry for telling you to go, sorry for telling you that I wished I hadn't introduced you to my kids. I'm sorry that I broke us, I'm sorry that I bowed out when things got hard, but they're so, so, *so* much harder without you, and I just want to get past these hurdles and be together again because I love you so much, and my kids love you, and I want to figure out how to make this work, and I know I had goals and dreams and aspirations but none of them seem to matter at all without you. I put the blame in the wrong place. I want you to forgive me, and I want to be with you, and I didn't mean to say all this right here, right now, but I can't seem to stop myself."

Jesus, Cassie. Get a grip on yourself.

That was *not* the speech I practiced on the plane ride here.

His jaw opens and then slams shut, and he's obviously grappling for words here while my own words are vomiting all over this hotel lobby.

"You...you love me?" he asks tentatively.

"Of course I do," I say softly. And then I think...well, I may as well go all in here. I came all this way, and I've already experienced what it feels like to lose it all. The only way to go from here is up. "I've never loved anyone the way I love you."

He takes the final step to close the distance between us, and one of his hands moves to my hip while the other moves to my cheek. His eyes search mine, and they're hot there, full of heat and lust like always, but with something else there, something warm and lovely. Something like hope and love all rolled into one.

"I've never loved anyone the way I love you, either," he says softly. His lips crash down to mine, and my chest that felt so tight and crushed for the last week feels like it's opening as wave upon glorious wave of love pour out of me and into him.

He pulls back, and his eyes search mine again. "I can't believe you're really here," he says.

"I just wanted to be here for you, Tanner. I can only imagine what you're going through, and even though I was certain you'd moved on, if I could make this tragedy just the tiniest bit easier on you, then I knew I had to be here."

"Moved on? From...you?" he asks.

I lift a shoulder.

He shakes his head. "No, Cass. You don't just move on when the love of your life walks away. You fight like hell to win her back, and I was planning to head home tomorrow and head straight to your house to start that fight."

My mouth breaks out into a huge smile. "But I beat you to it?" I guess.

He chuckles. "You beat me to it." He drops a soft kiss on my lips.

"You can still fight if you want. I won't stop you, and I kind of want to see what that fight entailed."

He slips a hand into his pocket, but then he glances out toward the front of the hotel. He pulls his hand back out of his pocket and reaches for my hand instead. "I'll fight every goddamn day to make sure you know how loved you are. That's a promise."

I squeeze his hand, and then we walk together toward the doors. We get outside just as a car pulls up, and I spot Charles and Sandra as they walk over toward it with Miller trailing behind. The three of them glance up at us as we approach, and Miller raises his brows when he spots us.

"You shooting my shots for me now?" Tanner asks him.

He just grins and shrugs.

"Two can play that game," Tanner mutters, and I wonder what that's all about, but before I get the chance to ask, he ducks into the car, and then we're on our way to the funeral home.

Tanner introduces me to all his half-brothers—including Grayson, with whom he shares a lot of similarities—and *damn*, this family has good genes, all thanks to the man we're here to celebrate. Tanner also meets some cousins, or half-cousins, I suppose, along with his uncle, a man who also played in the NFL.

The service is short and sweet, and Mrs. Nash planned a luncheon at a restaurant nearby, so we all head there after.

It's a long day that feels short because my hand is firmly planted in his, and the more time we spend together, the more I know how very much I never want to let go again.

But today isn't for us. Not really. It's for family, and in the moments when he's occupied, Miller talks with me, or Sandra and Charles do. They make me feel like I belong here, like I'm a part of things.

And I don't miss the secret look his mother shoots Tanner when she thinks I'm not looking.

She approves, and he's forgiven her, and everything is starting to fall into the right place once again.

"Do you have any hot sauce?" Miller asks our server as she sets a fancy plate of pasta in front of him.

"Dude, that's disgusting," Tanner says before she can answer.

"We have Tabasco," she offers, and Miller makes a face.

"No Cholula?" he asks, and he sounds like he's practically begging.

She shakes her head and offers an apologetic smile. "I'm so sorry."

He sighs heavily, and as she walks away, he pulls a tiny, travel-sized bottle out of his pocket. "Don't leave home without it," he says as he shakes it all over his noodles, and Tanner and I just laugh as we watch him. He holds up the bottle. "Want to try?"

I shake my head. "I'm good, thanks." I can't help my giggle as I think about all the future meals I'll have with Tanner's brother as we watch him pour hot sauce all over everything.

It's a future I can't wait for.

Chapter 59: Tanner Banks

To the Future

It's just the two of us after a long day together, and I'm nervous.

I have a question to ask her. A proposition of sorts.

Miller and Spencer headed out right after lunch and flew directly to Seattle to meet up with the rest of our teammates. I watched the game with Cassie and my parents in the sportsbook, the part of the casino with huge television screens set up for betting on the outcome of games, and after the Storm pulled out a victory, I knew it was time to finally ask my question.

I shouldn't be nervous. This is Cassie, and she showed up for me today. But what I want to ask her isn't just about *her*. She comes as a package deal, and the whole idea of all of this is still really new.

But it also feels right.

I just hope it feels right for her, too.

The timing may not be perfect on a day like this, but the events of the last few days also proved to me that there is no perfect time. If you don't say what you need to say when you have the chance, it may be too late to ever say it.

And I won't make that mistake again.

I'm taking her to Skybar, one of my favorite rooftop lounges in Vegas. We can look down over the Strip as we sip tequila and talk, and I can finally give her what's been setting my pocket on fire for the last few days.

We're shown to the table I reserved, and it's nestled in a private corner. The chairbacks are high, so it's like we're in our own little world as we stare out over the view together, and the service is top-notch as my tequila and her margarita arrive shortly after we order.

I hold up my glass, and she mirrors my movements.

"To the future," I say, and she taps her glass to mine.

"To the future," she echoes, and we each take a sip.

I take a second and a third before I set my glass down and turn away from the view and toward the beautiful woman sitting beside me. "How have you been over the last week?"

"Awful," she admits, and she shoots me a wry smile.

"Same. Where are Luca and Lily?" I ask.

"With my parents tonight, and they'll go to Alex's this weekend." She glances up at me from lowered lashes. "They miss you, you know."

My chest tightens at that. "I miss them, too."

"I just want to clarify what I meant when I said those awful things, Tanner. I regretted that they were going to be hurt, not that I introduced you to them. You are incredible with them, and they adore you."

I nod as her words confirm what I had suspected but didn't really believe. "Thank you for saying that. To be honest, those were the words that cut the most, even though eventually that was the conclusion I came to."

"I'm sorry for what I said."

"Water under the bridge," I say with a shrug, quoting Missy Nash in some attempt to model the forgiveness I saw between her and my mom. "Can I ask you a question?"

She takes another sip of margarita, and then she asks, "Is it a one sip or a finish my drink first type of question?"

I chuckle. "Just a sip. I know how important your career is to you. Have you found a job?"

She blinks and averts her gaze to the window as she shakes her head, and she drinks a little more margarita. "Jess suggested maybe I look into working with student-athletes at the place where Lily does gymnastics, but they're not hiring. I'm not really sure what I want to do, but I do know sitting at home sulking over losing everything in one fell swoop isn't it."

"You didn't lose everything, and maybe you didn't lose anything," I say quietly.

Her eyes dart to mine, and her brows are pushed together in confusion.

"Come work for me. Be my personal physical therapist until I'm able to get back on the field, and then you can shift to my trainer. It'll be a full-time position, and I know I'm no picnic to work with, but I need someone who can handle me. You're the only one, Cass. And it'll be reduced hours so you can be with the kids and still have time for your own life."

"Tanner, that's not a full-time position," she protests.

"Okay, then open your own practice," I blurt. "And I'm just one of your clients. You could work with other injured athletes, or you could bond with the wives of athletes, or you could work with gymnasts. And I can help you get started."

Her eyes widen as she stares at me like I have two heads for a beat, but she seems to soften a bit as she thinks it over. "Your trainer *and* my own practice?"

I reach into my pocket and finally pull out the little box, and I flip it open and remove its contents. I slide it across the table toward her, and she stares down at it as the shiny metal glints in the dim light in here. "And my roommate."

She gasps as she picks up the key and turns it over in her hand. "Roommate?" Her eyes shift from the key to me.

"I bought a place in San Diego, and I was hoping maybe you'd be interested in moving in with me. I haven't even told Miller yet. It's close to your place so the kids won't have to change schools, and it has a pool so we can partake in our favorite swimming activities, and there's a kid-friendly fence around the pool. It's got a few extra bedrooms for, you know…growth, or guests, or an office, or whatever. And if it's too soon and you don't want to, that's totally fine, too, but I felt like Miller and I deserved our own spaces, but I'd love for this space to be yours and the kids', too, and—"

She cuts me off. "Oh my God, Tanner, stop. Yes!" She leans across the table and presses her lips to mine. "Of course yes. To all of it," she says, holding her forehead to mine for a beat, and then she moves to pull away, but I pull her back into me for a lingering kind of kiss. She looks a little dazed once I let her go, and she finishes her margarita. She glances over at me. "Can I be honest with you about something?"

"Always. Everything."

"But I need you to promise me you aren't going to go all caveman apeshit on me."

My brows furrow. "When have I ever gone caveman apeshit?"

"Any time I bring up my ex."

I drain my drink at the mention of his name. "Okay," I say icily. "Bring it on."

She sighs. "He's been watching me via the doorbell camera, and it made me wonder if he has other cameras around the house."

"I'll fucking kill him."

She purses her lips and rolls her eyes. "See? But anyway, I've been thinking maybe it would be best to move. Start over. I just wasn't sure where to go, and I didn't want to uproot the kids when they're in the middle of a school year."

"I get that. And if you want to move in first to get used to it with the kids but without me there, that's fine too. I want to make sure everyone is comfortable with the living situation. Except Alex. I want him to hate it with every fiber of his being."

Her brows pinch together. "Without you there? Hell no, Tanner Banks. It's *your* house that you invited us to."

I shake my head. "No, Cass. It's *our* house. I bought it for us."

She looks surprised at that. "What if I said no?"

"Then I would've sold it." I shrug. "But I told you, I was gearing up to fight for you. I know what we shared, and somewhere deep down, I knew that house was where we belonged together."

"Can I see it?" she asks softly.

I pull my phone out of my pocket, and I navigate to the listing to show it to her. She gasps at the first picture, and I do have to admit, it's pretty damn impressive.

I know I'll need to tell Miller, but we've been here before. When I moved out of the place we shared together in Arizona after I moved in with Heather, I signed over my half of the house to Miller. We'll do the same thing here if he wants to stay, or we'll sell it and move on.

Who knows? Maybe he'll even end up in the house we're sharing now with Sophie.

If he ever gets up the nerve to shoot his shot. Maybe I need to do it for him like he did for me.

But not tonight. Tonight, my focus is entirely on the woman sitting beside me and the future that we're going to create together.

Chapter 60: Cassie Fields

Chicken Tenders and Sweet Potato Fries

It's really all falling into place. I stare at the water spraying into the air at the fountains outside the Bellagio as I slide my hand into his, and it feels like a full-circle moment.

We weren't meandering down the Strip that time like we are this time, but we ended up at the same hotel.

Last time, we took in the conservatory. This time, we're taking in the fountains.

Even though we both want to get up to the room for what comes next, these little moments together where we're just enjoying the scenery feel just as important as we create the kinds of memories that will only strengthen our bond.

He leans over and presses a soft kiss to my cheek, his familiar soft, woodsy scent overpowering my senses. I lean into him, not really sure how I got quite so lucky, but sure I want to cling onto this moment with him.

He tightens his arm around my shoulders, and I feel this sense that I'm exactly where I'm supposed to be.

I didn't know whether he'd forgive me for the things I said when I came out here, but the second I got the call from Miller, there was no other option but to show up.

And that's what we'll continue to do for each other moving forward. Show up.

Once the fountain show is over, we head into the hotel. We bypass the conservatory this time and head for the elevators. He pauses before he hits the button to head up to his room. "Do you need chicken tenders and sweet potato fries first?"

I chuckle as I slowly shake my head. "I just need you, Tanner."

His eyes heat as they fall onto me, and he doesn't stop looking at me even when he moves to press the button to take us up to his suite.

Our elevator is filled with other people, so we keep our composure. We head down the hall toward our room, and the very second the door clicks shut behind us, he's on me. His lips are on my mouth, and his body is backing me up until I feel the wall behind me, and I'm consumed by him.

He drags his lips from mine down my neck and into my cleavage, and he breathes in as I hold his head near my heart for a beat.

"God, I missed you," he says, his hands moving along my torso.

I duck my head to meet his eyes, and he straightens. "I missed you, too," I say.

His eyes study mine for a few seconds before his mouth crashes back down to mine, and then all bets are off.

He's a hungry animal, and I'm the desperate prey ready to let him take whatever he wants from me.

He doesn't move us from the wall. Instead, he bucks his hips wildly against me, and I moan at the feel of his erection as it slams against me. The need to feel him inside me again pulses heavy as an ache throbs down low, but I barely have time to focus on it because his tongue is thrashing against mine as his hands move to clutch my breasts over the dress I'm wearing.

He reaches under the dress and slides my panties to the side before pushing a finger into me, and I ride his hand as I take in all the other sensations—his mouth on mine, one hand still massaging my breast, the other hand under my dress as he fingers me. It's a lot of different things plowing into me at once, and he uses some combination of his hand and his mouth to move my breast over my dress. He sucks my nipple into his mouth, using his tongue to tweak it into a tight bud, and I cry out as heat starts to ripple through my core.

"Oh, God, yes, Tanner," I moan, and my voice seems to spur him into action.

He pulls his hands from my body as he grapples with his belt, and then he reaches in and pulls out his cock. It's hard and heavy in his hand. "Get naked," he demands as his hand slides along his cock a few times.

He yanks at his shirt, and buttons go flying everywhere, but he's not to be bothered as he continues to stroke his cock. He slips out of his shirt as I scramble out of my dress and underwear set.

I'm about to get down on my knees and suck him into my mouth when he reaches for my hand.

"I want to fuck you up against the wall, but I'm assuming it's not recommended since I'm just under eight weeks post-surgery," he says.

I try not to put on my medical hat even though I just accepted his job offer. "Best to keep weight off your knee," I say lightly, and he nods as he moves toward the bed.

He sits. "Climb on," he says, and I chuckle as he raises a challenging brow.

I do as I'm told, loving the way he commands me again in this moment, and I wrap my legs around his torso as he reaches under me to align his cock with my body. I'm slightly above him, completely naked, and I wrap my arms around his neck as he buries his face between my tits.

He grunts as he starts to move, sucking one of my tits into his mouth as I ride him. It's intense as he moves to ignite every zone of my body.

He lets go of the hold he has on my nipple as he drags his lips to my neck, and he sucks on the skin there for a few hot beats as he continues pumping into me. "Fuck, Cass, this pussy was made for my cock. You're so hot and wet for me, baby," he murmurs against my skin. "I feel you getting tighter and tighter. Come for me, Cass. Come all over me so I can fuck you until you come all over me again."

"Oh God, Tanner, yes!" I cry as my body bends to his provocative request. The climax tears through me, and even though it hasn't even been two weeks since the last time we were together, it feels like it's been forever as we reconnect.

My orgasm is vicious as my pussy clenches onto him. The rest of my body does the same as my legs tighten around him and my nails dig into the skin on his back. He thrusts into me relentlessly, riding out wave after wave of intense, brutal pleasure.

"Fuck, that's so tight. I love it when you come," he murmurs, his lips returning to my neck as the waves start to slip into the warmth as it spreads through my body. I continue holding onto him since he's still delivering thrust after glorious thrust.

He reaches between us to thumb my clit just as my body starts to come down from the high, and it's like he knows exactly what to do to make my body do what it was created to do.

I cry out at the feel of another impending orgasm, and he grunts as he closes in on his, too. "Fuck," he groans, drawing out the word. "Oh yes, I'm going to come so hard, baby. Take it all," he says, and he stops thumbing my clit to slip a finger into my pussy along with his cock. It's a stretch that hurts with a side of pleasure as he fingers me and fucks me at the same time, and when he pulls his finger out to finger my clit again, the relief of having his cock moving in me again without the finger is an intense sort of pleasure that propels me straight into my second orgasm.

I grip onto him tightly, my body hot for him everywhere as this climax is even more ferocious than the first. I can't make sense of anything as a string of words grunt out of my body, I hear his words as he tells me that he's coming, coming so hard, that only I can make him come like this.

I'm sure his words are gorgeous and beautiful, but my head rings as my body seems to grab onto the focal point of pleasure between our bodies, and I collapse into him as the climax wanes into a soft afterglow.

He holds me in his arms as he lays back onto the bed, cradling me even though he's still inside me, and once he shifts so he falls out of me, I feel his come as the wet heat rushes out of me.

It's intimate and sexy, and he leans over and presses his lips to mine. He pulls back to look me in the eyes, and as our eyes connect, I see the sort of future I never thought would be within my grasp—sexy nights like this, a true friendship, a partnership. Things I thought I had but never really did—not like this, anyway.

It's another pure, intimate moment where my soul seems to connect a little more with his. I'm not sure I ever really believed in soul mates…but then I met mine.

Chapter 61: Cassie Fields

Christen the Kitchen

It's a whirlwind weekend in Vegas. Between putting in hours with the Nash and Banks families and spending a lot of time naked with the quarterback—plus catching a couple of shows while we're in town—the weekend flies by.

I find myself walking through the airport with Tanner. He's recognized, and I don't have to hide. I can hold his hand in public, and there's something both sweet and empowering about it.

I'm more than just his physical therapist, though that designation also applies. For the record, I did make Tanner do his stretches. Some of them were naked. That whole *rehab before romance* line doesn't have to apply anymore since we're making the rules as we go.

In fact, he seems extra motivated when he's naked. Or when I am. It's a toss-up.

We land back home in San Diego on Sunday evening, and instead of heading right for my place or his, he takes us to *our* new place.

He closed on it last week before he went to Vegas. It was a quick sale, all cash, and I had no idea it had been in the works for quite some time.

He's quite the secret keeper, I guess.

The house is perfect with its panoramic sea views, eight bedrooms, training room, and sparkling pool, and as I twirl around the gourmet kitchen, I can't help my wide smile. I can't believe this is really ours.

It feels like some sort of dream—a fantasy, really. The hot, young quarterback falls for the older single mom as she navigates her new life post-divorce.

Yet here we stand in the house he bought for us to build our future in.

"When are you thinking we should move in?" I ask as I take it all in. It's huge—over eight thousand square feet—and this might be some sort of dream. I'm trying to make sense of it all as if making the plans around it will make it real.

"Whenever you're ready. Tomorrow? This weekend? Next month? Whatever you're comfortable with."

"God, why are you so perfect?" I whine, and he chuckles.

"Born this way. And by the way, it came furnished, so we can keep it as is or make it our own."

"Maybe a combination," I say as I glance around. The kitchen is perfect, but I know the kids will want to pick bedrooms and bring all their stuff from our current home when we move.

"Can I ask you a question?" he asks as he moves in behind me, setting his hands on my hips.

I lean back into him, my head settling near his neck, and he nuzzles me a little. "Of course."

"Are you okay with us sleeping in the same bed together when the kids are here?"

I spin around in his arms. "Just you try to stop me," I say, my voice full of sass.

He chuckles as he leans down to press a kiss to my lips. "I wouldn't dare." He moves to lift me onto the counter, and I stop him by holding up a hand.

"No lifting," I remind him, nodding to his knee, and he rolls his eyes as I lift myself up onto the counter.

He pushes my legs open with his body as he moves in between them, and he slides his hands along my torso as he leans down for a kiss. "There are eight bedrooms here, you know," he says softly.

"For guests?" I guess.

"Well, I figured you and I will share one." He holds up one finger as he ticks off which bedrooms are in use. "One for Lily, one for Luca. We can convert one to an office for you, maybe another one for me."

"That's five," I say, threading my fingers through the open hand he's holding up. "What about the other three?"

"One can be a guest room."

"And the other two?" I whisper. I think I know where he's going with this, but it's not really something we've ever discussed, and I don't want to make assumptions.

He's only twenty-nine. He's still young, and maybe someday he'll want kids of his own.

And maybe someday I'll want those kids with him.

But I'm not getting any younger, and if we're going to do this…well, we don't have endless amounts of time.

He clears his throat. "I know we just got back together like five seconds ago, and I know this is still new, but I also know that you are my future. And I was never sure what that future looked like until I met the person who was meant to be in it. Well, the people. You, Lukey, and CC."

My chest warms at his nicknames for my kids.

"You're such a good mom, and if it's in the cards for us, and if it's something you want, I think it would be a blessing to fill those other two rooms with a couple more kids."

Tears pinch behind my eyes. His words mean everything to me. He's really thinking about a future with me, with my kids, and with the potential for more kids, and the more time I spend with him, the more I see it. The more I *want* it.

"I thought I was done after Lily," I admit. "But the more time I spend with you, the more I see more kids. Ones with your eyes and your charm. Ones with your smile and that great hair of yours."

His lips turn up into a smile before they collide with mine, and as his mouth opens and his tongue glides along mine, I can't help but think that right now seems like the perfect time to start practicing.

We christen the kitchen counter before we head out, and he comes to my place with me to stay the night.

We spend Monday getting things in order around my house, and when it's time to pick up the kids from the bus stop, he walks with me to the corner to wait for them.

Jess's eyes look like they're about to fall out of her head when they spot his hand clutching mine, and as each new parent walks up to the area where we gather daily to see our kids off to school and welcome them home, I introduce them to my boyfriend.

He gets involved in a conversation with one of the dads while we wait, and it's incredible how he just seems to fit into every aspect of my life.

Jess leans in toward me. "Looks like the trip was successful?"

I smile. "Oh, girl. I've got news. Big news."

Katie walks up, spots my rather tall and lean hunk of man, and raises her brows at me. "Does that belong to you?" she whispers.

"In fact it does." I can't wipe the silly smile off my face, and it only gets wider as the bus pulls up and *both* my kids spot Tanner standing beside me and run to him first.

"Tanner!" Lily squeals, and he grabs her up into a big hug as Luca tugs at his arm.

"Come on, let's get home so I can show you what I built in Minecraft!" he practically begs, and the two of them start walking toward home—Lily still in his arms as he carries her, backpack and all, and Luca's little hand in his.

"Mama!" Lily says, reaching her hand out toward me, and I squeeze it before she loops it around Tanner's neck.

I absolutely love the fact that they love him.

And he loves them. I see it in the way he grins at Lily as he holds her in his arms, at the way he looks down at Luca as he chatters on about Minecraft, tugging on Tanner to get him to the house.

They don't know the background here, and they have no idea that we're about to tell them that we're moving in with Tanner at a new place. They don't know that I ended things only to realize my mistake and find a way to get him back in my life. They don't know that I had these visions of what I wanted my future to look like when my marriage ended, and how one person completely flipped all that upside down in just one night.

I still want financial independence, and I'll have that with the salary Tanner's going to pay me. I still want what's best for my kids, and I'll have that as we work on becoming a new version of a family, maybe even with more kids in it down the line.

I see my entire future as I watch them walk away. There will be hard times, for sure, but there will also be the easy times like this one, where he just takes charge and somehow makes life just a little easier on me.

"Damn, that ass is *fine*," Jess murmurs as she watches him walk away.

I purse my lips and glare at her. "That's *my* ass you're talking about there."

"Yeah, but he's got a twin brother, right?"

I laugh, and I'm about to reply with something about how I don't know if our family is ready for two football players when Lily starts to yell.

"Stop it, Luca! Let me talk!"

And then Luca fires back. "All you do is talk!"

I giggle as Tanner turns to look back at me rather helplessly. "I guess that's my cue," I tell Jess.

"Saved by the fighting kids," she mutters, and I laugh as I rush over to intervene.

I grab Luca's hand and ask him about his day as Lily babbles on to Tanner, the close call with the arguing children averted. Tanner glances over Lily's head at me with a smile as his free hand slides into mine, and I can't help but think back to the night we met in Vegas.

When I walked hand-in-hand with the football star whose real name I didn't even know as we looked at flower arrangements at the Bellagio before he took me upstairs for a one-night stand, I never imagined this would be where we'd end up just five months down the road.

But here we are, so much more than just a one-night stand, more than a physical therapist and her patient, more than a football star and his trainer. This is just the start of forever.

Epilogue: Tanner Banks

Happy Birthday to Me

Three Months Later

"Happy Birthday!" everyone around us says at the same time, and we all hold our glasses in the air.

And then my brother and I proceed to chug the contents of each of our glasses.

I empty mine first and slam it on the table, and I know chugging tequila is a stupid plan, but it's my thirtieth birthday in Vegas, and I'm not here to make smart decisions. It's our first drink of the evening, anyway, and I need a little liquid courage for what I have planned.

But first, it's a family reunion of sorts at the same club where I met Cassie last July. She's drinking a margarita, and we both laughed as we stood side-by-side at the bar when we first got here.

What a difference eight months makes.

Hell, eight months ago I thought I'd never be in another serious relationship, and then Cassie Fields mistook me for my half-brother, and the rest is history. Now I have this perfect little instant family, complete with the woman I love and two amazing kids who keep us on our toes and fill our lives with love and driving.

Lots of driving.

And apparently, it gets worse the older they get, at least according to Cassie's friends.

My rehab is going well, and my knee is getting stronger by the day with the help of my incredible physical therapist. I'm closer than ever with my family, including my half-brothers, and just when it felt like I'd hit rock bottom, a pair of hands belonging to the woman by my side seemed to reach in to pull me out of it.

Thirty isn't looking so bad right about now. For a while, it was. But Cassie somehow makes everything better without even trying.

And that's why I'm committed to spending the rest of my life with her.

It doesn't matter if it was two days or eight months or six years—when you know, you know. And after I missed out on the chance to get to know my biological father, I don't want to miss out on anything ever again.

Life's too short to sleep on the things that matter.

And Cassie matters. Her kids matter. Our love matters. Our life together matters.

Which is why I'm proposing to her tonight.

It's my birthday, and the greatest gift I could ever think to ask for is her hand in marriage.

My brother pulls me aside. "When are you going to do it?" he asks.

Miller is the only one who knows.

I shrug. I figured we'd party here for a while, and then I'd execute my plan. But last time I was here with these same people, the plan was to party for a while before we headed off in our separate directions. I left early—with Cass. No reason the same can't be true tonight.

"I think I'm ready," I say.

He's about to reply when he slides his phone out of his pocket. His brows are furrowed when he looks at me, and he flashes his phone to show me who's calling. "Soph?" he answers, and he holds a hand over his ear to hear her. "I'm in Vegas."

I feel Cassie as her arms slip around my waist from behind, and I'm about to turn around in her arms when my brother's alarming tone stops me.

"Who did this to you?" he demands. "I'll be right there." He ends the call and looks at me. "I need to go."

"Where?"

"Phoenix."

"Is everything okay?" I ask.

He shrugs, and he looks wildly around the room for a beat. "I don't know. Happy birthday, bro." He slaps my shoulder, and he leans in so Cassie can't hear. "Good luck tonight. We'll celebrate when we're back in San Diego." He bolts out of the room, and I turn around to face Cassie.

"What was that about?" she asks.

I lift a shoulder. "No idea. It was his best friend from back home and sounded like something was wrong."

"I thought you were his best friend," she teases.

I chuckle. "I am. I guess I should clarify by saying this is the woman he's been in love with since we were freshmen in high school."

"Oh," she says, drawing out the word knowingly. "That kind of friend."

I nod. "Exactly. Except they've never slept together, so probably not what you're thinking."

"Hope he gets the girl," she says.

"He will. Someday. Just like I did." I lean down and drop a kiss to her lips. "Want to go for a walk with me?"

She nods, and we don't bother with goodbyes since we have brunch planned in the morning with my half-brothers anyway.

We hop in a rideshare toward the Bellagio, and then we're in the midst of the conservatory just like the night we met.

The theme is different this time with an entirely new display, and we stroll slowly through the gardens as I memorize everything about this night, from the smell of flowers wafting through the air to the way Cassie's hand fits so perfectly into mine.

I draw in a deep breath, her vanilla comingling with the floral scent, and I know this is my moment—especially as we come upon a display of avocados made entirely out of flowers.

I turn toward the woman I love as I take her hands in mine.

"I love you, Cassandra Lynn Fields."

"I love you, too, Tanner James Banks."

I smile as the words I've practiced no less than a hundred times seem to fall right out of my head. I go with words from the heart instead. "I knew there was something different about you the night I met you. I walked around these very gardens with you, and even though I wanted to take you upstairs to rip your clothes off, I equally wanted to get to know you, to find ways to make you laugh, to treat you to chicken tenders and sweet potato fries and hit the slots. You struck me as someone worth knowing, and that time we spent apart before I hurt my knee was dark as I couldn't get you out of my head. And I've realized ever since then that any time I don't get to be with you, life feels a little darker. But when you're with me, everything is vivid and bright because _you_ are vivid and bright. You're a great mom to those two amazing kids, you're an excellent physical therapist, you're smart as hell, and you're an animal in my bed."

I lean in close to her ear as I say the last part, and then I kneel down on my right knee—not my left—and she gasps.

"I want to spend the rest of my life holding hands with you, Lily, and Luca, and I want to hold your hand as we walk around gardens laughing, and talking as we eat chicken tenders, and showing up for each other just when we need each other most. Will you marry me?"

I reach into my pocket and hold out the ring I bought last week, and she gasps yet again as her hand flies to her mouth in surprise.

She nods as tears start to stream down her face, and then she squeaks out, "Yes!"

I lift to a stand, slide the ring onto her finger, and pull her into my arms, dropping my lips to hers as we hear clapping, cheering, and even some whooping all around us.

That's when I feel a slap on my back, and I pull out of the embrace to find Grayson behind me with Ava. Beside the two of them are Asher and Desi, Spencer and Grace, Lincoln and Jolene.

The only one not here is Miller, and I can't help but laugh.

"How did you all know?" I ask.

"Miller," Grayson admits. "Congratulations, man," he says, and he's the first to give me a hug, followed by the rest of the family.

"Ah!" Cassie yells beside me as she hugs Desi first.

Eventually we wind up back in each other's arms, and we walk around the conservatory with my half-brothers and their wives before we head to the snack bar for some chicken tenders.

"Happy birthday," she says as she holds up a tender. I hit it with one of mine as we both laugh. "You know, the worst thing I ever tried to do was quitting the quarterback, but soon I'll be married to the quarterback."

I grin. "And that's when our happily ever after will truly begin."

The End

Want more Tanner and Cassie?
Scan this QR code to download a bonus epilogue!

Scan this code to join Lisa on Facebook at Team LS: Lisa Suzanne's Reader Group!

Acknowledgments

Thank you first as always to my husband! I couldn't do this without you. And a special thanks also to our kids who all this is for.

Thank you to Valentine PR for your incredible work on the launch of this series and this book.

Thank you to Valentine Grinstead, Diane Holtry, Christine Yates, Billie DeSchalit, and Serena Cracchiolo for beta and proofreading and to Michele Begeman for your PT expertise. I value your insight and comments so much.

Big thanks to my ride or die bestie, Julie Saman. We'll always push each other to hit those deadlines no matter how impossible they may seem!

Thank you to Renee McCleary for all you do.

Thank you to my ARC Team for loving this sports world that is so real to us. Thank you to the members of the Vegas Aces Spoiler Room and Team LS, and all the influencers and bloggers for reading, reviewing, posting, and sharing.

And finally, thank YOU for reading. I can't wait to bring more football and more Nash family! Miller is up next, and I can't wait for you to read his story.

Cheers until next season!

xoxo,
Lisa Suzanne

About the Author

Lisa Suzanne is an Amazon Top Ten Bestselling author of swoon-worthy superstar heroes, emotional roller coasters, and all the angst. She resides in Arizona with her husband and two kids. When she's not chasing her kids, she can be found working on her latest romance book or watching reruns of *Friends*.

Also by Lisa Suzanne

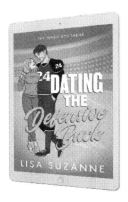

DATING THE DEFENSIVE BACK
(The Nash Brothers #1)

WEDDING THE WIDE RECEIVER
(The Nash Brothers #2)

FIND MORE AT AUTHORLISASUZANNE.COM/BOOKS

Made in United States
Troutdale, OR
04/03/2025

30302789R00233